The Regency

LORDS & LADIES
COLLECTION

_Two Glittering Regency
Love Affairs_

Mistress of Madderlea
by Mary Nichols
&
The Wolfe's Mate
by Paula Marshall

The *Regency*

LORDS & LADIES

COLLECTION

The Regency

LORDS & LADIES
COLLECTION

Mary Nichols &
Paula Marshall

MILLS & BOON®

*First published in Great Britain 2006 by
Harlequin Mills & Boon Limited,
Eton House, 18-24 Paradise Road, Richmond, Surrey TW9 1SR*

THE REGENCY LORDS & LADIES COLLECTION
© Harlequin Books S.A. 2006

The publisher acknowledges the copyright holders of the
individual works as follows:

Mistress of Madderlea © Mary Nichols 1999
The Wolfe's Mate © Paula Marshall 1999

ISBN 0 263 84427 7

138-0506

*Printed and bound in Spain
by Litografia Rosés S.A., Barcelona*

Mistress of Madderlea
by
Mary Nichols

Born in Singapore, **Mary Nichols** came to England when she was three and has spent most of her life in different parts of East Anglia. She has been a radiographer, school secretary, information officer and industrial editor, as well as a writer. She has three grown-up children, and four grandchildren.

Chapter One

1817

'This is no good, no good at all,' William Hundon muttered, reading a letter which had just been brought to the breakfast table. 'Something must be done.'

'My dear, do not frown so,' his wife said, glancing up from the piece of toast she was buttering to look at him. 'You will give yourself wrinkles.'

'Wrinkles!' he exclaimed. 'If that were all I had to concern me, I should count myself fortunate...'

'That is a letter from Mr Sparrow, is it not?' she went on. 'Only Mr Sparrow could put you in such an ill humour.' Although an invalid and a martyr to rheumatics, his wife insisted on coming downstairs in a dressing gown to have breakfast *en famille,* which included their daughter, Charlotte, and her niece, Sophie, who had lived with them for the last two years.

Sophie, alerted by the mention of Mr Sparrow's name, looked up at her uncle. 'Is there something untoward at Madderlea, Uncle William?'

'There is always something untoward at Madderlea.' He stopped speaking to tap at the letter with the back of his hand. 'This time he wants money for repairs to the stable block, last week it was the roof of the west wing that was leaking. I do not know whether he is incompetent or criminal...'

'Surely not criminal?' his wife asked, taken aback by his vehemence.

'Could you not employ another agent to manage Madderlea?' Sophie asked.

'And how could I be sure another would be any better? It is a highly unsatisfactory arrangement. We live too far from Madderlea for me to be constantly going to and fro to see that the man is doing his job. Besides, he does not own the place and one cannot expect him to have the same care as the family.'

'But, Papa, there is no family, except Sophie,' Charlotte put in, then stopped in confusion when her mother gave her a look of disapproval. The loss of her family was hardly ever mentioned in Sophie's hearing to save her pain.

'Precisely,' he said.

Madderlea Hall was the home of generations of the Roswell family. Her father had always referred to it as home, even when they lived in Brussels, and it was to Madderlea he had taken her when Napoleon's conquests and tyrannical rule had made living on the continent too dangerous for an Englishman. It had been a terrifying journey for a fifteen-year-old.

Because of the blockade of European ports, they had been obliged to travel eastwards to Gdansk where British ships were bringing guns and ammunition to the Russians who were retreating before Napoleon's march on Moscow, and she had seen sights which were indelibly printed on her memory. Troops were left to forage for food from a countryside laid waste by its people in order not to feed the invaders. The fields remained untilled or scorched by fire, the livestock slaughtered. Men and horses starved, even during the advance.

It had taken all her father's savings and her late mother's jewellery, everything they possessed, except the clothes they wore, to buy food and a passage home in a cargo ship which pitched and tossed on the rough sea until she was sick as a dog. From London, where they landed, Papa had taken her to her uncle, the Earl of Peterborough, and then gone off and got himself killed fighting in Spain.

The experience had made her seem older and wiser than her years, able to take the ordinary ups and downs of life in her stride, resourceful and unafraid. Nor was she often sad; life was too short for that and the serious side of her nature was balanced by a sense of fun.

Uncle Henry had treated her like the daughter he never had and she had loved him and his wife as a second set of parents. It did not diminish the fond memories she had of her mother, who had died years before, nor of her brave and loving father, but Madderlea had become her home too, a safe haven, a beautiful and happy place, the villagers content because the people at the big house cared about them. Until…

She didn't want to think of that day, but it would

always be there in the back of her mind, a day in her life she would never forget, a day which had transformed her from a bright happy young lady looking forward to her first Season, into a quiet, withdrawn woman, who was never free of pain, both physical and mental. Almost two years on, her body had miraculously healed, but the mental images were still with her and would be to the day she died. Even now, sitting at the breakfast table in her Uncle William's comfortable but unpretentious house, they returned to haunt her.

They had been on their way to London for the Season and she was to have a come-out. She had been full of happy anticipation, making plans, talking about the gowns and fripperies she was going to buy, confident of finding a husband among the many *beaux* who would attend all the social occasions. Aunt Margaret had assured her she would be the catch of the Season and she had no reason to doubt her.

She did not consider herself beautiful, being rather too tall and slim for the current fashion, and her hair was red-gold at a time when dark locks were favoured, but she carried herself well and her complexion was good. Her greeny-grey eyes were her best feature, or so her aunt had told her. She had been promised a considerable dowry too, provided her choice met the approval of her aunt and uncle, but that was only fair and she had no qualms about it.

The weather had been fine when they set out in the family coach from Madderlea in Norfolk, but by the time they reached Newmarket Heath, black clouds had gathered and it became almost as dark as night.

Long before it began to rain, lightning flashed across the heath and thunder rumbled ominously. There was nowhere to stop and take shelter. Her aunt had wanted to turn back but, as Uncle Henry pointed out, the clouds were moving northwards and turning back would mean travelling with them instead of against them; if they kept going they would soon be under clear skies again.

It was the most terrible storm Sophie had ever witnessed and the terrified horses, intent on turning away from the flashes that continually rent the air in front of them, galloped off the road across the rough heathland, bumping the carriage up and down so that the occupants were hard put to hold onto their seats. They had heard a scream as the coachman was thrown off and though the groom who sat beside him on the box tried to retrieve the reins, he could not. Helplessly, they hung on until a wheel hit a rock and the whole vehicle turned over to the sound of rending wood, screaming horses and cries of terror, hers as well as her aunt's. And then there was black silence.

How long Sophie had been unconscious she did not know. She had come to her senses when she heard rough voices. 'They're dead, every last one of them.'

'Well, we can't leave them here. Best find out who they are, send for help.'

It was then she had cried out, unsure whether she had made enough sound to alert them, but then a man's head peered at her over the edge of the mangled vehicle, where she had been trapped with the dead weight of her aunt on top of her.

'There's one alive in here. Help me get her out. There, there, miss, you're safe now.'

Safe yes, but badly injured. The rest of that day and the weeks that had followed were a blur of pain and misery, but there had come a day when she had woken to find herself in a pretty bed chamber and the sun shining in through the window. Aunt Madeleine, her mother's sister, had been smiling down at her, her pale face full of gentle concern.

'How did I come to be here?'

'We fetched you, just as soon as we heard the dreadful news that you were lying at death's door in the infirmary at Newmarket.' Her aunt had lived in England since her marriage and her English was perfect but there still remained a trace of a French accent which reminded Sophie of her mother.

She had a hazy memory of being carried, of being put in a vehicle of some kind, of groaning at the pain and of wishing only to be left alone to die in peace. But then there had been soft sheets and someone stroking her brow and muted voices, of returning consciousness which was too painful to bear and of drifting back into sleep. 'When?'

'Two months ago.'

Two months! 'Uncle Henry? Aunt Margaret?'

'I'm sorry, Sophie, you were the only one found alive and we thought we might lose you too. Now you are going to get well again. Charlotte will come and sit with you.'

Only later, when they thought she was strong enough, did they tell her that she had inherited Madderlea Hall. 'It is not entailed,' Uncle William had

'We'll walk through the woods,' Sophie said, as they donned cloaks to cover their light wool morning gowns and buttoned their feet into sturdy boots. 'Round over Corbury Hill, down through Little Paxton and back through the village. We can call on old Mrs Brown on the way and see how she is. What do you say?'

'But, Sophie, it's all of five miles. Are you sure you're up to it? '

'Of course. I'm perfectly well now, or Uncle William would not have suggested going to London. I am persuaded one needs a great deal of energy for all the balls and *soirées* and visits to the theatre, not to mention picnics and riding in the park.'

Charlotte laughed as they left the house behind and made for the footpath to the woods which ran alongside the garden. 'You have left out the most arduous exercise of all, Cousin.'

'Oh, what is that?'

'Finding a husband, of course.'

Picking her way carefully over the damp grass, Sophie contemplated the prospect. The only men she had really been close to were her father and her two uncles and the thought of being touched or kissed by anyone else sent a frisson of fear, mixed with a strange surge of excitement, through her whole body. And then she thought of Madderlea and her fortune and knew that those two facts alone would ensure a flock of suitors. But how to choose? How to be sure that whoever offered for her was looking at her for herself and not her inheritance?

'It will not be easy.' She sighed. 'There are times

when I almost wish I had no fortune, no Madderlea.
It is a weighty responsibility, you know.'

'How so?'

'It is not only Madderlea Hall which is old and
always in need of repair—there are servants, indoors
and out, and the tenants, who look to the Hall to repair their cottages and keep the land in good heart,
and the villagers, whose welfare must be considered,
and the parson, whose living is in the gift of the Lord
of the Manor. I must choose a husband who will be
as careful of all those responsibilities as Uncle Henry
was, who will love Madderlea as much as I do.'

'You have not said one word about him loving you.
Do you not believe in marrying for love?'

'Of course I do, but how can I be sure of any man?
Madderlea will be a great enticement to deceive,
don't you think?'

'Oh, Sophie, you must look for love as well. You
will be so unhappy if you do not.'

They had entered the woods, taking a well-defined
track between the trees. Sophie lifted an overhanging
branch, its new leaves glistening with raindrops, and
stooped to pass beneath it, holding it for Charlotte to
follow.

'Oh, Charlie, I should not care if he were as poor
as a church mouse, if he loved me. In fact, I think I
should be averse to a man with a fortune. Men with
deep pockets are almost always arrogant and unfeeling and think that money will buy anything, even a
wife. I am thankful that money is not one of the attributes I shall be seeking.'

'Oh, and what qualities would you be looking for in a husband?'

'He must be handsome and well turned out, but not vain of his appearance as some dandies are. I think it is far more important that he should have an interesting face and be able to converse sensibly without being condescending. He must allow me to be myself and not try to mould me to his idea of womanhood. He must, of course, be honourable in everything he does. He must be good with children, for I should like children, and be kind to his servants.'

Charlotte raised an enquiring eyebrow. 'Oh, is that all?'

'No, he must be considerate and tenderhearted and not haughty or domineering. But not soft. Oh, no, definitely not soft.'

'Goodness, Sophie, where are you going to find such a paragon? You ask too much.'

Sophie sighed. 'I know, but I can dream, can I not? Don't you ever dream?'

'Yes, but only of Freddie.'

'Mr Harfield, ah, yes, I had almost forgot him. You will be able to enjoy your Season, safe in the knowledge that you have him to come back to.'

'I am not so sure, Sophie. Freddie told me that his father wants him to marry someone with a substantial dowry; you know I don't have that.'

Sophie laughed. 'I have not heard that Mr Harfield is making any push to obey his papa. He has never so much as looked at anyone else.'

'No, but Sir Mortimer is the squire of Upper Corbury, which I own is nothing compared to Madderlea,

but in our little pool, he is a big fish, and no doubt
Freddie will have to give in in the end.'

'Then he is not the man I took him for,' Sophie
said.

They had come out of the woods on to a lane which
wound up and over Corbury Hill. The dark fields,
here and there showing the tips of winter wheat,
stretched on either side of them. On the skyline, they
could see the hunt, galloping behind the yelping
hounds.

'Do you think they've found the scent?' Charlotte
asked, as the sound of the hunting horn drifted across
to them.

'I hope not. I feel for the poor fox.'

'Oh, Sophie, and you a country girl!' She stopped.
'There's Freddie. Don't you think he is handsome,
the way he sits his horse?'

Sophie smiled. 'I am persuaded that you do.'

The young man had spotted them and turned his
horse to meet them, pulling it up in a shower of damp
earth, almost at their feet.

'Freddie!' Charlotte said, brushing down her cape.
'You have made us all muddy.'

He grinned, doffing his hat to reveal blond curls.
Two years older than they were, he still had the slim
figure and round face of a youth, but had been rapidly
maturing over the previous two years and would soon
have all the mamas for miles around looking at him
with an acquisitive eye.

'I beg your pardon, Miss Hundon.' Then, to Sophie, 'Miss Roswell.'

Sophie smiled. 'Mr Harfield.'

'It is so pleasant to be out after all the rain,' Charlotte said, teasing him. 'And we might not be able to do so much longer.'

'What do you mean?'

'We are both going to London for a Season. What do you think of that?'

'Season?' he echoed in dismay. 'You mean you are to have a come-out and mix with all the eligibles?'

'I mean exactly that,' she said, laughing.

He dismounted and walked over to grab both her hands, a gesture which Sophie knew she ought to discourage as being highly improper, but she had no heart to do it.

'Charlie,' he said, using the familiar name of childhood. 'You wouldn't… Would you?'

'Now, who's to say? I might…'

'Oh, no, please say you are only teasing…'

'I am only teasing.' She looked at him with her head on one side, while Sophie pretended to examine something in the hedgerow. 'But you know, Freddie, if your papa has his way, I should be holding myself back in vain.'

'I will bring him round. Promise me you will be patient.' He could hear the hunt fading in the distance. 'I must go.' He put her hands to his lips and reluctantly released them. The next minute he was astride his horse and galloping away.

'You know, that was highly indecorous conduct,' Sophie said, as they resumed their walk. 'If anyone had seen you…'

'But they didn't, did they?' Charlotte was smiling at the memory of her swain.

'No, but it will be very different in London, you know. What might be acceptable behaviour in Upper Corbury would be enough to ruin your reputation in the capital. Do remember that, Charlie.'

'There is no need to ring a peal over me, Sophie, I know I must be prim and proper when we go to London. Besides, Freddie will not be there and I shall not be tempted to stray.'

Sophie was not so sure. Temptations there would be, she was certain, not only for Charlotte but for her too—she must not allow herself to forget Madderlea and why she was there.

Three weeks later, they set off for London in the family coach, accompanied by Anne, who had been promoted from parlour maid to ladies' maid, and escorted by Joseph, Mr Hundon's groom, riding Sophie's grey stallion. Joseph's nineteen-year-old son, Luke, was riding Charlotte's smaller horse. Joseph and the coachman were to return with the carriage immediately because William needed it, but Luke was to stay in London to look after their mounts. They would be relying on their hostess's equipage to convey them around town.

'Her name is Lady Fitzpatrick,' William had told them on his return. 'She is a distant cousin on my mother's side. You have not met her because she moved to Ireland on her marriage and we did not correspond. She was widowed some years ago and returned to live in London. I went to ask her advice and she offered to sponsor you herself, which is very agreeable of her and saved me a great deal of time and trouble. She has a town house in Holles Street, not a top-of-the-trees area, but respectable enough.'

'Some years ago,' Charlotte echoed. 'Does that mean she is old, Papa?'

'No, I would not say old,' he told them. 'Mature and well able to deal with high-spirited girls.'

'A dragon.'

'Certainly not. In fact, she is a sympathetic sort and will stand well *in loco parentis*. I believe she might be a little short-sighted, for she uses a quizzing glass all the time, but that is of no account. I am sure you will like her; she impressed me very much with her sensibility and knowledge of what is right and proper.'

This description hardly filled the girls with rapture, but it could not have been easy for him, a country gentleman not used to the *haute monde*. They were going to London for the Season and that was all that mattered.

'Now, Sophie, you will have a care, will you not?' he had said the day before, when they were in the throes of last-minute packing. 'There will be unscrupulous men about and I do not want you to be gulled. Be guided by Lady Fitzpatrick and, whatever you do, do not commit yourself to anyone until I have seen and approved him. You do understand?'

'Of course, Uncle.'

'And the same goes for you, my love,' he told his daughter. 'And though you will not be the object of fortune hunters, you are a lovely girl and perhaps susceptible to flattery…'

'Oh, Papa, I am not such a ninny. Besides, I am

going to enjoy myself, not look for a husband. The man I want is in Upper Corbury.'

He had laughed at that and said no more, though Aunt Madeleine, tearfully coming out to the carriage to wave goodbye to them, had reinforced everything he had said and more, extracting a promise from them that they would write every other day.

'Oh, this is so exciting,' Charlotte said, when they stopped for their first change of horses. Anne, who was a bad traveller, had curled herself up in the corner and gone to sleep. The girls allowed her to slumber on; it was easier to exchange confidences without eavesdroppers, however unintentional. 'What time will we arrive, do you think?'

'With luck, before it becomes dark,' Sophie said.

'I do hope Lady Fitzpatrick is not a dragon. I mean to enjoy myself, meeting all the eligibles. It will not hurt Freddie to think he has some competition.'

Sophie envied her cousin her untroubled mind. 'You may look forward to it, Charlie, but I am not so sanguine.'

'Why not? You are rich as Croesus. Think of all the splendid gowns you will be able to buy, the pelisses, riding habits, bonnets and silk shawls. A new dress and a new bonnet for every occasion. And you will have all the young men dangling after you. In your shoes, I would be in ecstasies.'

'I wish you could be in my shoes, Cousin, dear, for I would willingly trade places.'

'You surely do not mean that.'

'I do. Then I could choose a husband without him knowing who I am.'

'And afterwards? He would have to know in the end.'

'Yes, but by then we should have discovered we suited and he would not mind.'

'No, I do not suppose he would, considering he had landed an heiress and not the simple country girl he thought he had won. Oh, Sophie, if you go about with that Friday face, you will surely put them all off.'

Sophie laughed, her greeny-grey eyes danced with light and her face lit up with mischief. 'I must not do that, must I?'

'Certainly you must not, if you wish to catch that paragon you told me of.'

They talked on as the coach rattled through the countryside, which gradually became more and more inhabited as one village followed another in quick succession. Then they were travelling on cobbles and there were buildings each side of the street, houses and inns and shops, and the streets were crowded with vehicles and people, in spite of the lateness of the hour. They leaned forward eagerly to look about them when they realised they had arrived in the metropolis. Sophie had seen some of it briefly on her way from Europe to Madderlea, but to Charlotte it was new and wonderful.

Fifteen minutes later they turned into Holles Street and the carriage drew to a stop. The girls, peering out, saw a tall narrow house with evenly spaced windows and steps up to the front door, which was thrown open when Joseph lifted the knocker and let it fall with a resounding clang. A footman and a young lad ran down the steps to the carriage and be-gan unloading their luggage, while the girls extricated themselves and made their way, in some trepidation, up the steps and into the front hall, followed by Anne, still half asleep.

'Ladies, ladies, welcome. Come in. Come in. Is that your maid? Tell her to follow the footman, he will show her your rooms. She can unpack while you take some refreshment. I do hope the journey has not tired you excessively.'

The rush of words ended as suddenly as they had begun and the girls found themselves staring at a dumpy little woman in a mauve satin gown and a black lace cap, who was peering at them through a quizzing glass. Her eyes, small and dark, were almost lost in a face that was as round and rosy as an apple.

'Good evening, Lady Fitzpatrick.' Sophie was the first to speak. 'We—'

'No, don't tell me, let me guess,' their hostess said, lifting her glass closer to her eyes and subjecting them to individual scrutiny. They were dressed similarly in plain travelling dresses and short capes, though So-phie's was a dark russet, which heightened the red-gold of her hair, and Charlotte's was rose-pink. So-phie's bonnet was dark green straw, trimmed with matching velvet ribbon, and Charlotte's was a chip bonnet, ruched in pale blue silk.

Her close inspection completed, her ladyship pointed her lorgnette at Charlotte, who was standing silently trying not to laugh. 'You are Miss Roswell. I can tell breeding a mile off.' She turned to Sophie. 'And you are the country cousin.'

Charlotte was too busy trying to smother her giggles to contradict her. Sophie dug her sharply in the ribs with her elbow and smiled at their hostess. 'Why, how clever of you, my lady. I did not think it so obvious.'

'Sophie!' breathed Charlotte in alarm, but Sophie ignored her and smiled at Lady Fitzpatrick.

'I can see that no one could gull you, my lady. Not that we should try, of course. I am, indeed, Miss Hundon.'

Her ladyship leaned towards her, cupping a hand round her ear. 'You must learn to speak clearly, child, it is no good mumbling. I am sure Miss Roswell does not mumble.'

Sophie realised that, besides having poor eyesight, Lady Fitzpatrick was also hard of hearing. Had Uncle William known that?

'Charlotte, for goodness' sake, don't stand there giggling,' she murmured. 'Say something.'

'What can I say? Oh dear, Sophie, what have you done? You have landed us in a bumblebath and no mistake.'

'Bath,' said Lady Fitzpatrick. 'Of course, you may have a bath. I will order the water to be taken up to your rooms. But first, some refreshment.' She led the way into the drawing room, where a parlour maid had just arrived with a tea tray which she put on a low table beside a sofa. 'Now, Sophie, you sit here beside me and Charlotte can sit in the armchair opposite.'

Charlotte obeyed and then gasped when her ladyship looked askance at her. 'I meant you to sit beside me, my dear, but it is of no real consequence.'

Sophie relinquished her seat and motioned Charlotte to take it. 'My lady, you have misunderstood,' she said, speaking very precisely. 'I am Sophie. This is Charlotte.'

'Oh, I see. You know, Mr Hundon spoke very quickly and I did not always catch exactly what he said. So Miss Roswell is Charlotte and Miss Hundon is Sophie, not the other way about. No wonder you were amused.'

'But…' Charlotte spluttered and then dissolved into the giggles she had been trying so hard to suppress and Sophie found herself laughing. It was the first time for two years that she had really done more than smile a little, and it felt wonderful.

Lady Fitzpatrick, mistaking the cause of their laughter, allowed herself a rueful smile. 'I have it right now, do I not?'

'Yes, indeed,' Sophie said, accepting a cup of tea and sipping it. She knew Charlotte was staring askance at her, but refused to look her in the eye.

'Sophie, whatever are we going to do?' Charlotte, unable to sleep, had padded along to Sophie's room in her nightdress. 'We cannot possibly keep up the pretence.'

'Why not? Lady Fitzpatrick's mistake is fortuitous and it would be a shame to disillusion her. You said you would like to be in my shoes, so now you may.'

'But, Sophie, Anne and Luke know which of us is which…'

'Oh, I told Anne when she queried why you had

been given the best room. I promised her five guineas and assured her she would not be in trouble over it.

'Five guineas! Why, that is a small fortune to her!'

'It would not serve to be miserly. As for Luke, he thought it was a great lark, when I offered him the same inducement.'

'Sophie, I cannot do it, really I can't. I shall die of mortification when we have to go out and about and meet people.'

Sophie thrust her conscience firmly into the background. Fate had taken a hand in the matter and made Lady Fitzpatrick make that mistake. It could not and should not be ignored. 'No one knows us in town and you will manage wonderfully. Wouldn't you like to play the heiress for a few weeks? It will flush out the fortune hunters and we can have a little fun at their expense. And, who knows, I might even meet that paragon.'

'And when you do?'

'Why, we will confess the truth and the toadeaters will come home by weeping cross and serve them right.' She paused. 'Charlotte, say you will do it. At the first sign our ruse is not working, I shall make a clean breast of it, I promise, and I shall say it was all my doing.' She could see the idea growing on her cousin and pressed home her advantage. 'Go on, tell me you are not tempted by the thought of playing the lady and having all the eligibles at your feet. You will, you know, because you are very fetching. You will return to Freddie with such a tale to tell, he will be filled with admiration and no harm done.'

Charlotte laughed and gave in.

* * *

Lady Fitzpatrick's carriage was old, creaky and scuffed and the unmatched horses leaner than they should have been. It took them safely about town to do their shopping but the image it created was certainly not the one Sophie had in mind. Even though she intended to stay in the background, she wanted Charlotte to shine, for how else were they to flush out the fortune hunters as she had so succinctly put it to Charlotte the night before?

Mentally she put a new equipage on their shopping list, though that would have to wait for another day; buying gowns for morning, afternoon, carriage rides and balls, not to mention riding habits, bonnets, pelisses, footwear, fans and underwear took the whole of their first day.

Sophie's choice of garments, while not exactly dowdy, was certainly not in the first stare of fashion. She chose plain styles and muted colours and let Charlotte be the peacock, encouraged by Lady Fitzpatrick.

'Charlotte, my dear,' her ladyship said, as the young lady eagerly pounced on a pale-green crepe open gown over a satin slip, while Sophie chose brown sarcenet, 'I do not wish to scold…do you not think you could be a little more generous towards your cousin? She is to be brought out, too, you know.'

'But Sophie is…' Charlotte, who had been going to say Sophie held the purse strings and could buy whatever she wanted, stopped in confusion.

'I am quite content, ma'am,' Sophie said, all innocence. 'Any man who offered for me must take me as I am. It would be wrong of me to pretend I am of greater consequence than I am.'

'Sophie, Lady Fitzpatrick is right,' Charlotte said. 'It will look mean of me, if you do not choose at least one or two fashionable gowns for special occasions.' Blue eyes twinkling, she added, 'Please do not consider the cost, you know I can easily afford it.'

Sophie choked on a laugh; Charlotte was doing better than she had hoped. 'Very well, but I shall not be extravagant.'

They returned home with the carriage piled high with their purchases and more to be delivered the following day, all to be paid for on Miss Roswell's account, which would, of course, go to her uncle. The only thing they lacked was that first important invitation.

It arrived the following day. It was for a *soirée* being given by Lady Gosport, an old friend of Lady Fitzpatrick's.

'It will only be a small gathering, but it will set the ball rolling,' her ladyship said.

The girls looked at each other. The time had come to test their masquerade and they were half-eager, half-fearful.

Chapter Two

The two men had enjoyed a morning gallop across the heath. The horses had gone well and now they were walking them back towards town. Both were tall and sat their mounts with the ease of cavalry officers used to long hours in the saddle; both wore impeccably tailored riding coats of Bath cloth, light brown buckskins and highly polished riding boots. Richard, Viscount Braybrooke, the older at twenty-nine, and slightly the bigger of the two, had been silent ever since they had turned to go back.

'What ails you, Dick?' Martin asked. 'You've been in the dismals ever since you went home. You found no trouble there, I hope?'

'Trouble?' Richard roused himself from his contemplation of his horse's ears to answer his friend. 'No, not trouble exactly.'

'Then what is wrong? Grandfather not in plump currant?'

'He says he isn't, but that's only to make me toe the line.'

'What line is that?'

'Marriage.'

Martin shrugged. 'Well, it comes to us all in the end.'

'It's all very well for you, you haven't got a dukedom hanging on your choice. It would not be so bad if I had been born to inherit, but Emily was the only child my uncle had and the estate is entailed. My own father, who was the second son, died when I was still in leading strings and my uncle died of a fever while we were in Spain, so I came back to find myself the heir.'

'You knew it might happen one day.'

'Of course I did, but I thought I would have plenty of time to look about for a wife. The old man is holding my cousin Emily over my head like the sword of Damocles.'

Martin grinned. 'Quite a feat for an elderly gentleman. I believe she is quite a large girl.'

Richard smiled in spite of himself. 'You know what I mean.'

'She is not to your taste?'

'She was a child when I went away to war and it is as a child that I think of her, my little cousin to be petted and indulged, not as a wife.'

'She is of marriageable age now, though.'

'Seventeen, but her mother has spoiled her abominably and she is still immature, without a sensible thought in her head. I should be miserable legshackled to her and so would she.'

'Has His Grace given you no choice?'

'Oh, I have a choice. Find a wife of whom he will

approve before the end of the Season, or it will have to be Emily.'

'Why the haste? You have only just returned to civilian life, a year or so enjoying the fruits of peace would not come amiss.'

'So I told him. I also pointed out that Emily should be allowed more time to grow up and make her own choice, but he says he has no time to waste, even if I think I have. He is an old man and likely to wind up his accounts at any time. He wants to see the next heir before he goes.'

They had arrived at the mews where the horses were stabled and, leaving them in the charge of grooms, set out to walk to Bedford Row where the Duke of Rathbone had a town house.

'Do you know, I begin to feel sorry for Emily.'

'So do I. Choosing a wife is not something to do in five minutes at a Society ball. It needs careful consideration. After all, you have to live with your choice for the rest of your life.'

'Some don't,' Martin said, as a footman opened the door of the mansion and they passed into a marble-tiled vestibule. A magnificent oak staircase rose from the middle of it and branched out at a half-landing to go right and left and up to a gallery which overlooked the hall. 'They marry someone suitable to continue the line and then discreetly take a mistress. Look at the Prince Regent...'

'I would rather not look at him, if you don't mind,' Richard said, before turning to the servant who had admitted them and ordering breakfast for them both before leading the way to the library, a large room lined with bookshelves and containing a reading table and a couple of deep leather armchairs either side of the fireplace. 'I may be old-fashioned, but I would rather find a wife I could care for and who cared for me. Emily has no feeling for me at all but, with my uncle's death, my aunt was deprived of her chance to be a duchess and so she is determined on her daughter fulfilling the role. She will hound me to death as soon as she hears of my grandfather's edict.'

Richard sprawled morosely in one of the chairs and Martin, always at ease in his friend's company, sat opposite him. 'Then there is no alternative, my friend—you must mix with Society as one of the eligibles and hope for the best.'

'The best,' Richard echoed. 'Oh, that I could find such a one.'

'A great deal depends on your expectations, Dick. Tell me, what attributes will you be looking for in a wife?'

Richard gave a short bark of a laugh, as if considering such a thing had never crossed his mind, though he had been thinking of little else since the interview with his grandfather. 'Let me see. It goes without saying she must come from a good family, or Grandfather will never sanction her. Beautiful? Not necessarily, but she must have a pleasing face, a certain style and presence, so that I can be proud to have her on my arm in public. She must be able to converse intelligently; I should hate anyone vacuous or missish.'

'An educated wife…that might be asking for trouble.'

'A little education does no harm, but I wouldn't

want a blue stocking; they are always trying to score points. She must want and like children because the whole object of the exercise is to beget an heir and I do not hold with women who have babies and then hand them over to nurses and governesses to rear.'

'That's quite a list.'

'I haven't done yet. I would expect her to be considerate towards those beneath her and tenderhearted when they are in trouble, but not soft, not easily gulled. She must enjoy country pursuits because I shall wish to spend much of my time in Hertfordshire on the estate. Not a hoyden, though. Don't like hoydens above half.'

Martin was smiling at this catalogue of virtues. 'What about a dowry?'

'Most important of all she must not be a fortune or a title hunter. In fact, it would be a decided advantage if she had her own fortune.'

'Why? You are a pretty plump in the pocket already.'

'I know, but if she has her own fortune, she will not be marrying me for mine, will she? I want someone accustomed to wealth so that she will fall easily into my way of living and not be overawed by it. Besides, I will not be truly wealthy until I inherit and, for all his protestations to the contrary, my grandfather is fit as a flea.

'It would be better if my wife could afford all the extravagant fripperies she needs without my having to go to him for an increase in my allowance. If she is already independent, she would not fetter me with extravagant demands. She would be prepared to let me go my own way in return for being able to lead her own life, within certain decorous limits, of course.'

'Do you know, I am sure I heard you say you were not interested in taking a mistress.'

'I should like to keep the option open.' He spoke so pompously that Martin burst into laughter. 'You may laugh,' Richard told him. 'You aren't constrained by other people's expectations.'

'It is your own expectations which are the more demanding, old fellow. Such a paragon of virtue does not exist.'

'More's the pity.'

A footman came to tell them that breakfast was ready and they got up to go to the small dining room, where a repast of ham, eggs, pickled herrings, boiled tongue and fresh bread was laid out for them.

'Then you do agree that you must be seen in Society?' Martin queried, watching Richard fill his plate. His problem seemed to have had no effect on his appetite.

'I have no choice.'

'Well, do not sound so reluctant, you will never attract your paragon like that. You must be agreeable and well turned out and...'

'I know, my friend, I do not need a lecture on how to conduct myself.'

'Then we'll start this evening. Mama has arranged a little gathering at home and I promised to attend. It is very early in the Season, but she assures me there are to be several young ladies up for their first Season and a one or two of the competition too, I'll be bound.'

'Then I had better do something about my wardrobe. Everything I had before I went into the army is far too tight.'

'That's hardly surprising,' Martin said laconically. 'You were little more than a boy when you left and a man when you returned.' He looked critically at his friend's large frame. 'Not a small one, either. Do you wish me to accompany you?'

'No, of course not, I am perfectly able to choose clothes. I'll meet you at Jackson's at four. There will just be time for a short bout before dinner at five.'

Martin laughed. 'Do you expect to have to fight for your lady's hand?'

Richard smiled. 'No, but it is always a good thing to maintain one's ability to defend oneself.'

'Oh, come, Dick, you have no enemies, a more affable man I have yet to meet.'

'It would be a fortunate man who managed to go through life without acquiring a few enemies,' Richard said.

'Name me one.'

Richard needed time to consider. He was indeed fortunate that he was popular and well-liked by his peers and the men he had commanded, except for those who had flouted the tight discipline he maintained as an officer. 'There was Sergeant Dawkins,' he said, remembering the man he had had courtmartialled for looting, something Wellington had expressly forbidden.

The offence had been exacerbated by the fact that

the goods the man had stolen had come from a Portuguese family who were allies. His defence, which had not been upheld, was that the family had been consorting with the enemy. The sergeant had been flogged and dishonourably discharged. Left to find his own way home from Lisbon, he had threatened Richard with revenge.

'That threat was made two years ago and in the heat of the moment,' Martin said. 'You surely do not think he meant it?'

'No, of course not, the poor fellow likely never made it back to England. He probably settled down in the Peninsula with a Spanish señorita. You asked for an example and I gave you one.'

'Point taken. But I hope you will rid yourself of your aggression and ill humour against Gentleman Jackson in the boxing ring this afternoon and present yourself in my mother's drawing room at seven this evening, in a sweet temper, ready to act the agreeable.'

'Have no fear, my friend,' Richard said, as both men left the table. 'I shall be a model of the man about town.'

Sophie and Charlotte had arrived at Lady Gosport's in Denmark Place a few minutes after seven to find her drawing room already buzzing with conversation. Most of the company seemed to be of Lady Fitzpatrick's generation and Sophie's spirits sank. This was not her idea of London Society at all. She looked across at Charlotte and exchanged a rueful grimace, before their hostess caught sight of them and hurried over to greet them.

'Harriet, my dear, so glad you could come.' She kissed Lady Fitzpatrick on both cheeks and then looked at the girls, taking careful note of Charlotte's white crepe open gown trimmed with silk forget-me-nots over a pale blue slip, and moving on to examine Sophie's cambric high gown with its overskirt of pale green jaconet, which her ladyship considered more suitable for day than evening wear. 'So, these are your charges.'

'Good evening, Beth.' She took Charlotte's arm and drew her forward. 'May I present Miss Charlotte Roswell. The Earl of Peterborough's niece. God rest his soul.'

'Indeed, yes. My commiserations, Miss Roswell.'

Reminded of her superior station by a dig in the ribs from Sophie, Charlotte executed a small polite bob, not the deep curtsy she had intended. 'Thank you, my lady.'

'You are fully recovered from your ordeal?'

'Yes, thank you.' It was obvious that the girl was painfully shy and would have to be brought out of her shell if she were to take well. Her ladyship turned to Sophie. 'Then you must be Miss Hundon. Miss Roswell's companion, I collect.'

'Oh, no,' Charlotte put in. 'Sophie is my cousin and friend, not a paid companion. We share everything.'

'That is to your credit, my dear,' Lady Gosport said. 'But you will find that the possession of an estate and great wealth, as I believe you have, will make your advance in Society very unequal.' Then to Sophie, 'I do hope, dear Miss Hundon, you have not been led to expect the same attention as your more illustrious cousin?'

'No, indeed,' Sophie said, though she longed to bring the lady down to size with some cutting remark. Only the thought of their masquerade being exposed stilled her tongue.

'Come, let me introduce you to the company.'

There were a few young ladies present, they realised, as they were conducted round the room, and one or two young men, who stood about posing in tight coats and impossibly high pointed cravats, twirling their quizzing glasses in their hands and speaking in affected voices which made the girls want to laugh aloud. Instead, they bowed politely and exchanged greetings and longed to escape.

'This is quite dreadful,' Sophie murmured to her cousin when they had done the rounds. 'If the whole Season is to be like this, I shudder to think how we shall go on.'

'It is early in the year,' Charlotte whispered. 'The Season is not yet under way.'

'I hope you are right.'

Just then a commotion by the door heralded the arrival of latecomers. 'Why, it is Martin,' Lady Gosport cried, hurrying over to drag her son into the room. 'You are very late. I had quite given you up.'

He gently removed her hand from the sleeve of his green superfine coat and smiled at her. 'I am sorry, Mama. Pressing business delayed me. May I present my friend, Richard, Viscount Braybrooke?'

The man behind Mr Gosport stepped forward and the whole roomful of people gave a combined sigh, including Sophie, who had told herself she was immune to masculine vanity. If vanity it was. He seemed unaware of the impression he had created, and yet, as she looked more closely she realised he did know, for there was a twinkle of amusement in his brown eyes and a slight twitch to the corners of his mouth.

He was clad in a blue satin coat which fitted him so closely the muscles of his broad shoulders could be detected as he bowed over her ladyship's hand. His waistcoat was of cream figured brocade and his blue kerseymere trousers, in the latest fashion, reached his shoes and were held down by straps under the instep, making his legs seem impossibly long. His cravat, though nothing like as high and pointed as those she had noticed on the other young men, was so skilfully tied, it drew exclamations of admiration from them.

His dark hair, cut short so that it curled about his ears, was the only slightly dishevelled part of him, but Sophie knew it was a style much favoured among the gentleman of the *ton*, called Windswept. Here was a tulip of the first order, and tulips were very definitely not what she was looking for, but beneath all that finery she sensed a man of great strength and power. She had a sudden vision of him unclothed, all rippling muscle, and a flood of colour suffused her cheeks.

She turned away to scrabble in her reticule for a handkerchief in order to compose herself. Whatever was the matter with her? She had never ever thought about a man's nakedness before. Had he deliberately set out to have that effect? It was disgraceful in him if he had and even more disgraceful in her to succumb.

Charlotte, beside her, was openly staring. 'My, would you look at that peacock,' she murmured. 'Oh, goodness, Lady Fitzpatrick is bringing them both over.'

Sophie, struggling to regain her usual serenity, was aware of Lady Fitzpatrick presenting the two men to her cousin. 'Miss Roswell is the niece and ward of the late Earl of Peterborough,' she was saying. 'Being abroad, you will not have heard of the tragedy two years ago which left poor Miss Roswell all alone in the world.'

'Not quite alone,' Charlotte said, determined to include Sophie, not only because she felt overwhelmed, but because it wasn't fair on her cousin to shut her out, as Lady Gosport seemed determined to do. 'My lord, may I present my cousin, Miss Sophie Hundon?'

Sophie found herself subjected to a brown-eyed scrutiny which made her squirm inside and when he took her small hand in his very large one, she felt trapped like a wild bird in a cage which longed to be free but which hadn't the sense to fly when the cage door was opened. Here, she knew, was a very dangerous man. Dangerous because he could make her forget the masquerade she and Charlotte had embarked upon, could make her disregard that list of virtues she had extolled as being necessary for the man she chose as her husband, dangerous for her peace of mind. And all in less than a minute!

She hated him for his extravagant clothes, for looking at her in that half-mocking way, for his self-assurance, for making her feel so weak. But no one would have guessed her thoughts as she dropped him a deep curtsy and then raised her eyes to his. 'My lord.'

'The cousins are to be brought out together,' Lady Fitzpatrick told him. 'Which I hold very generous of Miss Roswell.'

'Indeed,' he said, though she could not be sure if he was expressing surprise or agreement.

'Not at all,' Charlotte put in, making him turn from Sophie towards her. 'We have always been very close, ever since...' She stopped in confusion. She had been going to say ever since Sophie's accident brought her to Upper Corbury, but checked herself. 'Since the tragedy.'

'Your soft heart does you credit, Miss Roswell,' he said. 'May I wish you a successful Season?'

'Thank you, my lord.' She curtsied to him and he moved off. Sophie breathed again and managed a smile for Mr Gosport as he followed in his friend's wake.

'What do you make of that?' Sophie whispered, watching the backs of the two men as they were introduced to the other young ladies.

Sophie made sure their sponsor had moved out of earshot, which, for her, was not very far. 'I think Lady Fitz fancies herself as a matchmaker.'

'Who?'

'Why, you and Lord Braybrooke, of course.'

'But she thinks I am you. Oh, Sophie, we are truly in a coil now.'

'No, we are not. You do not fancy him for a husband, do you?'

'No, I do not. He is too high in the instep for my taste. Besides, he might already be married—he is surely nearer thirty than twenty.'

'Yes, but you heard Lady Fitz mention he had been away in the war. And she would not have dragged him over to us if he were not eligible.'

'What are we going to do?'

'Nothing. Enjoy ourselves. If he offers for you, you can always reject him. I'll wager that will bring him down a peg or two.'

'You do not like him?'

'No, I do not think I do.'

'Why not?'

Sophie was hard put to answer truthfully. Across the room the two men were enjoying a joke with a young lady and her mother to whom they had just been introduced and Sophie felt her heart contract into a tight knot, which she would not recognise as anything but distaste.

'He doesn't fit my criteria in any respect.'

'How can you possibly know that?'

'I just do.'

The two men were taking their leave. Lady Fitzpatrick returned to the girls after talking to Lady Gosport. 'What a turn up,' she said, smiling broadly, making her round face seem even rounder. 'We could not have hoped for a better start. Lord Braybrooke will undoubtedly be the catch of the Season. He was particularly interested in you, my dear Charlotte.'

'Oh, no, I think not,' Charlotte said. 'He did not say above a dozen words to me and those most condescending…'

'There you are, then! We must make what plans we can to engage his attention, and soon too, before he is snapped up.' Sophie burst into laughter and received a look of disapproval. 'Sophie, finding a husband for such as Miss Roswell is a very serious business and not a subject for mirth.'

Sophie straightened her face and remembered to speak very clearly, close to her ladyship's ear. 'You are quite right, my lady, marriage is a solemn undertaking. I beg your pardon.'

'If you are lucky, you may engage the attention of Mr Gosport, though from what I have seen, he does seem to be tied to his mother's apron strings and disinclined to wed. I should not say it, of course, for Beth Gosport is my friend.'

Sophie wondered why she had said it, unless it was to emphasise what a difficult task lay ahead in being able to suit the less important of her two charges.

'I think we can safely take our leave now,' Lady Fitzpatrick went on. 'It is polite to arrive a little late and leave early if one means to stamp one's superiority on to these little gatherings.'

'As his lordship has done,' Sophie said, winking at Charlotte, a gesture which was lost on the short-sighted Lady Fitzpatrick or she would have earned another reproof.

* * *

'God, Martin, is that what I have to do to find a wife? I'd as lief forget the whole thing. I would, too, if it didn't mean falling into a worse case and having to marry Emily.'

The two men were walking towards St James's Street, where they intended to spend the remainder of the evening at White's.

'Oh, it was not as bad as all that,' his friend said, cheerfully, 'There was that little filly, Miss Roswell. Pretty little thing, blue eyes, blonde curls and curves in all the right places. And a considerable heiress, to boot. My mother told me the story.'

'I collect Lady Fitzpatrick saying something about a tragedy.'

'Yes. Her father, the second son of the second earl, married a Belgian lady and Miss Roswell was born and raised in Belgium…'

'Really? She does not give the impression of a well-travelled young lady. I would have taken a wager that she has not stirred beyond the shores of England. More, I should have been inclined to say she had never come up to Town before.'

'How can you possibly tell?'

'The polish is lacking. She has a simple charm that is more in tune with country life.'

'That is good, surely? It fits in well with your criteria.'

'Does it?' Richard turned to grin at him. 'And are you going to remind me of that whenever we meet and discuss one of the hopefuls?'

'Probably.'

'Then carry on. I might as well know the rest.'

'I believe her mother died some years ago. Her father brought her to England to stay with her uncle and his wife and then bought himself a commission and died in the Battle of Salamanca, a hero of that engagement, I am told. Her uncle, the Earl of Peterborough, adopted her.'

'What do we know of him?'

'Nothing out of the ordinary. He was a quiet gentlemen who stayed on his estate most of the time. I have heard nothing against him. On the contrary, he was well respected, even loved, on his home ground.'

'Go on.'

'Two years ago they were all travelling to London for Miss Roswell's come-out when they were caught in a terrible storm; the horses took fright and the carriage turned over. Miss Roswell was the only survivor. Unmarried and seventeen years old, she inherited Madderlea. Quite a catch, my friend.'

'Then why is she being sponsored by that antidote, Lady Fitzpatrick? Are they related?'

'I do not think so.'

'Related to the country cousin, maybe?'

'I don't know that either. I suppose it is possible. Since the accident, Miss Roswell has lived with her cousin.'

'Miss Hundon,' Richard murmured, finding himself remembering the feel of her small hand in his, the colour in her cheeks and the flash of fire in greeny-grey eyes which had looked straight into his, as if challenging him. She made him feel uncomfortable and he didn't know why.

'Yes, but she is of no consequence, not out of the

top drawer at all and must be discounted. Your grand-father would not entertain such a one.'

'No. So, I am to make a play for Miss Roswell, am I?'

'You could do a great deal worse. It was fortuitous that we went to my mother's *soirée*. Unless you make a push she will be snapped up.'

'I do not intend to make a push. I cannot be so cold-blooded.' They had arrived at the door of the club and turned to enter. 'But if, on further acquaintance, I find myself growing fond of her…'

'Oh, I forgot that love was an item on the list.'

Richard laughed and punched him playfully on the arm.

'Very well, I shall call on Lady Fitzpatrick tomorrow and suggest a carriage ride in the Park. And now, do you think we can forget the chits and concentrate on a few hands of cards?'

Lady Fitzpatrick and the two young ladies were sitting in the parlour the following morning, discussing the previous evening's events, when the footman scratched at the door and, flinging it wide, announced in a voice which would have done justice to a drill sergeant, 'My lady, Lord Braybrooke wishes to know if you are at home.'

'Braybrooke?' her ladyship queried, making Sophie wonder if she was losing her memory as well as her other faculties.

'He was at the gathering last evening, Lady Fitzpatrick,' Charlotte said. 'Surely you remember?'

'Oh, Braybrooke! To be sure. Rathbone's grandson. Show him in, Lester. At once.'

He disappeared and she turned to Charlotte. 'Who would have thought he would call so soon? He must have been singularly taken by you. Now, do not be too eager, nor too top-lofty either, my dear. Conduct yourself decorously and coolly.' Fussily she patted her white curls and adjusted her cap, took several deep breaths and fixed a smile of welcome on her face, just as the footman returned.

'Viscount Braybrooke, my lady.'

Richard, dressed in buff coat, nankeen breeches and polished hessians, strode into the room and bowed over her hand. 'My lady.'

'Good morning, Lord Braybrooke. This is a singular pleasure.' She waved a plump hand in the general direction of the girls. 'You remember Miss Roswell and Miss Hundon?'

'How could I forget such a trio of beauties, my lady? Quite the most brilliant stars in the firmament last evening.' He turned and caught Sophie's look of disdainful astonishment before she could manage to wipe it from her face and his own features broke into a grin. He was bamming them in such an obvious way, it made her furious, all the more so because Lady Fitzpatrick was simpering in pleasure and Charlotte's cheeks were on fire with embarrassment. He plucked Charlotte's hand from the folds of her muslin gown and raised it to his lips. 'Miss Roswell, your servant. I hope I see you well.'

'Quite well, thank you, my lord.'

'And, Miss Hundon,' he said, turning to Sophie almost reluctantly, 'you are well?'

'Indeed, yes.' He was having the same effect on her as he had had the previous evening. A night's sleep and time to consider her reaction had made not a jot of difference. He exuded masculine strength and confidence, so why act the dandy? Why pretend to be other than he was? This thought brought her to her senses with a jolt. She was acting too, wasn't she?

Lady Fitzpatrick indicated a chair. 'Please sit down, my lord.'

'Thank you.' He flung up the tails of his frockcoat and folded his long length neatly into the chair.

Sophie watched in fascination as he engaged Lady Fitzpatrick in small talk. To begin with he was frequently obliged to repeat himself, but as soon as he realised her ladyship was hard of hearing—a fact she would never admit—he spoke more clearly, enunciating each word carefully, winning her over completely.

Sometimes he addressed his remarks to Charlotte, smiling at her and flattering her, but rarely turned to Sophie. She was glad of that. He was far too conceited for her taste and she sincerely hoped Charlotte would not be such a ninny as to fall for a bag of false charm.

It was several minutes before he could bring himself to speak of the true reason for his visit. It had been a mistake to come, but Martin had nagged at him unmercifully, reminding him of his grandfather's ultimatum and in the end he had concluded it could do no harm. Little Miss Roswell was pretty; she had a rosy glow about her and an air of insouciance he found at odds with her position as heiress to a great estate.

But the other, the country cousin, disturbed him. Her eyes, intelligent, far-seeing, humorous, seemed to follow his every move, to understand that he was playing a part dictated by Society. He was not behaving like his normal self and he was afraid she would call his bluff and expose him for the clunch he felt himself to be, a feeling with which he was not at all familiar. How could she do this to him?

He had come to ask Miss Roswell to take a carriage ride with him, but she would have to be chaperoned and it was evident that was the role Miss Hundon was to play. Her watchful eyes would be on him every second, protecting her cousin, reducing him to an incompetent swain.

'My lady,' he said, addressing Lady Fitzpatrick. 'I came to ask if you and the young ladies would care to join me in a carriage ride in the park tomorrow afternoon.'

'Why, how kind of you,' she said, while both girls remained mute. 'I should very much like to accept, but… Oh, dear, I am afraid I have undertaken to visit Lady Holland.' She paused. 'But I do not see why you should not take the young ladies. Miss Hundon will chaperone Miss Roswell and their groom can ride alongside. If you are agreeable, of course.'

'I shall look forward to it.' He rose and bowed his way out, leaving two thunderstruck young ladies and a very self-satisfied matron behind him.

'Well…' Lady Fitzpatrick let out her breath in a

long sigh. 'I never thought you would engage the attention of someone so high in Society so soon.'

'No doubt he has heard of my...' Sophie paused and hastened to correct herself '...my cousin's fortune. Madderlea is a prize worth a little attention, do you not think?'

Charlotte's face was bright pink. 'That is unkind in you, Sophie,' she said. 'Do you not think he likes me for myself?'

Sophie was immediately contrite. 'Of course, he does, my dear, who could not? But you must remember that you, too, are superior and have something to offer.'

'Quite right,' her ladyship said, after asking Sophie to repeat herself. 'Now, we must discuss clothes and what you will say to him, for though it is one thing to attract his attention, it is quite another to keep it.'

'What do you know of the gentleman, my lady?' Sophie enquired, for Charlotte seemed to be in a daydream, and someone had to ask. 'Apart from the fact that he is grandson to the Duke of Rathbone. Is he the heir?'

'Indeed, he is. His father was a second son and did not expect to inherit, particularly as the heir was married and in good health, but the old Duke outlived both his sons. There is a cousin, I believe, but she is female.'

'Can she not inherit?' Charlotte asked.

'Unlike Madderlea, the estate is entailed. Richard Braybrooke came back from service in the Peninsula to find himself Viscount Braybrooke and his grandfather's heir.'

'A position, I am persuaded, he finds singularly un-congenial,' Sophie put in.

'Yes, he is a most congenial gentleman,' Lady Fitzpatrick said, mishearing her. 'Such superior address and conduct can only be the result of good breeding.'

Sophie choked on a laugh, making Charlotte look at her in alarm. 'If good breeding means one is insufferably arrogant, then he is, indeed, well-bred,' she murmured, while wiping tears of mirth from her face with a wisp of a handkerchief.

'I do not know what ails you, Sophie,' her ladyship said. 'Your cousin is also well-bred and she is most certainly not arrogant. Indeed, it were better if she could adopt a more haughty attitude, for she is far too shy.'

'I cannot change the way I am,' Charlotte said.

'Nor should you,' Sophie said. 'If the gentleman cannot see that you are sweet and kind and would not hurt the feelings of a fly, then he is blind and does not deserve you.'

The gentleman could see it. He was well aware of Miss Roswell's virtues and it only made him feel unworthy. She deserved to be wooed for herself, by some young blood who appreciated the very qualities he found so cloying. He wanted and needed someone with more spirit, someone to challenge him as Miss Hundon had done. When he had said as much to Martin, his friend had laughed and reminded him of his list of requirements. Challenge had not been mentioned at all. 'You have hardly had time to make a reasoned judgement, Dick,' he had said. But then reasoned judgement and instinct did not go hand in hand.

He called for the young ladies the following afternoon, not at all sure he was going to enjoy the outing. It might be the way Society dictated a man should court a lady, but it was not his way. It was too artificial. He felt a sham, dressed to make a killing in double-breasted frockcoat of dark green superfine, soft buckskin breeches and curly-brimmed top hat. He was not averse to dressing well, but to do so to catch a young lady smacked of hypocrisy.

Sophie and Charlotte were waiting in the drawing room for him. There was still a keen edge to the wind and so Charlotte had chosen to wear a blue carriage dress in fine merino wool which almost exactly matched the colour of her eyes. It was topped by a blue cape and a fetching bonnet trimmed with pink ruched silk in a shade that echoed the rose in her cheeks. She looked delightfully fresh and innocent.

Sophie, on the other hand, determined not to shine, was dressed in grey from head to foot and would not be persuaded to change her mind, when Charlotte said she had made herself look like a poor relation.

'But that is exactly what I am, Charlotte dear,' she had said. 'I am your chaperon, after all.'

There was no time to go back to her room and change, even if she had wanted to, for his lordship was announced at that moment and, after the usual courtesies, they made their way out to his lordship's barouche. And what a carriage; it made Lady Fitzpatrick's town coach, which stood beside it ready to convey her ladyship to her appointment, look even shabbier.

It was a shining black affair with the Rathbone coat of arms emblazoned on both doors and seats comfortably upholstered in red velvet. The driver, in impeccable uniform of tailcoat, striped waistcoat and knee breeches, was sitting on the box, whip in hand. His lordship put a hand under Charlotte's elbow and helped her into her seat, then turned to do the same for Sophie, but she was already climbing in, disdaining his assistance. He smiled at this show of independence and took his own seat and, giving the driver an almost imperceptible nod, they set off, with Luke riding demurely half a head behind on Charlotte's little mare.

Chapter Three

It was a perfect late spring day and the carriageway in the park was crowded with vehicles of all shapes and sizes, and as they were all going at little more than walking pace it was almost like a parade. Richard seemed to know or be known by almost everyone and they frequently drew to a halt for the girls to be presented to the occupants of other carriages. They were also hailed frequently by riders from the nearby gallop, who reined in to speak to Richard, while casting admiring glances at Charlotte, who sat smiling beside him, enjoying every minute.

Sophie hardly rated a second look, but that had its advantages in that she could take time to gaze about her, to make her own assessment of the wide range of characters who took part in the traditional afternoon procession. They ranged from dowagers to schoolgirls, not yet out, Lady This and the Countess of That, as well as some whom Sophie was sure came from the *demi-monde* and rode by with all the aplomb and self-confidence in the world, twirling their parasols.

There were dandies and rakes, army officers resplendent in uniform, a few naval officers and more than a sprinkling of hopefuls who did not fit into any category but wished they did. Not one took her eye…except the man sitting in the seat opposite her and conversing so easily with her cousin at his side.

He was handsome in a rugged kind of way, his features lined by exposure to sun and wind. He exuded masculinity; it came over so strongly it took her breath away. If only… She sighed and suddenly found his attention focused on her. 'You do not agree, Miss Hundon?'

She had not been attending to the conversation and found herself at a loss. 'I beg your pardon, my lord, I was daydreaming.'

He smiled. Her eyes had held a faraway look, as if she were thinking of some absent admirer. In Upper Corbury in the county of Leicestershire, perhaps. He had just learned from Miss Roswell that that was where the Hundons had their home. 'Miss Roswell was commenting on the number of officers still in uniform and expressing the hope that the peace may last and they will no longer be needed to fight.'

'Oh, to that I most heartily agree, but my sympathies are with the common soldiers, who know no other means of earning a living. I think it is shameful just to turn them loose, after they have fought so well for their country. We worry about Spain and Portugal, France and Austria, send delegates to the Congress of Vienna to ensure justice on the continent and we ignore the problems nearer home. It is no wonder there are riots. And ranging militia against unarmed men and women who are only trying to have their voices heard is not the way to go on.'

He was inclined to agree with her, but the challenge was there, in her voice and in her greeny-grey eyes, and he could not resist the temptation to rise to it. 'Law and order must be kept or we will descend into anarchy.'

'Oh, that is the answer we are given for every act of repression. Shoot them, cut them down. Throw them in prison and hope everyone will forget them. Suspending the Habeas Corpus Act was a monstrous denial of justice.'

He smiled. 'I collect your father is a lawyer. Have you learned such sentiments from him?'

In her fervour, she had forgotten her uncle's profession and she had not heard him express any views on the subject. He was not a man to discuss either his clients or the state of the economy with his daughter and niece. Young ladies, in his opinion, did not need to know of such things. She glanced at Charlotte from beneath the brim of her bonnet, but her cousin was staring straight ahead, a bright pink spot on each cheek.

'No, my lord, but I read a great deal and have always been encouraged to think for myself.' She knew she was on dangerous ground and hurriedly reverted to the original subject under discussion. 'If work could be found for the discharged soldiers, they would not be discontent.' And then, because she could not resist having a dig at him. 'It is all very well for the officers, for they have families and estates and education to help them…'

He laughed. '*Touché*, my dear Miss Hundon. But, you know, families and estates bring their own responsibilities.'

She smiled at that, thinking of her own situation, but he saw only sparkling greeny-grey eyes and a mouth that was made for smiling. And kissing. God in heaven, what had made him think that? She was nothing more than a country mouse, a little grey one. No, he amended, that description was inaccurate, for she was tall and her movements were not the quick scurrying of a tiny rodent, but the measured movement of a stalking cat.

'Yes, my lord, the responsibility to marry well, to produce heirs. It is, I am persuaded, a form of vanity.'

'Sophie!' Charlotte cried. 'How can you say that when you—'

'Miss Hundon is entitled to her opinion, Miss Roswell. Do not scold her.' He was looking at Sophie as he spoke and she felt herself shrink under his gaze, though she would not let him see it. 'You are surely not implying your cousin is vain?'

'Nothing was further from my thoughts, my lord,' she said truthfully. 'No one could be less vain or more sweet-natured than my cousin. But her case is exceptional. She is a young lady who has inherited a large estate, but cannot have the governing of it. Society has decreed that that can only be done by a man. She must have a husband or give up her home entirely.'

'Sophie, please…' Charlotte begged. 'You are being excessively impertinent, when Lord Braybrooke has been so kind as to invite us to share his carriage. He does not wish to hear…' She stopped in confusion.

'Oh, my dearest, I did not mean to put you to the blush,' Sophie said, contrite. 'I don't know what came over me.'

What had come over her was a strong desire to pierce Lord Braybrooke's self-assurance, to stop him looking at her in that half-mocking way and take her seriously. But why? Why did it matter so much?

They had come to the end of the carriageway and the driver turned the barouche skilfully and set out on the return journey, while the two girls chatted, their disagreement forgotten.

Richard was intrigued, not only by Miss Hundon, but by the relationship which existed between the two girls. That they were close he did not doubt, but they were so different. Miss Hundon was outspoken and opinionated, almost the blue stocking he had decried, and her dress sense left a great deal to be desired but as he was not considering her for a wife, he told himself it was of no consequence.

On the other hand, Miss Roswell, who did have many of the attributes he had so carefully listed to Martin, including her own fortune, did not stir him to any kind of passion, either of desire or anger. Her skirts, brushing against his leg in the carriage, did not make him want to increase the pressure, to touch her, to kiss her, pretty though she was. Perhaps that would come, when he came to know her better, when she relaxed a little in his company and opened out to him.

At the moment she was stiff and tense, almost as if she were afraid of him. Miss Hundon was not afraid.

He pushed thoughts of Miss Sophie Hundon from him and turned to converse with Miss Roswell, trying to bring her out, to show her there was nothing to fear, but she had suddenly gone mute. He could get nothing out of her but 'Yes, my lord' or 'No, my lord' or 'Indeed?'

Sophie, now that his attention was engaged elsewhere, was able to relax a little. The carriage bowled smoothly along and she found herself thinking that they must be seen in the park more often, but it would not do to be too frequently in the company of Lord Braybrooke. He was not the only eligible in Town and he needn't think he was! They certainly could not drive out in Lady Fitz's town coach; they would be a laughing stock.

She would buy an equipage of her own, one with the Roswell crest emblazoned on the door, and drawn by matched cattle which would be the envy of the *ton*. The thought brought a smile to her lips, a smile not lost on Richard Braybrooke, who was taken aback by the way it lit her whole countenance and made what he had hitherto considered a somewhat unexceptional face into a beautiful one. He was lost in wonder and a sudden arousal of desire which made him squirm uncomfortably in his seat. It was the second time she had done this to him, and he resented it.

He was supposed to be searching for a wife, a wife with very particular virtues, not lusting after a poor country cousin. Did she know the effect she was hav-

ing on him? Was it deliberate? If so, she might be
agreeable to a little dalliance if he made it worth her
while. It might serve to bring him back to his usual
salubrious self and he could then concentrate on the
task in hand, wooing the heiress.

He allowed himself to savour the prospect for a few
delightful seconds before banishing it. He was not in
the army now, he could no longer take whichever
wench fluttered her eyelids at him in invitation. He
had never had to pay for his pleasures, but neither
had he bedded an unmarried gentlewoman. The idea
was unthinkable. And yet he had thought it. He shook
himself and made more strenuous efforts to engage
the attention of Miss Charlotte Roswell.

'Tell me about Madderlea,' he said, deciding that
was surely a subject on which she would find it easy
to converse, but apart from telling him that it was near
the north Norfolk coast and very extensive, she vol-
unteered no information. In fact she seemed very agitated. Did she think he was more interested in her
inheritance than in her? He smiled and dropped the
subject.

When they drew up outside Lady Fitzpatrick's
front door, he jumped out to hand Charlotte down
while the coachman knocked at the door, then turned
to help Sophie.

About to step down behind her cousin, she held out
her hand for him to grasp, but instead she found his
lordship's hands spanning her waist. Startled, she said
nothing as he lifted her down and deposited her on
the pavement. He did not immediately release her, but
stood smiling down at her, his brown eyes looking

into hers, almost as if he were trying to read her thoughts. She moved her gaze to his mouth and wished she had not. It was a strong mouth, so close to hers, she could feel the warmth of his breath. Even as she looked, it seemed to move closer. Surely he was not going to kiss her, not here, in the street? Why couldn't she move away? Why couldn't she speak?

'Miss Hundon,' he said, and managed to convey a deal of meaning in it. 'I enjoyed our little sparring match. I hope you will afford me the opportunity of a return bout before too long.'

She had no idea what he meant and her legs were so shaky she thought she would fall if he released her, but she did not intend to be intimidated. She stepped back and found the ground stayed beneath her feet, the sky was in its correct position above her head and, though her breathing was erratic, she was in no danger of swooning. She forced a smile. 'My lord, such a manly pursuit as fisticuffs is hardly in my repertoire.'

He grinned and turned to escort her to the door, where Charlotte stood looking back at them. 'You and Miss Roswell do ride, though?'

'Yes, indeed.'

He looked up at Charlotte as they approached her. 'Miss Hundon tells me you both ride,' he said. 'Would you care to join Mr Gosport and me for a gentle canter tomorrow morning? If you have no mounts, I can easily find some for you.'

Charlotte hesitated, looking to Sophie to indicate whether or not she wanted her to accept. 'I am not sure what engagements we have,' she said.

'Why, Charlotte, we said we were going to bespeak a carriage tomorrow and Lady Fitzpatrick recommended Robinson and Cook, don't you remember?'

Charlotte remembered no such thing, but she smiled and said, 'Oh, yes, I had quite forgot. I am sorry, my lord.'

'Another time, then,' he said, smiling affably. 'But, forgive me, who will advise you on your purchase? Lady Fitzpatrick…' He left the sentence hovering in the air.

'We shall take Luke, our groom, with us and he will consult the proprietor,' Sophie said.

'I doubt that will ensure a satisfactory deal,' he said. 'Allow me to offer my services.'

Charlotte appealed to Sophie and, receiving a slight nod, turned back to him. 'That is excessively kind of you, my lord, we should be most happy to accept.'

What else could she have done? Sophie asked herself, after he had arranged to call for them the following morning at ten and taken his leave. It would have been ungracious to have spurned his help, especially when she acknowledged they probably needed it.

'He has fastened himself to us like a leech,' Charlotte said as they went up to their rooms to divest themselves of their outdoor clothes. 'It is Madderlea and your fortune he has in his sights and I wish it were not so. We shall both be ruined when the truth comes out that I am not mistress of Madderlea and have no fortune.'

'Why?' Sophie threw her bonnet on the bed and followed it with her cloak, glad to be rid of the outmodish garments. 'Young gentlemen of the *ton* are forever playing tricks on people. They bam their way into select gatherings, pretend to be coachmen or highwaymen and no one thinks anything of it. Why shouldn't we?'

'We are not young gentlemen.'

'No, but we have gone too far to turn back now. We will tell everyone when we return to Leicestershire at the end of the Season. No harm will be done because you are going back to Freddie and as for me…'

'Yes? What about you?'

'Unless I can find a man who comes up to my expectations and has humour enough to laugh at our masquerade, I shall go back single.'

'What about Lord Braybrooke? Are you not a little taken with him?'

'No, I am not,' Sophie retorted, far too quickly to be convincing. 'He is too arrogant and you heard all those questions about Madderlea. He is undoubtedly counting his chickens.'

'He does not need Madderlea, he is heir to a dukedom.'

'Then he is also greedy.'

It was all very well to find fault with the man, to try to convince herself that he had not come within a mile of her expectations; the truth was that, in the space of two days, he had touched a chord in her, made her aware of feelings and desires she never knew she had. The pressure of his hand, the light in his eye, the soft cadences of his voice when he was not sparring with her, even his disapproval, excited her and lulled her at the same time. He was a threat to her peace of mind. She must remember Madderlea and her responsibilities and perhaps the danger would go away.

'He is not the only fish in the sea,' she said. 'We must make a push to meet more people and buying a carriage is the beginning of our crusade.'

'Chickens! Fish!' Charlotte laughed. 'Are we to make a tasty dinner of him?'

They both fell on to the bed in paroxysms of mirth at the idea. 'Served with potatoes and cabbage and a sharp sauce.' Sophie giggled. 'Followed by humble pie.'

There was nothing humble about Viscount Braybrooke and Sophie was obliged to acknowledge that when he called to accompany them to buy the carriage. He was dressed in frockcoat and pantaloons with a neatly tied cravat peeping over a yellow and white striped waistcoat. His dark curls were topped by a high-crowned hat with a curled brim which made him seem taller and more magnificent than ever. She was determined not to let him undermine her confidence and treated him with cool disdain, an attitude he seemed hardly to notice, being equally determined to pay particular attention to Charlotte.

But when it came to discussing the different carriages on offer at Robinson and Cook's premises in Mount Street, Charlotte, aware that it was Sophie who would be paying for it, once again fell silent. It was Sophie who found questions to ask about the advantages and disadvantages of curricles, phaetons, high-perch and low-slung barouches, landaus and tilburys, and their comparative prices, and it was Sophie who asked about horses once they had chosen a barouche because it could seat four easily and Lady Fitzpatrick would inevitably be accompanying them on most of their jaunts.

Once the arrangements had been made for it to be finished in dark green and the Roswell coat of arms to be painted on the doors, they left and were driven by Richard to Tattersall's where he purchased a pair of matched greys on their behalf and arranged for them to be delivered to the mews which served the houses in Holles Street. Luke would be in seventh heaven looking after them, Sophie knew, and prompted Charlotte politely to decline his lordship's offer of interviewing coachmen.

They arrived home in good time for nuncheon and he stopped to pay his respects to Lady Fitzgerald, treating her with great courtesy and earning her enthusiastic approbation.

'We are beholden to you, my lord,' she said on being told of the successful outcome of their visit to the coachbuilder. 'I am sure Miss Roswell could not have made such a bargain without you.'

'Indeed, no,' Charlotte said. 'We are in your debt.' He smiled and bowed towards her. 'Then, if you wish, you may discharge it by coming riding with me tomorrow morning. Mr Gosport has said he will be delighted to escort Miss Hundon.'

Surprisingly she did not consult Sophie before accepting. 'Thank you, we shall be delighted.'

Sophie's feelings about that were so ambivalent she spent the remainder of the day going from depression to elation and back again in the blinking of an eye. Richard Braybrooke had, all unknowingly, wormed his way into her heart while so patently wooing the Roswell fortune embodied in her cousin. Mentally she went over the list of attributes she had decided were required for the master of Madderlea and incidentally, the husband of its mistress, and realised she knew very little about Richard, Viscount Braybrooke.

True, he was handsome and well turned out, but he was also conceited and arrogant. Was he kind to his servants, good with children, an honourable man? She did not know and only further acquaintance would tell her, a prospect that filled her with joyful anticipation, until she remembered that his attention had been almost entirely focused on Charlotte, the supposed heiress, which made her wonder if his grandfather, the Duke, was not as plump in the pocket as everyone had supposed and her fortune was the main attraction. Or was she maligning him—was his heart really set on Charlotte?

Jealousy and her love for her cousin raged within her so that she could not sit still, could not sew or read, was snappy with everyone and then immediately sorry. Charlotte could not bring her out of it, because Charlotte herself was worried about the deception they were practising and what she was going to say to his lordship should he offer for her.

'I like him well enough,' she told Sophie in the privacy of her room. 'But I would never consider him as a husband. I am determined on marrying Freddie and nothing and no one will change that. Besides, as

soon as he discovers that you are the heiress and he
has been deceived…'

'He will want neither of us,' Sophie snapped. 'So
there is no need to put ourselves into a quake over
it.'

It was a relief to find a pile of invitations on the
breakfast table the following morning. Lady Fitzpatrick, in a housegown and with her hair pushed under
a mob cap, was delighted. 'I knew it would happen,
as soon as you were seen out with Lord Braybrooke,'
she said. 'None of the mamas of unmarried daughters
are going to let you have a clear field where he is
concerned. And the ladies with sons will not allow
him to take all the limelight when you have so much
to offer, dear Charlotte.'

She chuckled. 'Oh, this is going to be a very interesting Season. Now, girls, go and dress for your
ride. I have already sent for your mounts to be
brought to the door.' She waved the bundle of invitations at them. 'When you return we will decide on
which of these to accept and make plans for your own
come-out ball.'

'A ball?' queried Charlotte as they mounted the
stairs together. 'How can we possibly have a ball
here? There is no ballroom and the drawing room is
too small, even if we moved all the furniture out.'

Sophie was too tense to worry about the answer to
that question. 'No doubt her ladyship will find a way.
Let us take one day at a time. Today is the day for
riding.'

In spite of her mental anguish, Sophie longed for

the exhilaration of a good ride and made up her mind that she would enjoy it and not spend precious time worrying about what could not be helped. She had not bought a new riding habit because the one she already had was perfectly serviceable. Frogged in military style with silver braid, it was of deep blue velvet and fitted closely to a neat waist, becoming fuller over the hips. Her beaver hat, trimmed with a long iridescent peacock feather which curled around the brim and swept across one cheek, was a creation to turn heads.

Without revealing her true identity, she would set aside the undistinguished country cousin and be more like herself, just for a day. It was vanity, she acknowledged, but necessary if she were not to sink into self-induced oblivion. She went downstairs when she heard his lordship arrive, determined to be cool, but her resolve was almost overturned when she saw Lord Braybrooke looking up at her from the marble-tiled hall.

He was neatly but not extravagantly dressed for riding, in a double-breasted coat with black buttons, supple leather breeches and boots with enough polish to mirror whatever was immediately above them, in this case, his outstretched arm as he came towards her hand to take it in greeting.

'Miss Hundon.'

'Lord Braybrooke.'

Why was it that even the small touch of his fingers could bring a hot flush of colour to her cheeks and turn her legs to jelly? She was vastly relieved when Charlotte, becomingly attired in leaf green, followed

her downstairs and distracted the viscount, giving her
time to give herself a severe scolding and collect her
scattered wits. She picked up her crop from the hall
table and led the way outside, where Martin and Luke
stood with the horses.

Luke, who naturally knew that the stallion was her
mount, threw her up, leaving Richard, taken by surprise, to see Charlotte into her saddle, then the three
men mounted and the little cavalcade set off at walking pace, carefully weaving its way in and out of the
traffic until they reached the gates of Green Park.

Sophie on horseback was a very different person
from Sophie playing the country cousin in a Society
drawing room, or being a nondescript companion riding in a carriage. Sophie on a horse was strong and
fearless and competent. Before long she became impatient with their steady plod and, as soon as she saw
a wide expanse of green in front of her, set off at a
canter, which the others were obliged to follow.
Laughing, she increased the pace to a gallop.

Richard was torn between going after her and staying with Charlotte, who showed none of the reckless-
ness of her cousin.

Reckless perhaps, but magnificent. When he had
first seen the stallion he had thought it too strong for
either of the girls and assumed the young groom
would ride it. His initial astonishment at Miss Hundon's changed appearance was increased when he
realised the big stallion was hers. She sat it easily at
a walk, as if moulded into the saddle, but now she
was flying away from them, a born rider.

Martin, at his side, chuckled. 'Go on after her, you

know you want to,' he said in an undertone. 'I'll stay with Miss Roswell.'

Richard spurred his mount and was gone, leaving Martin to turn ruefully towards Charlotte. 'He will see she comes to no harm.'

'Oh, I doubt Sophie will fall, she is too good a rider. At home she always outruns me.'

'I suppose it is not to be wondered at. Leicestershire is good hunting country and if you have been all your life among hunting folk, you have a feel for it.'

'Oh, but Sophie has not…' She stopped in confusion and began again. 'She does not care for hunting.'

'And you?'

'I follow it sometimes, but in truth, I fell off when I was little and broke my arm. I was lucky it was no worse, but it has made me a nervous rider. Sophie is very good, she encourages me and does not usually gallop off like that, but I expect she could not resist the opportunity to stretch Pewter's legs.' She looked up to where the two riders could be seen approaching a small copse of trees. 'See, she is pulling up and his lordship has caught up with her.'

'Are you run mad?' Richard demanded, pulling his own horse to a quivering stop beside the big grey at the very edge of the trees. 'You could have been thrown.'

She smiled mischievously and slid easily to the ground. 'Did I look in danger of falling off, my lord?'

He had to admit she had not and that his annoyance was not so much directed at her as at his own strange emotions. He wanted to shout at her, to tell her she had frightened him to death, to shake her until her teeth rattled, but that was tempered by another desire, one so strong it was almost overwhelming him. He dismounted and stood beside her, looking down into her face which showed more animation than he had seen in her before.

Her greeny-grey eyes sparkled, her cheeks glowed and her mouth, slightly open, tantalised him with a glimpse of white teeth and the tip of a pink tongue. Did she know how provocative she was being? Was it a well-rehearsed ploy? God in heaven, he was not made of stone! Throwing off his hat, he reached out and pulled her into the cover of the nearest tree where he took that smiling mouth in a kiss which was almost brutal in its intensity.

She was taken completely by surprise and did not move, could not move. His mouth on hers was hard and unyielding, borne of anger, but as the kiss went on, the tension drained from him and the pressure of his lips softened. When she could have pulled herself away, she did not. She found herself responding, allowing him to explore her mouth with a feather-light tongue which swept her into heedless rapture. Her surroundings disappeared and only their two bodies, so close she could feel his heartbeat against the material of her habit, held any meaning for her.

Somewhere, deep inside her, she felt herself turn to liquid. It was as if the very essence of her was dissolving, merging, becoming one with him. The hands she had raised to push him away crept up and round his neck. Her fingers tangled themselves in his hair and pulled him even closer. Her skirt became entangled round his legs as if they were one being. Time and place were irrelevant; who he was, who she was, were irrelevant. She could smell the maleness of him, taste his saliva and it was like a drug. She was lost.

The sound of horses alerted him and he thrust her from him, breathing heavily. She stood staring at him, unable to speak.

What she ought to have been was furious with him, but that would have been hypocritical, when she had wanted the experience as much as he did. It would be more to the point to be furious with herself, for betraying her feelings, for succumbing, for forgetting she was mistress of Madderlea.

He was the first to regain his composure, but not for a moment would he admit, even to himself, that she had bewitched him, that forces stronger than reason had impelled him to act as he had. But an apology was called for. 'I beg your pardon,' he said softly. 'I did not mean to hurt you in any way.'

'What did you mean, then?' she demanded, brushing her hand against her swollen lips and trying very hard not to cry.

'Nothing, Miss Hundon.' He was almost back in command of himself. 'Temptation in the guise of a beautiful and enticing young lady is always hard to resist and I am weak when it comes to resisting temptation.'

Before she could think of a suitable reply, Charlotte's voice came to them from the other side of the bushes. 'Sophie! Where are you? Have you hurt yourself? I saw you disappear...'

Sophie sank to the ground—her legs were weak in any case—and smiled up at Charlotte as she ducked under the overhanging branches of the tree to join them. 'I twisted my ankle on a hidden root when dismounting,' she said. 'It is nothing.'

'Oh, dear, do you think you can ride?'

'Of course, it was only a little twinge. And it is not my stirrup foot.' She made to rise unaided, but Richard was at her side in a moment, picking her up effortlessly and setting up such a jangling of her nerves that she was hard put to appear calm. He carried her to her mount and set her in the saddle. Neither of them spoke.

Luke and Martin were waiting by the horses and they set off for home, silent now because every single one of them had thoughts they could not utter. Richard and Sophie were deep in contemplation of what had happened and what it might mean; Martin, guessing the truth, wondered whether his intrepid friend had at last found his match; Charlotte, surmising that something important had passed between the viscount and her cousin, worried about the deception they had perpetrated; and Luke was fearfully hoping that he would not be blamed if Miss Sophie had really hurt herself.

When they arrived at Holles Street, Richard declined Charlotte's invitation to come in and have some refreshment and the two men saw the young ladies safely indoors and turned to leave.

'Well?' Martin demanded, as they walked their horses back to Bedford Row.

'Well, what?'

'Miss Hundon did not stumble, did she? Except into your arms. I wonder you were so cork-brained, considering Miss Roswell was only a few yards behind. It was all I could do to hold her back when you both disappeared from view.'

'I do not need a scold from you, my friend, and if that is all you have to talk about, I would as lief you remained silent.'

'Then silent I shall be. But I won't stop thinking.'

They rode on without speaking for about fifty yards, then Richard laughed. 'I am sorry, Martin, you are too much of a friend to be treated in that rag-mannered way. And over a little bit of muslin.'

'Only she is not just a little bit of muslin, she is a gentle young lady, an innocent.' He turned to Richard with a gleam of humour in his eye, though he did not yet feel comfortable enough with him to laugh outright. 'And she does not meet your criteria.'

'She is lovely when she chooses to leave off those dowdy country-cousin clothes and she is fond of outdoor pursuits. She sits a horse better than some troopers I have met.'

'That could be construed as being hoydenish and I distinctly recall you saying you do not like hoydens. Besides, her family, though undoubtedly respectable, are not out of the top drawer and she has no dowry to speak of. Insuperable obstacles, my friend. And what about Miss Roswell, who has hitherto been the object of your attentions?'

'I said I was sorry, I did not ask you to renew your attack. If you must challenge me, let's go and have a few rounds at Jackson's.'

They left the horses to be rubbed down, watered and fed by grooms at his lordship's stables and walked to Bond Street where they stripped off and spent an hour in the ring, then they dressed and wandered to St James's to have coffee in Hubbold's and read the newspapers. It was late in the afternoon when they finally left and parted. Martin had undertaken to dine with his mother and Richard decided to go for a walk. He wanted to be alone to come to terms with that revealing kiss and what it meant.

Sophie, sitting in Lady Fitzgerald's drawing room, was tired of discussing balls and routs, musical evenings, visits to the opera and theatre, not to mention the gowns they would wear and the people they might meet. Her mind was too full of Richard Braybrooke to think of anything else. Indeed, she had developed a dreadful headache which was exacerbated by having to speak loudly and clearly to Lady Fitzgerald while avoiding meeting Charlotte's eyes. She knew her cousin was longing to ask her about the incident in the park and she knew she could never bring herself to speak of it.

The last straw was when Lady Fitzgerald began talking about their own ball, telling them that her old friend, Lady Gosport, had offered the use of her ballroom. 'It is excessively kind of her,' she was saying. 'And will suit our purpose well, for young Martin is a close friend of Lord Braybrooke's and the tabbies can make what they will of that. For my part, I do not subscribe to the common opinion that his lordship is a rake and is only looking for a wife to please his grandfather. The right gel will soon make him change his ways and if you should be so fortunate, my dear Charlotte, as to take his fancy, I shall consider my efforts well rewarded.'

Charlotte began a half-hearted protest, but Sophie could not stay and listen; she rose and excused herself. 'I have a dreadful headache, my lady, I need some fresh air.'

'Would it not be more efficacious to lie down and take a tisane, my dear?'

'No, my lady, I have sometimes had these headaches before and the best remedy is a walk.'

'Very well, but if you leave the garden, make sure Anne or Luke accompanies you. Charlotte and I have much to discuss and will remain here.' Her main responsibility was towards Miss Roswell, Mr Hundon had made that clear, and if the cousin chose to go out, then her duty was to see she had an escort, no more.

Sophie had been counting on that. Throwing a burnouse over her afternoon gown of striped jaconet and donning a small brimmed chip bonnet tied beneath her chin, she let herself out of the house, conveniently forgetting to alert either Anne or Luke. She wanted to be alone to think.

Where her footsteps took her she could not afterwards have said, but half an hour later she found herself in Covent Garden. The stalls and barrows had long since gone and it was not yet time for the theatregoers to begin arriving. The huge open space was comparatively free of crowds. The only people about were one or two walkers, like herself, a crowd of barefoot children playing tag and two or three beggars. It was only when one of them accosted her, dirty palm uppermost, that she realised that they were wearing the tattered remnants of uniforms.

She smiled and dug into her reticule for a few coins. 'You are soldiers?' she queried.

'Were soldiers, miss,' one of them answered her. 'Soldiers no longer, there being no call for military men now there's peace.'

'Where do you come from? You do not sound like a Londoner.'

'Norfolk, miss, but tain't no good going back there, is it? They've troubles enough of their own.'

'You have no work?'

'No, miss.'

She handed over all the money she had with her, which was only a couple of sovereigns and some smaller coins. 'I'm so sorry. I wish I could do more.'

'Oh, no, you don't.' The coins were snatched from the man's hand. 'Be off with you or I shall feel obliged to call a constable.'

She turned towards the speaker, eyes flashing angrily. 'Lord Braybrooke, how *dare* you interfere? I gave the men that money of my own free will and I wish I had more to give them. Please return it to them.'

'They did not threaten you?'

'No, of course not. Why should they?'

He handed over the money with a wry grin. The man tugged at his forelock and gave Richard a wink of understanding, which only a few short months before he would never have dared to do. 'Thank you, lady. God bless you.' And with that he turned on his heel and joined the others who had been watching the exchange with interest.

Sophie turned to Richard, still angry enough to ignore the swift beating of her heart at his unexpected appearance. 'Did you follow me?'

'No, why should I do that? I merely saw what I perceived to be a lady in trouble and came to the rescue. I apologise if I mistook the situation, but you should not be out alone. Where is your escort?'

'I do not need an escort, my lord. I have nothing worth stealing.'

'Except your good name.' It was out before he could stop it and he knew he had laid himself open to a sharp retort and he was not disappointed.

'That, my lord, was stolen earlier in the day and by someone I should have been able to trust.'

'It was not stolen, it was freely given,' he said, equal to the challenge.

'Lady Fitz said you were a rake and how right she was,' she said, ignoring the truth of his remark.

'And you are a tease.' He was angry now. He had thought she was in danger from ruffians, had expected gratitude, not this bitter exchange of accusations. Rake, indeed! 'If you behave like a demi-rep, then you must expect to be treated like one.'

It was as well Sophie did not understand the epithet or she would undoubtedly have stung his face with the flat of her hand. As it was, she was hard put to desist. He was the outside of enough. Not a gentleman. Not kind and considerate, not even honourable. Dastardly. She turned on her heel and walked away, tears stinging her eyes.

She had gone only half a dozen paces when she realised he was still beside her. 'Why are you following me? Are you hoping I will be so weak as to succumb a second time?'

'I wish I could be so fortunate,' he said, with a melodramatic sigh. 'Your generosity does you credit as I have just witnessed, but twice in one day is more than I can expect or deserve.'

'And there you are right, sir, so why dog my footsteps?'

'I may well have dug my own pit as far as you are concerned, Miss Hundon, but I am not so lacking in sense as to allow you to continue alone. You have given away all your money—what will the ruffians demand next, I wonder?'

She shuddered at the prospect. 'I am going home.'

'Then allow me to escort you.'

She nodded, unable to bring herself to admit she would be glad of his company. In spite of their harsh words, she felt safe with him, safe and protected.

At her door, he bowed with a flourish and strode away. She watched him go with a terrible ache in her heart. He failed her expectations in so many ways, but she loved him and everything else paled into insignificance beside that bittersweet knowledge.

Chapter Four

The Season began in earnest and the girls found themselves caught up in a flurry of social engagements. Accompanied by Lady Fitzpatrick, they drove out in the new carriage on most afternoons when the weather was fine, either in the park or to make calls. They left cards all over the place, went out to tea, visited the theatre with supper afterwards, attended musical gatherings and simple country dances but, until they had officially come out, they could not attend the big balls, which was where the higher echelons of the eligibles gathered. Lady Fitzpatrick, anxious to remedy that, was deep in negotiations with Lady Gosport to hold their come-out ball early in the Season.

It was thus that Martin was privy to all the arrangements and gossip that went on between his mother and the girls' sponsor, which he passed on to Richard. 'It is going to be a fearful crush,' he told him one day when the two men were relaxing at their club. 'Lady Fitzpatrick is determined that Miss Roswell will be launched in style.'

Richard laughed. 'What does she know of style, unless it be thirty years out of date. She will have us in knee breeches like they do at Almack's.'

'It is to be a costume ball. And she is being guided by Mama, so you need not fear being made to look foolish.'

'I am not concerned for myself, but the young ladies. Do they really suppose Lady Fitzpatrick is all the crack?'

'No, they are not blind. And both have a sense of refinement, particularly Miss Hundon. There is a quiet dignity about her which would be more appropriate in the heiress than the country cousin. Miss Roswell, on the other hand, delightful though she is, does not have that presence, that spirit of independence, which is so evident in her cousin.'

'Fustian! Miss Hundon is a hoyden, you said so yourself.'

'I was simply reminding you of the requirements you listed, I did not say I agreed with you.'

'I wish I had never spoken to you about them, if you are to be continually flinging them in my face. They are not writ in stone, you know. I may be flexible.'

'I am glad to hear it.'

'Why are you extolling the virtues of Miss Hundon? You know my grandfather would not countenance the daughter of a lawyer.'

'Have you asked him?'

'Certainly not. There is no need, I have no plans to offer for Miss Sophie Hundon.'

'Miss Roswell, then? She is excessively wealthy,

but you would not know it to speak to her, for she is
modesty itself. And Madderlea is a great house, I am
told, though, according to Mama, it needs repairs and
renovation. She really must marry soon or it will go
to rack and ruin for want of someone to care for it.
Once the Season gets underway, the competition will
be fierce.'

'I thought it already had.'

'No, what we have had are only preliminary skirmishes, the real battles are to come. I am looking
forward to it.'

'So you may be. You are not constrained by duty
as I am.' Richard chuckled suddenly. 'But I intend to
mix duty with pleasure. I shall flirt lightly with every
unmarried miss between the ages of seventeen and
thirty and keep them all guessing. I shall sometimes
be disdainful and superior and sometimes flattering
and eager and see what transpires. It will serve the
dowagers right for putting wealth and title before
character. Time enough to be serious when I have
made up my mind.'

'By then you will have earned the reputation of
being a rakeshame and none will have you. Certainly
Miss Roswell will not.'

'I am persuaded that is already my reputation,' he
said, reminded of Sophie's accusation. 'I may as well
live up to it.'

'Why?'

'Why?' he echoed. He did not know. He was not
a conceited man, nor was he vindictive, but he hated
this notion that a single man in want of a wife must
parade himself before hopeful mamas, his address and

conduct scrutinised, his prospects and fortunes ana-
lysed, until it was impossible to sneeze without it being the subject of gossip. If he were not the Duke of
Rathbone's heir, if he were still a simple soldier, no
one would be the least interested in him.

'I suppose it is because I dislike the idea that my
faults should be weighed against my title and fortune
and not against my virtues,' he said slowly. 'I am
curious to know how far the scales will tip before one
outweighs the other.'

'That is a dangerous game to play, my friend. You
may put off the avaricious, though give me leave to
doubt it, but you will also give the lady of your choice
a hearty aversion to you.'

He had already done so, he realised with a jolt that
shook him to the core. Miss Hundon, the country
cousin, an entirely unsuitable young lady in the eyes
of his grandfather, had never been far from his
thoughts ever since he had met her. She had more
than most to gain by becoming the Duchess of Rathbone. Had she deliberately set out to trap him into
that kiss, hoping for a declaration? Had she galloped
away, knowing he would follow and that if she fluttered her eyelashes at him, he, being a man, would
be bound to do what he had? It was easier to convince
himself of that than to admit he had fallen in love.

His conviction was sorely shaken when he next
came across Miss Roswell and Miss Hundon after a
visit to the opera one evening when he discovered
they were included in the supper party Lord and Lady
Howard had arranged afterwards. Paying attention to

the Howard daughter while uncomfortably aware that Sophie stood only a few yards away and could hear every word was unnerving. He felt an almost uncontrollable urge to turn towards her and tell her he was only acting the part, to grab hold of her and hurry her away some private place where he could taste her lips again, feel her body pressed up against his, to know her passion matched his.

Instead he completed his conversation with Miss Howard and, turning as casually as he could towards the object of his discomfort, swept her a leg of such exaggerated proportions that he made her smile. 'Why, Miss Hundon, I did not know you were to be here. How do you do?'

'Well, my lord, thank you.' Having had a few moments to compose herself while he talked to Miss Howard, her voice was cool and distant. He must not know how his very presence in the same room set her heart fluttering uncomfortably in her throat. Lady Fitzpatrick's informant had been correct: his behaviour, now the Season's events were following each other thick and fast, was definitely rakish. His eye roved over the company at every gathering, stayed on her for a second that seemed like a month, and moved on. He danced with every debutante, talked a great deal of nonsense, leaving the mamas twittering and the young ladies sighing.

How had she come to be so deceived in him? Why, even now, did she tremble whenever he was near? Why could she not be like Charlotte, relieved that his attention had moved on, able to laugh at his antics and thank goodness for her escape?

'Has this been your first visit to the opera?' he queried, almost at a loss for a safe subject for conversation.

'No, my lord, my father took me to…' Goodness, she had almost said Vienna '…the local operatic society amateur performances but, naturally, they were nothing like this. I enjoyed tonight's singing very much, but I did think the soprano had a tendency to shriek on the high notes.'

'So she did.' He smiled, thankful not to have to flirt with her. He could talk to her in a sensible fashion about all manner of subjects and he allowed himself to enjoy the experience. She was not in the running for Duchess of Rathbone and he did not have to pretend she was. 'Her talent is fading now, but she had a fine voice when she was younger. I heard her sing in Milan years ago, just before the war, when I went on the Grand Tour. But when hostilities began, her planned visit to London had to be cancelled.'

'The war spoiled so many pleasures, took so many good men's lives,' she said softly, thinking of her father. 'And many of those that survive are in dire straits.'

'You are thinking of those soldiers you spoke to?'

'Yes, and others. I cannot get them out of my mind. Surely something could be done to help them?'

He decided to humour her, simply to prolong the discussion. 'What do you suggest?'

'Work could be created. Repairing the roads, for they are in a parlous state, building houses. Give them plots of land so they may be self-sufficient…'

'My goodness, a Radical!'

'I did not expect you to agree with me,' she said, stiffly. 'Brought up as you have been in comfort. You cannot know what it is like to be poor.'

'Not poor, perhaps,' he said. 'But my father was a second son and had to make his own way and I have been a soldier myself. Do not brand me a humbug.'

She felt the colour flare in her cheeks at this put-down but, though she knew she deserved it, she was not yet ready to apologise. 'I notice you did not follow my example and give a little money to those beggars.'

'No, because they would spend it all on drink. It is the soldier's panacea for everything. Believe me, I know. It is not charity they need, but work. You said so yourself.' He smiled. 'My dear, if you must indulge in deep debate do, at least, be consistent.'

'Oh, you are the outside of enough!' she exclaimed, proving to his satisfaction that, faced with logic, she reverted to being entirely feminine. He could have told her that whenever a vacancy occurred at any of his grandfather's properties, priority was always given to ex-soldiers, particularly those with families. It had taken him more than a little effort to persuade the Duke to agree, but the policy had paid off with loyal and hard-working staff. He didn't tell her because he did not want to score points over her. And he knew what her reply would be if he did: what he had done was a drop in the ocean compared to what needed doing.

They were interrupted by Lady Howard who felt that her chief guest had been monopolised long enough by Miss Hundon who had no fortune and no prospects and should never have been encouraged to share dear Miss Roswell's come-out. It was giving her ideas above her station.

'Do come and allow me to introduce you to Miss Greenholme,' she said, dragging him away. 'She is the Marquis of Bury's granddaughter, you know.'

'And I am the granddaughter of an earl,' Sophie muttered to Charlotte who had, at that moment, come to her side.

'Then why not say so and be done with this charade?'

'Charades! What an excellent idea!' Lady Fitzpatrick exclaimed, catching only the last word.

'Charlotte did not mean this evening,' Sophie said, enunciating carefully. 'It is far too late.'

'Yes, you are right, my dear,' her ladyship agreed equably. 'We will arrange something for another day. Now, I think it is time to take our leave.'

The girls dutifully did the rounds of the company, saying goodbye, but Lord Braybrooke had gone to play cards in an adjoining room and was nowhere to be seen. Sophie told herself she was glad; the less she saw of that pompous young man the better.

Richard spent almost the whole night at the gaming tables, but his mind was not on the cards; though he did not lose too heavily, he realised that playing whist was not the way to take his mind off a certain young lady. He needed to think. Declining Martin's offer to accompany him, he returned home just before dawn, bathed, changed into riding clothes and ordered his horse to be saddled. A long ride into the country might serve to clear his head.

The sky was shot with pink and mauve as the sun rose slowly in a great orange orb above the horizon as he rode out on to the Hampstead road. The trees were in full leaf and the air was heady with the scent of blossom. The heath, when he reached it, was dotted with grazing cows and goats, and in the clear air, the birds were in full song, greeting the dawn. There was nothing to beat the English countryside in early summer, he decided, breathing deeply. It was something he had dreamed about in the heat and dust of Spain, England's green and pleasant land and his home in Hertfordshire.

He walked his horse, allowing it to have its head and go where it willed, reflecting on those dreams of home and how he had felt when he was told he had become his grandfather's heir. The war had been coming to an end at the time, but he would have been expected to give up his commission in any case, to come back and prepare to take up the responsibilities of administering a vast estate, to learn how to be a landowner, to care for his people, to do his duty.

He was a military man, an officer; he knew the importance of doing one's duty even when it was disagreeable. He had punished men for failing the high standards of courage he expected of them. He could not be any easier on himself. And his duty was clear; he must marry. It was all very well to joke with Martin about his requirements in a wife, but it was a deadly serious business and he would do well to take stock of his situation.

He was thirty years old next birthday, wealthy and titled. He was strong and healthy, not ugly by any means, and he dealt well with almost everyone. He would not make unreasonable demands of his wife, but she must be up to being a duchess and that took breeding. Being cool and level-headed about it, he could see that Miss Hundon was already out of the running. Miss Greenholme was a possible, but she was hardly out of the schoolroom and terrified of him. There were others, but the one who stood out as being the one his grandfather would most likely sanction was Miss Roswell.

Charlotte. If there had been no Miss Hundon, no kiss in the park, he might have been very content with Miss Roswell. Perhaps he still could be. He would stop being frivolous and seriously set about wooing that young lady.

His horse whinnied, reminding him that the sun had climbed high in the sky and food and water were required for both of them. He stopped at an inn on the other side of the heath for refreshment, before riding back to town, his mind made up. Duty before love.

Because Lady Fitzpatrick had her hands full concentrating on Charlotte, Sophie was often left to her own devices, a state of affairs she found very agreeable, even though Charlotte frequently protested. 'You are the heiress, not me,' she said. 'You should be the one to be paraded before all the eligibles.'

'And very glad I am not to be,' she said, watching her cousin change to go out with Lady Fitzpatrick.

'You can sum up their characters for me and weed out the hopeless ones.'

'And how am I to know who they are?'

'You know my criteria.'

'If I am to adhere to that, then every single man I have met so far falls a long way short.' She paused. 'There is Lord Braybrooke, of course.'

'Him! No, he was the first to go. We will not mention him again.'

Charlotte sighed heavily. 'Very well. But if I am to pay calls with Lady Fitz this afternoon, what will you be doing?'

'I am going to see the sights: the Tower and London Bridge, Westminster Abbey, St Paul's, the waxworks and Bullock's Museum. I believe Napoleon's coach is on view there.'

'You cannot do that in a single afternoon, Sophie.'

'Naturally I cannot. Hatchett's is sure to have a guide book to help me find my way about. Shall I find a book for you while I am there?'

'Sophie, I am not given time to read, you know that, nor for sightseeing, though I would dearly love to accompany you, and it is all because of this masquerade you have embroiled me in. It rates more than a scolding and I dread to think what Mama and Papa will say when they find out.'

Sophie felt exactly the same, not so much for herself because she did not care two pins for Society's conventions, but for her cousin, but whenever she thought she could play the part no longer, she thought of Madderlea and why they had come to London. Choosing a husband who would be good for Mad-

derlea was one thing, falling in love quite another.
And she had fallen in love, she could not deny it. She
had fallen in love with the most unsuitable man in
the whole of London, if her list of requirements were
to be the yardstick.

He was a dandy, a fortune hunter, a flirt, a man
without honour who could take a gently brought-up
young lady into the bushes and kiss her without so
much as a by-your-leave or any sort of declaration
and then accuse her of being a tease! And all that
when he was clearly trying to fix Charlotte's attention,
believing her to be the heiress. Would he, as soon as
he knew the truth, suddenly turn to her? She didn't
want him on those terms. No, she did not! She would
find herself a husband and then reveal who she really
was and that would serve everyone right for engaging
in this affectation they called the Season.

'Wait until after our ball, Charlotte, please. I promise I will not prolong it after that.'

Charlotte agreed. In truth, she enjoyed playing the
heiress and found it very gratifying to have every eligible young man in London paying her court, but she
was not such a goose as to imagine their attentions
were sincere and she had a great deal of sympathy
for her cousin's predicament. She smiled and picked
up her reticule. 'But I will not have you crying off
outings to go to staring at old buildings, it is no way
to go on if you want to find yourself a husband. Tonight we are invited out to supper and entertainments
at Mrs Whitworthy's and you must come.'

Sophie had every intention of going to Hatchett's,
but there was something else she wanted to do as

well, something she knew perfectly well Lady Fitzpatrick and her cousin would not approve of and it
had nothing whatever to do with social engagements
and finding a husband. Before she set out, she went
to the mews to find their groom who was busy har-
nessing the greys to the carriage.

'Sorry, Miss Sophie, I was told two o'clock,' he
said, finding that mode of address easier than her fic-
tional one of Miss Hundon. What Mr Hundon would
make of it all when he heard, Luke dared not think.
But he was very fond of both girls and the five guineas would go a long way to allowing him to propose
to the young lady he had set his heart on. 'I will have
the carriage ready in a shake of a lamb's tail.'

'I am not using the carriage this afternoon, Luke.
It is Lady Fitzpatrick and Charlotte who are going out
in it and they are not yet ready. I came to ask you a
question.'

'Oh, and what would that be, miss?' he queried,
his heart in his boots in case it was another outrageous
request like pretending she was her cousin.

'There are a great many discharged soldiers in
town, begging in the streets…'

He looked startled. 'Yes, miss, there are. But, cra-
vin' your pardon, miss, you should not be bothered
by them.'

'But I am bothered. I cannot stop thinking about
them. What I wondered…' She stopped and swallowed. 'Do you know where they congregate?'

'I'm sure I don't know, miss, and you shouldn't be
asking me such a question.'

'I want to help them.'

He forgot to be subservient and stared at her in astonishment. 'How?'

'I don't know. I need to ask them. Food, lodgings, work. Luke, I am a very rich young lady and it is not fair that I should have so much when they, who have fought so gallantly and achieved such a fine victory, should have so little. So tell me, where can they be found? I saw some in Covent Garden a week or so ago. Is that where they are?'

'Lady Fitzpatrick would never agree to let you go there!'

'I do not intend to tell her.'

'You don't mean to go alone? No, miss, it is not to be thought of. You will be set upon, robbed. Worse. I could not have that on my conscience. I shall be obliged to tell her ladyship.'

'I won't be alone if you are with me, will I? Lady Fitzpatrick's coachman can drive the carriage this afternoon and you can come with me.'

'Oh, Miss Sophie, I dursn't.'

'You are quite right,' she said, realising it was not fair to the young man to bully him so. 'Forget I asked.'

He breathed a sigh of relief and watched her as she left the mews. But she did not go back towards the house, but carried on to the main thoroughfare and he knew she intended to go alone. It wasn't as if he didn't know the answer to her question. His brother had died out in Spain and he had often, when he had an hour or two off duty, gone to drink and chat with the veterans, hoping that he might meet someone who had known and fought alongside Matthew. Hastily he called to Lady Fitzpatrick's coachman to take over and hurried after her.

'There is a soup kitchen I know of, where the men line up for a hot bowl of soup and a hunk of bread,' he told her when he caught up with her. 'It is run by a Mrs Stebbings.'

'Good. Take me there. You will be well rewarded. And I am not Miss Roswell, nor yet Miss Hundon, I shall be Mrs Carter. A widow. An officer's widow, I think. Do you understand?'

He scratched his head in perplexity. 'Yes, miss.'

Mrs Stebbings, thin as a rake and dressed from head to foot in black, except for a huge white apron, was serving the men from the back of a wagon parked in an alley off Covent Garden. She was the widow of an infantry sergeant, she told Sophie, after Luke had introduced her. 'Some of his men came to visit me after the war ended and I was appalled at their condition. The poor things were in rags and almost starving. They were men my husband had lived and fought with and naturally I fed them, but they told me of others, some in even worse straits, so I started a little subscription fund to buy the ingredients for the soup. Most of it is scrag of mutton and vegetables, but it is hot and nourishing.'

'How long have you been doing it?' Sophie asked, taking off her cloak and donning a sacking apron to help.

'Almost a year, but the line of men and their families waiting to be served does not grow any shorter.

Indeed, with the withdrawal of the occupation troops earlier this year, it has become even longer.'

'And you have very little shelter against inclement weather.'

'No, but they take no account of that, though I have noticed that many of them are ill when the weather is bad—some are still suffering from their wounds. What they need is shelter and medical care, but the fund will not stretch to that.'

'Then more money must be found.'

'I have tried, but most people look upon the poor men as a nuisance and want to see them off the streets.'

'The best way to do that, surely, is for them to have work and homes.'

'Oh, if only it were possible.'

'I will undertake to raise enough for one refuge, at least.'

'You can do that?' Mrs Stebbings's astonishment was comical, making Sophie smile.

'I think so. I have some visits to make now, but I will be back.'

She had sounded so positive when talking to Mrs Stebbings, but making good her promise would not be easy, she knew. Her allowance, though more than generous, was not a bottomless purse. Most of London was owned by aristocratic landowners, even the poor districts, and they employed agents to look after their interests. Accompanied by a bemused Luke, she set off to find such a one.

She wanted to rent a house, she told him. It had to be very cheap so it did not have to be in good repair, because she was sure the tenants would be only too pleased to make it habitable, and it ought to be somewhere around Covent Garden.

The poor man did not know what to make of this extraordinary request from someone who was obviously a gentlewoman. Had she run away? Had she been abandoned by a lover and was too frightened to go home?

'I would advise you to return to your parents, miss,' he said. 'You do not know what you are embarking upon. You would never survive living in such a district.'

'I do not intend to live there, sir,' she said, perfectly able to read his mind. 'I am representing an association of philanthropic ladies dedicated to looking after out-of-work soldiers. We wish to make a refuge for them to stay until they find work.'

'Then I think I have the very property,' he said, breathing a huge sigh of relief which made her smile. 'It is in Maiden Lane. I will conduct you there, if you would not object to waiting while I arrange for my clerk to take over in my absence.'

When Sophie saw the house her disappointment was acute. It was in a dreadfully run-down state, with broken windows and doors, tiles missing from the roof and damp everywhere. The agent assured her she would find nothing cheaper, so she paid a deposit and returned to Mrs Stebbings with the good news.

She would write to Uncle William and tell him their expenses had been much higher than they had calculated and she needed an increase in her allowance. He would not refuse her, knowing how important this trip to London was for the future of Madderlea and the lifting of his burden as trustee. Later she would tell him the truth, along with a confession about her change of identity with Charlotte. If, by then, she had secured a husband, he would not be too angry.

Securing a husband was the main stumbling block. The Season was already well underway and she had not done a thing to advance that cause. In fact, she had been dilatory to the point of standing still. And the reason for that was a tall, handsome man who set her nerves tingling and turned her legs to jelly. She must stop thinking about him, she really must. She saw him everywhere, expected him round every corner, wanted him to be there, was disappointed when he was not. She longed for him and knew that whatever her future life held, she would never love anyone else. Was Madderlea worth the anguish?

Richard had been in Holles Street, intending to pay his respects to Lady Fitzpatrick, and request Miss Roswell's company for a carriage ride in the park, when he saw Sophie leave the house alone. He had dived, like a thief, into the cover of the nearest bush and watched her.

She was dressed in that awful grey gown and cloak, but she walked with a purpose and held her head high, her red-gold curls peeping out from beneath a small straw bonnet. Martin had been right, she did have dignity and presence, but that covered a very passionate nature as he knew to his cost. He could not put that kiss and the feel of her body held against his from his mind. It eclipsed everything else, made nonsense of his coldly calculated list of requirements for a wife, turned him from a man of the world into a boy in the throes of first love, and he resented it.

As he watched, the young groom had joined her and they set off together, talking animatedly. He felt an uncontrollable envy of her young escort and had set off after them, intending he knew not what. She had no business going out with no other escort but a servant; he had told her that when he had intervened over those begging soldiers. Did she never listen to advice?

He had followed them, keeping out of sight, while they made their way along Oxford Street and down Charing Cross Road towards Seven Dials. Surely she was not going to venture into that notorious den of iniquity? He had quickened his pace. She must be stopped and that groom called over the coals for taking her anywhere near the place. He smiled grimly, remembering the last set down she had given him for interfering. Well, he would interfere again and chance her wrath.

He had been relieved when she safely negotiated the corner, but the danger was not over and he kept close behind, ready to pounce on anyone who so much as lifted a finger against her. When she turned down Long Acre and into Covent Garden, he guessed it was the discharged soldiers she was thinking of. Her compassion did her credit, but he did not see what good giving them a handful of sovereigns would do. They would never leave her alone once they realised she was a soft touch.

He watched in amazement as she approached the soup kitchen where she took off her cloak and donned an apron to serve food to the line of men. It was magnificent of her and his annoyance turned to admiration and a burning desire to stand at her side and do likewise. But he desisted, knowing she would not welcome him.

He stood, lost in admiration of her cool perfection, knowing there would never be another woman for him and, however much his grandfather blustered and threatened, however often Martin reminded him of his rash and arrogant list of requirements, he would marry no other. But how to win her? Was it already too late?

He had been a thorough-going fool and ruined his chances with his brash conduct and his half-hearted efforts to engage the attention of other hopefuls, including her very rich, very pretty, but somewhat uninspiring cousin, who deserved to have a husband who loved her. He could not love her, or anyone else, while Sophie Hundon lived and breathed.

And he had insulted her with that kiss. It had been intended to hurt for making him feel as he did, to let her know who was master, not only of her but of his own emotions. Her response had been unintentional, a physical reaction down to his own practised ability and her innocence. And he had called her a tease— worse, a demi-rep! Would she ever forgive him for that?

The men to whom she was administering were rough and unkempt but they treated her with extraordinary courtesy and good humour, and she was in no danger with Luke glued to her side. He waited until she left, assuming she was returning home, then turned and strode away, unaware of the next call she made.

He must see his grandfather, tell him the truth and beg to be allowed a free choice. If the old man met Sophie, he would surely understand. He could put an end to the charade he had been playing and be himself. But first he needed to know how Sophie really felt about him, whether, she held him in complete aversion or whether if he tried to explain, she might understand. It was going to be decidedly tricky, especially as she was so evidently very fond of her cousin and would do nothing to hurt her.

He arrived back at Braybrooke House in the late afternoon. Leaving his horse for a groom to stable he strode indoors, intending to order the tea-tray to be taken to his room, where he could drink it while he changed. He was puzzled to find a mountain of luggage in the hall.

'What's that?' he demanded of the footman who had opened the door to him.

'Lady Braybrooke is here,' the man said. 'She and Miss Braybrooke arrived earlier this afternoon. They are taking tea in the drawing room.'

Aunt Philippa and Emily! They were the last people he wanted to see. 'Tell them I will join them directly I have changed,' he told the servant, before bounding up the stairs two at a time.

Half an hour later he entered the drawing room,

bathed and dressed in a modest kerseymere frockcoat and matching pantaloons. He bowed to his aunt before kissing her hand and then turned to do the same to Emily, noticing the colour flare in her pale cheeks when he asked her how she did.

'We have been hearing such tales, Richard,' his aunt said, when the courtesies had been completed. 'I determined to come at once and scotch them.'

'Rumours, Aunt? About whom?'

'You, of course. Tell me you have not been flirting with every unmarried girl in town, making a cake of yourself…'

He laughed, though the sound was a little cracked. 'Grandfather ordered me to find a wife and that is what I am doing. How I go about it is my affair.'

'And that includes making up to dowds who are no more than paid companions…'

He did not doubt she was referring to Sophie, though how she had found out about her he did not know. He supposed tattle was as easily spread by writing letters as by word of mouth. 'If you mean Miss Hundon, she is far from a dowd.'

'She is highly unsuitable. You know perfectly well what your grandfather's wishes are and acting the park saunterer will not endear him to you. I only wish the estate had not been entailed, then Emily would hold all the cards, not you.'

'Marriage is not a game of cards, ma'am,' he said sombrely. 'Though I own it is a great gamble.'

'Of course it is not. You simply do your duty.'

'Mama…' Emily began. 'Please, you are putting me to the blush.'

'Then go and do your embroidery. I came to speak my mind and I intend to do it.'

'Aunt, you are being unkind to Emily,' he said. 'Given a free choice she would not choose me, I am quite sure.'

'How do you know? You haven't offered for her.'

Emily, overcome with embarrassment, fled from the room in floods of tears.

'There! See what you have done,' his aunt said. 'She will make her face all blotchy with weeping and we are meant to be going out this evening.'

He did not answer. What was the good? His aunt was in no mood to listen. In fact, she continued to scold. 'I think you might at least make a push to be agreeable to your cousin and let the world see that you are not the scapegrace they think you are. A little conduct would not come amiss.

'Escort us both to Mrs Whitworthy's this evening. We were invited to supper, but I was afraid we would not arrive in town in time and undertook only to join the company for the entertainment afterwards. It is just as well because it will take some time to repair the ravages to Emily's complexion.'

He was not aware that he had been disagreeable to Emily. In fact, he had always been scrupulously careful in his conduct towards her. He was fond of her in a cousinly sort of way and had done nothing to encourage her to think of him as a husband. It was her mother who had put the idea into the old duke's head and kept it there with constant nagging.

To save his cousin from any more scolding from her mama, he agreed, but that didn't mean he would abandon his plan to go to Hertfordshire to see his grandfather. Escorting his aunt and cousin was simply an unwelcome diversion.

Sophie and Charlotte, in a whispered exchange, agreed that the supper party was extremely dull. The young men were either peacocks, making no secret of their need for a rich wife, or were already very rich and looking only for a breeding machine to produce the mandatory heir. Some were extremely silly. The young ladies were their counterparts and, in Sophie's opinion, they deserved each other. It was a bigger masquerade than ever she and Charlotte were perpetrating and she hated it.

'We shall have to do something to liven it up, or I shall die of boredom,' Charlotte murmured, as they applauded a very out-of-tune duet. 'Shall you play and sing for us?'

Mrs Whitworthy, catching the end of what Charlotte had said, turned to Sophie. 'Oh, Miss Hundon, do entertain us. It is always nice to listen to a new talent.'

'I am not very talented, ma'am.'

'Oh, she is, she is,' Charlotte put in.

Sophie rose reluctantly and took her seat at the pianoforte, wondering what to play. And then an imp of mischief jumped into her head and nudged her. 'You wanted to liven things up,' it said. 'Then go on and do it.'

She struck a chord, then her fingers danced over the keys and her melodious voice began to sing in French. It was not until she repeated the chorus that the assembled company began to fidget. Few of them were able to translate accurately because the song was in patois, but the tune and the rhythm was quick and lively and her manner of delivery was enough to alert them to the fact that this was not a song for the drawing room. After a time she heard a murmur in the room behind her, then the rustle of skirts and a cough or two and then a chuckle. Someone appreciated it.

At the end she turned in her seat, with a smile which could almost have been construed as triumphant, to receive the applause which was more enthusiastic from the young men than the ladies who were present. It was when she rose to go back to her seat she saw Richard standing at the back of the room, an expression of delighted surprise on his face. How long had he been there? Had he understood the words of the song? She could feel the colour burning her cheeks and wished she had not been so lacking in decorum. What must he think of her?

'Viscount Braybrooke, Lady Braybrooke and Miss Emily Braybrooke,' the footman announced.

'His lordship's aunt and cousin,' she heard Lady Fitzpatrick whisper to Charlotte as she returned to sit with them. 'There is talk that the old duke would like to see a liaison there. If the gossip is right, it is a great shame. But I cannot think why else they have come to town. You are going to need your wits about you, my dear, if you are to prise him loose.'

'My lady,' Charlotte returned, 'if that is where his heart lies, I have no wish to detach him from her. In truth, I…'

'Fustian!' her ladyship said, bracingly. 'It is all part of the game. You will see.'

Game! Sophie grimaced. Was that how Lord Braybrooke saw it? Had he simply been amusing himself until his cousin arrived in the capital and put an end to the fun? If so, she had been right to discount him. But it hurt, it hurt so much she didn't know how she was going to keep her composure for the rest of the evening.

Chapter Five

Mrs Whitworthy, who had not seen her new guests arrive, hurried forward to greet them, all a-twitter. 'My lady,' she said, 'please forgive me, I did not see you there. And Miss Braybrooke, how charming you look.' Emily, in a white muslin open gown over a pale pink underskirt, inclined her head at the compliment. Their hostess turned to Richard. 'Lord Braybrooke, I had not expected you to honour our little gathering with your presence. You are welcome.'

'Thank you, ma'am.' He bowed towards her, immaculate in an evening coat of mulberry velvet and dark pantaloons, his cravat a masterpiece of his valet's art.

'I believe you are acquainted with most of the company,' Mrs Whitworthy went on, almost dragging her ladyship round the room, to meet her guests one by one. Stopping opposite Charlotte, she said, 'But I do not think you know Miss Roswell. Allow me to present her.'

Lady Braybrooke, in mauve half-mourning for a

husband lost over three years before, lifted her lorgnette and subjected Charlotte to a thorough inspection. 'Earl of Peterborough's niece, I believe. Inherited the lot when his lordship stuck his spoon in the
wall. Not that it isn't a millstone round your neck, for
I am persuaded it is in a parlous state of repair and
needing a man's hand.'

Charlotte, taken aback by her ladyship's outspo-
kenness, curtsied but could find nothing to say. Richard gave her a wry smile of sympathy as they passed
on to Sophie, who was bubbling with indignation.
'This is Miss Roswell's cousin, my lady, Miss Hundon.'

The quizzing glass went up again and Sophie, unlike her cousin, returned the gaze unwaveringly, looking from a mauve satin turban topped with a tall black
feather, down over a thin face and thin lips to a rake-
like figure which was held very upright. It was meant
to intimidate, but she would not be intimidated, especially as Richard was standing just behind his aunt,
smiling enigmatically. Was he laughing at her or with
her? She could not tell. Her chin went up. 'How do
you do, Lady Braybrooke.'

Her ladyship's answer was almost a snort. Top-
lofty in the extreme, Sophie decided, watching her
move away, followed by her daughter, a tall dark-
haired girl who had not yet rid herself of her puppy
fat. She had her hand on Richard's sleeve in an un-
equivocal gesture of possession. So Lady Fitz had
been right and that was where the wind lay!

'This is Lady Fitzpatrick, Miss Roswell's sponsor.'

'Oh, we have known each other since we were

girls,' Lady Braybrooke said. 'How do you do, Harriet?'

'I am well, thank you, Philippa. What brings you to town?'

'Family affairs, my dear. Must keep the young people up to the mark, must we not?'

'Indeed, we must.'

'I did not realise you were acquainted with the Earl of Peterborough.'

'I was not. Mrs Hundon is a distant cousin and Hundon is Miss Roswell's trustee. I am acting *in loco parentis* for both girls.'

'Oh, so that is the connection.'

Sophie was beginning to worry that somehow other truths might be revealed and the last thing she wanted was for anyone to begin digging deeper. The deception was hard enough to maintain as it was.

Lady Fitzpatrick, equally reluctant to be quizzed, came to her rescue. 'I was about to suggest charades, my lady,' she said, then, turning to Mrs Whitworthy, 'What do you think, Annabel?'

'Capital idea!' their hostess exclaimed. 'Perhaps Miss Braybrooke and his lordship would care to take part.' And without giving the new arrivals time to respond, she added 'I shall select teams of four.'

This took some organising because the good lady was mindful of the main reason for the gathering, to bring hitherto single young men and ladies together and she had already mentally paired everyone off, except Sophie and Charlotte.

Sophie found herself in the same team as Richard and Emily, probably because it was deemed more prudent, in view of Emily's arrival, to keep Richard away from the heiress of Madderlea than from the poor cousin, a situation Sophie might have found amusing, if she had not been worried about the fact that the viscount was standing next to her, his head bent towards her as the group decided on the adage they were going to enact.

He was stirring her insides up in such a froth she could hardly breathe. If his close proximity did this to her, whatever would happen if he touched her? But, remembering that kiss, she knew the answer to that. She would melt, just as if she hadn't a bone in her body and everyone present would see and guess what was the matter with her. She would be a subject for derision; the poor relation who had the temerity to wear the willow for the Season's biggest catch. The fact that she wasn't the poor relation was neither here nor there. Whatever happened, she must remain cool.

They chose 'a bird in the hand is worth two in the bush' at Richard's suggestion. Three chairs were set side by side and a large potted plant placed behind them to represent the bush. Sophie and Emily and one of the young men sat side by side pretending to preen themselves and flutter their wings, oblivious of Richard stalking them. He reached out suddenly and grabbed Sophie by the hand, pulling her to her feet, while the two remaining birds twittered nervously.

They had expected the company to guess the answer at this point, but when they did not Richard cupped Sophie's hand in his, stroking the back of it, as if stroking a nervous bird. She was meant to cheep like a bird, but the sound she made was more a strangled cry of distress. The gentle pressure of his fingers was playing havoc with her resolve. She was shaking and prayed that everyone would assume it was part of the play-acting because she could not stop it. Was he also play-acting when he looked down into her eyes with such gentle concern for the bird he had trapped?

He released her at last and made an effort to catch the two in the bush, but his efforts ended in failure. He spread empty hands to the company and shrugged his shoulders in defeat, as they began murmuring among themselves.

'Have you not guessed it yet?' he enquired, forcing himself to sound normal, though Sophie's little hand trapped in his had had the most disturbing affect. 'Must we do it all again?'

Sophie didn't want a repeat performance, especially as Emily was looking at her with venom in her dark eyes as if it were her fault Richard had chosen to 'capture' her. 'Oh, Charlotte, you surely know,' she said. 'It is a very common truism.'

'They were birds, were they not?' one of the young ladies said. 'And one of them was trapped in Lord Braybrooke's hand.'

Charlotte laughed and clapped her hands. 'Oh, I know what it is. A bird in the hand is worth two in the bush.'

The players bowed and took their place in the audience while the next team, which included Charlotte, began their charade, but Sophie could not concentrate—she was too aware that Richard had chosen to sit beside her, even though he seemed to be concentrating on the players. She hid her hands in the folds of her gown so that he would not see that they were still shaking, and tilted her chin up.

'I enjoyed your little song, Miss Hundon,' he whispered, proving that he was paying no more attention than she was.

'Thank you, my lord.'

'You learned the French accent very well.'

'You understood it?'

'Oh, yes, I understood most of it. The point is, did you? Or did you simply learn it by rote?'

She could not admit that her French was perfect or that she knew the song to be a little *risqué*. She smiled. 'I learned it by rote, my lord. I have a good ear.'

'Indeed you have and a very pretty one,' he said, looking at that organ. He leaned towards it to whisper. 'Miss Hundon, I must speak to you. It is important.'

He had a guilty conscious, she told herself, and all he wanted to do was to excuse himself and explain about his attachment to his cousin and how he had been amusing himself with the young ladies of the *ton* until her arrival. Sophie did not want to hear it. Besides, it was Charlotte who deserved an explanation, not her. 'Shush, my lord,' she whispered. 'You are disturbing the others.'

He sighed and turned his attention back to the charades. It was not the right time to unburden himself to her, he must wait for a more appropriate moment. But no such moment presented itself that evening.

Charlotte's team managed to portray 'too many cooks spoil the broth' and this was followed by 'pride goes before a fall' and then the party broke up. As everyone was saying their goodbyes and arranging to meet at other social occasions, Sophie heard their hostess invite Lord Braybrooke and Miss Braybrooke to a ball and the young lady's enthusiastic acceptance.

She watched his lordship closely. He gave no indication that the arrangement was not acceptable to him. Indeed, he seemed to have lost his light-hearted air of dalliance and though he smiled, it was a smile of serious intent, as if his wings had truly been clipped. And by Miss Braybrooke! Sophie was more sure than ever that was what he had wanted to speak to her about.

She turned away to fetch her pelisse and bonnet, feeling as though her heart were breaking. All her play-acting, her masquerade as her cousin, had been to no purpose. She could not have the man she loved; though there were others eager to become master of Madderlea and her fortune, they thought Charlotte was the heiress, not she. Not that she wanted to marry any of them, so that did not signify.

She could return to Upper Corbury unattached but that would certainly displease her uncle who had been so good to her, giving her a home and looking after Madderlea, but he could not be expected to continue to do so now that she had recovered her health and was of marriageable age. Madderlea was a burden he should not have to bear, especially when he would rather be spending more time with his invalid wife.

Oh, what a coil she had got herself into! And she had embroiled Charlotte. She had not been fair to Charlotte. She was thankful that her cousin had not fallen in love with any of the young bloods she had met, that her mind was as firmly fixed as ever on marrying Frederick Harfield.

The cure for her ills, she decided, during a sleepless night, was to immerse herself in the problems of others and perhaps, in trying to solve those, a solution to her own would present itself to her.

The keys to the house in Maiden Lane had been handed to Mrs Stebbings the day before and she and her helpers were going to start preparing it for its new role. It was not enough to provide the money, Sophie decided, she must become actively involved.

'I would like to go shopping,' she told Lady Fitzpatrick and Charlotte after breakfast the following morning. 'There is a law book Papa was interested in and I thought I would buy it for him. It is quite a rare book and I might have to visit several shops, so do you mind if I take your coach, my lady?'

Charlotte gave her such a look of blank astonishment that Sophie was glad her ladyship was concentrating on her correspondence and did not notice. 'A book for Papa?' she queried.

'Yes,' Sophie said firmly. 'I remember him saying he needed it.'

'Why should she not buy her father a book?' Lady Fitzpatrick put in, proving that her loss of hearing was inconsistent. 'I am sure it is a very daughterly thing to do.'

'And I collect you and Charlotte are taking the carriage out this morning,' Sophie went on. 'So may I borrow the coach? Luke will drive me, I am sure.'

'Very well,' her ladyship agreed. 'But do take care, won't you?'

Sophie went to fetch her cloak and then made her way to the kitchen where she made sure the servants were busy elsewhere before delving in the store cupboards for brooms, scrubbing brushes, dusters and soap. Putting the smaller things into a bucket and carrying the two brooms, she hurried out to the mews and instructed Luke to put the horses to the old coach.

If he was surprised at the strange collection of implements Miss Sophie was carrying he did not express it, nor did he question why she was taking the coach which, in his opinion, was fit only for the dustheap; he was becoming immune to the young lady's little peccadilloes. Ten minutes later they were trotting down the road on their way to Maiden Lane.

Because there was bound to be many more men than they had places for at the refuge, they had decided to limit a stay to one night. The men would be given a bed, a bath and a healthy breakfast before going on their way. Feeling clean and refreshed, they might find it easier to obtain work.

Sophie also intended to try and set up an agency to find employment for them, but that would mean talking to prospective employers and she was not sure if she were the right person to do that. They needed a man to help them, a man of some substance, who would understand what was needed and, more importantly, had a persuasive manner.

The only man who came to mind was Richard Braybrooke, but he came to her mind whatever she was doing, sleeping or waking, so that did not signify anything except that she was not making a very good hand at forgetting him. Asking for his help would only make her shattered emotions worse. And he would very likely refuse on the grounds that what she was doing would not make a scrap of difference.

As soon as she arrived at the house she rolled up her sleeves, donned an apron and worked with a will, sweeping and scrubbing alongside Mrs Stebbings and two other women, while Luke helped some of the soldiers, recruited for the purpose, to assemble beds, put up shelves, fill palliasse covers with straw, chop firewood, put bolts on the doors and generally do everything the women could not. By the middle of the afternoon, the house was beginning to look habitable, if not exactly homely.

Sophie was exhausted, but it was a contented kind of exhaustion. Chatting to the women and the soldiers about their lives while they worked had put her own privileged existence into perspective. She was fortunate she had her health and a roof over her head and was in no danger of starvation and for that she must give thanks.

She was about to suggest they finish for the day and go home, when she heard a crash coming from the adjoining room where Luke was putting up a curtain rail. She dropped the broom she was using and ran into the room to find Luke sitting on the floor, tangled in the steps he had been using, and broken glass everywhere.

'Luke, are you hurt? Oh, my goodness, you are bleeding.' He was holding one hand in the other and blood was pouring down his arm. 'It's nothing, Miss Sophie. The steps gave way an' I put out my hand to save m'self.' He grinned ruefully. 'Straight through the window.'

'We must bandage it up.' She looked round as Mrs Stebbings came in from upstairs where she had been making up beds. The good lady took in the situation at a glance and told one of the men to fetch her basket and a bowl of water. The men had been to the pump several times during the day and there were some buckets of clean water still in the kitchen.

'I always carry ointment and bandages,' she said. 'It's being a soldier's wife, I suppose. When we were out in Spain—' She stopped speaking as the water and basket were brought to her and she set about washing the wound, which was quite deep, and picking out tiny shards of glass, which made Luke bite his lip in pain. 'I preferred to treat my husband's minor wounds myself, rather than let him go to the army sawbones. If I'd been with him at the end instead of coming home ahead of him, he might have survived.'

'I am so sorry,' Sophie murmured, squatting down to support Luke's hand.

'Curtains!' one of the men said, watching her. 'I said we didn't need curtains. Now, we've got a wounded man and a window broke. This ain't Carlton House, nor yet Grillon's Hotel. And it ain't a bit of use pretending it is.'

Sophie was too worried about Luke to argue with the man. It had been her idea to have curtains and rugs on the floor to make it more homely, less like the workhouse which was what the men dreaded most of all.

'Dawkins, you are the most downpin man I ever did meet,' Mrs Stebbings said. 'If Mrs Carter is so good as to provide curtains, then why brangle about it? She did not know the steps would collapse, did she? It was an accident.' She finished bandaging Luke's hand. 'There, it's the best I can do, but perhaps you should see a physician.'

'No, no, I'll mend,' Luke said, trying to move his fingers and grimacing when he discovered it hurt him. 'They be a bit stiff. I'll be right as ninepence tomorrow.'

'Then we'd better get you home,' Sophie said, reaching down to help him to his feet.

Aghast that she should do such a thing, he scrambled up on his own.

'You'll never manage the horses with one hand,' Dawkins said. 'Shall I drive you?'

Sophie looked at Luke, as the realisation dawned that he could not drive and she could not allow anyone else to see where they lived. Her identity was secret and she wanted it to stay that way. Luke caught her eye and gave her an imperceptible nod of understanding. 'I can drive,' he said. ''Tain't nothin' but a scratch.'

Sophie smiled at the sergeant. For no reason that she could explain, he made her nervous. It may have been the scar on one side of his face which gave him a permanent leer, or it may have been that he was constantly finding fault, even when people were trying to help him. To give him his due he had worked

hard during the day and his offer was a kind one—
she ought not to be ungrateful. 'Thank you, Sergeant,'
she said, allowing him the courtesy of his rank,
though he had long since been discharged. 'But if
Luke is incapacitated, I can drive myself.'

'Are you sure?' Mrs Stebbings asked.

'Yes, I often drive, don't I, Luke?'

He could hardly call the young lady a liar and so
he muttered that, yes, Mrs Carter was used to amuse
herself by taking the ribbons occasionally.

He walked beside her to where the old coach had
been left and she climbed up on the driving seat with
Luke beside her. She had driven the new carriage in
the park once or twice, but not this bulky coach and
not in heavy traffic and she was more than a little
nervous. But she had to pretend to be confident because Mrs Stebbings and several of the others had
come out to see them go.

She waved cheerily to them and picked up the
reins, while Luke muttered instructions. It was not as
bad as she feared. The horses were nearly as ancient
as the coach and they were quite content to set off at
a steady plod.

'Keep 'em walkin', Miss Sophie,' Luke said. 'But
keep a tight rein in case they're spooked by the traffic.'

She obeyed and slowly the nervousness left her and
she began to enjoy herself. This was better than sitting
over the teacups listening to the latest *on dit*. In fact,
the whole day had been very rewarding, except for
Luke's accident. She felt responsible for that and very
concerned about him.

'How do you feel?' she asked him, when she had safely negotiated the worst of the traffic around Covent Garden, most of it empty farm carts, which were being driven home after a successful day's trading in the market. 'Is it very painful?'

'It ain't too bad, Miss Sophie,' he said stoically. 'But what are we going to tell Lady Fitzpatrick? If she was to ask me to drive the carriage this evening...'

She hadn't thought of that. 'Goodness, we shall have to think of something. How could you have sustained a cut like that while driving me out shopping?'

'I don't know,' he said gloomily. 'I wish I'd never let you coax me into this humbug, Miss Sophie. It'll get me the bag for sure.'

'You won't be turned off, Luke, you are employed by Mr Hundon, not Lady Fitzpatrick.'

'But we gotta tell 'er something.'

'Yes, we must,' she said, turning into Oxford Street. It was crammed with vehicles of all kinds, from high-perch phaetons to sedan chairs, heavy drays to stage coaches laden with passengers. There were beggars in the gutter, pedestrians on the pavement, hawkers plying their wares from trays and here and there a stationary vehicle to negotiate. It was a minute of two before she felt confident enough to put her mind to other things besides her driving. 'I think you must have done something heroic,' she said, at length. 'Then everyone will be all sympathy and allow you to rest and recover.'

'On my life, Miss Sophie, I ain't no 'ero.'

She had enough to do concentrating on the road

and trying to think of something Luke could have done to sustain his injuries, without further distraction. But there was no mistaking the tall figure of Viscount Braybrooke, standing on the side of the road, watching her with a such a look of amazement on his face, she could not help breaking into a smile. He was elegantly dressed in a dark green superfine frockcoat and biscuit pantaloons, his dark curls peeping beneath a shiny brown beaver. Mischievously she wondered whether to stop and offer him a lift and if he would be too proud to accept it, but before she could pull the horses up she heard shouting ahead of her.

She looked up to see a curricle bearing down on them at great speed. There was no driver but a little boy was clinging to its sides, so terrified he could not even cry out. Everything in its path was being frantically pulled to the side out of its way. Pedestrians were fleeing in all directions, some of them screaming. Lady Fitzpatrick's old coach was too cumbersome and the horses to old to move fast and though Sophie did her best, it seemed a collision was inevitable.

Sophie's only thought was for the poor little boy. She hauled on the reins, helped by a one-handed Luke and the curricle hurtled alongside so close they almost touched. Luke was down like a shot long before they pulled to a halt and made a grab for the reins of the runaway horse, as it passed. He was not alone. Richard had moved equally fast and was on the other side. Sophie watched in horror as the terrified horse dragged them both along the street.

The vehicle was bouncing from side to side and the little boy in danger of being thrown out. Sophie jumped down and ran along the road, desperate to save him, though how she thought she could do it, she did not know. The panicking horse, trying to throw off the two men who impeded its progress, halted suddenly and reared up. The curricle turned over and Sophie heard the little boy scream. Then everything stopped.

The horse stood still; the curricle lay on its side, the uppermost wheel still spinning; Luke and Richard, both battered and bruised, were too winded to move. The bystanders were doing no more than gape. To Sophie, running towards it, the whole thing seemed like a set tableau and she was the only one capable of action.

And then everything started again. The little boy began to cry, proving he was still alive, Richard left Luke calming the horse and ran to the overturned curricle, the bystanders began to crowd round all talking at once, and Sophie reached Richard's side. Without speaking, they lifted the little boy out. He was about six or seven years old, his small face deathly white and his eyes wide with terror.

Sophie picked up one of the seat cushions which had been thrown out and put it on the ground, so that she could sit down and nurse him. He was badly shocked and there was a nasty bruise on the side of his head, but a quick examination by Richard established that no bones were broken.

'Thank heaven for that,' she said, stroking the boy's tumbled curls away from his face and wiping his tears away with her handkerchief, while Richard dispersed the spectators with such an air of authority it did not occur to them to do other than obey. 'He's had a lucky escape. I wonder where his parents are.'

'I don't know,' Richard said grimly, looking back along the street. 'I shall certainly have something to say to them, when I see them. How could they be so irresponsible as to leave a small child alone in a vehicle like that?'

He looked down at Sophie. Her face was dreadfully pale and there were smudges below her eyes. Her gown, visible beneath the grey cloak, was grubby and her hands, tenderly ministering to the child, seemed workworn, her usually well-buffed nails broken. What in heaven's name had she been up to? But the child did not care about that. He was lying in her arms, his head against her soft breast, while she stroked his hair and talked soothingly to him, with an expression of such compassion and love, Richard's heart turned a somersault in his breast.

'What's your name?' Sophie asked him but he looked blankly at her.

'Ne comprends pas.'

Sophie smiled and tried again. *'Qu'est-ce que t'appelle-toi?'*

'Pierre Latour.'

'Je m'appelle Sophie,' she said. 'You are quite safe now. Where are your parents?'

He turned and buried his head in her breast, crying for his mama and talking in rapid French, which Richard found very difficult to follow, punctuated as it was by sobs.

'He says his papa left the carriage to ask directions and the horse bolted. His father tried to stop it but was hit by the wheel,' Sophie translated without even thinking.

'Then he must be lying injured in the road. I'll go and look for him.'

But before he could go, a man limped towards them, his fine clothes torn and muddy and his expression distraught. He rushed up to the child. *'Pierre! Mon pauvre fils!'*

'Papa!' The boy reached out and was enfolded in his father's arms.

'Merci, merci, madame,' the man said to Sophie.

Sophie smiled and, relieved of her burden, stood up. Now it was all over, she felt weak and stiff. She took a step and stumbled, but before she could fall, Richard reached out and pulled her towards him, supporting her with his arm around her. It was comforting there and she did not move away.

Monsieur Latour had been speaking to his son and now he turned to Richard and Sophie to thank them, explaining that he was a diplomat and had come to England as part of a delegation. His wife had never visited England and so he had brought her and their son with him. He had hired the curricle to show them some of London. He had left his wife at the mantua-makers and taken Pierre for a turn about the park before returning for her and they had lost their way.

He had stepped down to ask directions and something had spooked the horse. He was eternally grateful to *monsieur* and *madame* for looking after the child. Now, he must go and find his wife, she would be beside herself with worry. All this was said in rapid French which Richard had great difficulty following. Not so Sophie, who answered so fluently he was astonished.

Luke had calmed the horse and enlisted the help of bystanders to right the vehicle, but it was in a sorry state. 'The wheels might turn, but I wouldn't like to try and drive it,' he said.

Sophie immediately offered to take the Frenchman to his destination, forgetting that Luke could not drive. In fact, his struggle with the horse had set his hand bleeding again and the bandages were stained red with his blood.

'Very tender-hearted of you, my dear,' Richard murmured close to her ear. 'But perhaps the gentleman does not have my confidence in your ability as a whipster.'

'What are we to do then?' she asked. 'We cannot abandon them.'

'Then I had better drive.'

'My lord, I am sure you have other things to do. An appointment perhaps.'

'Nothing of any import,' he said. 'I cannot simply walk away, can I?'

'N…no, but—'

'Your French is unquestionably better than mine,' he went on before she could find any more objections. 'Tell the gentleman I shall be pleased to drive him. Then lead the way back to that bone-breaker you call a coach. The sooner we reunite the boy with his mama, the better. He should see a doctor and so should your groom. We shall take him, after we have discharged our duty to the Frenchman.'

She knew it would do no good arguing with him but, in truth, she was feeling very shaky and very tired and thankful to have someone with an air of authority to take charge. The Frenchman and his son took their places with her inside the coach alongside the brooms and bucket, while Richard hitched the horse from the curricle to the back of the coach. The vehicle itself was abandoned and would have to be fetched by the hire company. Luke managed to climb up to the driver's seat, where Richard joined him.

It took Sophie a few minutes to establish which mantua-maker Madame Latour was visiting, but it was not far away and the little boy was soon reunited with his mother, who had been standing outside the shop looking this way and that in growing panic. When she saw the state of her husband and son, she all but fainted and then burst into tears. It took Monsieur Latour a little time to convince her that he was not hurt and there was nothing to get into hysterics about. Eventually she joined him and their son in the coach and were conveyed to their hotel where a doctor was sent for and the runaway horse was handed over to one of the hotel staff to return to the hire company.

They insisted on Luke, the hero, being administered to after the doctor had treated Pierre and given him a sleeping draught, and it was very late when they took their leave.

'I am afraid Lady Fitz and Charlotte will be wondering what has become of me,' she said, as Richard escorted her back to her coach.

'That, my dear Miss Hundon, is an understatement. The sooner we have you safely home, the better.'

It was then she realised that he intended to continue his mission of mercy. And though half of her wanted him to stay, wanted his support, the other half told her it would be dangerous to her hard-won independence. 'My lord, there is no need to accompany me,' she protested. 'I admit I was a little shaky, but I am fully recovered now and perfectly able to drive.'

He smiled. 'I should be a poor tool, indeed, if I allowed that. And no doubt you will have some explaining to do to your patroness. I should hate to see you roasted, so I shall come to lend you support.' He turned to Luke, who was looking decidedly green after having his old dressing removed and several stitches inserted in the wound to his hand. 'Get inside, old fellow. Miss Hundon can ride on the box with me. It is a position she seems to prefer.'

'Yes, do it, Luke,' Sophie said, as he hesitated. 'I do not want you fainting and falling off.'

Reluctantly he climbed in and Richard helped Sophie up on the driver's seat before taking his place beside her.

'Now,' he said, as he took up the reins and the coach moved. 'I should very much like to know what deep game you are playing.'

'Game, my lord,' she repeated innocently. 'There is no game. I came out shopping and you saw what happened.'

'Shopping for buckets and brooms, I assume.'

So he had noticed them! 'Yes, my lord.'

'What a hum!'

'My lord,' she said, mustering her dignity, 'I am not accustomed to being called a liar.'

'Then you had better become accustomed to it or resolve to tell the truth from now on.' He turned to glance down at her. 'Do you usually go shopping in dirty clothes, with smudges on your face?'

'Have I?' she asked, momentarily diverted and scrubbing at her cheeks with the handkerchief she had used to mop up Pierre's tears, which made her even grubbier.

He laughed, loving her whatever she was wearing and however dishevelled she was. In fact it made her even more appealing. 'You look like an urchin.'

She managed a wan smile. 'It is not to be wondered at, is it? I have been sitting on the ground, comforting a small boy.'

'Oh, it didn't happen then,' he said airily. 'Certainly not all of it.'

It was not a question and so she declined to confirm or deny it. 'And you are no picture of elegance, my lord. In truth, I do not think you are in a fit state to go visiting. Your sleeve is torn and you have lost your hat, not to mention scratches and bruises on your hands.' She glanced down at them as she spoke. Big, tanned, capable hands, hands which had recently been about her waist, hands which had caressed her and comforted her, hands that bore the scars of his efforts to stop the runaway curricle; hands she longed to take in her own and put to her lips.

'*Touché*, my dear,' he said with a smile. 'But the

more determined you are that I shall not take you home, the more determined I become that I shall. I am interested to know what Banbury tale you will tell to explain your tardiness.'

'The overturned curricle, my lord. You can bear witness to that.'

'Oh, I am to compound your mischief by telling half-truths, am I? And I suppose your coachman sustained his injuries stopping the runaway horse.'

'It certainly made his hand worse, it was only a scratch before that.'

'Do you take me for a flat, Miss Hundon? You would hardly put half a yard of bandage on a scratch and you forget I saw it when the doctor stitched it. It is a severe cut. And whatever your activities this afternoon, they were not those usually indulged in by well brought-up young ladies.'

She had to put an end to his questions somehow. 'My lord, you said you would hate to see me roasted and then you proceed to do exactly that. It is very uncivil of you. What I do with my time is my own business; if it had not been for the accident, I would have been home in good time for dinner at five and no explanations would have been necessary. I beg of you to desist from quizzing me.'

'And will you desist from bamming me?'

She did not answer and he turned in his seat to look at her. There were tears glistening on her lashes and he was suddenly filled with compassion. He wanted to stop the carriage, to take her in his arms and tell her that whatever she did made no difference to how he felt about her, that his search for a wife had been no more than a half-hearted effort to appease his grandfather and he had long ago become heartily sick of it. 'Oh, my dear Miss Hundon, forgive me. I had no right to go on so, when you have had such a dreadful day.'

'I have not had a dreadful day,' she contradicted, regaining her spirit suddenly. 'I have had a very good day. It is others who have suffered, not me. That poor little boy and Luke. Even you. You must be in great haste to return home to change your clothes and put some salve on your hands, I am sure they are very painful. Do see if you can put a little life in the horses.'

'I comprehend the game must be played to its end,' he said, as he urged the horses into something resembling a trot. 'I do hope, my dear Miss Hundon, you will not come out the loser.'

It was no comfort at all to her; she was already the loser and though she wanted to tell him that she was not his Miss Hundon, dear or otherwise, she decided she had nothing to gain by confession. She wasn't the only one playing a game; he had been indulging in one himself, pretending to be looking for a wife, setting all the young ladies into a twitter, when his choice had already been made.

The rest of the short journey was made in silence. At its end he saw her safely into the drawing room, paid his respects to her ladyship and withdrew, leaving Sophie to tell the tale in whatever way served her purpose. But it wasn't the end; his curiosity had been aroused and until he had satisfied it, he would not say anything of what was in his heart.

Chapter Six

Lady Fitzpatrick and the girls were taking tea with Lady Gosport and a group of her friends two days later and the talk was all of the accident to the curricle.

'Poor Luke was dreadfully injured,' Lady Fitzpatrick said. 'And Sophie came home covered in blood and dirt and with her hair all falling out of its pins. I never saw the like.'

'I was not hurt, my lady,' Sophie said, squirming uncomfortably. 'I beg you do not refine upon it.'

Her ladyship ignored her. 'And it was so late I had twice put back dinner and then Cook said if she did not serve it at once it would be quite spoiled, so I allowed Tilly to bring it in. But I could not eat a morsel of it, fearing some terrible fate had befallen Sophie. Charlotte was weeping and would not be comforted, not that I had any comfort to offer, for I had not. There are so many villains about, especially with all the soldiers abroad on the streets.'

'The soldiers cannot help it if they have no work

and nowhere to go,' Sophie said. 'It is not right to blame them for every misdemeanour in town. I was in no danger with Luke beside me.'

Her ladyship was intent on telling her tale and would not be sidetracked. 'Monsieur Latour came to call the very next day. Such a fine gentleman and so grateful.' She laughed suddenly. 'He asked for Monsieur Hundon and it was a minute or two before I realised he thought Viscount Braybrooke was Sophie's husband. Can you imagine it? Why, it was a mere coincidence that they were both at the scene of the accident. I own I was glad of it, though, because Luke was so badly hurt he could not drive and his lordship drove the carriage home.'

'Yes, so his lordship told Martin,' Lady Gosport put in, proving that Lord Braybrooke, however much he disapproved, had confirmed that Luke had sustained his injuries at the scene of the accident. Not that Sophie had lied about it; in telling the story, she had simply allowed everyone to make the assumption.

'He was to meet Martin at White's at eight o'clock and did not arrive until nearly ten,' her ladyship went on. 'Martin said he seemed a little bemused. He was surprised, he said, for Dick is not one to make a Cheltenham tragedy of something of so little consequence. He was a soldier after all and, according to Martin, he was always cool in battle. He would not tell Martin what was on his mind but, whatever it was, he did not stay for cards, made his excuses and left.'

'Perhaps he is in love,' Verity Greenholme suggested with a giggle which made Sophie feel like slapping her.

'Who do you suppose can have gained his affection?' Verity's mother asked archly, while smiling at her daughter.

'I think it might be his cousin Emily,' Charlotte said.

'No, my dear,' Lady Fitzpatrick said, patting her hand. 'That is by no means decided. You must not give up as soon as a rival appears on the scene.'

'I heard he was very particular about his requirements,' Lady Gosport said. 'He gave Martin a long list of them.'

'What might they be?' Mrs Greenholme queried.

'Oh, I cannot remember them all, but I know she was to be wealthy—that seemed important, though he is already plump in the pocket. It had something to do with disliking being constantly dunned for lady's fripperies.'

'How mercenary that sounds,' Charlotte said. 'I never would have believed it of him.'

'Was there anything else?' Verity asked. 'Was she to be fair or dark?'

'Martin did not say. But he did say she was to have presence and dignity befitting a future duchess and hoydenish behaviour certainly would not do.'

'There you are, Charlotte,' Lady Fitzpatrick said. 'I am sure you fit the bill exactly.'

This remark served only to make Charlotte blush to the roots of her blonde curls and fumble in her reticule for a handkerchief. Sophie, who had been telling herself that she had been totally mistaken in Viscount Braybrooke who was nothing but a cold-hearted pinchcommons if all that concerned him was not having to pay for his wife's clothes, heartily wished the subject of Lord Braybrooke could be dropped.

It was abandoned the very next minute and in the last way Sophie could have wished. The door was flung open and a footman announced, 'Mr Frederick Harfield, my lady.'

'Freddie!' Sophie and Charlotte exclaimed in unison, looking at each other in dismay as he strode over to bow before their hostess and exchange civilities with her.

'What are we to do?' Charlotte whispered. 'We are undone.'

His greetings done, he turned to survey the company and spotted them on the far side of the room. 'Miss Roswell. Miss Hundon,' he said, hurrying forward, a broad smile on his face. 'What an agreeable surprise it is to find you here.'

Charlotte had gone very pale and Sophie very pink. Oh, dear,' Sophie said, rising from her chair and stepping forwards. 'It is so hot in here, I do believe I...' She put a hand to her brow and, timing it to perfection, fainted in Freddie's arms.

He was obliged to gather her up before she reached the floor and looked round for somewhere to deposit her.

'Oh, poor Sophie, I do believe she has not fully recovered from that dreadful accident,' Charlotte cried, realising what Sophie intended. 'Freddie, do bring her outside where the air will revive her.' She pulled urgently on his sleeve and he followed her through the door which led onto the terrace, with the whole company trooping out behind them.

'Get rid of them, Freddie,' Sophie whispered. 'We must speak to you alone.'

Startled, he looked down at her, but her eyes were closed and she gave every appearance of being in a deep swoon.

'There is a seat down the garden a little way,' Lady Gosport said, while Lady Fitzpatrick clucked around like a worried hen. 'She will recover there.'

'My lady, we do not need to trespass on your kindness. Do, please, take your guests back indoors and drink your tea before it becomes cold,' Freddie said. Sophie was becoming very heavy and he would have to put her down soon or drop her. 'I am sure Miss Roswell…'

'Of course I shall stay with her,' Charlotte interposed quickly. 'All she needs is a little air.' Then in an undertone to Lady Gosport. 'Lady Fitzpatrick fusses so and she is really no help at all, though she means to be, I know. Please persuade her to go back indoors with you.'

While she was speaking, Freddie had gained the seat and thankfully lowered Sophie onto it, took off his coat and folded it beneath her head, as Charlotte joined them and sat on the bench beside Sophie.

'Now, you may put an end to the dramatics, Miss Roswell' he said. 'I ain't such a cake as to think you would swoon at the sight of me, even though I was the last person you might expect to see.'

'That's true,' Charlotte said. 'What *are* you doing here, Freddie?'

'M'father sent me to get a little town bronze and find me a rich wife.'

'Oh, Freddie,' Charlotte cried. 'You didn't agree?'

'No choice in the matter, my dear, besides, I couldn't see it would do the least harm. I wanted to come, had a great fear you might take a liking to one of the *ton* and accept his offer. Couldn't allow that.'

'Oh, Freddie, you are absurd!' Charlotte said, delighted by this statement. 'As if I would! But that doesn't explain why you came to this house.'

'My father asked me to pay his respects. Lord Gosport is a particular friend of his. They were at school together. Didn't expect to find you here, though.' He paused, looking from one to the other. 'And it's plain as a pikestaff you didn't expect me.'

'No. Oh, Freddie, are your parents in town too?'

'No, they ain't. Came up alone, staying in lodgings. Now, are you going to tell me why you staged this little charade? Miss Roswell is no more unconscious than I am.'

'We had to stop you letting the cat out of the bag, Mr Harfield,' Sophie murmured, still pretending to be feeling ill because, although everyone else had gone back to the house, they were undoubtedly watching from the window.

'I told you we should never have embarked on this masquerade, Sophie,' Charlotte said in a voice which was certainly not one of solicitude for an invalid, although she was waving her open fan over her cousin's face. 'Someone was sure to put the cat among the pigeons. What are we to do?'

'Cats, bags, pigeons,' Freddie exclaimed. 'Be so good as to explain. If you have got yourselves into a scrape…'

'Oh, you will have to know, though what you will think of it, I dare not imagine,' Charlotte said. 'You see, we changed identities. I am known in town as Miss Roswell and Sophie is Miss Hundon.'

He stared from one to the other for several seconds, taking in the fact that Charlotte, in pale blue muslin with a ruched frill of silk decorating its neckline, was far more modishly dressed than Sophie in a dove-grey cambric round gown. 'In the name of heaven, why?'

'It will take too long to explain,' Sophie said. 'And Lady Gosport is coming out again. But whatever you do, do not address me as Miss Roswell or Charlotte as Miss Hundon.'

'But we have kept our own given names,' Charlotte put in quickly. 'It would have been too easy to make a slip if we had not. But you must not be too familiar with me, because I am the heiress and…'

She stopped as Lady Gosport approached. 'I see you have come round, Miss Hundon,' her ladyship said. 'Please do come indoors again, it is becoming much cooler and you will catch a chill. If you wish, you may rest in my boudoir and I will have a restorative sent up to you.'

'It is very kind of you, my lady,' Sophie said, standing up. 'I am perfectly recovered.'

'I think we should go home,' Charlotte said decisively, while Freddie retrieved his coat and stood looking with dismay at the creases in it. 'I am persuaded that the accident knocked you up more than you will admit, Sophie, and you ought not to have come out today.'

'Yes, that must be it,' her ladyship agreed. 'Perhaps

you should fetch a doctor to your cousin, Miss Roswell.'

To which Freddie said he would call on the young ladies the following day to see how they did, but he was hard put not to laugh aloud and his eyes were twinkling mischievously.

During the flurry of solicitous enquiries when they rejoined the other guests before taking their leave, he managed to whisper to Charlotte, 'I shall expect a full account tomorrow.'

The carriage was called for and Lady Fitzpatrick hustled the girls into it. She was not at all pleased with Sophie making a scene just when she was in full flow over the fascinating Monsieur Latour. It was her opinion that the lowly Miss Hundon was trying to steal Miss Roswell's thunder with her antics and that could not be borne. And if, as she had been led to believe, Sophie had an understanding with Mr Harfield, it was not to be wondered at that she had fainted at the sight of him.

It was her bounden duty to warn that young man to make his offer as soon as maybe and secure the young lady's hand before she could cause any more mayhem. It was her ladyship's aim to attach Miss Roswell to Viscount Braybrooke and she would not be thwarted. After all, she had been paid to find a suitable match for the heiress and she was determined to discharge her obligation.

Freddie, in his best superfine coat and grey check pantaloons, arrived in Holles Street soon after noon the following day and was ushered into the drawing room, expecting to find the two girls alone with Lady Fitzpatrick, but it seemed half the *haute monde* was there, sitting over the teacups, continuing the gossip started the day before, much to Lady Fitzpatrick's satisfaction.

He made his bow and turned to discover Miss Hundon and Miss Roswell deep in conversation with Martin Gosport, whom he knew slightly, and another gentleman, whose easy manner, superbly tailored coat and pristine neckcloth proclaimed him a pink of the *ton*.

'Lord Braybrooke, may I present Mr Frederick Harfield,' Charlotte said, after Freddie had stood before them to make his bow.

The two men bowed slightly, eyeing each other warily. 'And this is Mr Martin Gosport,' she went on. 'But perhaps you are already acquainted?'

'We met when we were boys, before the war, when Sir Mortimer brought him to London on a visit,' Martin said. 'How d'you do, Harfield? Sorry I was not at home when you called yesterday.'

'You are from Miss Hundon's home town?' Richard enquired of Freddie.

'Indeed, yes.' Suddenly remembering it was Sophie the viscount meant, Freddie tore his gaze from Charlotte and smiled at Sophie. 'We have known each other since we were in leading strings.'

'And we have so much to tell you, Freddie,' Sophie said, eyes brimming with laughter. 'I know it has only been a few weeks since we came to London, but we have met so many people and seen so much, it is difficult to know where to begin. I shall carry you off to talk in private, if his lordship will excuse us.'

Richard nodded and watched with growing alarm as she took Freddie's arm in a very proprietorial way and led him to a quiet corner of the room, sat down beside him and began an animated conversation with him.

'Miss Hundon seems to have recovered her spirits remarkably since the accident,' he commented drily.

'Oh, yes,' Charlotte said, as a sudden idea occurred to her. 'Yesterday she was in the dismals and then, lo and behold, Mr Harfield arrived and put the blue devils to flight.'

'My mother said she fainted at the sight of him,' Martin put in. 'Now, I would not have said she was the swooning sort.'

'Nor I,' Richard agreed. 'But she did have a very nasty experience three days ago, and the effects were, perhaps, delayed. That sometimes happens, I believe.'

'And you, my lord?' Charlotte queried, keeping one eye on the two people in the corner and wondering what Sophie was saying to Freddie. 'Have you sustained any ill effects?'

'No, only to my jacket and a little to my pride to think that your groom was there before me. Nothing of consequence.'

'We are very grateful to you, my lord. Sophie is sometimes a little headstrong and perhaps it was unwise of her to go out with only Luke for company, but she is used to being independent, you know.' She smiled disarmingly. 'I am afraid Freddie will have his hands full with her.'

'Has she fixed on Mr Harfield, then?' He tried to make the question sound casual, but was obliged to admit to himself that the answer was of considerable interest to him.

'No, not exactly. You see, Sir Mortimer is determined that his son shall marry money and Miss Hundon has no fortune, as you must know. How they will contrive, I do not know.'

Richard assimilated this piece of information with mixed feelings. If Sir Mortimer had his way and forbade the marriage, would Miss Hundon be consoled by another suitor? And did he want to be second best? 'But Miss Hundon has scarcely been out of Leicestershire,' he said. 'She can have little experience of the world. Do you think it is possible that she might find she was mistaken in him? After all, he is little more than a green boy and if he cannot stand up to his father…'

'He is not a green boy,' she contradicted hotly. 'Freddie is…' She stopped suddenly, her face on fire. She had so nearly given the game away, when all she had wanted to do was make Lord Braybrooke just a tiny bit jealous, so that he would see Sophie's merits. Sophie might deny she had a *tendre* for the viscount until she was purple, but Charlotte knew better.

If only Sophie had not been so particular about the man she wanted for a husband and looked into her heart instead, she might be happier and they could call off this subterfuge. 'I believe he is at a stand, that is all.'

Richard smiled. So the heiress was jealous of her own country cousin! Sir Mortimer might be gratified to know it, but it did Miss Roswell credit that she was prepared to stand back for her cousin's sake. Or was there more to it than that? He glanced over to where Mr Harfield and Miss Hundon were still deep in conversation and decided it was time to intervene.

He strolled over to them, catching the end of the conversation before they became aware of him.

'Freddie, we shall neither of us speak to you again, if you breathe a word,' Sophie was saying. 'You must wait until after our come-out ball. It is only three weeks away.'

'Three weeks!' It was an exclamation of anguish. 'I shall never manage it.'

'Of course you will.'

Richard coughed lightly, making them both look up at him. He was intrigued to see that both faces bore unmistakable signs of guilt. 'Mr Harfield,' he said smoothly. 'We cannot allow you to have Miss Hundon all to yourself, you know.'

Freddie rose with alacrity. 'No, beg pardon, thoughtless of me. We had so much to impart, but the rest can wait. Come Sophie, let us rejoin the others.'

Sophie rose and they moved across the room to where Charlotte and Martin were in conversation with Lady Fitzpatrick. Her ladyship was regaling Martin with a colourful account of Monsieur Latour's visit and saying she intended to invite him and his wife to the girls' ball, if they were still in England when it took place. Seeing Freddie, she lifted her quizzing glass to peer at him.

'Ah, Mr Harfield. So glad you have come. I may count on you to be Miss Hundon's escort to the ball, may I not?' Without waiting for an answer, she turned to Richard. 'And Lord Braybrooke, you will honour us, will you not?'

'It promises to be the event of the Season and I would not miss it for worlds,' he said. 'I shall be honoured if Miss Roswell will stand up with me for a waltz.'

'Of course,' Charlotte said, ignoring Freddie's black looks.

Lady Gosport was trying to escape from Verity Greenholme and her mother, who had been quizzing her about Miss Roswell's supposed wealth and wondering why the young lady did not put it about a little more. 'Not a bit like an heiress,' Mrs Greenholme said. 'No different from the country cousin. Why, it is sometimes hard to tell one from the other. You would think someone with the blunt she is supposed to have would have a little more style.

'If you ask me, it is all hum and what Lord Braybrooke will say when he finds he has been taken for a flat, I dare not think. Let us hope someone opens his eyes before he discovers the truth for himself.'

'I am sure I do not know what you mean,' her ladyship said miffily. 'Miss Roswell is a charming young lady and it is to her credit she don't advertise her prospects.'

'I am persuaded his lordship would be well advised to enquire into the details of her inheritance.' She looked round suddenly when she realised the room had gone very quiet and everyone except Lady Fitzpatrick had heard her last remark. Unable to back down, she laughed shakily. 'Lord Gower is making a cake of himself over Miss Thomson, you know. And no one knows the least thing about her, except what that silly woman who says she is her aunt spreads about. Can't take people on face value, can you? Not that I ain't sure everything is right and tight as a drum.'

'Oh, dear,' Charlotte murmured. 'What am I to say?'

'I should not dignify it with a reply,' Richard said, bowing towards Mrs Greenholme and smiling silkily. 'Indeed, ma'am, one would be very unwise to play one's hand unseen.'

Sophie was put in mind of a tiger, sleek, muscled and dangerous. But what if his lordship were to take the lady's advice and make enquiries about Miss Roswell? What could he discover? Nothing but the truth, she told herself, as long as no one was able to identify her. Freddie could, but Freddie was sworn to secrecy.

'Is Lord Braybrooke going to play cards?' Lady Fitzpatrick enquired, gazing about her short-sightedly. 'Is it not a little early in the day for that?'

'Much too early,' Richard said, with heavy emphasis which could have been for her ladyship's benefit, but which seemed to Sophie to be loaded with another meaning and she felt her heart lurch uncomfortably.

'I have been thinking of arranging a little outing to Vauxhall Gardens on Saturday,' Lady Gosport put in before the conversation became even more fraught. 'Would you care to join us, Miss Roswell? And Miss Hundon? I believe there are to be tableaux representing the Battle of Waterloo and fireworks afterwards.

Lord Braybrooke, would you consent to be one of our escorts?'

'Delighted, ma'am,' he said bowing. Then, to Lady Fitzpatrick, 'Regretfully, I must take my leave.' He bowed over her hand, then took Charlotte's and raised it to his lips. 'Miss Roswell. Until Saturday.'

'I shall look forward to it, my lord.'

'Miss Hundon.' He turned to Sophie. 'I am glad to see you recovered. But I beg of you, be more careful in future.' In spite of her efforts to hide her hands in the folds of her skirt, he managed to possess himself of one of them and raise it to his lips. The gentle pressure was enough to set her tingling with sensations she could not control; a warmth spread from the top of her head to the tips of her toes and her stomach churned itself into knots. The smile on his face told her all too clearly that he knew what he was doing to her and it angered her.

'My lord, I am always careful and it was hardly my fault the curricle overturned. Indeed, it might very well have collided with us if it were not for my...' She stopped, gulped and went on, 'Luke's quick thinking.'

'Yes, the inestimable Luke,' he murmured. 'How is he? I think I shall have to ask him how he hurt himself so badly.'

'No, my lord.' It was out before she could stop it. She flushed, but forced herself to face him out. 'He hates a fuss and becomes quite irritable if anyone makes a to-do over him. He will be bound to say he was only doing his duty.'

'Then I must not embarrass him,' he said, eyes twinkling. 'Good-day, Miss Hundon.'

There was something havey-cavey going on, he was sure of it. Both young ladies were behaving in a most unnatural manner, answering for each other and threatening that pup, Harfield, who seemed not to know where his interests lay, either with the heiress or the country cousin. As for Sophie, she was playing the deepest game of all and he would not rest until he knew all. And if that meant allowing himself to be inveigled into escorting Miss Roswell, then he would do it. Miss Roswell, he felt, was the weak link in the chain.

He was riding down Oxford Street towards home after a canter in the park the following morning when he saw Sophie come out of the end of Holles Street. She was on foot and dressed very plainly in dove grey and wore sturdy half-boots and a small straw bonnet with no brim to speak of. Luke, walking half a pace behind her, looked decidedly uneasy.

Richard reined in and watched as she set off at a fair pace in an easterly direction. Walking his horse, he followed, though he could make a good guess at her destination. Would she never learn! Only four days ago she had been in a fair way to being run down and though she had eschewed that monstrosity of a chariot on this occasion, she was still courting danger and flying in the face of convention.

True, she was not high-bred, but she was a gentlewoman and should not be allowed to wander all over London at will. London was not Leicestershire, where perhaps things were done differently, it was a great cosmopolitan city full of strange characters, footpads, cut-throats, pickpockets and worse. Even some who appeared the height of respectability were nothing of the sort.

He had a good mind to speak to Lady Fitzpatrick about it. But the thought of the scolding Sophie would receive and his own curiosity prevented him. He would see she came to no harm, even if it meant following her everywhere she went.

Sophie, unaware of her second escort, continued on her way to Maiden Lane, where they were to open the house to their first lodgers. Determined to be there, she had told Lady Fitzpatrick that because of the accident and having to take the Latour family back to their lodgings, she had not been able to purchase the book she had set out to buy. Her ladyship, deep in discussions about food and flowers and musicians for their ball, hardly raised an eyebrow.

Charlotte was expecting Freddie to call and was all on edge, even though Sophie had assured her Freddie would not let them down, and had not wanted to accompany her. It was only Luke who raised any sort of objection and she had been obliged to order him to do as he was told in her best Mistress-of-Madderlea manner.

She saw the long line of men waiting to be admitted to the house long before she reached it. She hurried past them to join Mrs Stebbings and her helpers.

'What are we to do?' the good lady asked when

Sophie had taken off her cloak and donned an apron. 'We cannot look after them all.'

'Then it will have to be first come first served and those admitted today must be barred tomorrow.'

'There will be arguments.'

'Then we will enlist those who helped us prepare the house to keep discipline. The men are used to obeying orders, they will not cause trouble if they see we are being fair. In the meantime we can feed as many of them as we can. I shall send Luke to the market for more supplies.'

Sophie was so busy serving the men with the food cooked by Mrs Stebbings's helpers, she did not notice the passage of time. It was only when she heard the church clock strike noon that she remembered she had promised to be back at Holles Street for nuncheon. She hurriedly took off her apron and left, promising to return as soon as she could, though how it was to be achieved, she did not know. She could hardly use the excuse of going to the bookshop again.

Richard had walked his horse up and down the street for what seemed an age and, tiring of that, had purchased a news sheet from a vendor on the corner of the road and was sitting on a wall opposite the house, reading it. The Luddites were busy in the north again, wreaking destruction, and he wondered how long it would be before their activities manifested themselves in the south. Already there were rumblings of discontent. If there were riots in London, the unemployed soldiers were bound to join in and Sophie would be in even more danger.

He folded the paper when he saw her depart with Luke at her elbow, but instead of following immediately, he crossed the road and entered the refuge where he introduced himself to Mrs Stebbings as Major Richard Braybrooke and expressed an interest in the work she was doing.

Flustered, she apologised for not being able to offer him proper refreshment, or even a comfortable chair. 'We have been rushed off our feet, Major,' she said. 'We did not expect so many.'

'Good news travels fast, ma'am,' he said, smiling. 'But tell me, how have you been able to accomplish so much? You must have a very generous benefactor.'

'Yes, indeed, though we do not know who she is. Mrs Carter is acting for her, but she dare not reveal her identity, being sworn to secrecy.'

'Mrs Carter?' he enquired, raising a well-defined eyebrow. 'Who is she?'

'A war widow, my lord. She is companion to the lady in question but that is all I know.'

'Could it be the lady I passed on my way in? She was wearing a grey cloak and a small bonnet. Red-gold curls, I recall.'

'Yes, that would be Mrs Carter. A lovely lady, so compassionate and not afraid of getting her hands dirty.'

'So, I collect,' Richard murmured under his breath, then pulling a purse from his pocket, he laid it on the table beside the dirty plates and beakers. 'Please accept this towards your expenses. It is all I have on me, but I will arrange for a larger donation to be sent to you.'

She thanked him effusively and he left, mounted his horse and set off after Sophie.

Companion to the lady in question, he mused. That could only be Miss Roswell. So, the heiress of Madderlea was also a philanthropist, which was to her credit, but it was Sophie who was doing all the donkey work, while she cavorted about town in her new carriage, making calls and gossiping over the teacups. It was easy to be generous when you had a great deal of blunt; Sophie gave something more precious than money, she gave her time. Oh, how he loved her for that, misguided as she was.

Did Harfield know what she was about? Yesterday she had been swearing him to secrecy, so undoubtedly he did know, but why was he not escorting her instead of going sparring with Martin? It was a dashed ungentlemanly way of going on and he might very well find an opportunity of telling him so.

Sophie, late back for nuncheon and still unable to produce the book she went out to buy, told Lady Fitzpatrick that it was out of print and she must needs give up on it, to which the good lady replied, 'Well, your papa cannot say you did not do your best for him. Now, perhaps you will settle down with Charlotte to discuss the arrangements for the ball and your costumes. Rattling around town on your own is not the thing, you know, not the thing at all. Why did Mr Harfield not accompany you this morning?'

'I believe he was otherwise engaged, my lady,' Sophie said demurely. 'His father has given him endless commissions.'

'He does have to find a rich wife too,' Charlotte put in with a giggle.

'And so does Braybrooke,' her ladyship retorted. 'You would do better, miss, to make a push to engage his attention instead of worrying about what don't concern you. I shall be very disappointed if you have not brought him to an offer by the time your ball is over. And so will Mr Hundon.'

'I cannot make him want me, if he has set his sights elsewhere.'

'Of course you can. You know, my dear, you are too modest for an heiress and the future mistress of Madderlea. You must assert yourself more or you will be despised.'

'If modesty is to be despised, then I scorn those who despise it,' Charlotte said with some heat. 'I am who I am and cannot change.'

At this point Sophie could stand no more and was obliged to excuse herself on the pretext of having to change for their carriage ride in the park. Once in her room, she burst into laughter.

Charlotte, following her, did not share her amusement. 'Sophie, it is all very well for you to laugh, but you have not been looking for a book for Papa, that I know. It is all a hum. And you are not making the smallest effort to find a husband.'

'I have not met anyone I would even consider.'

'And that's a whisker. You are wearing the willow for Lord Braybrooke, I know that.'

'And Lord Braybrooke is looking for a rich, com-placent wife who will allow him to continue his bachelor existence unhampered by considerations of faith-fulness,' Sophie snapped.

'Wherever did you come by that idea?'

'Mr Gosport said so. He seemed to think that being a duchess would be enough to compensate for any shortcomings in his lordship.'

'And that has sunk you in the suds and why you have been going out all alone to brood. Oh, Sophie, I am so sorry. Perhaps if he knew you were really a considerable heiress...'

'Do you think I would want him on those terms? He is the very opposite of the man I want for a hus-band. He is arrogant and vain and unfeeling and...' She stopped, remembering that kiss and how she had melted into his arms and enjoyed every delicious sec-ond, and how her whole body tingled with excitement when he so much as took her hand or looked at her with those liquid brown eyes.

'And what?' Sophie asked, curious.

'He thinks he has only to snap his fingers and every young lady in town will prostrate herself before him. Did you ever hear such a conceited recital as that list of requirements he wants in a wife? Beauty. Wealth. Deportment. And what is he prepared to offer in re-turn? The dubious pleasure of one day becoming a duchess.'

'And Lady Fitz exhorts me to set my cap at him,' Charlotte put in. 'I am no more likely to acquiesce to such Turkish treatment than you are and so I shall tell him if he deigns to make an offer. Not that I would accept him, even if he behaved like an angel, because I am already engaged.'

Sophie, diverted, stared at her cousin. 'Engaged?'

'Yes. Freddie called while you were out and we contrived to have a few moments alone when Lady Fitz left the room to speak to Cook about something she had forgot about the ball—something to do with poached salmon, I think.'

'Never mind about the fish, tell me what happened.'

'Nothing happened. Freddie said he was not going to make any sort of push to make the acquaintance of this year's debutantes and unless I agreed to marry him then and there, he would reveal all to Lady Fitzpatrick the minute she came back into the room.'

'And you agreed.'

'Of course I agreed, it is what I have always wanted, though it will have to remain a secret until he has been home and confronted his father. He has already spoken to Papa.' She giggled suddenly. 'He even promised to pretend to pay particular attention to you.'

'Me?'

'Well, he has been dangling after Miss Hundon ever since he came down from Cambridge, everyone knows that. What more natural that he should be seen often in her presence?'

'Oh, I see. I thought you were tired of our masquerade?'

'So, I was, but now Freddie is part of it, it might be fun. And besides, I have not yet brought Lord Braybrooke to an understanding.'

'You can't have them both!'

'I don't want them both. I mean to make him understand the error of his ways and realise what a treasure he will have in Miss Sophie Hundon and when I speak of treasure, I do not mean anything so vulgar as money. Nor will it hurt him to become just a little jealous of Freddie.'

'Charlotte, I beg you to do no such thing. He will be so angry.'

'Then you must contrive to turn it to your advantage. He is to escort me to Vauxhall Gardens on Saturday and Freddie is to escort you. We shall see what transpires. And please, Sophie, do not dress in the unbecoming fashion you have adopted since we came to London. It is enough to put Freddie off, not to mention Lord Braybrooke.'

Sophie sighed, knowing she had lost control of the situation. She had been almost ready to agree with Charlotte that they must reveal their true identities and take the consequences when Charlotte changed from being an unwilling accomplice to an enthusiastic accessory. And what she was planning was even more hazardous. Well, she would go down fighting.

She dressed for the visit to Vauxhall Gardens with particular care in a gown of amber crepe over a cream satin slip. The short bodice had a round neck and tiny puff sleeves and was caught under the bust with a posy of silk flowers from which floated long satin ribbons in amber. Her hair was dressed *à la Grecque* and threaded with more ribbon. Her accessories were a single strand of pearls around her neck, long white gloves, white satin slippers, a small satin drawstring bag and a fan which had once been her mother's.

'Beautiful,' Charlotte said when Sophie came to her room to see if she was ready.

'You too. That rose pink is exactly right for your complexion. Freddie will fall in love with you all over again.'

'I hope he may, but it would be fatal to show it. I do believe I heard the front-door knocker. Are you ready?' Sophie took a deep breath and together they descended to the hall where Lady Fitzpatrick was greeting their escorts.

Richard, who had himself risen to the occasion and clad himself in a lilac evening coat of impeccable tailoring and dove grey pantaloons, looked up when he heard the rustle of their gowns and his breath caught in his throat as he beheld Sophie.

Here was no dowdy country cousin, here was a young lady with the face and figure of a goddess, who came down the stairs as if she were floating. If he had had any doubts about his choice of a wife, they fled at the sight of her.

What he most wanted to do was take her away somewhere private and declare his intentions before taking her in his arms once more and kissing her. He needed to feel her soft lips on his, her pliable body close to his so that he could enjoy her heart beating against his as he had done once before. But would she have him? Apart from her response to that kiss she had never given any indication she would welcome an offer from him.

It was neither the time nor the place and Freddie was hurrying forward to take her hand and claim her, showering her with compliments which were a little too effusive to be sincere. There was nothing for it but to make his bow to Charlotte and offer his arm to escort her to the waiting carriage.

Chapter Seven

The tableaux of Waterloo were impressive for the uniforms of the protagonists, for the simulated noise of the wooden guns and the smoke which threatened to obscure the whole thing. The actor who played Wellington sat impassively upon his horse doing nothing at all except look superior and Napoleon, short and stout and wearing his cockaded hat sideways, strutted about waving his arms ineffectually, while the armies rushed about pretending to fire muskets and stabbing each other with their bayonets. The English died stoically, while the French screamed and flung themselves about. The audience, standing in the darkness beyond the flambeaux-lit stage, were convulsed with laughter.

'Such realism! Such heroics!' Richard laughed, as the whole thing came to an end with Napoleon fleeing in his coach and the English soldiers cheering. 'If that is how the general populace see our hard-won victories, it is no wonder they have so little sympathy for our returning soldiers.'

'You would have everyone frightened to death by the truth?' Sophie asked him. 'The blood and the stench and the screaming of wounded horses, men torn limb from limb and dying in agony? It is supposed to be an entertainment, not a history lesson and it does no harm to remind people how brave our soldiers were. They might be a little more generous towards them.'

That she could describe such things, he put down to her taste in reading and a vivid imagination, not experience. She had spoken with spirit, her eyes glowing in the darkness, so vividly alive that he was obliged to clench his fists at his sides to stop him from pulling her into his arms. The tension he felt clamped his jaw, so that he could not trust himself to speak.

'You are silent,' she went on. 'Do you not agree?'

'Oh, you are right,' he said, forcing himself to respond. 'I can find no fault with your argument.'

'There is nothing more to see,' Charlotte said, laying her fingers lightly on his arm. 'Shall we walk a little? The coloured lanterns in the trees are so romantic, don't you think?'

'Miss Roswell, forgive me,' he said, turning to smile down at her and leading the way along one of the many pathways which wound around the gardens, many of them ending in little arbours. 'I am persuaded you share Miss Hundon's particular concern for the destitute soldiers.'

'Oh, I cannot believe they are destitute,' she said. 'Surely they have been given pensions?' She looked up at him coquettishly. 'You do not look like a man who is impoverished. I do believe you must outdo Mr Brummell, though I have never met that gentleman.'

'It is different for Lord Braybrooke,' Sophie said from behind them where she was walking with Freddie and Lady Fitzpatrick. 'He is an officer and a gentleman of independent means.'

'Of course he is,' Charlotte said. 'Did I say he was not?'

'Miss Roswell, you are putting Lord Braybrooke to the blush,' Freddie put in, annoyed with Charlotte for playing up to the viscount. 'Pray desist.'

'I was only bamming.' She turned to walk backwards in order to face him and Sophie. 'And I do not know what he means when he says I share your particular concerns, Sophie. Have you voiced concerns to his lordship?'

'I expect his lordship was referring to our conversation the first time he was so good as to take us to the park in his carriage,' Sophie said.

'Fancy him remembering that. I had quite forgot it.'

Either Miss Roswell was very good at dissembling or she was not the benefactress he had supposed her to be, Richard decided. Then who was it? Not Miss Hundon herself, for she had no money with which to be munificent. Lady Fitzpatrick, perhaps? It might account for her allowing Miss Hundon to go out alone, but her ladyship did not give the impression of being a philanthropist, or plump in the pocket. Ten to one she had been paid to chaperone the young ladies.

The mystery occupied his mind to such an extent that he lost the thread of the conversation going on about him. Charlotte, who had resumed walking at his side, had to speak to him twice to bring him back in line. 'I beg your pardon, Miss Roswell.'

'I said the fireworks are not to be let off until midnight and I suggested we might go to the bandstand and listen to the orchestra. I believe we might buy refreshments from a tent nearby.'

'By all means.'

They had barely taken their seats when Charlotte nudged Sophie. 'Is that not Monsieur Latour over there, Sophie?'

'Goodness, so it is. He is with his wife and little boy.'

'Oh, do introduce me to Madame Latour and the little boy, Sophie. I do not think I have ever met a real live French family.'

'Of course you have. London is full of *emigrés*, has been ever since the Terror. Why, the French king was exiled here until he returned to France at the end of the war.'

'Well, I never met him, did I? Oh, he has seen us and is coming over.'

Monsieur Latour was indeed making his way over to them, his wife on his arm. Pierre skipped ahead and made a formal bow before Sophie. 'Ma'amselle Hundon. Papa has brought us to see the sights. It is past my bedtime but he says it does not matter for I may sleep late tomorrow. Did you see the battle?' All this was said in breathless French.

Sophie smiled. 'Yes, and I am sorry for it.'

'Why?' He turned as his parents came up behind him. 'Ma'amselle did not like the tableaux, Mama.'

'Did she not?' Monsieur Latour smiled and bowed. 'Miss Hundon. Viscount Braybrooke. It is a pleasure to meet you again.'

Sophie left her seat to shake hands with Madame Latour and introduce her to Lady Fitzpatrick, Charlotte and Freddie. It was only when they sat down they realised the language would be a barrier to conversation. Monsieur Latour spoke a little English, but his wife and son none at all.

Richard tried manfully to keep up with them, but it was left to Sophie to translate, which she did without hesitation, moving fluently from one language to the other. It was only when the Frenchman commented on it that she realised she had probably made a dreadful mistake. 'I had a French governess,' she said, trying to retrieve the situation.

'She is to be congratulated,' he said. 'I could almost take you for a native, though the accent is not Parisian.'

'I believe Madame Cartier came from Brussels,' Sophie said, wishing the ground would open and swallow her because Richard was looking at her with a strange gleam in his eye.

'Miss Roswell did not share your teacher?' Madame Latour asked.

'No. We have not always lived together. My cousin did not come to live with us until her guardians died in a tragic accident two years ago.'

'*Pauvre fille.*' Madame Latour patted Charlotte's hand sympathetically. 'Lady Fitzpatrick is not your guardian, then?'

Because Charlotte had not understood the question,

it was left to Sophie to reply. 'No, only while we are in London for the Season. We are to come out into Society at a masked ball in three weeks' time.'

'Ah, yes, the invitation we 'ave received. Lady Fitzpatrick is very agreeable to ask us. *Malheureusement*, we expect to return to France the week before.'

Sophie hoped fervently that her relief did not show as she expressed her regret.

The conversation was interrupted when the first of the fireworks burst upon the sky and Pierre cried out with excitement. Richard hoisted him on his shoulders and pushed his way through the crowd to be near the front and the little boy sat perched on his vantage point, his eyes round with wonder as, one after the other, the fireworks fizzed skywards and fanned out in brilliant colours of red, yellow and green before dropping to earth.

Sophie's heart contracted as she watched them. What had she said to Charlotte all those weeks ago when they walked in the woods at Upper Corbury? He must be good with children. Viscount Braybrooke was giving every appearance of enjoying the company of the little boy and was not at all concerned about Pierre's boots dirtying his lilac coat.

She found herself with an image of Richard at Madderlea, playing in the garden with several children. Their children. Oh, if only... But being good with children was not the only requisite she had expounded. There had been a whole list of them. How vain and top-lofty she had been! But he had been no less arrogant in his requirements and she must remind herself of that when she felt herself weakening.

The endpiece of the display was a huge wheel which spun round emitting brilliant sparks and illuminating a huge set-piece of Saint George slaying the dragon, which breathed fire and smoke. Richard, who had explained the story to Pierre, set him down and took his hand to return him to his parents; soon afterwards the Latours took their leave. It was very late for Pierre to be out, Monsieur Latour explained, and now he had seen the fireworks, he must be taken home to bed.

'I think it is time we went too,' Freddie said, looking daggers at Charlotte who was hanging on to Richard's sleeve and looking up at him for all the world as if she adored him. It was all very well to say she was pretending for Sophie's sake, but she was doing it too brown. And he didn't see that it would do a pennyworth of good. 'Lady Fitzpatrick is already slumbering.'

They turned to look for the dowager and discovered her sitting on a bench with her head dropped on her chest and her bonnet all askew. 'As a chaperon, she is hardly to be recommended,' Richard laughed. 'Why, we could have carried you off and she none the wiser.'

'One must suppose she took you both for gentlemen,' Sophie said, though he could not tell if she were indulging in sarcasm or not.

'I suggest you wake her and bring her to the entrance, while I call up the carriage, before the temptation to prove otherwise overwhelms me,' he said.

She looked up at him, eyes glittering. 'Again, my lord?' The words were said in an undertone and not heard by Charlotte and Freddie who were gently shaking her ladyship awake.

Furiously he turned and strode away to find the carriage among the long line waiting for their owners to tire of the entertainment and ask to be taken home. Some would still be there at dawn, he well knew. It was a place for secret assignations and declarations and stolen kisses in the dark, but all he had managed was a stringent exchange of words which told him nothing except that she had not forgiven him.

But he had learned something. He had learned that she spoke fluent French and Miss Roswell did not. Miss Roswell professed never to have met a French family and yet, according to the *on dits* which were current about town, she had spent her childhood in Belgium. He was beginning to wonder if she had ever been abroad. But if not, where had she lived the first fifteen years of her life?

And had Miss Hundon really had a Belgian governess? And one called Cartier, a very similar name to the one adopted by her at the refuge. Tonight she had not looked or behaved like a country cousin; her clothes had not been flamboyant but elegantly understated. She had a presence, a stature which demanded attention. And lips that asked to be kissed, too. And he had not even managed one private word with her! He had wanted to ask for her forgiveness for the kiss he had stolen and to try and explain himself, but all he had done was to confirm her disgust of him.

The only way he would succeed in returning himself to favour, if he had ever held that exalted position, was to forget all about that embarrassing list of requirements and begin again, as if he had only just met her, to take this business of courtship seriously. But was it already too late?

'Richard!' He looked up at the sound of his name and was appalled to see his aunt and cousin bearing down on him.

'Richard,' his aunt said, tapping him with her fan. 'We did not know you were to be here. Why did you not say? We could have come together.'

'I am in company, Aunt.' He made his bow to both ladies. 'Good evening, Emily.'

'Whose company? Shall we join forces for supper?'

'We are on the point of leaving. The ladies are fatigued.'

'Ladies, eh?' She laughed. 'Barques of frailty. Oh, well, sow your wild oats, if you must, but do remember what is expected of you before the Season is out.'

'How could I forget?' He was on the point of explaining that his companions were not barques of frailty, when Frederick hove into view with Sophie on one arm and Charlotte on the other, followed by a somewhat sleepy and dishevelled Lady Fitzpatrick.

Lady Braybrooke laughed, making the tall plume on her turban nod. 'My goodness, what a handful you have there, Richard. I do hope you can manage them.' She gave Charlotte an unctuous smile, while ignoring Sophie. 'Good evening, Miss Roswell. Lady Fitzpatrick. I was about to suggest supper, but my nephew tells me you are fatigued and are going home.'

'Yes, my lady,' Charlotte said. 'The night is well advanced.'

'Oh, I had forgot, in the country you go to bed at sunset and rise at dawn. You must find town hours very irksome.'

'Not irksome, my lady,' Sophie said sweetly. 'Unhealthy perhaps. I have heard it said that rest taken before midnight is more efficacious than that taken during the morning. It makes for a smoother complexion and a better temper.'

Richard laughed aloud and earned a swift look of annoyance from his aunt. 'You live in the country three parts of the year yourself, Aunt Philippa, so you must have heard the expression.'

'Of course I have heard it, it is not meant for the *haute monde*, but the labouring classes. Take the ladies home, Richard, but I shall expect you to escort Emily and me in the park tomorrow afternoon.'

'Ma'am, I am…'

'Oh, please do,' Emily said. 'We have been in town nearly a week and you have not taken me out once.'

Richard's inbred good manners would not let him give his cousin a set down. He bowed to her and to his aunt in acquiescence and turned to offer his arm to Sophie, only to find she had taken Freddie's arm and was strolling towards the carriage with him, her bonnet so close to his cheek they were almost touching. He gave his arm to Charlotte.

Sophie could not sleep. Plagued with visions of Richard, she went over every conversation they had ever had, every look they had exchanged, remembered the taste of his lips on hers, the vibrant masculinity of his body when he held her in his arms. She argued with herself that it meant nothing except that she was a total innocent when it came to men and was no more to him than a mild flirtation. It must be so, for he seemed to be able to turn to Charlotte, his cousin Emily or Miss Greenholme with perfect ease of manners.

She tossed about so much the bedclothes were heaped around her, the pillows flattened. She sat up and pummelled them angrily. It was nearly dawn; she could see the light through the curtains, the outlines of the furniture and the reflection of the bed in the long mirror. She rose and went to the window to draw the curtains back and sat on the window seat to watch the pink light come up over the roof tops.

Was Lord Braybrooke still out on the town, playing cards at his club perhaps, or had he gone home to bed? Why was she so obsessed by him? The lamp lighter went down the street extinguishing the lamps; a cat padded along the street with a mouse in its mouth; a milkmaid led a cow to the back door of the house across the other side of the road, its udder heavy with milk. A chimney sweep, black as the soot he shifted, walked down the road, a sleepy-eyed young boy in his wake. A hackney stopped on the corner to set down a late-night reveller. Another day had begun, another day to live through.

She turned, slipped on a house robe, and went downstairs. A skivvy was clearing out the grate in the dining room, humming tunelessly under her breath.

'Oh, miss, you startled me,' she said. 'Did you want something?'

'No, Hetty, you carry on.'

She wandered all over the ground-floor rooms, her legs as heavy as lead. She desperately wanted to sleep, but she could not. It was all her own fault, this mull she had made of her life. She had been so sure of herself, so sure of what she wanted, so determined to put Madderlea first, she had embroiled not only herself but Charlotte, too, in a game of make-believe without considering what the consequences might be. It had all been intended to find the husband of her dreams, but it had turned into a nightmare. Only she was wide awake!

She went back to her room and sat on the rumpled bed. Lady Fitzpatrick and Charlotte would not be awake for hours. Suddenly making up her mind, she flung open her wardrobe door and pulled out her riding habit. She would go riding and blow the blue devils away in a gallop.

Luke, who had a room above the stables at the mews, was still fast asleep when she made her way there. Rather than wake him, she saddled Pewter herself with a man's saddle and set off alone, trotting through the quiet streets towards Hyde Park.

It was going to be a warm day, but now the air was pleasant with a slight breeze which lifted her red-gold curls as she set her horse to canter along the almost-deserted ride. But cantering was not enough. She turned off the path and spurred Pewter to a gallop across the grass.

It reminded her of the rides she had taken with her

Uncle Henry around the estate at Madderlea. She had not been back since that dreadful accident because Aunt Madeleine considered it would be too upsetting for her. But she ought to go back. She should know what was going on there even if she was debarred by law from having control of it. She ought to test her memory, find out if it really was worth all the heartache she was suffering. Supposing when she saw it again, she discovered it was no more than bricks and mortar, a millstone, as Lady Braybrooke had suggested? Then what?

She drew up and jumped down to rest her horse, sitting with her back against a tree trunk while he cropped the grass close by. Bricks and mortar. What did Richard think of bricks and mortar? But it was a heritage too and there were people involved, flesh and blood like she was, people who worked and ate and drank and loved. Love. What exactly was it? Her eyelids drooped as her thoughts went round and round, going nowhere.

Richard found her there, under the spreading branches, fast asleep.

After he left the ladies at Holles Street, he had felt too restless to go home, knowing his aunt and cousin would be waiting for him, fussing over him, questioning him. He had sent the carriage back to Bedford Row with the coachman and walked about for hours, so deep in thought he had no idea where his steps had taken him, except that just before dawn he had found himself back at Holles Street as if he had been drawn to it like a magnet.

All the contradictory aspects of Miss Hundon and

Miss Roswell's characters had been going round and round in his head until he was dizzy. He was almost to the point of believing they were not Miss Hundon and Miss Roswell at all, but two imposters, out to trap him. But why?

Was there anything in his past which might account for it? Had he ever done anything to cause two apparently innocent young ladies to want to play games with him? He was no greenhorn and there had been several ladies in his life, little bits of muslin, barques of frailty, as his aunt had so succinctly put it, but he had never knowingly hurt any of them. And he had never met Miss Hundon before; he would certainly have remembered her if he had.

He had stood outside the house, staring up at the windows, wondering which one was Sophie's. He had been answered when he saw the curtains being drawn and just managed to duck out of sight as the subject of his contemplation looked out. He was not the only one who was sleepless.

A few minutes later she had come out and darted down the lane to the mews, the skirt of her riding habit bunched up in her hands. Keeping hidden, he followed and saw her mount and trot away towards the park. His doubts were forgotten and he hurried after her, but by the time he reached the ride she was nowhere to be seen.

The first thing that came to his mind was that she had an assignation. Why else creep out alone at so early an hour? Angry with himself for being such a sousecrown, he had turned to leave but, hearing hoof-beats some way off, turned in the direction of the sound and saw the rump of her horse as she galloped towards the centre of the park and disappeared into a copse. He went after her, but being on foot it was some time before he came upon her, seated on the ground with her back against a tree. So, it was an assignation!

Curious, he had stayed out of sight and watched. Fifteen minutes went by. She did not seem to be anxious or looking about her as if expecting her lover. He had been both relieved and horrified when her eyes closed and he realised she was slumbering like a child.

He came out from his hiding place and stood for a moment, watching the gentle rise and fall of her breast, wondering how to wake her without startling her. Sitting on the grass at her side, he leaned on his elbow and allowed himself the luxury of studying every inch of her face. He noted the arched brows, the straight nose, the perfectly shaped lips, slightly parted now, even the dimple in her chin and the light sprinkling of freckles on her cheeks and the soft curve of her throat as it disappeared into the frill of the blouse which peeped above the collar of her habit.

He picked a stem of grass and tickled her chin with it. She twitched like a sleeping puppy but did not wake. Slowly he bent his head and put his lips to her forehead. She did not stir. Becoming bolder, he kissed her lips very, very gently. Her eyes flew open. He leaned back as she came fully awake, sat up and stared at him as if she could not believe what she was seeing. 'It's you!'

He inclined his head, smiling. 'As you see.'

She had been asleep. And dreaming. She had dreamed he was bending over her, kissing her, a look of such tenderness in his eyes, she had been in ecstasy. And then she woke to find him sitting beside her, laughing at her. And still wearing the lilac coat and the dove-grey pantaloons of the evening before. Was she awake or still asleep? 'Where am I? What are you doing here?'

He smiled. 'I am sitting on the ground in the middle of Hyde Park, the same as you.'

'I know that. What I meant was, why, for what reason? I'll take my oath you have not been home to bed. You are still wearing your evening coat and you have not shaved.'

'If I had known I might meet Sleeping Beauty, I might have attired myself as Prince Charming.'

'I was not asleep, I was merely resting my eyes.'

He did not bother to contradict her; they both knew the truth. 'I was out walking. What reason can you give?'

'I could not sleep. I decided to take a ride.'

'All alone?'

'Why not? I did not want to wake the rest of the household.'

'And so you came here, to one of the loneliest parts of the park, and fell asleep like the Babes in the Wood. What do you think might have happened if someone other than me had found you? Unless you were expecting someone else. If so, you must be sadly disappointed he did not arrive.'

'An assignation? Whatever gave you that idea?' She was so genuinely astonished, he realised he had been mistaken. 'Sir, I think it very uncivil of you to suggest that I would meet up with someone secretly, and at this hour. But then, I collect, you have no great opinion of me…'

'Miss Hundon, that hit is below the belt. And unworthy of you.'

'I told you before I know nothing of pugilism, but how clever of you to turn the tables and put me in the wrong. You would have me apologising to you next for discommoding you.'

'That was certainly not my intention and I beg your pardon if I mistook the matter, but I was, and am, concerned for your safety. What madness possessed you to come out at this hour? Good God, you might have been robbed or your horse stolen. Worse, you might have been attacked.'

'But I wasn't, was I?' She sounded a great deal more spirited than she felt.

'It was your good fortune that I was on hand.'

'How did you come to be on hand? Have you been following me?'

'I saw you leave the house; it behoved me to make sure you came to no harm.'

'And what, pray, were you doing outside our house at so early an hour?'

He laughed. 'Now, you are turning the tables. Let us say I was on my way home after a night out.'

'And you saw me and immediately jumped to the conclusion I was meeting a lover—not that it is any concern of yours. You are not my keeper.'

'No, I am not, but if this morning is a yardstick,

you are certainly in need of one. The sooner you find
a husband to take you in hand, the better.'

'Do you think I might not find one willing to undertake the task?' she asked mischievously.

'He would certainly have his hands full. A greater
hoyden I have yet to meet.'

'And I collect you dislike hoydens excessively.'
She scrambled to her feet and began dusting down
her skirt. The conversation was so barbed, she could
not bear to continue it. 'I must go.'

'Then allow me to escort you.'

'Oh, please do not trouble yourself, my lord, I am
sure you must be in some haste to be elsewhere.' She
looked about for Pewter, who was nibbling a dande-
lion a few yards away.

'It would be very disobliging of me to be in a hurry
when I meet a young lady who so obviously does not
know how to go on and needs assistance.'

'I need no assistance,' she said, catching Pewter's
reins and preparing to mount by herself. The horse
stepped sideways and she found herself hopping after
him with one foot in the stirrup.

He strode up to her and grabbed the bridle, making
the horse stand still. 'Allow me.' He bent to offer his
cupped hands for her foot. 'Do you ever observe the
proprieties?' he asked, noting the man's saddle. 'Who
taught you to ride astride?'

'Papa,' she said without thinking.

'Really? You surprise me. Lawyers always seem to
me to be rather stuffy gentlemen.'

'That just shows one should not jump to conclu-
sions,' she retorted, spreading her skirt.

He smiled a little grimly. She was the most infuriating chit imaginable. And the loveliest. 'Yes, you would have thought I would have learned that by now, would you not? Nothing is ever what it seems.'

She was feeling tired and confused and did not know how to answer that and so she clicked her tongue at Pewter and set off at a walk, back towards the Stanhope Gate.

He took hold of the horse's bridle to lead him. 'Miss Hundon,' he said, walking purposefully beside her. 'I want you to promise me you will not go out riding alone again. If you feel like early morning exercise, will you tell me? I shall be happy to accompany you.'

'Oh, I do not think that would be at all the thing, my lord. We shall have the tattlers talking and that would certainly not please Lady Braybrooke. And besides, this morning's ride was not premeditated. It was a whim and unlikely to be repeated. You need not concern yourself with my eccentricities.'

She had given him a disgust of her and instead of meekly accepting his scolding and thanking him for seeing her safely home, she had snubbed him. He was angry, she could tell by the set of his jaw as he strode beside her horse, looking straight ahead.

When they reached the mews, he turned to help her dismount, putting his hands about her waist and lifting her to the ground as if she weighed no more than thistledown. They stood together looking into each other's faces, trying to read thoughts that were hidden, desires which could not be expressed, hope where there was none. Or so it seemed.

'Miss Hundon…' His voice was soft and gentle, making her heart jump into her throat.

'My lord?'

'We have made a poor start, you and I, have we not? I should like to…' He got no further because Luke came hurrying out of the stable towards them.

'Miss Rosw—' He stopped, his mouth a round O of dismay at his mistake.

Sophie, turning to face him, said the first thing that came into her head. 'What about Miss Roswell, Luke? Has she been looking for me?'

'Yes, miss.' His relief was obvious. 'She couldn't find you in the house. I didn't know where you were, but Pewter were gone and…'

'I went for a ride to see the sun come up,' she said. 'I am sorry if I worried anyone. I'll go in and see Charlotte straight away.' She turned to Richard. 'Thank you, my lord, for seeing me safe.'

Dismissed, there was nothing to do but take his leave.

Lady Fitzpatrick and Charlotte were still abed and Sophie was not required to explain her absence. She hurried to her room and dressed in a striped cambric morning dress with a high neck and straight sleeves, one of those Charlotte had decried as being dowdy, and was brushing her hair before the mirror when Anne came in with her morning chocolate.

'I thought I heard you moving about, Miss Sophie, and Hetty said you were downstairs before it was even light.'

'Too much excitement, Anne. I could not sleep.'

'That's just what I thought, so I've brought your chocolate early. Shall I do your hair?'

'Please.'

Anne took over the brush. 'Goodness, this is in a tangle. What shall I put out for you to wear today, miss?'

'This will do for this morning. I am going out. As for the afternoon, I shall have to see what Lady Fitzpatrick has arranged.'

'I doubt she will stir before noon. Nor Miss Charlotte neither.'

'Good. Let them sleep as long as possible, Anne. I have some business to see to.'

'I ain't so sure you should be rushing about on your own, Miss Roswell. And pretendin' to be Miss Hundon. What Miss Charlotte's mama would say if she knew…'

'But she doesn't know, does she? And we shall all come to rights before the Season ends. If anyone asks for me this morning, I have gone to Pantheon's Bazaar because I have been told they have some new lace come in and I need to buy some for my costume for the ball. It's a secret, so I do not want anyone to come with me.'

'Very well, miss.'

Putting on a light pelisse and a plain bonnet, she picked up her reticule and left the house again, ignoring the fact that less than an hour before Richard had scolded her for going out alone. She could not see that she was in any more danger on the streets of the metropolis than she had been in Upper Corbury.

And as for the conventions, she had already flouted them too often to worry about conforming now.

His lordship had said it would be a good thing when she found a husband, but he had no more thought of offering for her himself than he would of offering for her maid. She was beneath his notice, except as a sparring partner, a nuisance who was for-ever inconveniencing him, a hoyden who sometimes amused him; it was too late to turn herself into the kind of genteel young lady he would take as a wife. Nor did she want to. If he did not like her as she was, then there was no point at all in sighing after him.

Remembering the last time she had said she was going shopping, when she had returned without the book she had expressly set out to buy, she called first at Pantheon's Bazaar and selected several yards of lace to be put on Miss Roswell's account and deliv-ered to Holles Street, then went on to Maiden Lane.

The refuge was busy as always. Mrs Stebbings and her helpers were serving what could be called either a late breakfast or an early nuncheon. Sophie took off her cloak, donned an apron and stood beside the giant stewpot, ladling out food on to plates, smiling at each recipient as she did so. They passed by so quickly that all she really saw of them was a hand and an arm and perhaps a grubby coat.

'Thank you, miss.'

She raised her head at the sound of the voice and almost fell over in surprise as she found herself look-ing into the laughing eyes of Richard Braybrooke. He was wearing a very dirty uniform coat with a torn sleeve. He had still not shaved and his hair was un-kempt.

'Go away!' she hissed at him. 'You have no right to come here, pretending to be poor. This food is for the sick and needy and you are neither.' She reached out to take the dish from him, but he held it out of her reach.

'No, but then this is not for me. It's for poor Davy, over there.' He nodded towards a legless, one-armed man who sat on the floor in a corner. 'He can't stand in line like everyone else.'

'Oh.' She was chagrined, but quickly recovered. 'Then why dress like that?'

He smiled. 'Do you suppose they would welcome me if I came in a coat tailored by Scott and Hoby's tasselled hessians?'

'No, but why come at all?'

'You have come. And you dress the part.'

'That's different.'

'Why? You are not the only one to feel compassion for those less fortunate.'

'Compassion?' She did not try to conceal her sur-prise.

'Do you find that idea so very difficult to grasp, Miss…Mrs Carter?'

'Hey, will you stop your jabberin' and move on,' the man behind him grumbled.

Richard apologised gruffly and moved away. 'I should like to speak to you when you are free,' he murmured to Sophie.

She went on with her task, but part of her was watching Lord Braybrooke as he knelt beside the legless man and helped him to eat. There was nothing arrogant about him now; he was considerate and caring.

'Who would have believed it?' Mrs Stebbings said beside her. 'It just goes to show, don't it?'

'Goes to show what?'

'That a true gentleman don't need fancy clothes and there's more to compassion than handing out money.'

'You know who he is?' she asked, doling out potatoes on to the next plate.

'Yes, he is Major Richard Braybrooke. He was an aide to Wellington, you know, and a fine officer, so I have been told, though very strict on discipline. He came here a few days ago and asked who our sponsor was.'

'What did you tell him?'

'Only what you yourself said we might say, that the benefactress wished to remain anonymous and you were acting for her. He seemed exceedingly interested and promised a further donation himself, though I shouldn't tell you that. He wishes to be incognito, but there can be no harm in you knowing, I am sure, if you are known to him.'

'He is an acquaintance of my employer.'

'Then he will have guessed the name of our benefactress?'

'Very possibly,' she said, realising he would conclude that it was the heiress of Madderlea, which was all very well, but now she would have to tell Charlotte and her little secret would be out. Unless she could persuade his lordship to say nothing to her cousin.

The legless man had finished his meal and Richard was helping him on to a kind of platform on wheels which he used to propel himself about the streets, paddling it with his one hand. As soon as he had gone, Richard brought the empty plate back to Sophie, who had just served the last of the long line of men. There would be another batch of supplicants later but others would serve them. She had been absent from home long enough and she was nearly asleep on her feet.

'When you are ready, I will take you home,' he said. 'I left my curricle round the corner.'

She was too tired to argue. Taking off her apron, she allowed him to help her into her pelisse and, saying goodbye to Mrs Stebbings and the other ladies, she stepped outside and took the arm he offered. Neither noticed Sergeant Dawkins ambling up the street towards the refuge.

He stopped when he saw them. 'Well, well, well,' he muttered. 'If it ain't Major Braybrooke. And with the little filly, too. Now there's a turn up.' He forgot all about his rumbling stomach and set off after them, keeping well to the rear. The last thing he wanted was to be seen and recognised.

When they climbed into a carriage and trotted away too fast for him to follow, he cursed under his breath. But it did not matter; the chit would return and, unless he missed his guess, so would the Major.

He had forgotten all about his threat of revenge made three years before in the heat of Lisbon where his court martial had been held, but seeing and recognising Major Braybrooke had brought it all back:

the stifling heat of the prison, the humiliation of being flogged before his men, the loss of pay and the fact that he had lost the only job he had ever had. He was a good soldier and loved the life now denied to him. And, on top of that, he had been obliged to find his own way back to England. And all because of a few tawdry ornaments and a silver brooch.

His resentment rekindled, he determined to have his revenge.

Major Braybrooke, who always knew where his next meal was coming from, who could throw coins to beggars with gay abandonment, would die a slow and painful death. And he would know why he was dying too. He, George Dawkins, would make sure of it. He grinned and went back to the refuge to stand in line for a meal and try his luck for a bed for the night.

Chapter Eight

The tiger, in his yellow and black striped waistcoat, had been walking his lordship's equipage up and down the street for the best part of two hours and was relieved to see his employer appear.

Sophie watched as Richard stripped off the ragged coat and donned a frockcoat of brown superfine which he had left on the seat and, running his hand through his hair, found his tall beaver hat and set it upon his dark curls. 'Behold, the transformation,' he said. 'It would not be at all the thing for a tramp to be seen escorting a lady in the Braybrooke curricle.' He handed her up and climbed in beside her; the tiger jumped on to the back step and they set off at a brisk trot.

She was still annoyed with him for appearing at the refuge as he had and she was determined not to soften towards him. That way lay more heartache than she thought she could bear. 'In the absence of the husband you spoke of, have you appointed yourself my keeper?' she asked.

He was unsmiling as he guided the carriage through the traffic. 'Someone has to watch out for you.'

'So you followed me again.'

'No, for I was sure you were safe home in bed and making up for lost sleep.'

'It was too late to go back to bed and I had promised Mrs Stebbings I would help her this morning, not that I think it is the least necessary to explain myself to you.'

'Such stamina fills me with admiration.'

'You have not been to bed either.'

'No, but I am—was—a soldier, accustomed to remaining alert for two days without sleep.'

'If you did not follow me, how did you know about the house?'

'Oh, I came upon it quite by chance about a week ago. It seemed to me to be a very worthy cause and one I could support.'

'Do you mean that?'

'I am not in the habit of saying things I do not mean.'

'I was thinking that besides a place to eat and sleep, what the men need most is work. I had thought of setting up an employment agency, but that would mean finding out what the men could do and talking to employers and persuading them to take them on. It would need to be done by a man who knew what he was about. Do you know of such a one?'

'You thought of that yourself?'

'Why, has it been done before?'

'There are agencies…'

'Yes, for domestic workers and people like that,

not specifically for ex-soldiers and ex-sailors. I am sure it will help them, especially if you sponsor it.'

'Because you ask it of me, I will give it some thought.'

'Thank you.'

'I make no promises—there are many aspects to be considered before a decision is made. It would have to be done in a businesslike way, not by a chit of a girl who has more compassion than sense.'

'That is unfair, my lord, I am not without sense.'

'You have shown little evidence of it in the short time I have known you. It is certainly not sensible to walk about the streets of London alone. I cannot allow it to continue.'

'You cannot allow it!' She was so incensed she turned towards him, her face flushed with anger. 'And, pray, what gives you the right to dictate to me, Lord Braybrooke?'

'Someone must. Lady Fitzpatrick has obviously failed to have the correct influence upon you and though Mr Harfield has but lately come to town, I would have expected him to have more care of you. Such a ramshackle way of going on, I never did know.'

'Then I am surprised you allow yourself to be seen with me,' she said. It was easier to be angry with him than to sit in silent misery. 'I can do your reputation no good. I am not in the running for the next Duchess of Rathbone and that must surely be your first consideration. Countenance and elegance and presence, I am informed, are requisites, along with a fortune and turning a blind eye to infidelity. My goodness, I fail in every respect.'

'Where did you learn that tarradiddle?'

'*On dits*, my lord. Your list of requirements is the talk of the town and all the mamas are busy trying to make their daughters conform in order to please you.'

He cursed Martin, who must have told his mother—that inveterate gossip had tongue enough for two sets of teeth. 'Which just goes to show how silly they are,' he said. 'Do you think I cannot tell false from true?'

Her little gasp of shock amused him, but he let the remark hang in the air, waiting for her to find a response. 'Then it is true, you have made a list of your requirements and are busy ticking them off, one by one against all the possibles. I never met such a top-lofty, conceited man in all my life.'

'Then you have not met many men, for I am the soul of modesty.'

It was said in such a light-hearted way, she found herself laughing. 'And that boast itself is proof of the contrary.'

'You have a very caustic tongue for a young lady brought up in the seclusion of the country.'

'I do not see why I should sit meekly saying nothing while you scold me, my lord, especially as I do not, nor ever will, attempt to conform to your list.'

'I would be disappointed in you if you did.'

'Nor will Charlotte.'

'No, but we were not talking about your cousin, were we? Charlotte is a delightful young lady, pretty as a picture and as mild as you are sharp, but I have

no intention of earning Mr Harfield's undying enmity
by making an offer for her.'

'Mr Harfield?'

'I am not blind, you know. I have seen the way
they look at each other and two people more in love
I have yet to see. I wish them well. They will deal
famously with each other.'

'If his father allows it.'

'Why should he not?' he asked, testing her. 'Miss
Roswell has a fortune, does she not? And a large estate. Sir Mortimer could hardly quarrel with that.'

Oh, how she wished she did not feel so tired. She
might know how to answer that without giving the
game away, except it was not a game but a deception
of terrifying magnitude. How was she going to endure
staying in London a moment longer, knowing he was
ticking off those attributes in every other eligible
young lady he knew and had discounted her right
from the start. But Charlotte, at least, would be glad
to know she was not being considered.

'No cutting response?' he queried after a moment
or two of silence. 'No set down to put me in my
place? No turning of the tables? No denying the
truth?'

'My lord, I am too tired to bandy words.'

'Yes, my poor Sophie, I know you are and it is
unkind in me to tease you. You will soon be home
and then you may rest.'

'What are you going to do?'

'Do?' he queried, as they turned into the end of
Holles Street. 'Why, I think I shall go home to Bed-

ford Row, have a bath and a shave and then I might well take to my bed for an hour or two.'

'No, I meant what are you going to do about my secret. Will you tell Lady Fitzpatrick?'

He turned to grin at her. 'Which secret?'

'My work with the veterans, of course—what other secret would there be?'

'Now, do you know, I thought there might be something else.'

'I cannot think what you mean. I was always taught that good should be done by stealth and that is why I have said nothing about the enterprise to anyone, not because I am ashamed of it. Besides, I doubt Lady Fitzpatrick would understand.'

'Then she is not the unknown benefactress?'

'No.'

'Who is?'

'Would you have me betray a confidence?' she queried evasively.

She was good at being evasive, he mused. 'No, I am sure you would never do that.'

'Then are you going to tell her ladyship?'

'No, but there is one condition.' He brought the curricle to a stop outside Lady Fitzpatrick's front door. 'You will not go to Maiden Lane alone again. It is a most unsavoury district.'

'I have seen worse,' she said, referring to her journey through war-torn Europe.

'I wonder where?' he mused.

'Every city and town in the land has it slums,' she said, though she wondered how much longer she could keep thinking of answers to his awkward questions.

'True, but that does not make it acceptable for you to wander about the streets alone. If you must indulge in philanthropy, then we will go together.'

'But, my lord, if we are seen too much in each other's company, there will be gossip…'

'There is one way to silence it,' he said slowly, turning in his seat to face her. He was feeling reckless. Sitting there, wanting to take her in his arms, wanting to confess his love for her, it was immaterial to him whether it was Miss Hundon or Miss Roswell he was proposing to; names meant nothing. It was the person she was that drew him to her; rich or poor, it was all one to him. But she was also a clever prevaricator. He did not want to believe it was anything reprehensible, but a woman who could keep a secret was a rare specimen. Until he knew the reason for it, oughtn't he to hold his horses?

'How?' she asked.

He reached out and touched her cheek. 'My lovely Sophie, I do believe you are too fagged to continue sparring with me and I am not one to take advantage of an opponent's weakness. We will leave it for another day. I believe you are to be at Almack's on Wednesday?'

'Yes, Lady Fitzpatrick obtained vouchers two days ago. Do you go?'

'I have to leave town for a day or two, I have pressing business in Hertfordshire, but I hope to return in time to be there. If I am not, rest assured I will call on you the next day.'

'Why?' she demanded bluntly.

He laughed. 'Why, for the next round, of course. I shall expect you to be in fine fettle again and leading with your chin as always.'

'It is all very well to amuse yourself roasting me,' she said. 'but if there are paragons who fit your criteria, they will surely all have been snapped up by the time you come to realise that bamming me is not the way to find yourself a wife.'

'I am not looking for a wife, much less a paragon. How dull life would be leg-shackled to such a one.' He jumped down and held out his hand to help her down. 'Come, allow me to escort you indoors.'

She put her hand in his and let him to lead her to the door, so weary that she was almost stumbling. 'My lord, I beg you, do not stay. You are as tired as I am and you cannot go into Lady Fitzpatrick's drawing room unshaven as you are.'

'Do not fret so, little one, her ladyship is too short-sighted to notice, you know that.'

'But Charlotte will notice.'

'She will be too polite to mention it.'

They reached the door as a footman opened it but he was too well trained to show any sign of shock or disapproval.

'Where is Lady Fitzpatrick?' Sophie asked him.

'I believe she has gone shopping with Miss Roswell, Miss Hundon. The Pantheon Bazaar, if I understood correctly.'

'Oh, then I must have missed her.' Relieved, she turned to Richard, who obviously could not stay under the circumstances. 'Thank you for your escort, my lord.'

'My pleasure, ma'am.' He swept her an elegant bow and ran lightly down the steps and back to his curricle, fired with determination to see his grandfather.

He did not need to go to Hertfordshire to do so, for when he arrived home he found Lady Braybrooke hurrying upstairs behind a chambermaid who was carrying a pile of bedlinen. She caught sight of him as he came in and handed the footman his hat.

'Richard, where have you been?' she demanded, returning downstairs. 'The Duke is here and asking for you.' She looked at his dishevelled appearance and the stubble on his chin in disgust. 'Really, Richard, you look like a vagrant. Have you been out all night?'

He smiled and bowed. 'As you see.'

'Then you had better go upstairs to change and be shaved before seeing His Grace. I will tell him you are home.'

'Why has he come to town? He hates London.'

'I have no doubt he will tell you. He is in the library.'

Richard hurried to make himself respectable and presented himself in the library twenty minutes later, a picture of studied elegance in a frockcoat of green superfine, biscuit-coloured pantaloons, yellow kerseymere waistcoat and a neat but not flamboyant cravat. His chin was smooth and his hair carefully arranged.

His grandfather was sitting in an armchair by the hearth, fortifying himself with a glass of brandy. The tragedy of losing both his sons had taken their toll on him and he seemed to have shrunk a little, so that his dark brown nankeen coat hung loosely on his shoulders. His own, very white hair was covered by a dark wig, but for all that he was upright and alert and his knowing brown eyes missed nothing.

Richard stood before him and bowed from the waist. 'Your Grace, I did not expect you or I would have been here to greet you.'

'Didn't expect to be here. Don't like the Smoke above half. Sit down, boy, sit down.'

Richard obediently sat in the chair opposite him. 'I am pleased to see you, sir, but why are you here?'

'Your aunt asked me to come. Seems you have been making a cake of yourself, rattling round town, playing fast and loose with every unmarried wench…'

'Your Grace, I have simply been doing as you asked and looking for a wife.'

'With an impossible list of requirements which has the whole *haute monde* buzzing with conjecture.' He smiled suddenly. 'I cannot blame you for that, but why make it so public?'

'It was only a jest between Martin Gosport and me, not meant to be taken seriously, but he must have told his mother…'

'That gadabout. Tell her and you tell the world.'

'Yes, I should have known. But it has certainly had some revealing consequences…'

His Grace held out his glass. 'Fill that again, will you? And have one yourself. I must speak bluntly and you may have need of it.'

Richard, who had never known his grandfather to be anything else but blunt, went to obey.

With the newly replenished glass in his hand, His Grace leaned back in his chair and surveyed his grandson for fully a minute before speaking. 'Well, what have you got to say for yourself?'

'In what respect, Your Grace?'

'In respect of finding a wife. Though why you should feel the need when I have already made known my thoughts on the subject, I do not know.'

'You mean Emily?'

'Yes, whom did you think I meant?'

'But, sir, Emily is my cousin; we grew up together as children. She is little more than a child now. She needs more time and you have told me to make haste…'

'Marriage will soon mature her.'

'Grandfather, you are being unfair to her. Given a year or two more and a free hand, I am sure she would not choose me.'

'And what would happen to the noble families of England if their daughters were allowed to pick and choose? Why, they would be so diluted they would die out, the estates would be broken up and, before you know where you are the proletariat would be running the country. Your Aunt Philippa understands that, if you do not.'

'You did give me an alternative.'

'So I did. And what have you done about it, except earn yourself the reputation of being a rakeshame?'

'I have met someone…'

'Ah, if my information is correct, you mean the

Roswell filly, niece of the late Earl of Peterborough. Coming out with her cousin Miss Hundon, under the wing of that antidote widow of an Irishman, are they not? She's as queer as Dick's hatband. If Miss Roswell is as high in the instep as rumour says, why could her guardian not find someone more *au fait* with Society to bring her out?'

'Lady Fitzpatrick is short-sighted and a little deaf, but good-hearted enough.'

'So good-hearted the chits are allowed to do as they please. You have not made an offer, I hope.'

'No. There are complications...'

'Indeed, there are. There is Philippa, for one. Not that I can't deal with her, if I have to. But Emily is also my grandchild and I am fond of her.'

'As I am, Your Grace. That does not mean we should suit.'

'You know your aunt is bringing forward Emily's come-out and giving a ball for her next week? I am persuaded she means to steal a march on Miss Roswell and bring you to the mark before that young lady's own come-out.'

Richard sighed. 'I was afraid of that.'

'I have told her she must invite Miss Roswell. I want to look her over.'

'And Miss Hundon, I hope.'

The Duke, in the act of setting down his empty glass, looked up at him sharply. 'Miss Hundon? The country cousin? I thought it was Peterborough's niece you were dangling after?'

'She will not come without her cousin. They are

inseparable.' He smiled. 'Sometimes it is difficult to tell one from the other.'

'Then invite them both. Invite the whole *ton*. Let me see them all at once. The sooner I meet them all, the sooner I may return to the country.'

'You may see them before the ball, if you wish. They will be at Almack's on Wednesday and I have said I will meet them there.'

'You want me to dress up in evening clothes and sit around drinking lemon cordial all evening?'

'You need not stay the whole evening.'

'No, I should not do so in any case.' He sighed heavily. 'Oh, well, we might as well get it over with. But if I have come on a wild goose chase and you change your mind, I shall not be pleased.'

He would never change his mind about Sophie, he told himself as his grandfather released him; the thought of marrying anyone else was abhorrent, but he knew instinctively that she would never agree to marry him if he had to defy his grandfather to do it. But how to bring about the metamorphosis from country cousin to Madderlea heiress without upsetting the whole applecart, he did not know. He could not humiliate her by revealing her secret, but on the other hand, if she could not bring herself to confide in him, then could he trust her at all?

'Well?' His aunt accosted him in the hall. 'What did he say?'

'Nothing of import. Where is Emily?'

She gave a smile of unconcealed relief. 'Why, I do believe she is in the garden. Go and find her, Richard. She will be so pleased to see you.'

He bowed and hurried away to find his cousin. She was sitting on a swing in a little arbour at the end of the garden, dreamily pushing herself with her toe. She looked like a gangly child, all arms and long legs. Her dark hair had been fastened back with a ribbon, but it had come undone and her tresses were spread across her shoulders.

'Emily.'

She looked up and he noticed she had been crying. 'Oh, it's you.'

He went over to her and put his hand under her chin to lift her face to his. 'What is wrong?'

'Nothing.'

'I do not believe you are the sort to weep for nothing.'

'I am not weeping.'

'That is a whisker. Has your mama been scolding you?'

'Not exactly.'

'No, for you never do anything to invite a scolding, do you? Do you not sometimes feel like rebelling?'

'Oh, no.'

'So, if you were told to marry someone you hold in aversion, you would do it, simply because your mama says you must.'

She looked up at him with startled green eyes. 'I do not hold you in aversion.'

'But you do not love me.'

'Of course I do.'

'Yes, but as your big cousin who carried you on his shoulders when you were very small, who taught you to ride and fish and fall into scrapes, not as a husband.'

'Mama says…'

'I do not want to know what your mother says. I want to know what you think. If I was to offer for you, would you throw yourself into my arms in delight or run away and hide and wish you could die rather than share my bed?'

'Richard!' she exclaimed, shocked by his bluntness, as he knew she would be.

'Marriage is for life, my dear,' he said. 'You may please your mother, you may even please Grandfather, but you would certainly not be storing up happiness for yourself in marrying me.'

'I wish you would not roast me so. I have had enough of that already.'

'I am under pressure too, you know.'

She raised pleading eyes to his. 'Yes, but you will not give way to it, will you?'

'You do not wish me to? You would refuse me if I did?'

'Oh, Richard, please do not ask me, then Mama cannot blame me if it does not come to pass.'

'Then I won't. We will remain friends and cousins.'

She jumped off the swing and threw her arms about his neck. 'Oh, thank you, Richard, thank you. But, you know, Mama will fly into the boughs over it.'

'Then we shall not tell her of this conversation,' he said, gently disengaging her. 'Wait until after your come-out ball because I am sure there will be other young men there more to your liking. Aunt Philippa will come about.'

'Oh, I do hope so. You see, there is someone…' He smiled indulgently at her. 'Is there, now? And am I to be taken into your confidence?'

'You will not laugh?'

'Now, why should I do that?'

'Because he is older than me and has told everyone he is not in the petticoat line, which is a good thing because I must grow up first. But I have known him for years and years…'

'My dear Emily, you intrigue me. I cannot, for the life of me, think who it might be.'

'Can you not? You have known him for years and years too. You introduced us the day before you both left for the war…'

'Martin! Do you mean you have set your cap at Martin Gosport? The sly old dog!'

'I knew you would laugh.'

'I am not laughing, my little one. I wish you happy. He will inherit his father's title one day and, though he is not so wealthy as I shall be, his income is certainly not to be disdained. Your mama can have no objection to him.'

'You must not say anything to her. It is a secret.'

He took her hand and linked his arm with hers. 'Then a secret it shall remain until you give me leave to felicitate you. Now, let us go back inside and no more tears, eh?'

Lady Braybrooke, watching them approach the house arm in arm, smiling at each other, felt thoroughly pleased with herself and returned to her escritoire to add the names of Lady Fitzpatrick, Miss Roswell and Miss Hundon to her guest list, as her father-in-law had instructed. It did not matter now and the downfall of those two young ladies would give her immense satisfaction.

Sophie was woken by Anne coming into the room. She had been dreaming of Madderlea, but instead of the usual peace and calm it was the centre of a pitched battle. Guns had been going off and there had been smoke and men falling and screams and she was trying to find someone, moving about in the mêlée, searching faces. The nightmare had been brought on by her conversation with Lord Braybrooke and the talk of fighting and soldiers and memories of her flight from Europe. She shook off the dream and looked at the clock. It was gone six.

'Her ladyship put off dinner to give you longer to sleep, Miss Sophie, but Cook won't keep it back above another quarter of an hour, so I came to wake you and help you dress.'

Sophie scrambled off the bed. 'Goodness, have I slept all afternoon? Whatever will they think of me?'

'Nothing, why should they?' She was busy pouring hot water into the washbasin. 'Her ladyship and Miss Charlotte slept most of the afternoon themselves. It's what happens when you stay up most of the night. Now, you have a wash while I lay out your clothes. What shall you wear?'

'The brown striped jaconet, I think. We are not going out and there is to be no company tonight.'

Fifteen minutes later she was dressed and went downstairs.

She had reached the hall and walked across to the dining room door when she heard Lady Fitzpatrick's voice. She paused with her hand on the doorknob.

'I hope your cousin is not ailing,' her ladyship was saying. 'Why, when I was your age I could stay up all night and think nothing of it.'

'I believe she did not sleep well, my lady. Anne said she was wandering round the house in the early hours. She took her some hot chocolate.'

'So she went out shopping as a cure for insomnia. My dear, I know you are very fond of your cousin, but she is not doing you any favours, behaving as she does. She seems to flout every convention. I fear I shall have to write to her papa about it.'

'Oh, no, my lady, I beg of you not to do that. He will be so displeased.'

'Displeased with me, I shouldn't wonder. Not that I haven't done my best…'

'And so you have, my dear Lady Fitzpatrick. You have been the very best sponsor we could have had— I should hate having him make us return home with the Season only halfway through. It would be such a waste of time and money and nothing to show for it.'

'You are right, I cannot let you go back unspoken for. I fully expect Lord Braybrooke to declare himself at your ball. We will contrive to keep your cousin on a tighter rein until then. Do you think Mr Harfield will offer for her? I should like to think I had discharged my duty to you both.'

Sophie went into the room before Charlotte could

reply and smiled at them both. 'Why did you not wake me?'

'You looked so peaceful,' Charlotte said, as Lady Fitzpatrick rang the bell for the first course to be served. 'Anne told us you had not been able to sleep. It was probably all to do with that accident and meeting Monsieur Latour again and Mr Harfield turning up so unexpectedly. And we have no engagements this evening, so we decided to let you sleep. Do you feel refreshed now?'

'Yes, thank you.'

'Did you find what you wanted at Pantheon's? We went there ourselves, you know, expecting to find you, but there was no sign of you.'

'I expect we passed each other on the way. I bought some lace and a few yards of muslin. It is being delivered tomorrow.'

'Sophie, I have told you before about going out alone,' Lady Fitzpatrick said. 'It is not the thing, you know. Please don't do it again.'

'I came to no harm, my lady.'

'But you might have. And supposing someone saw you…'

Sophie smiled. 'Someone did. Lord Braybrooke met me in the street and brought me home in his curricle.'

'Lord Braybrooke!' exclaimed Lady Fitzpatrick. 'And Charlotte not here to receive him. Oh, how mortifying! Did he leave a message?'

'No, except to say that he had business in Hertfordshire which would keep him out of town for a day or two. He said he hoped to be back in time to join us at Almack's on Wednesday. And if he did not return in time, he would call on us the next day.'

'There you are!' her ladyship exclaimed in triumph. 'He has gone to visit his grandfather to tell him of his intention to offer for Charlotte and ask his blessing. I knew he was coming to the point, I told you so. Ten to one he will go on to Leicestershire and speak to Mr Hundon too.'

'Oh, no!' Both girls spoke together.

'Why not? You must surely know he must ask your trustee, Charlotte, though I am surprised he has not spoken to me of it first, for I am your sponsor while you are in town.'

'Perhaps you mistake the matter,' Charlotte said, 'for I am convinced he means to offer for his cousin.'

'That chit! She is no more than a schoolroom miss. No, no, my dear, that is only a wish of her mama, not realistic at all.'

'But, my lady, I do not want to marry him.'

'Fustian! Of course you do. Any girl would.'

'Ma'am, I do not love him and I am sure he does not love me.'

'Oh, that is of no consequence. Love will come later, if you are lucky. You must remember you are not like other young ladies who have nothing more than their dowries to recommend them. You have a fortune and a large estate as your portion. You must leave falling in love and such frivolity to your cousin who has no such assets.'

'I begin to think I am unmarriageable,' Sophie said, as a servant brought in a tureen of mulligatawny soup.

'So you will be if you insist on cavorting about

town on your own,' Lady Fitzpatrick retorted. 'Such behaviour is eccentric and gentlemen of any standing do not like eccentricity in the least. I beg you to conform or you will spoil your cousin's chances, for they will say it runs in the family.'

'The last thing I want is to be the cause of Charlotte's unhappiness, my lady.' She dare not look at Charlotte for fear of bursting into laughter.

'Then oblige me by observing the proprieties in future. You may go out with me or with Charlotte, escorted by gentlemen of whom I approve and always chaperoned.'

'Yes, my lady,' she said meekly, wondering how she was going to be able to go to Maiden Lane again. Mrs Stebbings could manage the work with her helpers, but when the next month's rent was due, she would have to be there or arrange for someone else to pay it on her behalf.

Lord Braybrooke sprang immediately to mind. He had said he wanted to help, had offered her his escort and, though he sent her emotions into a wild spin whenever she was near him, she must put her feelings aside and ask him. She would try to behave in a businesslike manner and refuse to let him bait her. But what of the gossip? He had said there was a way to deal with it, though he had not answered when she asked him how.

Oh, if only he had meant that he wanted to marry her. Once the engagement had been announced, the tattlers would lose interest and he could come and go as he pleased. But that was an idle dream. Men of consequence did not like eccentrics and, if Lady Fitz-

patrick was right, she was on the way to becoming
one. And he had called her a hoyden, a tease, a demi-
rep, someone to amuse him, not to be taken seriously.
And when the truth about the switch in identities became known, he would know he had been right in his
conjecture. Her spirits were as low as they could possibly be.

Satisfied that she had made her point, Lady Fitzpatrick picked up her spoon and began on the soup.
The rest of the meal was eaten with little conversation
and afterwards they retired to the drawing room.
Charlotte picked up her crewel work, Sophie idly
turned the pages of the latest *Lady's Magazine* without taking in a word and Lady Fitzpatrick sat reading
Miss Austen's latest novel with the aid of a large
magnifying glass. Before long the hand holding the
glass dropped and then the book fell to the floor. Her
head fell on her chest and light snores told that she
was fast asleep.

'What are we going to do?' Charlotte whispered.

'Leave her, she looks comfortable enough.'

'No, I meant about Lord Braybrooke. You don't
think he means to go to Leicestershire, do you? Papa
will think he is offering for you when he speaks of
Miss Roswell and he would mean me. Oh, Sophie,
what a coil we have got ourselves into.'

'He isn't going to Upper Corbury, Charlotte. He
told me he knew you and Freddie were in love and
he has no intention of coming between you.'

'Oh, thank goodness. But what about you?'

'We should not suit. Charlotte, we may both forget
all about Viscount Braybrooke.'

'Why, what else has he said? Oh, Sophie, I am quite sure if he knew the truth, he would offer for you.'

'If he did that, then I should hold him in contempt, changing his mind just because he has discovered I have a fortune, when he would not dream of having me without it. You remember Lady Gosport telling us about his list of requirements for a wife? I taxed him with it and he did not deny it and when I said I failed in every respect, he did not repudiate that either.'

'Poor Sophie! But you made a list too, I recollect.'

'Yes, but that was meant as a jest…'

'No, it was not, you were in deadly earnest. And as far as I can see, his lordship qualifies perfectly. And you are not so far off a good match for his.'

'He does not know I have the fortune he requires, nor would I tell him, simply to make him offer for me. Neither would I agree to shut my eyes to infidelity.'

'I do not believe he is the kind of man to play fast and loose with a lady's affections. Once married, I dare say he will become a paragon of virtue.'

'Charlotte, I am beginning to think you are not so averse to him as you pretend.'

'I never said I was averse to him. He has many qualities I admire, but that does not mean I would marry him.' She reached out put her hand on Sophie's arm. 'Do not give up hope, my love, Lord Braybrooke is being very short-sighted, but he must surely see your worth soon and then all will be well.'

'How can it be, when we have deceived everyone

about who we are? It seemed such a good notion at the time, especially when fate seemed to be on our side with Lady Fitz making the mistake of thinking you were me, but now I realise that it was not only foolish, but really dangerous. I tried to play God and must be punished.'

'Fustian!'

'You are forgetting something, Charlotte. You are forgetting that whether he offered for you or for me, he would have to speak to your papa first and as he thinks Uncle William is my father and not yours…'

'Then the sooner we confess the better.'

'Yes, but to whom? Do we make an announcement? Do we put a notice in the *Gazette* or the *Morning Post*?'

Charlotte suddenly giggled. 'Tell Lady Gosport, that should do it. Much cheaper and quicker too.'

'I am glad you can laugh about it.'

Charlotte became serious. 'Oh, Sophie, I am so sorry. What shall you do?'

'There is nothing I can do. We shall return to Upper Corbury and the engagement of Miss Hundon to Mr Frederick Harfield will be gazetted and no one will be the wiser. As for Miss Roswell, she will live quietly in retirement, an ape leader and eccentric. If Uncle William does not want to remain my trustee, he will have to appoint someone else. Or sell Madderlea. I shall be able to live in comfort on the proceeds and leave what is left to your children, for they will be as close to me as my own.'

'Sell Madderlea! Oh, Sophie, you cannot.' Charlotte's voice rose in protest and Sophie looked at Lady Fitzpatrick in alarm. She slumbered on.

'It is that, or accept the first man who offers for me,' she whispered.

'I will not let you do it. Something must be done. There are other men, considerate, kindly men who would make good husbands. Lord Braybrooke is not the only fish in the sea.'

'He is for me.' And that was the last word she would say on the subject.

A few minutes later Lady Fitzpatrick woke up with a start and straightened her cap. 'Goodness, how late it is! I think I shall retire and I advise you to do the same. We are out tomorrow evening and at Almack's on Wednesday and it would never do for you to be seen with dark circles under your eyes. Come along, both of you.'

They rose and followed her upstairs.

Chapter Nine

Almack's was a disappointment. Everything was so
stiff and formal and there was nothing to drink but
tea and lemonade. And, what was worse as far as
Sophie was concerned, Richard, in black coat, white
knee breeches and dazzling white shirt, arrived with
Emily clinging to his arm and Lady Braybrooke looking like a cat in a cream bowl.

They were accompanied by an elderly gentleman
who, in spite of his outmoded satin breeches, high-
collared brocade coat and the black wig covering his
white hair, had a very formidable presence and the
patronesses buzzed round him like bees round a
honey pot.

Both girls' dance cards were soon full, but Sophie
perversely kept a dance free in case Richard should
ask her to stand up with him. She had been dancing
with Sir Peter Somersham and he was escorting her
back to her seat when she overheard one of the ma-
trons saying, 'Yes, I have it from Augusta Greenholme who had it from Philippa Braybrooke herself.

He has already offered for his cousin and the announcement is to be made at her come-out ball. It is why His Grace has come to London.'

So that was the reason for his visit to Hertfordshire. He had been summoned by the Duke to account for his tardiness and told to make his cousin an offer and, by the look of her, Viscount Braybrooke had obeyed. Was he so faint-hearted? She did not believe that for a minute. No one would make him do anything he did not want to do and she was forced to conclude that it had been his wish all along.

'His Grace is still a fine figure of a man, don't you think?' Lady Fitzpatrick said, as Sophie and Charlotte joined her between dances. 'But I never thought to see him here. We must contrive to be presented.'

'Oh, no, my lady, that would be too presumptuous,' Charlotte said, while Sophie remained silent. She had supposed that sooner or later Viscount Braybrooke would make an announcement, but however much she had prepared herself for it, she could not stop herself feeling thoroughly downcast.

'I do not see why that should be. No doubt he has come to bring Lord Braybrooke up to the mark and look over the possibles. I would be failing in my duty if I did not see that you were introduced. There! The viscount is looking this way. He is coming over.' She gave a little squeal. 'And His Grace is coming with him.'

Sophie's heart began to pound when she realised her ladyship was right and Richard and his grandfather were walking purposefully towards them. All three ladies stood up.

'Your Grace.' Her ladyship attempted a wobbly curtsy, as he stopped before her. 'May I present Miss Roswell.'

Charlotte executed a deep curtsey. 'Your Grace.'

'I am pleased to make your acquaintance again, Miss Roswell,' he said. 'I believe we have met. It was before the war. I was on a diplomatic mission to Belgium and your father and mother were so kind as to offer me hospitality. You were very small and naturally will not remember me. I was sorry to hear Captain Roswell perished in the fighting in Spain. A gallant soldier. You will be proud of him.'

Charlotte, her face crimson with embarrassment, could find nothing to say but 'Yes, Your Grace.'

'We will talk again later. Richard bring her to me at supper.'

Sophie, consumed by guilt and the dreadful fear that she was about to be found out in the worst possible way, wished she could cut and run, but there was no hope of that as Richard turned to present her to his grandfather. 'And this is Miss Hundon, sir.'

'How do you do, Miss Hundon.' The Duke lifted his quizzing glass and subjected her to a close inspection, while the musicians struck up for the next dance. She could not recall having met him and, if she had been a baby at the time, he would not remember what she looked like, would he? 'Miss Roswell's cousin, I collect.'

Refusing to be overawed, she met his gaze unflinchingly. 'Yes, Your Grace.'

'Close, are you?'

'Indeed, yes, Your Grace. I am very fond of Charlotte and I think she is of me. For the last two years we have done everything together.'

'Nothing much to choose between you, I dare say.'

'No.' She smiled, mischievously. 'Except a fortune, Your Grace, which makes deciding on a husband very difficult for her.'

'No doubt you are urging her to caution, but her trustees will no doubt make sure she don't make a ninny of herself. Her fortune or otherwise shouldn't trouble you.'

'Oh, it does not.' She was taken aback by her own temerity at hinting that the problems facing an heiress who must marry were as daunting as those of a nobleman. If Richard was going to marry Emily, it hardly mattered and she might as well go down fighting.

'Pert article, ain't you?' He smiled suddenly, making her realise how much alike he and Richard were. They had the same masculine good looks, the sharp nose and humorous eyes. 'Oh, you do not need to answer that. I shall sit here and talk to Lady Fitzpatrick.' He sat down on the seat Sophie had vacated and waved her away. 'Go and follow your cousin's example and dance.'

The ladies of Almack's had, at last, given up their opposition to the waltz and Freddie was whirling Charlotte round, his hand about her waist. Sophie, who had no partner for the dance, turned to find Richard at her elbow.

'Miss Hundon, please do me the honour of waltzing with me.'

She was about to point out that the dance was almost finished, but decided that she would be the loser if she refused. Even in they only managed one turn about the floor, it would be something to savour in the long, lonely years ahead of her. She curtsied and he slid his arm about her and turned her into the dance.

She felt light-headed, almost in a trance as they moved together in tune with the music. In tune with each other as well. Unwilling to believe that it was the end of everything for her, she tried pretending that it was only the beginning and that they had just been introduced: Miss Sophie Roswell and Viscount Richard Braybrooke, eminently suitable and about to fall in love.

'You are quiet,' he said.

'Was I? I am sorry.'

'Did your papa teach you to waltz as well as to ride astride?'

'No, the waltz was not considered quite proper when…' She stopped suddenly, realising she had almost given herself away by referring to her time in Belgium. 'Freddie—Mr Harfield—taught us both, Charlotte and me, when we knew we would be coming to London for the Season.'

'Oh, then he is a good teacher. Or you were a gifted pupil. I must congratulate you.'

'Thank you.' She paused, unable to bear not knowing for sure. 'May I offer my felicitations on your engagement?'

'Engagement? Where did you hear that?'

'It is the talk of the *ton*.'

He smiled. 'And who, according to the tabbies, am I engaged to?'

'Your cousin, of course.'

'Then the gossips are ahead of themselves as usual.'

'It is not true?'

'Does it matter?'

'No, of course not.'

'Liar!' he said softly.

She felt the colour flood her face. 'My lord, I am not accustomed to having my veracity doubted.'

'Then you must learn to be honest. I collect I have said that before.'

The pleasure of dancing with him was spoiled and she fell silent. He watched the fleeting expressions cross her face; guilt, perhaps, sadness, yes, and he longed to banish both. 'Miss Hundon. Sophie, I must speak to you.'

Her heart was beating almost in her throat and her voice came out as a croak. 'You are speaking to me.'

'Not here. When are you going to Maiden Lane again?'

Maiden Lane. Oh, then all he wanted to talk about was the refuge. Perhaps he had found someone to help with the employment agency. Her heart resumed its steady beat and she allowed herself to breathe again. 'I have promised Lady Fitz I will not go out unless I am escorted.'

'Then I will undertake to escort you.'

'I doubt her ladyship will agree. If she realises you are not affianced to your cousin, she will expect you to escort Charlotte, not me. She will not give up hope that you will decide your future happiness lies with my cousin.'

'And do you also subscribe to that view?'

If he was hoping she would let her guard drop, he was to be disappointed. Her expressive grey-green eyes met his in what could only be construed as indignation. 'My opinion is of no consequence, my lord. You said you knew she was in love with Mr Harfield and you would not come between them.'

'Did I?' he said blandly. 'Then just to be sure on that point, I shall ask Mr Harfield to come too. A sightseeing tour perhaps, taking in Westminster and the Tower and St Paul's.'

'Oh, no, that would mean telling them about Maiden Lane...'

He smiled down at her as the music came to an end and they stood facing each other. 'Oh, I think we can contrive to become separated, don't you?' He bowed low as she curtsied to him, then he offered his arm to escort her back to her seat.

She never felt so confused in all her life. He was so insufferably cheerful, as if life had suddenly dealt him a winning hand. And why, oh, why had he changed his mind about Charlotte? Was it his grandfather's doing? When he said they would contrive to become separated, did he mean he expected her to draw Freddie away, so that he could talk to her cousin alone? Did he intend to put pressure on Freddie to withdraw his suit? She would have to warn Charlotte.

Lady Fitzpatrick did not rise before noon and the girls breakfasted together. Usually they had much to talk about—their social engagements, the latest fashions, what so-and-so had said to such-and-such, who might offer for whom, the latest *on dit* about the Regent, news from Upper Corbury contained in Mrs Hundon's letters—but the morning after the visit to Almack's, Sophie was silent.

'Are you not well?' Charlotte enquired after she had twice spoken and received no response.

'What? Oh, I'm sorry, Charlotte. I have something on my mind.'

'I should just think you have! It is that dreadful hum we have been practising. Has someone found out about it?'

'No. At least, I do not think so, but Lord Braybrooke told me last evening that the rumour that he has already offered for his cousin is not true and he has not given up hope of marrying you.'

'He was gammoning you. He has been no more attentive to me than to any of the other young ladies in Society.'

'He was not teasing. He has involved me in contriving a way of speaking to you alone.'

'I shall reject him.' She laughed suddenly. 'I think that might be a new experience for him, so high in the instep as he is.'

'Oh, Charlotte, I think you do him an injustice. Whatever he is, he is not arrogant.'

'You said he was.'

'I have changed my mind.'

'Does he have no idea that you love him?'

'Certainly not! Do you suppose I wear my heart on my sleeve?'

'Perhaps you should.'

'Oh, Charlotte, please listen, for I have something else to tell you and we haven't much time. The viscount will be here at any moment.'

'Here? This morning? I shall refuse to see him. He must speak to Lady Fitzpatrick first and she is still abed. Sophie, we must tell the footman to say we are not at home.'

'No. His lordship is bringing Freddie with him and we are all to go on a sightseeing tour in the Braybrooke barouche.'

'Why is he bringing Freddie? They have not known each other above five minutes.'

'Freddie is supposed to be dangling after Miss Hundon and, as far as his lordship is concerned, that is me. So, it is not so strange. Some time during the morning, I am supposed to draw Freddie away so that his lordship may speak to you alone. At least that is what I think he meant. He was not at all clear.'

'We do not have to go.'

'But we must. I have an errand of my own and you know I promised Lady Fitz I would not go out unaccompanied.'

'What errand? Sophie, you are being very mysterious.'

Sophie took a deep breath and explained to her cousin about the soldiers and the house in Maiden Lane and how Viscount Braybrooke had found out about it and had offered to help. Charlotte listened with eyes growing wider and wider in astonishment.

'So that was where you were the morning after we went to Vauxhall Gardens? I knew Pewter had been out because I went to the mews to ask Luke if he had seen you. And later Anne told us you had gone to the Pantheon Bazaar. No wonder we could not find you there.'

'I did go there, you know I did, because the stuff I ordered was delivered the next day. But then Luke cut himself helping make the house ready and could not drive the carriage home. I was driving when Monsieur Latour's horse bolted with his little boy in the curricle and Lord Braybrooke suddenly turned up. I think he had been following me, though he denied it. He seems to have appointed himself my guardian.'

'There you are, then! It is you he favours or he would not take such good care of you.'

'Oh, Charlotte, he is only doing it to refine upon my faults, which he points out at every opportunity. I should not ride alone, nor walk unescorted, nor speak to beggars. He cannot allow it, he said, as if I would take a jot of notice of what he says.'

'But he is right, you know that very well.'

'That does not mean I enjoy having him ring a peal over me.'

'But if he had not been close by when that horse bolted… Oh, Sophie, you might have been killed. We are indebted to his lordship.'

'Yes, I know, but now he insists on escorting me when I go to Maiden Lane and I must go this morning to see how everything is and pay the rent. And if we are seen, the tattlemongers will have a field day, so you must come too. Oh, Charlotte, it is all such a mull…'

'But where has the money come from to pay for it all?'

'Donations from well-wishers. And my allowance. I wrote to Uncle William and told him I needed extra because our ball was going to be far more expensive than we had at first supposed. He sent me a draft for more, but most of it has been spent.'

'Then I am glad you insisted I had the same allowance as you because I have hardly touched mine. That is no problem. And neither is Lord Braybrooke. I can deal with any overtures from him.' Charlotte, who usually followed where Sophie led, had suddenly taken over the role of leader. Sophie smiled wanly, recognising that it stemmed from a new confidence brought on by the arrival of Freddie and his commitment to her, and a wish to have her cousin as happy as she was herself. 'Now, we had better go and change so that we are ready when the gentlemen come.'

Reluctantly Sophie agreed and followed her cousin upstairs. She dressed in the grey cambric round gown as she always did for a visit to Maiden Lane. The day was too warm for a cloak and instead she tied a fringed shawl about her shoulders. She was just leaving her room when she heard the front door knocker. Charlotte came out of her room at almost the same time. They smiled at each other in mutual reassurance and descended the stairs together.

The two men were waiting for them in the vestibule. Richard was dressed in a frockcoat of brown Bath cloth and buckskin breeches, his neckcloth was plain white muslin, not top of the trees in elegance.

Sophie understood the reason for this and so did Charlotte, but Freddie, not wishing to be outdone by a man whose sartorial reputation was of the highest order, had taken great pains with his appearance and now found himself considerably overdressed in a blue superfine tailcoat, white pantaloons and an elaborately tied cravat about a shirt collar whose points scratched his cheeks whenever he moved his head.

Charlotte, seeing this, hurried upstairs to change her cape for a pink sarcenet pelisse and to replace her plain bonnet for one with pink ruching below the brim and tied with a large satin bow. 'Now we are ready,' she said, rejoining the others who had waited in the hall.

Sophie might have been interested in the sights—Westminster Hall, Horse Guards, the Tower and its ravens, St Paul's, which was more impressive outside than in—if she had not been so aware of the viscount and her own rapidly beating heart. He was at his charming best to both young ladies, and very knowledgeable.

Freddie found a great many questions to ask him about the history and the architecture of the many buildings they looked at which he answered easily. At no time did his lordship suggest Charlotte might like to view something Sophie and Freddie did not.

When they came out of St Paul's, they crossed Covent Garden and though there were few stallholders so late in the day, the area was swarming with urchins, who scrambled in the piles of discarded fruit and vegetables for something edible.

'Poor things,' Charlotte said, throwing them a few

coins from her reticule which they pounced on with cries of delight. 'Is that how they live?'

'Yes. Scavenging in the mud of the river for flotsam and jetsam and begging.' Richard smiled. 'But now you have given them money, they will not leave you alone.'

He was proved right when the few were joined by many more, dancing round them, holding out grubby hands, calling, 'Me! Me too!' Charlotte, who had no more money in her purse, showed every appearance of being frightened to death and even Sophie, who was used to dealing with the soldiers, felt a frisson of alarm.

Richard showed them a guinea and then threw it as far as he could in the direction of a pile of garbage. The urchins raced after it. 'Come,' he said, taking Sophie's arm as rubbish flew in all directions and the children began to squabble. 'Let us make our escape while they are occupied.'

'I have to go to Maiden Lane,' she told him in an undertone as they made for the barouche which had been left in a side street. Freddie and Charlotte were close behind.

'Then I suggest you find some way of parting us from our chaperons.'

She looked at him quizzically, wondering if she had misheard him or whether he was being jocular but his expression told her nothing.

'Charlotte knows about the house in Maiden Lane.'

'Then you do not need to make excuses. Your cousin and Mr Harfield may take the barouche. We can make our own way home.' He smiled down at her. 'We have done it before, have we not?'

She was puzzled. 'But I thought you wanted to speak to Miss Roswell...'

'So I do. Later. Mrs Stebbings first.'

'Then we will all go.'

Richard was convinced that Sophie was deliberately avoiding being alone with him, probably because she guessed he was going to tax her with her deception and demand a reason for it. He sincerely hoped that the young ladies would not let the world know about the switch in their identities before he succeeded in speaking to Sophie. If it became the subject of gossip, then he would never persuade her he had not changed his allegiance as soon as he heard she was the one with the legacy and not Charlotte. If only he had spoken sooner! Now, there was nothing he could do but postpone his confrontation with her and agree.

The visit was not a success. The deputation was too big for Mrs Stebbings to handle calmly and the ex-servicemen looked on with undisguised suspicion. Freddie, in his finery, stuck out like a sore thumb, and Charlotte was so obviously repelled by the ragged men, some of whom had dreadful disfigurements, that she could do nothing but stand just inside the door with a wooden smile on her face, which deceived no one. Freddie, seeing this, took her out to wait in the barouche.

Sophie tried to behave as she usually did, helping serve food and listen to the men's woes, but she felt constrained and her previous natural compassion seemed forced. She was sure Charlotte was deliberately making it difficult for Richard to speak to her, and Freddie was not going to help, for which he could not be blamed.

She gave Mrs Stebbings the rent and Richard escorted her to join the other two, his hand lightly under her elbow, making her want to howl with misery, knowing it was no more than a gesture of chivalry, when she wanted so much more.

Sergeant Dawkins, who had been sitting unseen in a corner of the dining room, apparently tucking into meat pudding and potatoes, watched them go. An idea was forming in his mind. An idea based on the Major's obvious fancy for Mrs Carter; it was evident in the way his eyes followed her round the room and the way his features softened when he spoke to her. 'Fine feathers make fine birds,' he murmured to himself. 'And this one's ready for the plucking.'

Charlotte, taking off her bonnet in Sophie's room where they had gone as soon as the gentlemen had paid their respects to Lady Fitzpatrick and left, was thoroughly satisfied with their morning.

'There! You were worrying for nothing, Sophie, the viscount made no attempt to speak to me privately, nor even to part me from Freddie. He must know it would be a waste of time. Though how you can go near those filthy men, I do not know.' She shuddered. 'I feel dirty myself now and shall have to have a bath brought up and change every stitch. I cannot understand Lord Braybrooke encouraging you.'

'He feels as I do about the need to help the men.'

'Which only goes to prove how well suited you are. He is blind if he cannot see it.'

'He is guided by that ridiculous list of requirements and the only one I conform to is that I have a fortune, which he knows nothing about. It is a vicious circle, Charlie, without an end.'

'Then the circle must be broken. The first thing is to tell Lady Fitz and throw ourselves on her mercy. She might see a way out.'

'You are no doubt right, but I must be the one to do it. I won't have her giving you a jobation over it.'

But that was easier said than accomplished, as they soon discovered when they returned to the drawing room. The invitation to Lady Braybrooke's ball had come while they had been changing and her ladyship was in high dudgeon.

'She thinks she has stolen a march on us,' she said, tapping it furiously against her chin. 'Putting Emily's come-out before yours and the chit barely out of the schoolroom. Well, she will come home by weeping cross, for it is such short notice that no one will go.'

'Oh, I don't know,' Sophie said. 'I fancy a summons to attend the Duke of Rathbone's mansion will be a huge inducement to cancel all other engagements. It is sure to be the event of the Season.'

'But your ball was meant to be that,' her ladyship wailed. 'We had it all arranged, the musicians, the food, the flowers and everything.'

'I cannot see that anything has changed,' Charlotte said. 'Does it matter which comes first?'

'Of course it does. Philippa Braybrooke will have her nephew shackled to her daughter before they ever get to our ball. They will come together. Or not come at all.'

'But the invitations went out before Lady Braybrooke came to town, did they not? And Lord Braybrooke accepted.'

'Yes, but I was obliged to include Philippa and Emily as soon as I knew they were here.'

'Well, I do not think it is anything to get into a quake over,' Sophie said. 'I do not think Lord Braybrooke will allow himself to be bullied into offering for his cousin if he does not want her.'

'You are a goose if you think that,' her ladyship said. 'He is no different from any other man. He will give in if he is nagged enough.'

'Then I should hope that Charlotte would be glad of her escape,' Sophie said. 'I know I should not want to be married to a man who is so weak that he can be persuaded into something he knows is wrong.'

'And you, young lady, have not the first idea what you are talking about. Pray, keep your thoughts to yourself. Now, Charlotte, we must devise a way…'

'No, my lady,' Charlotte said, very loudly and very firmly.

'No? How can you say no?'

'Easily. My lady, I beg of you to forget all about Viscount Braybrooke. We should not suit.'

'But he is the catch of the Season.'

'I do not think so.'

'How can you say that? He will be a duke one day and the Rathbone estates are vast. Even Madderlea pales into insignificance beside them.'

'Wealth does not guarantee happiness, my lady. I

would rather have a poor man who loved me that a rich one who treated me like a chattel. Sophie agrees with me, don't you, Sophie?'

'Naturally, she would,' her ladyship put in before Sophie could speak. 'But she is not required to put it to the test.'

'Neither am I. I am determined on another.'

Her ladyship looked startled. 'Who is that?'

Charlotte looked at Sophie and received a small nod before answering. 'Mr Harfield.'

'Mr Harty? I never heard of him. And no title either. Has he prospects of one? A fortune? When did you meet him? Oh, Mr Hundon will be so displeased.'

Charlotte tried again, louder. 'Mr Frederick Harfield, ma'am.'

'Harfield! But I thought he was dangling after Miss Hundon. Everyone said he was. She fainted at the sight of him. And he has been much in her company.' She turned to Sophie. 'Did you know about this?'

'Yes, my lady.' She took a deep breath and went on. 'You see, we have been engaging in a ruse.'

'Engaging a what?'

'In a deception, my lady.' It was so difficult to confess while shouting; Sophie would rather have whispered her guilt. 'We have been pretending to be each other, making believe that Miss Hundon is the heiress.'

'Miss Hundon an heiress? I do not understand. Everyone knows who you are and certainly Mr Harfield must, for he comes from your own part of the country. If you have been putting it about that you are the heiress, Sophie, then you have been very foolish indeed.'

'I know that, my lady,' Sophie said. 'But you have not understood…'

'As if anyone would believe such a Banbury tale! The Roswells are a well-known aristocratic family and the Hundons, respectable though they may be, are certainly not one of the *ton*. And if Mr Harfield is such a cake as to believe such tarradiddle, more fool he.'

Sophie tried again. 'You misunderstand, my lady. I am…'

'Not another word. You are supposed to be young ladies with a modicum of good sense and I find you have been indulging in schoolgirl pranks. I shall make quite certain that any rumours that Miss Hundon is an heiress are quashed. No wonder Viscount Braybrooke is confused.'

'Is he confused?' Sophie asked, diverted for the moment from her task of trying to tell her ladyship something she did not want to hear.

'Indeed he is. Why, he has been paying as much attention to you as to Charlotte, as if he could not make up his mind.'

'But you said his mind would be made up for him by his grandfather.'

'Oh, that is enough, you are confusing me now. There is nothing for it, but we shall have to work on the Duke.'

'To what purpose, my lady?' Charlotte asked. 'Do you think he would condone Sophie?'

'Oh, you are talking in riddles, both of you,' her

ladyship said in exasperation. 'I can only pray you will come to your senses by the time we attend the Braybrooke ball.'

The girls looked at each other and gave up.

The morning of the ball came in wet and windy and Lady Fitzpatrick was gleeful. 'She will not be able to have the musicians on the terrace and lanterns in the garden,' she said. 'We shall be cooped up in the ballroom and it will be a dreadful crush.'

'I thought that was a good thing,' Sophie said, watching the raindrops sliding down the windows of her ladyship's boudoir where they were drinking their morning coffee. She had been planning a visit to Maiden Lane, but could find no excuse for going out in the rain. 'The greater the crush, the greater the success.'

'Yes, but there are crushes and crushes. One must be able to breathe and converse and dance.'

'But you said you did not think many would attend.'

'Perhaps they won't,' Lady Fitzpatrick said perversely.

Her ladyship was wrong on all counts. The ballroom at Rathbone House was large enough to contain a hundred guests in comfort and a hundred was about the number who had accepted. Whatever the tattlers' private opinions of her ladyship, she was known as a first-rate hostess and it was worth going for the food alone. Add to that the chance of a juicy snippet of gossip, such as the announcement of a betrothal or, more telling, the lack of an expected announcement, and the invitation was impossible to refuse.

Sophie had dressed in what she considered her plainest evening gown. It was made of a filmy pale green gauze which floated over a silk slip of a slightly darker green. It had a round neck, ruched with dark green and little puff sleeves, slotted with ribbon. Another ribbon was threaded through the high waist and was caught up under the bust, from which the ends floated free. More of the same ribbon and a few pearls were strung through her red-gold hair, which was drawn up and back into a Grecian knot that emphasised the long curve of her neck where a single string of pearls nestled against her creamy skin. The Madderlea family jewels, too ostentatious for a young lady not yet in Society, had been locked away by her uncle until such time as her engagement was announced.

This understatement had the opposite effect from the one she had intended. Instead of being dismissed as too plain, she was revealed as a young lady of stunning beauty. And Richard was stunned. She was poised and elegant and that bright hair shone in the light from the chandeliers so that he saw her as a flame of unmatched brilliance, drawing him like a moth. He was consumed with a desire so strong, he could hardly wait to have her to himself. But that was not possible until he had finished greeting their guests.

'Miss Hundon,' he said, bowing as she reached where he stood with his grandfather, his cousin and his aunt.

'My lord.' She was vaguely aware of a black satin

evening coat and muscular legs clad in black kerseymere trousers strapped under the instep, a white shirt
and an elaborately tied cravat as he bowed over her
hand. It was not his clothes which took her breath
away, but the touch of his hand as he raised it to his
lips and the look in his brown eyes which were scan-
ning every inch of her face as if trying to commit
every tiny feature to memory.

'I hope I see you well?'

'Yes, thank you, my lord.' So formal, so unnatural,
when they had shared so much—the work at Maiden
Lane, the accident with the curricle, the dawn encounter in Hyde Park, that kiss, the memory of which
still sent shivers of desire through her. But he was
being very correct and she supposed the ball marked
the end of that easy relationship. Now he meant to
keep his distance. Was that what his eyes were telling
her?

He took her card from her and scribbled his name
against two dances, before she followed Lady Fitzpatrick and Charlotte into the ballroom which was
ablaze with light and colour. The air was heavy with
perfume and the scent of hothouse flowers which
stood in bowls in the window recesses.

Dowagers sat in chairs surrounding the floor, peering through quizzing glasses at everyone else's
charges, comparing notes, their tongues as sharp as
razors. Young men, dressed like peacocks, stood in
groups, eyeing the young ladies in their flimsy gowns,
deciding which to choose, as the musicians, on a dais
at one end of the room, struck up the first dance.

As soon as Sophie and Charlotte appeared they

were besieged by young men wanting to mark their cards, including Martin Gosport and Freddie Harfield, who whirled Charlotte away before she even had time to draw breath or smile at her other admirers, all of whom believed she was Miss Roswell. Sophie found herself facing Martin Gosport.

He swept her an elaborate bow and held out his hand. 'Will you do me the honour?'

She allowed him to lead her into the country dance, noticing as she did so that Richard had come into the room with his cousin and was dancing with her. Emily was beginning to look more mature, more assured and she was smiling. Did she know Richard's intentions? If she did, she did not seem too unhappy about it.

'May I congratulate you, Miss Hundon?' Martin said, after they had taken their places and were moving down the room in step with the other dancers. 'I do believe you will break every young man's heart tonight. There is no one to hold a candle to you.'

'Mr Gosport, what a hum!'

'I mean it. If it were not for your lack of a fortune, you could have any man in the room.'

'Now you are being very foolish, Mr Gosport. Have you not been told that compliments should be more subtle than that?'

'I have always believed in being direct, Miss Hundon. It saves a deal of misunderstanding.'

'How right you are! But supposing it is not compliments you wish to impart, would you still be so outspoken?'

He smiled, circling round her. 'I think I might remain silent.'

She laughed. 'I shall remember that if you become mute.'

'Miss Roswell is in fine form, too,' he went on, having seen Charlotte in the next set, laughing into the face of Freddie Harfield, who was grinning happily. 'If I were Richard I think I would nail my colours to the mast before Harfield steals a march on him.'

Sophie forced herself to sound light-hearted. 'You think it is Charlotte his lordship has fixed upon then?'

'Who else fits his criteria?'

'Oh, that list. We have all heard of it. Tell me, is it true she must have a fortune?'

'Oh, I do not think that is of prime importance. He said it so that he would not be besieged by penniless fortune hunters. Why do you ask?' He looked down at her suddenly. 'Oh, surely you do not have aspirations in that direction yourself?'

'Certainly not!' she retorted. 'I was merely curious to know how a man can be so cold-blooded as to set out his requirements in so exacting a fashion.'

'Oh, it was only a joke. He did not mean any of it. A more warm-hearted and sensitive man I have yet to meet. Why, he has stood buff for me many a time.'

'Then you think he is capable of falling in love?'

'Oh, I am sure of it, given the right lady.'

'And would he be a faithful husband?'

'There would be none more constant and true. If you are worrying about your cousin, Miss Hundon, then do not. If he offers for her, she could not marry a finer man.'

Sophie was glad the dance ended at that point because she wanted to run away and hide. If what Mr Gosport said was true, Richard Braybrooke would not be proposing to Charlotte because he thought she had a fortune, but because he loved her. As soon as Martin had returned her to Lady Fitzpatrick, she excused herself and left the ballroom to find the ladies' retiring room.

Richard, who had been doing his duty by dancing with the most important of the young ladies, including Emily, Verity Greenholme and Martin's sister, as well as Charlotte who was pretty as a picture in rosebud pink Italian crepe, could hardly wait to claim Sophie for the next dance. He escorted his last partner back to her mama, bowed low to them both and turned to see the object of his desire disappearing from the room.

Now, what deep game was she playing? He went over to Lady Fitzpatrick, who was looking after Sophie with an expression of exasperation on her face. 'My lady, is Miss Hundon not feeling up to snuff?'

'Oh, my lord, I did not see you there.'

'I was expecting to have the next dance with her.'

'Were you?' Her ladyship sounded vague. 'I dare say she will be back soon. Why don't you stand up with Miss Roswell instead?'

'It would give me the greatest pleasure, my lady, but I believe Miss Roswell's card is already full. Please excuse me.'

As he hurried after Sophie, he found himself wondering if Lady Fitzpatrick knew about the deception. Was she part of it? It was a new thought and one which puzzled him. What had she to gain by it? What had anyone? Was it Charlotte's idea or Sophie's? Did they think it would increase Charlotte's chances of finding a husband? But that did not ring true, for that young lady had set her cap at Freddie Harfield.

He did not believe Sophie was capable of harming anyone, but surely a hoax of this magnitude was doing a great deal of harm. Had she been forced into it? Had it been conjured up specifically to test him? Did the whole *ton* know he was being gulled? Why? Why? Why?

Chapter Ten

$\approx\!\!\infty\!\!\approx$

The music faded behind Sophie as she made her way up to the next floor. The corridor in which she found herself was thickly carpeted and lined with doors. Which one had been set aside for the lady guests to recuperate, she did not know.

She wandered along its length, hoping to hear female voices which would help her, but everywhere was silent. She pushed open one of the doors, to reveal a bedroom, sumptuously furnished with a bed draped in muslin and lace, striped silk curtains, mahogany wardrobes and chests, a striped upholstered sofa and a long cheval mirror. Afraid to be caught prying, she withdrew.

'Looking for a place to sleep, Miss Hundon?'

She swung round guiltily. Richard was standing so close to her she could feel the warmth of him. 'Oh, you startled me.'

'Obviously. Are you unwell? Did you wish to rest?'

'Not at all. I did not mean to pry. I was looking

for the ladies' room. My hair needs attention. I…' She stopped because he had put a hand on each of her shoulders and was looking down at her with an expression on his face she could not fathom. Concern? Tenderness? No, that could not be. It must be annoyance.

'Your hair looks perfect as it is.' He reached out and touched a tendril which was too short to be included in the Grecian knot. 'You are in superb looks tonight.' The touch of his fingers on the soft flesh of her neck was devastating; she felt as if her whole body had become boneless and was a quivering jelly of desire. Her breathing became fast and shallow as if she was being deprived of air. She wanted to grab the hand away in order to stop the torment, but like someone mesmerised she could not move.

'Don't you know the effect you have on me?' His voice was hardly more than a whisper.

'Oh, yes,' she said, forcing herself to react as he expected her to. 'I exasperate you.'

He threw back his head and laughed. 'You never said a truer word. Just when I think I have your measure, you confound me again.'

'I don't know what you mean.'

'Oh, I am sure you do. Tell me you are not at playing cat and mouse with me.'

'I would not dream of doing such a thing.'

'Then why do your eyes say one thing and your words another? I could have sworn…' He stopped. 'No matter. Why did you run away just when it was my turn to dance with you? Am I so repugnant to you?'

'No, no, I had forgotten it was our dance.'

'You find it so easy to forget me?' He put his hand on his heart in a melodramatic gesture. 'I am deeply wounded.'

'Now who is teasing?'

'This is no tease.' He put his forefinger under her chin and lifted her face to his. Taken by surprise, Sophie opened her mouth slightly and then his lips were on hers, gently at first and then with more urgency, as his arms went round her and he held her fast against his body. She was helpless. Caught in the trap of her own desire, she responded with every fibre, putting her hands about his neck and pulling him towards her, wanting the kiss to go on and on, uncaring that she was betraying her innermost longings to this man who held her in thrall and who had every intention of marrying someone else.

He lifted his mouth from hers at last, but did not release her. He leaned back and looked into her face without speaking, as if he were trying to interpret something her eyes were saying. 'Perhaps you will not find it so easy to forget me another time.'

Furious at her own weakness and anxious to regain some of her composure, she put her hands on his chest and pushed him with all her strength. He remained rock solid.

'Is this how you go about courting a wife, my lord? Poor Charlotte. I thought you loved her, wanted her for a wife. I hope she has the good sense to see you for what you are, a philanderer who will take advantage of her cousin when her back is turned and expect that same cousin to succumb like a serving wench. I may not be out of the top drawer, not one of the *ton*, but that does not mean I will allow any Tom, Dick or Harry to take liberties…' She stopped suddenly, too breathless to continue and because he was looking at her with amusement in his dark eyes.

'I would strongly object to Tom and Harry, my dear, but Dick is another matter.'

In spite of her fury, she found herself laughing. 'Oh, you are impossible!'

'Impossible? I do hope not.'

'Let me go, please.'

'Not yet. I have something to say to you. Something I want to ask you. But you know that, don't you?'

'No, how should I?'

'Because every time I say I want to speak to you, you find a way of avoiding me.' He put his hands on the wall either side of her head, trapping her. 'Now, you will listen.'

'Very well, my lord, but make haste because if anyone should come along…'

'I do not give a damn.' He paused to marshal his thoughts. He must make her see that what she was doing was wrong, make her confess, but the memory of the way she had responded to his kiss made it doubly difficult. 'Sophie, I have no intention of offering for your cousin.'

'Good, it will save you the disappointment of being rejected.'

He ignored her retort. 'Do you not know that I have lost my heart to you?'

'No, I do not believe it. It is impossible.'

'Why impossible? Do you think I have not a heart to lose?' When she did not answer, he repeated, 'Do you?'

'No, my lord. I believe you to be compassionate to those less fortunate but...'

'At least, I have that in my favour, but it was not compassion I meant. I was speaking of love.' The words were said very softly, causing her heart to beat faster than ever.

'You fill my thoughts, day and night, wondering what you are doing, if you are thinking of me, until I am in purgatory.' He paused to find a way of shocking her into realising the seriousness of her deception. 'But offering for Miss Hundon would be a travesty. You must see that...'

'Indeed, I can, my lord.' She cut him off before he could finish. 'But if you think I am such a ninny as to consent to such a proposition, my lord, you are gravely mistaken. I would rather die.' She ducked under his arm to try and escape but he grabbed her hand. She stood still facing away from him, her breast heaving.

He gave a despairing laugh. 'You think I am so lacking in honour? Oh, dear, then what did that kiss tell me about you? That you are prepared to be opportuned by a rakeshame?'

It was all too much. She wrenched herself away and ran down the corridor, away from him, away from the torment which she had brought upon herself. Pulling open a door, she found herself in a room where ladies' cloaks and pelisses were heaped upon a bed and there were comfortable chairs and sofas and pots of powder and phials of perfume on a dressing chest. She had found the ladies' retiring room and it was empty. She went in and slammed the door behind her.

He stood outside for a moment, wondering whether to follow her, but then decided against it and turned to go slowly downstairs and back to the ballroom.

The dance he should have had with Sophie had just ended and the couples were returning to their seats. Lady Fitzpatrick was sitting with Lady Gosport, her round face even rosier than usual. She was fanning herself vigorously and looking around her, while appearing to be listening to her companion's chatter. Charlotte was returning to her on her partner's arm.

He crossed the room to them. 'Miss Roswell, I must speak to you.'

She looked startled and turned to Freddie for support but he was grinning knowingly and Lady Fitzpatrick was actually smirking. 'Go along, my dear, you may take a turn about the room with his lordship.'

'Miss Roswell,' he said, walking towards the door and not round the room in full view as he should have done. 'I do not want to alarm you, but I think your cousin is not feeling at all the thing.'

'Sophie, ill? Then I must go to her at once. Why did you not say straight away?'

'I did not think she would want a fuss and telling Lady Fitzpatrick would surely have that effect. Come, I'll take you to her.'

They left the room watched by almost everyone present, who assumed his lordship was taking her off to propose to her. Lady Fitzpatrick was gleeful, Lady

Braybrooke furious and Emily placidly content, her arm tucked through that of Martin Gosport as they perambulated round the room after dancing together.

'I hope, my lord, you have said nothing to upset Sophie,' Charlotte said, as they climbed the stairs.

'Not unless asking her to marry me is upsetting to her.'

She stopped and turned towards him. 'You proposed?'

'I tried to. But she deliberately chose to misunderstand.'

'Why?'

'I thought perhaps you might know the answer to that.'

'Only she can tell you that, my lord.'

'I thought she had some fondness for me, but it seems I was wrong. Unless she is holding back for your sake. She is so close to you, she might deny her real wishes if she thought it would help you.'

'Yes, I know she would, but in this case, you are mistaken. Sophie knows where my affections lie.'

They resumed their climb and stopped just short of the door which had been so recently slammed in his face. 'With Freddie Harfield?'

'Yes.'

'And Sophie knows this?'

'Of course she does. We have no secrets from each other.'

'Then you will know if your cousin has fixed her heart on someone else. Is there some secret love she dare not speak of? She is not affianced already? Or being coerced?'

'No.'

'Then we are at a stand unless you can persuade her to open her heart to me.'

'But the talk is that you are looking for an aristocrat with her own fortune.'

'Oh, that nonsense! Pay it no heed. It is your cousin I want, if only she will have me. But she would not even listen. Please persuade her that nothing will make me change my mind.' He opened the door to usher her inside, but there was no Sophie to be seen.

'Where can she have gone?' she asked.

'Perhaps she returned downstairs while we were in the ballroom,' he suggested. 'You do not think she would be so foolish as to leave the house alone?'

'I do hope not.' She turned and hurried downstairs but he passed her and was the first to question the footman on duty.

'Miss Hundon? You know Miss Hundon?'

'No, my lord.'

'A young lady in a green gown. Red-gold hair.'

'A young lady such as you describe did leave about fifteen minutes ago, my lord.'

'Was she alone?'

'Yes. I saw her into her carriage. She said she was feeling unwell and would send it back for the rest of her party. Her groom was with her, so I thought no more of it.'

Richard turned to Charlotte. 'I'm going after her. I mean to get to the bottom of this.'

'My lord, is that wise? She can hardly admit you with no chaperon in the house. And Lady Fitz and I cannot come until our coach returns.'

'I must see that she has arrived home safely, even if she will not see me. Please return to the ballroom, Miss Roswell. I do not want the rest of the company disturbed. There is enough gossip as it is.' He was tight-lipped and she was afraid his anger would spill over if he forced the truth from Sophie.

'Please, my lord, do not be unkind to her…'

'I? Unkind? All I want to do is marry her—is that unkind? Now, please try and behave as if nothing has happened. I shall be back before you know it.'

Sophie was in her room lying face down on the bed, sobbing uncontrollably. Richard Braybrooke had confessed to loving her in the same breath as saying he could not marry her. Martin Gosport had been wrong about him being a faithful husband and so had Charlotte. It had never been his intention. And though she tried to fuel her anger, it was diluted by misery.

She did not think she could bear watching him courting someone else, knowing he would never touch her again, never put his arms round her, never kiss her. It was time to leave London, to put this disastrous summer behind her, to pretend it had never happened.

An urgent hammering on the street door made her lift her head and listen. She could hear the footman on duty in the hall and the voice of the caller, and then Anne protesting that Miss Sophie had retired. The next minute the maid rushed into the room.

'Miss Sophie, it's Lord Braybrooke and he won't go away. He says he must see you, only he asked for Miss Hundon. He do mean you, don't he? It ain't right to bully me so. I told him you was abed and he said I must fetch you down or he'll come up.' She looked round as if half expecting him to be behind her. 'Oh, miss, he's surely up in the boughs and won't be denied.'

'Very well, go and show him into the drawing room. Tell him I will be with him directly.'

As soon as the maid had gone, she roused herself and went to the mirror. Her face was swollen and blotched from weeping. She washed it and dabbed it dry, gulping back more tears. But what did it matter? She was destined to lose the love of her life and all because of her own vanity. It had been nothing more nor less than vanity, she was ready to admit that, and he had squashed that very efficiently by suggesting she become his mistress! If he had known she was the Roswell heiress, would that offer have been one of marriage?

Well, she was glad, she told herself firmly but untruthfully; it had shown him in his true colours and she had had a lucky escape. She had stripped off her ballgown when she came home and was in her petticoat. She covered it with an undress gown of blue silk, brushed out her hair, picked up a fan so that she might have something to do with her hands and could possibly hide her face with it, then went downstairs to the drawing room.

He stood by the hearth, one hand on the mantelshelf, a foot on the fender, gazing down into the empty grate. He turned when he heard her. She was looking very pale and was obviously distressed, or she would never have come down in that flimsy *demi-*

toilette with her beautiful hair hanging loose about her shoulders. He longed to comfort her, to tell her it did not matter what she had done or why, but she stood just inside the door and looked ready to bolt if he were so foolish as to try and approach her. He spoke softly. 'Sophie.'

'My lord.' It took every bit of self-control to speak normally. 'It was very unwise of you to come. If you had not frightened Anne quite out of her wits, I should have refused to see you. Now you have seen me, please leave.'

'When you have answered my question.'

'And what question is that?'

'Why you will not consent to be my wife.'

'Your wife!'

'What did you think I meant?' He paused, wishing she would lower that silly fan and let him see her eyes. Her eyes gave her away every time. 'Good God! You surely did not think I was offering you *carte blanche*?'

She did not answer.

'You did, didn't you? You must think me the worst kind of coxcomb, if you thought I would do anything so contemptible.'

'We have already established that I do not meet your requirements in a wife, my lord, which is why I thought…'

'Oh, yes, you do. In every respect.'

She forgot her resolve to be cool. 'How can you say that?'

'Easily. You are beautiful and compassionate and good with children and those less fortunate; you ride as if you had been born in the saddle and you have a neat pair of hands with the ribbons. And you have courage. The only flaw that I can see is that you are too independent for your own good, but I can believe that has been forced on you by circumstances. And, in spite of what you say, I do think you have a little regard for me.'

'My lord, I never said that.'

'Your eyes speak more truly than your words, my dear, but if it was the manner of my address which displeased you, then I humbly beg pardon. Only say you will marry me and my whole life shall be devoted to pleasing you; there is nothing I wish for more. I love you.'

She could not make herself believe he was really saying what she had always hoped he would say. But it was too late, too late to come out of the affair with any honour. When he learned the truth, he would be very angry and not amused, as she had so confidently told Charlotte he should be. 'My lord, please do not go on.'

'Why not? I must know what your answer will be before I speak to Mr Hundon.'

'Oh, no!' she cried in desperation. 'You must say nothing to him, you really must not.'

'But I must.' He took a step towards her, but paused when she stepped back. 'Sophie, I am asking you to be my wife and that requires the consent of your guardian…'

She was too distressed to notice his deliberate use of the word guardian and not father or papa. She took a deep breath. 'Lord Braybrooke, I am sensible of the

honour you have done me, but the answer is no. I
cannot consent to be your wife…'

'Why not?' Fearing she would run away again, he
strode forward and grabbed her wrist. She turned
away from him but he held her fast. 'Do you find me
repulsive? Despicable? Ugly?'

At each question, she mutely shook her head, refusing to turn to face him.

'Then why, Sophie? Are you worried by a lack of
a dowry? That is of no consequence at all. And neither is your family background. None of it matters.'

Oh, if only she could believe that! But even now,
she was not ready to admit her deceit. She clung to
it as if she were drowning and it was her only lifeline.
'It matters to your grandfather.'

Having given her ample opportunity to tell him the
truth, it was hardly the response he had hoped for. He
took her shoulders and turned her to face him. 'Then
let us throw ourselves on his mercy. When he knows
how things stand he will not deny us. And even if he
did, it would make no difference. If you will have
me, I would stand against the world. There is no reason in the world for you to refuse me.'

'I am not obliged to give you reasons.'

He was angry now. 'You little ninny, do you think
I am so easily given the right about? You are having
a game with me and it goes ill with me, I can tell
you.'

'Then I am sorry for it.'

'Why can't you confide in me?' His anger faded
as quickly as it had come. 'I know there is something

troubling you and unless you tell me what it is, I cannot help you.'

She looked up at him and found herself looking into brown eyes which held nothing but gentle compassion and she knew she did not deserve it. It was all going to come out in the end and it would be better if she told him herself and did not let him hear it from tattlemongers. She took a deep breath and opened her mouth, but before she could utter a word, they heard the door knocker and Anne had burst into the room.

'Oh, Miss Sophie, Mr Hundon is here. What are we to do? He will so angry…'

'Oh, no!' Sophie gasped. 'My lord, he must not find you here. He would not understand.'

'But I must speak to him, explain…'

'Not tonight. He will be tired from his journey and not in a mood to listen. Please go.' She grabbed hold of his arm and pulled him towards the window, which was a low one and gave out on to the terrace. 'Go that way. Quickly. Quickly.' She tugged at the catch and flung the window open.

Reluctantly he disappeared into the rain, just as her uncle came into the room. Anne busied herself securing the window and shutting the curtain.

'What was that clunch of a footman talking about, Sophie?' William demanded. Although he had given his greatcoat and hat to the servant, he looked very wet. 'First he says Lady Fitzpatrick and Miss Roswell are out and then he tells me Miss Sophie is at home.'

'Uncle William, what a surprise to see you,' Sophie said, trying to sound normal and not quite succeeding;

her voice was a pitch higher than it usually was. 'I hope there is nothing wrong at home?'

'At home, no. Your aunt is as well as she can be, considering her affliction. Where are Lady Fitzpatrick and Charlotte and why are you at home alone?'

'They are at the Braybrooke ball, Uncle.'

'Did you not go?'

'Yes, but I felt a little unwell and came home early.'

'I must say, you don't look at all the thing. But surely her ladyship did not allow you to come home alone?'

'I did not want to spoil their enjoyment. I brought the carriage and Luke was with me as well as the driver, so I was in no danger.'

'But why did you not go straight to bed? And surely standing half-dressed by an open window is not a sensible thing to do, especially as it is raining quite hard. You will catch a chill.'

'I came down to ask Anne to heat up some milk for me and while I was waiting for it I felt a little faint and opened the window to get some air.'

William turned to the maid, who still stood by the window, her mouth open. 'Don't stand there gaping, girl, go and heat up the milk and take it to Miss Roswell's room. And then make a bed up for me.'

Anne scuttled away and he turned to Sophie. 'Now, you had better go up to bed. I shall wait for Charlotte and Lady Fitzpatrick.'

She could not let Charlotte bear the brunt of his anger, just because she had pretended to feel unwell.

'Uncle, why don't you retire too. There will be plenty of time to talk in the morning. It is very late.'

'So it is. I had intended to be here earlier, but the coach broke down miles from anywhere and the passengers were left stranded while the guard rode on with the mail.' He smiled wryly. 'His Majesty's mail takes precedence at all times, never mind that people are left wet and hungry in a hedge tavern which was no better than a pig-sty.'

'Then you must be very fatigued. Why not go to bed?'

'You seem to be very anxious to see the back of me, Sophie. I am beginning to think His Grace might be right.'

'His Grace?'

'The Duke of Rathbone. He wrote to me, told me there was something havey-cavey going on and if I didn't want my daughter and my niece to make complete fools of themselves and me too, I had better come and see what was afoot.'

His Grace had recognised her! 'But how—'

'Oh, so there is something. What is it, Sophie?'

She sank into a chair and put her head in her hands, unable to meet his gaze. 'I have been very foolish, Uncle William, and ruined my life.'

'Oh, come, it cannot be as bad as that.' He sat beside her and patted her hand. 'You had better tell me all about it.'

It was some time before she could begin, but then it all poured out, the fear of being married for her money, the need for Madderlea to have a benign master, her own longing to be loved and Lady Fitzpat-rick's mistake.

'It seemed as though fate was offering me a way out,' she said. 'I didn't realise how complicated it was all going to be, nor how much gossip there would be among the *haute monde*, watching and speculating...'

'I can hardly believe my ears,' he said. 'Sophie, this is dreadful. How did you suppose it would all end? You could not have allowed it to go on if either of you had an offer...'

'At first I thought I could tell whoever offered for me and he would not mind finding out I had a fortune when all he expected was a small dowry, but then when I realised I would not receive an offer, not from the man I wanted at any rate, I decided we need not tell anyone, because when we returned home, I should live in seclusion. I thought if Madderlea was too much for you, then you could find another trustee, or sell it.'

'Good Lord! I never heard such a fribble. I have a duty to you and your late uncle to do my best for you and I shall discharge that duty until you are married. Though how that is to be brought about after this I do not know. This piece of mischief has done untold damage to your prospects.'

'I know, Uncle, I know.'

'And what about Charlotte? I suppose she followed where you led, as usual. As for Lady Fitzpatrick, she must have lost whatever sense she was born with to be so easily gulled. I do not know who is the more to blame.'

'It was all my fault, Uncle, truly it was. Do not blame Charlotte, or Lady Fitzpatrick.'

'How in heaven's name did you manage to carry it off for a single day, let alone several weeks?'

'It became harder and harder, especially with Viscount Braybrooke a constant visitor and Freddie...'

'Of course, Frederick Harfield is in Town, I had forgot Sir Mortimer sent him to get a little town bronze. How did you silence him? No, you do not need to tell me—he would do anything Charlotte asked of him.'

'You know?'

'Of course I know. He came to see me before he left. I have no objection to a liaison if that is what Charlotte wants, but he has to deal with his father himself. And he will find it doubly difficult after this.'

They were interrupted by the return home of Lady Fitzpatrick and Charlotte who stood just inside the door, staring at him, her eyes wide with shock.

'Papa! What are you doing here? How did you get here? It is nearly dawn...'

'You may well ask. I sent you to have a Season, to learn how to go on in Society, perhaps to find a husband. Certainly I hoped Sophie would do so. Instead I find you indulging in a masquerade which is set to make us all a laughing stock.'

'You know?'

'Your cousin has seen fit to take me into her confidence,' he said laconically.

'Oh, Papa, I am so relieved you know. Poor Sophie...'

'Papa?' queried Lady Fitzpatrick. 'But surely…'
She looked from one to the other in puzzlement.

'We did try to tell you we had been hoaxing everyone,' Sophie said, standing up to take her hand and
lead her to a seat. 'I am afraid you misunderstood.'

It took some time to explain everything to Lady
Fitzpatrick, who was so distressed she had to be
calmed with several glasses of brandy.

'Lord Braybrooke must be told,' William said. 'I
shall go and call on him after I have had a few hours'
sleep. Now, off to bed, both of you.' He looked down
at Lady Fitzpatrick who was sprawled across a sofa,
moaning. 'Tell her ladyship's maid to come down and
help her. I fear the brandy has taken its toll. Tomorrow we will decide what is to be done. I sincerely
hope the Duke and Lord Braybrooke will agree to
keep silent and we may avoid a scandal.'

It was also Richard's wish, though how he could
obtain his heart's desire without everything being
made public he did not know. He walked home in the
rain, still pondering on the reason for Sophie's masquerade. He felt sure she had been going to tell him
when Mr Hundon arrived and thrown her into a spin.
Her uncle was obviously not party to the deception
and he wondered what he would have to say about it.
Was it all about to come out? It would be the story
of the year, of several years.

It was almost dawn and the last of the guests were
leaving as he arrived, wet and bedraggled from the
rain. Rather than be seen, he slipped in at a side door
and went up to his room, where he stripped off his

wet clothes without calling for his valet and climbed into bed. If there was to be a scandal, then it would be better if his grandfather knew of it before it broke.

He would seek an interview in the morning, tell him everything and see what they could contrive. He was as determined as ever to marry Sophie. He smiled to himself, remembering how beautiful she had looked, how spirited, not in the least overawed and able to give him as good as he gave. He fell asleep, reliving the feel of her lips on his, her body pressed close to his.

He woke in the middle of the morning to a room flooded with light. His valet had drawn back the curtains and was busying himself about the room, laying out shaving tackle and towels beside the bowl of hot water he had brought into the room. Richard yawned and stretched and climbed out of bed.

'Good morning, my lord.' The valet turned from the washstand. 'It is a fine day. The rain has gone and I believe it may turn out warm. What will you wear today?'

'Oh, anything, it's of no consequence. I shall be making calls later so perhaps the blue superfine. And trousers, yes, trousers. The light kerseymere, I think.'

The valet smiled; his master knew that trousers were more flattering than pantaloons and made his legs seem longer. Not that he needed to look taller— he was over six feet in his stockings. 'Very good, my lord.'

'Is His Grace up?' He knew his grandfather had only put in a token appearance at the ball and retired early as he would have done in the country and, as in the country, he would also rise early.

'I believe so, my lord.'

An hour later, shaved, dressed and with his hunger alleviated by a good breakfast, he presented himself in the library where his grandfather was reading the *Morning Chronicle*. He put it down when Richard entered.

'Ah, Richard, my boy, come in. Ball go according to plan, did it?'

Richard smiled. 'No, not exactly.'

'Philippa cut up rough, did she?'

'No, surprisingly she did not. Perhaps Emily managed to turn her up sweet.'

'So, it is to be Miss Roswell.' He peered into his grandson's eyes. 'Miss *Sophie* Roswell.'

The emphasis on Sophie's given name was not lost on Richard. 'You know?'

'There is not much escapes me.'

'But how do you know?'

'She is the image of her mother. The same features and the same colour hair, almost impossible to describe, but unforgettable.'

'Gold with red highlights, as if streaked with fire.'

His Grace smiled. 'Very poetic, Richard, but what have you done about her?'

'I have asked her to marry me.'

'An offer she had no hesitation in refusing, I'll wager.'

'Yes, but I am sure it was only because she has been playing this game of make-believe and it has gone wrong.'

'So I conjectured, which is why I alerted Mr Hundon.'

'He arrived this evening, but she would not let me speak to him…'

'Of course she would not. It would have meant her secret was out.'

'But you and I had guessed it, so did it matter?'

'I fancy she would like to come out of it with some remnant of dignity. Perhaps saving face is more important to her than marriage.'

'Perhaps. I should also like to avoid a scandal, for everyone's sake, not least Sophie's, but I do not see how it can be done.'

'Give up this idea of marrying her and allow her to return to Leicestershire where she can revert to her true identity without anyone of consequence knowing she had ever repudiated it.'

'I will not give her up. Grandfather, apart from this bumblebath she seems to have fallen in, you have no objection to her as a granddaughter, have you?'

'None at all. In fact, it would delight me. She must have a great deal of spirit to have embarked on such a hoax and to have carried it off so successfully for so long.'

'But why do you think she did it? Was she coerced?'

'Do you think she is a young lady easily persuaded? After all, you failed to induce her to marry you and most young ladies would sacrifice almost anything for the prospect of one day becoming a duchess.'

'Not Sophie, it seems,' he said bitterly.

'No, but is that not one of the things you find so endearing about her, that she does not behave in a conventional way?'

Richard smiled wryly. 'Yes, of course, but what can she have been thinking about to have embarked on it in the first place?'

'What were you thinking about when you made that list of attributes a prospective wife must have?'

'Oh, I don't know. Not being duped by fortune hunters, I suppose.'

'Then you have your answer.'

A broad smile lit Richard's face as he realised what his grandfather meant. 'Do you really think so?'

'Only one way to find out, my boy. Ask her.'

As he rose to go, a footman came to the door to say that Mr Hundon wished to see His Grace and asked if he would receive him.

'Yes, yes, show him in.' To Richard, he said, 'You might as well stay, hear what he has to say.'

William betrayed nothing of his unease as he was shown into the room. He bowed slightly to both men and took the chair offered to him.

'Your Grace, I am indebted to you for taking the pains to alert me to what was going on in my own household. I need not say I am mortified by it all. How we shall come about without a major scandal, I do not know. I am doubly sorry that you and yours have been involved.'

'Oh, we shall contrive to endure it,' His Grace said, with a twinkle in his eye.

'That is what we must do too,' William said. 'We shall return to Upper Corbury almost immediately.'

'You surely do not mean to go before the young ladies' ball?' Richard queried. 'That would only fuel the flames.'

'You are not suggesting I should condone the deception? My lord, I cannot pretend to be my niece's father, I really cannot. I am a lawyer, a man of integrity. And Lady Fitzpatrick has been in such a quake ever since she discovered how she had been gulled, she is in no state to be hostess to a Society ball. She has been resorting to the laudanum and the brandy bottle and lies on her day-bed, hardly aware of what is going on around her.'

'It is not to be wondered at,' His Grace murmured. 'She would not have been my choice for a chaperon for two such lively chits.'

'But that is the answer,' Richard said suddenly. 'Lady Fitzpatrick has been taken ill, so you have reluctantly been obliged to cancel the ball.'

William turned towards the young man. 'I am sorry you were duped, my lord.'

'Oh, I was not. I knew some time ago. But Sophie does not realise I know. I have been trying to encourage her to confide in me, but she would not.'

'She is too ashamed, my lord.'

'Did she tell you I had proposed to her and asked permission to speak to you and that she refused?'

'No. She said nothing of that. I wonder what else she decided not to tell me? I expect she realised she had thrown away any respect you might have for her—'

'On the contrary, I can only admire her the more for sticking to her guns.' He stood up. 'Mr Hundon, if I go to Sophie now and can persuade her to consent, may we have your blessing?'

William looked startled and turned to the Duke. 'Your Grace...'

'Oh, do not mind me, my grandson knows his own mind and I shall not interfere.'

'But what about the scandal?'

'Oh, we shall contrive something. If not...' He shrugged. 'Give the boy your blessing, Mr Hundon, and let him be on his way. I fancy he is a touch impatient.'

William nodded and Richard left the room, calling for someone to saddle his horse. It was not far to Holles Street, but walking would take too long.

Even so, he was too late. Everyone, except Mr Hundon, had been late rising and it was not until Anne went to wake Sophie and found her bed empty that they realised she had left the house. Charlotte, worried by her cousin's state of mind, was at her wits' end and pacing the drawing-room floor until her father should return. When Richard was shown in, she almost flung herself on him.

'My lord, Sophie has disappeared and Pa—' She stopped and began again. 'She was upset last night and I am afraid...'

He smiled. 'I know. And I know why too.'

'You do?' She looked at him, wide-eyed in astonishment.

'Yes.'

'Oh. Do you think she had run away because she could not face you? Oh, dear, whatever shall we do?'

'Calm yourself, my dear Miss Hundon. If I know

Sophie, she has pulled herself together, made up her mind to make the best of it and gone off to Maiden Lane.'

'Oh, yes, I had forgot Maiden Lane. But she was not supposed to go unescorted, was she?'

'No, but she might have thought it did not matter, after all. Now, you wait here for Mr Hundon. I left him talking to my grandfather. I will go and bring her home and we will sit down quietly and work out a strategy for coming about.'

He sounded more composed than he felt about it. He had never liked the idea of Sophie going among the soldiers on her own and today, for some reason he could not explain, he felt a tremor of unease, of danger lurking.

He rode to Maiden Lane with all the haste he could muster, almost colliding with a carriage as he galloped out of the street. He hoped he was right and she really was at the refuge. Sophie. Sophie. Her name went round and round in his brain as he rode in and out of the traffic. Sophie. Sophie.

Chapter Eleven

'Major, how good of you to come.' Mrs Stebbings, clad as ever in a huge white apron over her black mourning dress, was her usual cheerful self. 'Your legal man came to see me yesterday. I want to thank you on behalf of the Association and of the men. It will make so much difference to know that this refuge will always be here for them and others like them…'

'Yes, yes,' he said, a little impatiently. He had arranged to buy the freehold of the property and set up a trust to administer it. He had also engaged a man to act as an employment agent, much in the manner Sophie had suggested. But just at the moment he was not in the mood to listen to effusive gratitude. 'Where is Mrs Carter?'

'Oh, Major, I am sorry, but you have missed her. She was here earlier, but she seemed somewhat distracted, a little out of sorts, and I suggested she ought to go home.'

'Was she alone?'

'She came alone, but I did not like to think of her

walking back unaccompanied, when she was obviously not feeling at all the thing and Sergeant Dawkins offered to escort her…'

'Dawkins!'

'Yes.' She stopped when she saw the startled look on his face. 'Why, is there anything wrong, Major?'

Richard gritted his teeth and told himself to remain calm. Dawkins was not an unusual name; there must be dozens of Sergeant Dawkinses and, even if it were the same one, he probably would not remember making that threat of revenge. And if he did, he had no reason to connect Sophie with the officer who had had him court-martialled.

'I certainly hope not,' he said. 'How long ago did she leave?'

'Oh, some time ago. Two or three hours, I should think.'

'Three hours! Good God! Are you sure she meant to go straight home?'

'That is what I understood. She said she was leaving town tomorrow and came to say goodbye. She said she would see that the rent was always paid, but I told her about the trust and how you had bought the house for us and she seemed very pleased and said it was just the sort of kind action you would take.' She paused. 'I do not know where she lives, but if you do, you could check if she arrived safely.'

'I have just come from there. She had not returned home when I left.'

'Oh, Major, you don't suppose anything has happened to her? I could have sworn Sergeant Dawkins was reliable.'

'I must go,' he said, suiting action to words.

'Please let us know she is safe,' she called after him.

He returned to his horse and sprang into the saddle. Sophie had told Mrs Stebbings she was leaving town; had she meant immediately and not tomorrow? Would she go on her own? Travelling alone would not frighten her, he realised that, but she would not be so inconsiderate of her uncle and cousin as to go without telling them or leaving a message.

On the other hand, she had been very distressed when he had last seen her and that was probably increased when Mr Hundon arrived and she knew her hoax had been uncovered. Was it worth checking the coaching inns which, considering how many there were, would take forever, or should he concentrate on Sergeant Dawkins? First things first—he must return to Holles Street; she might have returned in his absence and he was worrying over nothing.

But she had not. He decided to say nothing of his suspicions to her family, who were all distraught enough as it was, and offered to recruit all his friends to help search for her. He sent Luke to rouse Freddie and Martin and enlist their help in looking everywhere a properly brought-up young lady might be found: the shops, libraries and dressmakers, and the drawing rooms of acquaintances. He sent other men servants to check the coaching inns and set off himself to search the less salubrious areas of the city.

He went home, picked up a pistol and ammunition, told the butler where he could be contacted if anyone should have news, then returned to the house in Maiden Lane in a closed carriage where he told Mrs Stebbings and those men who were in the house that Mrs Carter had not returned home and he was afraid for her safety.

'Did she say anything to any of you about where she was going, or of any fears she had?' he asked.

'No, Major,' they murmured.

'We'll find her, never fear,' Andrew Bolt said. He was a big, craggy-faced man with only one eye and a hand missing, but neither disability seemed to trouble him much. 'If we have to search the whole of London.'

'I think Sergeant Dawkins may have something to do with it,' Richard added. 'He bears me a grudge. Do any of you know where he might be found?'

None did, but the legless man, sitting by the door on his trolley, pushed himself forward.

'I did see the sergeant talking quiet-like to a cove yesterday, outside here,' he said. 'Didn't like the look of him, thought they might be up to something smokey, like robbing the house, so I followed them.' He grinned, tapping his wheels. 'I can move pretty fast on these here round legs, when I choose to, and nobody notices me, bein' so near to the ground.'

'Where did they go?'

'Into an alley off Seven Dials.'

'That was yesterday?'

'Yes. I know it don't prove nothin', but if we could find the other cove, he might lead us to the sergeant.'

'You can't go into Seven Dials in that flash rig, Major, and that's a fact,' Tom Case said. 'You won't take two steps before you're set upon and stripped bare. Besides, as soon as it's known you're looking for one of their number, the word will go round and every no-good footpad, pickpocket and cut-throat in the place will come to protect their own. It will take more than one man...'

'Are you volunteering, Trooper?' Richard asked with a smile. The man was skinny and stooped, but that did not mean he was weak, as Richard well knew. Like all of them, he was a good man to have with you in a tight corner.

'At your service, Major, and the service of the little lady.' It was a sentiment echoed by everyone present.

'I've got an old suit of clothes belonging to my husband, God rest his soul,' Mrs Stebbings said. 'I brought them here to give them to one of these men, but they might fit you. Very plain they are and a little shabby, but the better for that under present circumstances, wouldn't you think?'

'Thank you, Mrs Stebbings.'

She found them for him, and though the breeches were a little short so that his stockings barely reached them, and the cloth of the jacket was so tight across his shoulders that the seams began to spilt, that was all to the good, he decided. He rubbed dirt on his face, hands and boots, obliterating the shine which had taken his valet hours to produce.

After that, the search for Sophie took on the semblance of a military campaign, carefully planned. Men were dispatched to gather information. Others produced old muskets and rusty swords and expressed themselves willing to use them, but Richard, who did not think it was the right moment to ask how they had acquired them, forbade that.

'This is England,' he said. 'Criminals must be punished according to the law. I shall use my pistol only as a last resort.' He smiled a little grimly. 'Though if you were to find anyone mistreating or showing any indelicacy towards Mrs Carter, I should not object to them being taught a lesson.'

'Then what are we waiting for, Major?' Andrew Bolt said.

Even more impatient than they were, he forced a smile. 'For our runners to return. Reliable intelligence is half the battle, you should know that. Going off at half-cock will lose us our prize.'

Sophie had no idea where she was. All she knew was that it was dark and it smelled horrible. Her previous worries faded into insignificance as she wondered if she was about to die. What she did not know was why. Who wished her harm?

How long had she been there? How long before she was missed? She had rejected Lady Fitzpatrick's admonitions and Richard's scolding about going out alone so often, it was possible those at home would think nothing of her absence until she did not return for nuncheon.

Richard would not miss her at all because she had sent him away, rejected his proposal of marriage and refused to give him a reason. This was her punishment, to be tied hand and foot, her mouth gagged with a disgusting piece of cloth, and left to die in an empty room which stank of rotting garbage and excrement. Where had Sergeant Dawkins gone?

Why was he conspiring with that dreadful, leering giant of a man with a patch over one eye and huge rough hands? What did they want from her? She had offered them all the money in her reticule and promised more if they would only release her. When that failed, she had asked them what it was they wanted, had said she understood their problems and would try to help them, that if they released her unharmed she would not put the law on to them. Her only answer had been guffaws of laughter.

She had accepted Sergeant Dawkins's offer to escort her home only when pressed to do so by Mrs Stebbings, not because she was afraid of him—though he did make her a little nervous—but because she did not want him to know where she lived and who she really was.

It was her silly pride again, she supposed, and the fact that she had become so used to secrecy, to deceit, that she kept on with it even when it no longer mattered. Her true identity would be the talk of the town before the day was out. But would she live to hear it?

Dawkins had walked beside her as they made their way between the crowds in the market, pushing a way through for her, yelling at the urchins who had recognised her as one of the two ladies who had thrown coins for them. They wanted more. Dawkins clubbed one about the face, kicked another and swore at them all. Terrified, they fell back.

On the corner, Dawkins was joined by the second

man, who silently took up station on Sophie's other side; it was at this point that she knew something was wrong and became really frightened.

'Sergeant, I think I can manage to find my way home from here,' she said as calmly as she could. 'Thank you for your trouble.'

'Oh, it ain't no trouble,' he growled, pressing more closely to her, so that the smell of his unwashed body almost overpowered her. 'And we expect to be well rewarded.'

'Oh, yes, I am sorry.' She delved into her reticule for a coin.

'That!' He took it from her and threw it behind him, laughing as one of the waifs, bolder than the rest, dived on it. 'We'll have more than that before the day is out.'

They were opposite a narrow alley and the two men, each holding one of her arms, hustled her down it.

'Where are you taking me?'

'A short cut.' Dawkins grinned. 'A short cut to my just reward. I've got a score to settle.'

She had opened her mouth to scream, but that was a mistake. The second man clapped one enormous hand over her mouth, twisted her arm behind her back with the other and marched her forward. They left the busy market behind them and darted down one narrow alley after another. Tall tenements rose each side, blocking out the light and air. A few people stood about, but no one paid the least attention; they certainly showed no sign of wishing to intervene.

After a few minutes in which her futile struggles

weakened, they entered a doorway and she was carried, Dawkins at her shoulders and the other man at her feet, up several flights of stairs and into this room.

'Now, you'll stay 'ere until I come back,' Dawkins said when he had regained his breath. 'And if you're a good girl, Joe will bring you food and drink.'

She had made the mistake of struggling fiercely and yelling at the top of her voice, which resulted in her being tied and gagged and flung on to a filthy straw palliasse on the floor.

Now she was alone and her eyes were becoming accustomed to the gloom, she realised she was in an attic. There was a sloping roof above her, with some of the slates missing so that tiny beams of light played on the dust motes in the air. The room had no window and only one door and, apart from the mattress, the only furniture was a small table and a couple of rickety chairs with broken backs. In the corner lay a canvas bag and beside it a coil of knotted rope. It was unbearably hot and the gag had dried her mouth, so that she longed for a drink of water.

She heard footsteps on the stairs and Dawkins returned. He was carrying a small case from which he took pen, paper and a bottle of ink. 'Seemed to me that it would be better coming from you,' he said, in a chatty voice that took no account of her distress. 'I want you to write me a letter.'

She grunted and he sat down beside her on the mattress to look closely into her face while her eyes tried to convey that she wanted the gag removed.

'You want to speak, do you? Well, as to that, I

don't know. I'd need your promise not to yell out again.'

She nodded and he reached round her and untied the gag. She took several gulps of air but that hardly helped; the room was airless and she was parched. 'Water, please.'

He rose and went to the table where there was a jug and a tin cup. He poured water and came back to hold it against her face, but he made no attempt to tip it towards her lips. He grinned. 'You going to be good?'

She was so desperate for a drink, she would have agreed to anything. 'Yes, but untie me, please. I won't run.'

'Course you won't, there's nowhere to run to. There's the door and beyond it three flights of stairs and old Joe at the bottom of them and it's the only way out.'

He put the water down and untied her hands. She grabbed at the cup and poured the disgusting liquid down her throat, wiping her mouth with the back of her hand.

'I must say, for a genteel filly, you've got plenty of guts,' he said, watching her. 'A bit like my wife.'

'And what would you think of anyone who carried your wife off and held her prisoner?' she demanded.

'Couldn't do it. She died two years ago while I was stuck in Spain.'

'I am truly sorry.'

'Are you?' He looked closely at her. 'Maybe you are, so you won't mind writing a letter for me.'

'If it's only letter writing you want me for, you

could have asked me at the house in Maiden Lane. You didn't need to abduct me.'

'But this is a very special letter and the whole lay depends on you being hid.' He fetched a piece of broken floorboard and put the paper on it, took the lid off the ink bottle and offered her the pen. 'Write what I say.'

With a shaking hand, she took the pen and he began dictating. 'To Major Richard Braybrooke, Bedford Row.' He grinned at her gasp of astonishment. 'Go on, write it down.' He waited for her to do as she was told, then went on 'Dear Richard. Please do not try to find me or I shall be killed before you reach me.'

'Why do you think the Major would try and find me?' she queried, concluding he probably did not know Richard had come into a title since returning from Spain. 'He has no interest in me. We quarrelled.'

'Oh, you cannot gammon me, Mrs Carter. Or should I say Miss Hundon?'

'How did you find that out?'

'It weren't difficult. Followed you home, talked to the servants, watched the house, saw the Major visiting…'

'But he was visiting my cousin, not me,' she said, realising he did not know the whole truth, that she was not Miss Hundon, but Miss Roswell.

He laughed. 'One for the ladies, is he? It don't matter which one he was after, you were the easiest to pull in, bein' a mite more adventurous than the other. Aside for that, I've seen the way he looks at you. Now, go on writing.'

She dipped the pen in the ink again, just as heavy footsteps could be heard ascending the stairs. Dawkins scrambled to his feet and stood behind the door, drawing a knife from his boot. She held her breath, but it was only Joe who was tired of standing guard at the bottom of the stairs and wanted to know what was happening.

'You could 'ave got yerself killed,' Dawkins said, returning the knife to his boot. 'I told you to stay downstairs.'

'This is my room, I come to it when I want.' He looked down at Sophie. 'Ain't you got that letter writ yet?'

'Never will if you keep interruptin',' Dawkins said, returning to sit on the mattress again. 'Got that down, 'ave you?' he asked Sophie.

'Yes.'

'Then write this: "I shall be returned safely if you bring a thousand yellow boys to—"'

'Two thousand,' Joe muttered. 'Tell him two thousand.'

'He won't pay it,' Sophie said, guessing he meant guineas. 'Where would a major find that amount of money? And if he could, what makes you think he would pay it for my release? He would simply turn the letter over to the Bow Street Runners and forget about it.'

They looked at each other, wondering whether to believe her, then Dawkins laughed. 'Nice try, Miss Hundon. Now write: "Bring one thousand guineas to the steps of St Paul's tonight at seven—"'

'Two,' insisted Joe.

Dawkins turned on him angrily. 'I want him here, I want him to feel the lash as I felt it and if we're too greedy, he'll do as the chit says and hand the whole matter over to the law.'

'What do I care for your damned revenge?' Joe said. 'It ain't nothin' to me, what you did in the war, nor what he did neither. If you bring him here, to my lay, then my safe ken is blown and I need to find another a long way away and that takes blunt. He'll pay. Just look at her. She's a lady.'

'Yes, I am,' Sophie said, wondering what it was Sergeant Dawkins had against Richard. Whatever it was, it inspired powerful feelings of revenge stronger than mere greed. 'And a very wealthy one. I can give you more than Major Braybrooke who is nothing but a son of a second son, of no importance at all.'

She could see that Joe was interested. 'How much?' he demanded.

'You shut up and get out!' Dawkins shouted at him. 'Are you a cod's-head that you can't see she's trying to gull us to protect him? I want that man here. I want him to feel this.' He got up and went to the corner and picked up the rope by its handle. Sophie realised it was not an ordinary rope at all, but a cat o' nine tails. He swished it through the air a couple of times and then sat down again. 'I haven't finished the letter,' he said. 'Tell him to come alone and make sure he is not followed. If he brings anyone with him, I shall know of it and he may look for your body in the Thames. Tell him you know I mean it, beg him to come to your aid, say you are in mortal terror. Then sign it.'

She wrote slowly, trying to think of a way to warn Richard of what they planned for him. 'Come on,' he said. 'We ain't got all day.'

She wrote, her pen poised over the signature, but before she could write it, there was the sound of someone pounding up the uncarpeted stairs, making no attempt to be quiet. Joe hid behind the door, while Dawkins rose and faced it, standing poised with the lash in his hands, ready to use it. They could hear whoever it was banging on doors on his way up, shouting to the occupants.

'The Runners are coming down the street and they're searching all the houses.'

Joe flung open the door. A ragged man stood on the threshold, panting. 'If you've got anything to hide, you'd best make yerselves and yer booty scarce,' he said. 'The Runners are going from door to door looking for booty. I'm off meself.' He turned and clattered down the stairs again, but not before Sophie had recognised Tom Case. Was the refuge she had set so much store by, and worked so hard to create, nothing but a den of thieves? She cursed herself for her gullibility.

'I'm not waiting around for fool's gold,' Joe said, grabbing the canvas bag which clinked as he lifted it. 'But just you remember, you owe me, George Dawkins, and I shall find you, wherever you're laid up.' With that he disappeared down the stairs behind Case.

Dawkins was more cautious, but it was obvious he would be trapped if he stayed where he was. He stuffed the unsigned letter in his pocket, then bent to take Sophie's arm and hauled her to her feet, upsetting the ink bottle over her hand as he did so. 'Time we was gone,' he said, pushing her in front of him down the stairs, holding the cat o' nine tails at the ready. 'We'll finish this somewhere else.'

When they reached the street door, he poked his head out and looked this way and that, then up at the windows of the tenements. There was not a soul in sight. The cry that Bow Street Runners were in the road had been enough to send everyone to ground.

'Right, you first.' He pushed Sophie ahead of him, walking backwards himself. They had gone perhaps twenty yards when an arm shot out of a doorway and hauled her inside.

The next minute the street was full of men, some of whom she recognised, and children, dozens of them, converging on the cornered Dawkins, but Sophie was only half aware of them, as Richard, in an ill-fitting wool coat and worn leather breeches, held her tight against him. She felt breathless and weak and almost ready to faint. 'Are you all right?'

'Yes.'

'Stay there.' He left her and ran out to join the men who had Dawkins imprisoned by his arms. The cat o' nine tails lay on the ground. Richard picked it up. His expression was grim. 'So, this is what it was all about?'

The man was struggling fiercely while the children danced round, taunting him. Sophie, who had once again disobeyed and ventured out to see what was happening, was appalled to think Richard was going to use the lash.

'Let me do it,' Andrew Bolt, said, holding out his

hand for the cat o' nine tails. 'It would give me the greatest pleasure.'

'No!' Sophie shouted, appalled. 'You must not do that.'

Richard turned and for a moment she saw the old humorous look in his eye, but it was gone in an instant when he saw her torn clothing, her lovely hair hanging down, the pallor of her complexion. 'I told you to stay out of sight.'

'But he didn't harm me, just frightened me a little. You must not take revenge on him in that way. Vengeance is not for mere mortals.'

'No, but punishment is.' He threw the rope down and took off his jacket. To the men who held Dawkins, he said, 'Let him go.'

They released him and formed a circle round the two men, while Tom Case took Sophie's arm to draw her away. 'Don't look, ma'am.'

But she could not help looking. Peering between the circle of men, she saw Dawkins put up his fists to defend himself, saw Richard deliver a blow past his defence which rocked him on his heels. Enraged, the man flung himself at Richard, who neatly sidestepped and landed another blow. Dawkins, reeling, came again and again but, though he did manage to land a punch or two, he was outclassed as a pugilist.

Even in the midst of her anxiety and anger, Sophie could admire Richard's muscular body, the quick reactions as he danced out of his opponent's reach. His grim expression had relaxed and she realised he was enjoying himself. Dawkins, in desperation, made a lunge for the discarded cat o' nine tails, but Richard, watching his face, saw his eyes turn to the rope seconds before he reached for it, and put his foot on it.

'Oh, no, you don't. Fight fair or not at all.' Dawkins lowered his head like a maddened bull and hurled himself at Richard to bring him down, but in the process he stumbled and fell forward, hitting his head on the cobbles. He lay still. Richard calmly put on his coat. 'Look after him,' he told the men. 'Take him to the infirmary.' Then he made his way over to Sophie.

'Do you never do as you are told?' He stood in front of her, looking down at her, blood on his face and hands, though she could not tell if it was his or Sergeant Dawkins's.

'Is that all you can say, my lord, after—'

'No, it is not, but what I have to say is best said in private. Come, my carriage is waiting at the end of the street.' He turned to the men, busy hauling Dawkins to his feet. 'Thank you, lads. You shall be rewarded.'

'We want no reward, Major, it was our pleasure to help the lady who has been so kind to us,' Case said, grinning. 'We wish you happy.'

'How did you know where to find me?' she asked, as Richard put his arm about her take her to the coach.

'You have the soldiers to thank for that. Davie saw Dawkins plotting with his accomplice yesterday and followed him to this alley. We did not know for certain if this was where you had been brought nor, if we were right, which house you were being kept in, and we dared not make a frontal attack because we were not sure how many men were holding you and if they would harm you if they were alarmed.

'But the waifs knew which house it was because one of them followed you. As soon as they saw me and recognised me as the man you were with a few days ago, they ran to tell me. After that, it was a matter of luring him out into the open.'

'He was using me as bait to have his revenge on you. He made me write a letter to you demanding a thousand guineas…'

'It is just as well he did not know your true worth to me or I'd have been left without a feather to fly with.'

'I told them I meant nothing to you,' she said, smiling at his declaration that he would give all he had to save her. 'I said you would not come yourself, which is what Sergeant Dawkins wanted. I said you would simply hand the letter over to the Runners and let them deal with it. But he would not believe me.'

'Then you are not as good a prevaricator as you thought you were,' he said, helping her into the coach. 'Holles Street,' he told the driver and climbed in beside her.

She lay back on the cushions and shut her eyes, every ounce of energy drained from her. She was safe, but now came the recriminations, the harsh words. And she deserved them. She had put herself and the soldiers at risk, had deceived Society, had involved her cousin in her duplicity, had shamed her uncle and put poor Lady Fitzpatrick in an impossible position.

'Before you say a word,' she said, 'I know I have been excessively foolish. I can only say I am sorry and very grateful for your timely rescue.'

'Save your apologies for your uncle and cousin, Miss Roswell, they have more need of them than I.'

Her eyes flew open. 'Did you say Miss Roswell?'

'Indeed, I did.'

'You know, then.'

'Yes, I know.'

'How did you find out? When?'

'The clues were there for anyone to see. Your spirit of independence, your lack of squeamishness, your fluency in the French language—all attributes lacking in your cousin, who was supposed to be the one who had come out of France in the middle of a war. And Freddie Harfield playing the gallant with you, while keeping his eyes firmly on your cousin. Need I go on?'

'No.'

'And then, of course, my grandfather twigged it right away. He tells me you are the image of your mother. She must have been a very beautiful woman.'

'I suppose the whole world knows now.' She was too weary to put up a spirited defence or recognise the implied compliment. 'I deserve to be vilified, but not Charlotte, not Lady Fitz. Not Uncle William.'

'No, they don't.' It was becoming increasingly difficult to be severe with her, when all he wanted to do was take her in his arms, to feel her soft lips yielding to his, to repeat his offer of marriage. 'As for the whole world knowing, His Grace will say nothing and certainly Lady Fitzpatrick will not, she is too mortified. She is returning to Ireland, I believe. And you must return to Upper Corbury.'

'Yes, I know.' She said it with a sigh.

'Tell me, how *did* you intend to bring this débâcle to an end?'

'I thought, once we were back in Leicestershire, we would simply resume our proper identities. The engagement of Mr Harfield and Miss Hundon would be announced and Miss Roswell would live in seclusion…'

'And what did you intend if you should receive an offer while you were in town?'

'I should refuse it, of course.'

'Why of course?'

'I could not accept it under false pretences, could I? I could not say yes and then tell the poor man I was not the Miss Hundon he thought I was.'

'Is that the reason you refused me?'

She did not answer and he took that as an affirmative.

'Was that the only reason?'

She managed a twisted smile. 'That and the list of requirements you put about. I did not, do not, conform.'

'And if I were to tell you that I was not deceived, that the name you adopted had no bearing on my proposal at all, and neither had that list? There is nothing I regret more than dreaming that up, unless it was telling Martin Gosport of it.'

She stared at him unbelievingly. 'But, my lord, you cannot possibly wish to marry me after what has happened. There will be the most dreadful scandal.'

'We have been looking for a way of cancelling the rest of your Season without causing scandal…'

'We?' she queried.

'Your Uncle William, my grandfather and I.'

'Oh.'

'You have been through a dreadful ordeal—that much we can make public—and it has left you unable to continue your Season. Miss Roswell—I mean Charlotte, of course—is too upset to continue without you and the whole family has gone back to Leicestershire.'

She smiled wanly. 'It is an ill wind that blows nobody any good.'

'In a few months' time—not many, because I am an impatient man—I shall present myself at Upper Corbury and the engagement will be gazetted between Miss Roswell and Richard, Viscount Braybrooke.'

'But, my lord…'

He lifted her grubby, ink-stained hand and put it to his lips. 'I do hope you are not going to reject me again. I do not think I could bring myself to ask a third time.'

Her lovely eyes had regained some of their sparkle. 'Oh, my lord…'

'Richard,' he corrected her.

'I am not sure if I understand. Are you proposing in spite of what I have done?'

'You want me on my knees? Then I go on my knees.' He slipped to the floor and took both her hands in his. 'You want me to say I love you. I say it. I love you, love you, love you, have done since the day I met you. And rather than being in spite of what you have done, it might be because of it, because of your compassion for others, your fearlessness, your independence which is far too pronounced for your own good, for…'

'Oh, Richard, please do not go on with that tarra-diddle. And get up off the floor. It is dirty.' She laughed suddenly, realising that his breeches were already filthy, that his coat was torn and there was mud and blood caked on his face and hands.

He looked hurt for a moment, until he realised what she had said and joined in the laughter. 'Oh, Sophie, there will never be a dull moment married to you. You are going to say yes, aren't you?'

'Yes, Richard, yes, please.'

He resumed his seat beside her, putting his hands either side of her face and kissing her, tenderly, longingly, filling her with a surge of such happiness, she did not know how she could bear it. She was hardly aware that the carriage had stopped.

'Holles Street, my lord,' the driver said.

They were married at Madderlea six months later in a quiet ceremony attended by close family and friends, some of whom knew about the switch in identity and been sworn to secrecy. Mrs Stebbings and several of the soldiers who had known her only as Mrs Carter and were not in the least surprised that she turned out to be an heiress attended, along with the Madderlea villagers and the estate workers who had never known her as anything but Miss Roswell. Martin, amused by the way Richard had been hooked, had come, promising never to say a word to his mother, and also the new Mr and Mrs Frederick Harfield, who had married a month before. It was a happy

day, the service solemn, the wedding feast gargan-
tuan, a day full of laughter, as everyone toasted the
new master and mistress of Madderlea.

Later, when the old Duke died, they would be expected to move to the Rathbone estate, but Madderlea
would remain in the family, a home for their heir, the
next viscount. But that prospect was years and years
ahead, years they could look forward to with joy and
more laughter, without secrets.

*   *   *   *   *

The Wolfe's Mate
by
by Paula Marshall

Paula Marshall, married with three children, has had a varied life. She began her career in a large library and ended it as a senior academic in charge of History at a polytechnic. She has travelled widely, has been a swimming coach, and has appeared on *University Challenge* and *Mastermind*. She has always wanted to write, and likes her novels to be full of adventure and humour.

Prologue

'Jilted!' screeched Mrs Mitchell, throwing herself carefully backwards into the nearest comfortable chair. 'That a child of mine should be left at the altar. Call him out, or horsewhip him, do, Mr Mitchell, it is all he deserves.'

'Difficult,' responded her husband drily, 'seeing that his letter informs us that he was setting sail for France last night!'

His restraint was all the more remarkable because, until an hour ago, he had been loudly congratulating himself on getting rid of his stepdaughter to a husband who was, all things considered, above her touch, he being a peer of the realm, and she a merchant's daughter and not very remarkable in the looks department.

His wife's only response was to drum her heels on the ground and announce that she was about to faint—which she did with as much panache as Mrs Siddons performing on stage. Her two young daughters by Mr Mitchell stood helplessly on each side of her, sobbing loudly. Mrs Mitchell's companion was wringing her hands, and exclaiming at intervals, 'Oh, the wretch, the wretch.'

The only calm person in the room was the jilted young woman herself, nineteen-year-old Susanna Beverly, who coolly wrenched a feather from her mother's fan. She held it briefly in the fire and then placed it under Mrs Mitchell's nose to revive her.

Revive her it did. She started up, exclaiming loudly, 'Oh, Susanna, how can you be so unmoved when he has ruined you? The news will be all about town by tonight—it will be the sensation of the Season.'

'Really, Mother,' replied Susanna, who was clinging on to her self-possession for dear life, after just having been made the spectacle of the Season as well as its sensation, 'don't exaggerate. He hasn't seduced me, only left me at the altar.'

'Oh, Mr Mitchell,' shrieked her mother, sitting up at last, 'pray tell her that he might just as well have done so. Nobody, but nobody, will ever marry a jilted girl! Oh, whatever did you say to drive him away?'

She sank back into the chair again to be comforted by her companion, ignoring Susanna's quiet reply. 'Nothing, Mother, nothing. Perhaps that was what drove him away.' Only her iron will prevented her from behaving in the abandoned fashion of the rest of her family.

Her unnatural calm, however, annoyed her stepfather as well as her mother, however much it was enabling her not to shriek to the heavens at the insult which had been offered her. To arrive at the church, to wait for a bridegroom who had never turned up, and had sent a letter instead of himself—and what a letter!

'I have changed my mind and have no wish to be

married, but have decided to set out for France this evening instead. Convey my respects to Susanna with the hope that she will soon find a more suitable bridegroom than Francis Sylvester.'

It had been handed to her by the best man who, to do him justice, had looked most unhappy while carrying out this quite untraditional role.

Susanna had read it, and then handed it to her stepfather who had been there to give her away. He had read it, then flung it down with an oath, before shouting at the assembled congregation, 'There will be no wedding. The bridegroom has deloped and is no longer in the country!'

'Deloped!' Mrs Mitchell had shrieked. 'Whatever can you mean, Mr Mitchell?'

'What I have just said,' he had roared. 'Lord Sylvester has cried off. Failed to fire his pistol, or fired it in the air, call it what you will. Come, Susanna and Mrs Mitchell, we must return home before we become more of a laughingstock than we already are.'

Numbly Susanna had obeyed him. Noisily, Mrs Mitchell had done the same, abusing her daughter whose fault she claimed it to be.

Susanna scarcely heard her. Until an hour ago she had been secure in the knowledge that a handsome young man with a title and a moderate fortune, with whom she had just enjoyed several happy summer months, was going to be her husband. She had to confess that she did not love him madly, but then, who did love their husbands madly—other than the heroines of Minerva Press novels?

Nor did she think that he had loved her madly. Nevertheless, they had dealt well together, although their interests differed greatly. Francis Sylvester's life had revolved around Jackson's Boxing Salon and various racecourses in the day, and the more swell of London's gaming hells, where he was a moderate gambler, at night. Susanna's time, on the other hand, was spent reading, playing the piano, and painting—she was quite a considerable artist. These differences had not troubled either of them for they were commonplace in the marriages of the *ton*.

This being so, she could not imagine why he had behaved in such a heartless fashion. He had had ample time to cry off during the months of their betrothal when to have done so would not have ruined her as completely as his leaving her at the altar would do.

For Susanna knew full well that what her mother had said was true: to be jilted in such a fashion meant social ruin. Was it her looks? She knew that they were not remarkable—other than her deep grey-blue eyes, that was, on which Francis had frequently complimented her. Her hair was an almost chestnut, her face an almost-perfect oval. Her nose and mouth, whilst not exactly distinguished, were not undistinguished, either.

Her height was neither short nor tall, but somewhere in between. Her carriage had often been called graceful. Susanna, however, knew full well that she was not a raving beauty in the fashionable style which her two half-sisters promised to be. Both of them were blonde, blue-eyed and slightly plump: 'my two cherubs,' her stepfather called them.

Nor was her fortune remarkable. Like herself, it might be described as comfortable, her father having died suddenly before he had been able to make it greater. Her stepfather, having daughters of his own to care for—and still hoping for a son—had not considered it his duty to enlarge it.

She straightened herself and held her head as high as she could. There was no use in repining. What was done, was done.

'I am going to my room,' she said. 'Send Mary to me, Mother. I wish to change out of these clothes. They have become hateful to me.'

Even as she spoke, she saw by the expressions on her mother's and stepfather's faces that she had become hateful to them: a symbol of their disappointment. Not only had they lost an aristocratic son-in-law, but they were saddled with a daughter who had become unmarriageable.

As her mother said mournfully as soon as she was out of the room, 'No one will marry her now, Mr Mitchell. Whatever is to become of her?'

He shrugged his shoulders. 'Do not distress yourself further, my dear. Leave everything to me. I shall make suitable arrangements for her. We cannot have Charlotte and Caroline's reputations muddied by her continued presence. I have great plans for them, as you know.'

His busy, cunning brain had been working out how to deal with this *contretemps* ever since he had read Francis Sylvester's letter.

'Now follow Miss Beverly's example, my dear, and change out of your unsuitable bridal finery. Let us put this behind us. I shall speak to her in the morning.'

His tone was so firm that his wife immediately ceased her repining. Although he was usually indulgent towards her and all her three daughters, he invariably spoke to them as though they were recalcitrant clerks when he wished to make it plain that they must obey him immediately.

It was thus he addressed Susanna on the following morning when she arrived in his study in response to his request made over breakfast.

'It is necessary, Miss Beverly, that we discuss your unfortunate situation immediately. It brooks of no delay. I shall expect to see you in my room at eleven of the clock precisely.'

He had never called her Miss Beverly before. Indeed, in the past few months his manner to her had been particularly affectionate, but there was nothing left of that when he spoke to her then, or later on, when she arrived to find him seated at his desk writing furiously.

Nor did he stand up when she entered, nor cease to write, until he flung his pen down and said, 'This is a sad business, my dear. I was depending on this marriage to see you settled. I was prepared to find the money for your dowry, seeing that the match was such a splendid one, but, alas, now that your reputation has gone and you are unlikely to marry, such charity on my part is out of the question.'

Susanna listened to him in some bewilderment. She had always been under the impression that her father had left a large sum of money in a Trust for her which should have made it unnecessary for her stepfather to extend her any charity at all in the matter of a dowry.

And so she told him.

He smiled pityingly at her. 'Dear child, that was a kind fib I told you and your mother. Your father left little—he made many unfortunate investments before his untimely death. The Trust was consequently worthless. I was willing to keep you and even give you the dowry your father would have left you when I hoped that you would make a good marriage—as you so nearly did.

'But, alas, now that your reputation is blown—

through no fault of yours, I freely allow—there is no point in me continuing this useful fiction. I have the unhappy task of informing you that, whilst I will assist you towards establishing yourself in a new life, I cannot afford to continue to provide you with either a large income or a dowry.'

Susanna was not to know that there was not a word of truth in what her stepfather was saying. It was he who had made the unfortunate investments, not her father. He had been stealing from the Trust to help to keep himself afloat ever since he had married Susanna's mother and he now saw a splendid opportunity to annex the whole of it to himself.

His wife would suspect nothing, for her way of life would continue unchanged: Susanna would be the only sufferer.

'I shall,' he continued, 'settle a small annual income on you, for I would not have my wife's daughter left in penury. Indeed, no. What I have also done is write a letter to an elderly friend of mine, a Miss Stanton, who lives in Yorkshire. She has asked me to find her a companion and I shall have no hesitation in recommending you to her. She will give you a comfortable home in exchange for a few, easily performed, duties. You may even be fortunate enough to meet someone who, not knowing of your sad history, will offer for you.'

He smiled at her, saying in the kindest voice he could assume, 'You see, my dear, I continue to have your best interests at heart.'

Susanna sat in stunned silence, her heart beating rapidly. 'I had no notion,' she began. 'Had I been aware of my true position, I would have thanked you before now—as it is…'

Samuel Mitchell raised a proprietorial—and hypocritical—finger. 'Think nothing of it, my dear. I was but doing my duty. I shall send off the letter immediately, but have no fear, I am sure that Miss Stanton will be only too happy to employ you. Until then, continue to enjoy your position in my home as one of my daughters.'

Susanna nodded her head numbly. She felt deprived of the power of speech. The day before yesterday, she had been the only child and heiress of a reasonably rich merchant of good family. Yesterday, she had been about to become Lady Sylvester. Today, she had been informed that she was a poverty-stricken orphan who was to be sent away to be an elderly lady's companion— with all that that entailed. Running errands, walking the pug: someone who was neither a servant nor a gentlewoman, but something in-between.

Later, alone in her room, she began to question a little what her stepfather had just told her. Was it really true that her father had left her nothing? That the Trust had been false, nothing but a lying fiction? That she had been living for the past twelve years on her stepfather's charity? Surely she and her mother would have been informed of that if such had been the case.

She made up her mind to visit the family solicitors to discover the truth. She would not tell Mr Mitchell of her intentions, merely say that she needed to take the air in the family carriage.

But her stepfather, knowing her strong and determined character, so like her late father's, had foreseen that she might wish to do such a thing, and was able to prevent it by informing her mother that, until it was time for Susanna to travel to Yorkshire, it would be unwise for her to go out in public.

'The female mind is so delicate,' he said, 'that it might, in such a situation as Susanna finds herself in, be inadvisable for her to venture out of doors. A brief period at home, before she makes the long journey to Yorkshire, will do her a power of good.'

'If you say so,' her mother said falteringly.

'Oh, I do say so, Mrs Mitchell. After all, like you, I have her best interests at heart!'

It had been her mother who told Susanna of her step-father's decision.

Susanna had stared at her, more sure than ever that something was wrong. She had been about to refuse to obey any such ban and even considered telling her mother of her suspicion that Mr Mitchell had been lying about the Trust and her father's not having left her anything.

Then she looked at her mother with newly opened eyes and knew that she would not believe that her husband was lying, would simply see Susanna as trouble-making and ungrateful towards a man who had graciously taken the place of her father ever since she had married Mr Mitchell.

Not only would Mr Mitchell make doubly sure that she was confined to the house, but she would make an enemy of them both, to no profit to herself. He would simply assert that the misery of being jilted had un-hinged her mind—and she had no answer to that. She was helpless and knew it.

Susanna had taken her mother in her arms and kissed her childhood innocence goodbye. She would go to Yorkshire and try to make a new life there, far from the home which was no longer *her* home, and where she was not wanted.

Somehow, some day, God willing, she would try to repair the ruin which Francis Sylvester had made of her life…

Chapter One

1819

It had been one of Lady Leominster's most successful balls, as she afterwards boasted to her lord the next morning, who merely grunted and continued to read the *Morning Post*. His wife's conversation was only wallpaper in the background of his busy life. It would never do to let her know how useful her balls and other entertainments were, she would only get above herself and, heaven knew, she was too much above herself as it was without his praise elevating her even further.

'And even the Wolf, the Nabob himself, came—after refusing everyone else's invitations, even Emily Exford's.'

M'lord grunted again. This time in appreciation. He had spent a happy half-hour with Benjamin Wolfe, discussing the current state of England, gaining advice on where he might profitably invest his money as the post-war depression roared on, showing no signs of breaking.

'Not a bad move, that,' he conceded grudgingly. 'The

feller seems both knowledgeable and helpful. Invite him to our next dinner.'

'They say that he is looking for a wife.'

'Shouldn't have any difficulty finding one, my dear. With all that money.'

'True, m'lord, but his birth? What of that? Does anyone know of his family?'

'Well, I do, for one,' said Lord Leominster, smiling because for once he knew of a piece of gossip which his wife didn't. 'Same family as the General of that name. Poor gentry—went to India and made his pile there, or so he says. Besides, money sweetens everything. It's its own lineage, you know. Half the peerage goes back to nameless thrusters who received titles and consequence solely because of their newly gained riches—nothing wrong in that.'

Lord Leominster's distant ancestor had been a pirate with Francis Drake and was the founder of the family's wealth with loot wrested from Spanish treasure ships.

His wife shrugged and abandoned Ben Wolfe as a topic. 'They say that Darlington is about to offer for Amelia Western—that should be a meeting of money, and no mistake. He was paying her the most marked attention last night.'

She received no answer. Lord Leominster was not interested in idle gossip for its own sake. Ben Wolfe, now, was different. Such creatures had their uses.

Lady Leominster was almost right. The previous evening, George Wychwood, Viscount Darlington, had offered for Miss Amelia Western and been accepted. He had spoken to her father and received his blessing earlier in the day and had come to Leominster House solely to propose to her.

As usual, she had that dowdy goody of hers in tow. Well, she wouldn't be needing a duenna when she was his wife, as she surely would be soon, and the dowdy goody could be given her notice, move on either to be some old trot's companion or to shepherd some other innocent young woman and make sure that the wolves didn't get at her before the honest men did.

And speaking of wolves, wasn't that Ben Wolfe in earnest conversation with their host? George Darlington frowned. He had mentioned Ben Wolfe's name to his father, the Earl of Babbacombe, earlier that day, and the Earl had made a wry face and said, 'You would do well to avoid him like the plague. His father was a wretch, and like father, like son, I always say—although there were rumours that he was not Charles Wolfe's son at all, just some by-blow brought in when Wolfe's own son died at birth. I thought that he had gone off to India—enlisted as a private in that skimble-skamble Company army. What can *he* be doing in decent society?'

Uninterested, George had shrugged. 'Made a fortune there, they say. Became a Nabob, no less. Been put up for White's and accepted.'

He had little time for his father's follies and foibles, having too many of his own to worry about.

'Money,' said his father disgustedly. 'Whitewashes everything.'

His tone was bitter. There were few to know that the Wychwood family was on its beam-ends and desperately needed the marriage which George was about to make. Lady Leominster had been wrong in her assumption that money was about to marry money.

Certainly George had no knowledge of how near his father was to drowning in the River Tick and, if he had, would have thought Ben Wolfe a useful man to ask for advice on matters financial, not someone to despise.

As it was, he passed him by and concentrated on looking for pretty Amelia, whom he found sitting in a corner, her companion by her side. He ignored the companion and asked Amelia to partner him in the next dance.

'After that,' he said, 'I have something particular to say to you, if Miss—' and he looked enquiringly at the companion '—will allow you to walk on the terrace with me—alone. It is most particular,' he added with a meaningful smile.

'Oh, Miss Beverly,' said Amelia, 'I'm sure that you will allow me to accompany George on the terrace alone if what he has to say to me is most particular. After all, we have known one another since childhood.'

Susanna, who had been Amelia Western's companion and somewhat youthful duenna since her previous employer, Miss Stanton, had suddenly died, knew perfectly well what it was that George Darlington wished to say to her charge. She also knew that, although she and George had met several times, and even conversed, he would not have known her had he met her in the street. He had twice been told her name, but it had made no impression on him.

She rose to answer him and, as it chanced, stood on George's left. He had Amelia on his right. At that very moment, Ben Wolfe, who was looking across the room at them, asked Lord Leominster, who had just been joined by his lady, 'Is that George Darlington over there?'

It was Lady Leominster who answered him eagerly, 'Oh, indeed.' She leaned forward confidentially, saying,

'He is speaking to Amelia Western, the great heiress. I am sure that he is about to propose to her tonight.'

'He is?' Ben looked at them again, and asked, apparently idly, 'I see that he has two young ladies with him. Which is the heiress?'

Never loath to pass on information, Lady Leominster answered, 'Oh, the young woman on his left.'

She was, of course, wrong—but then, she had never known her right from her left—but before Lord Leominster could open his mouth to correct her, she had seized Ben Wolfe's arm and exclaimed, 'Oh, do come and be introduced to Lady Camelford, she has two beautiful daughters, both unmarried, and both, I am assured, well endowed for marriage'—so the mistake went uncorrected.

She was never to know that her careless remark would profoundly alter the course of several lives.

Ben had no further opportunity to see George Darlington or his future bride together, but later in the evening, as he was about to leave, Miss Western suddenly came out of one of the ballrooms. He was able to step back and inspect her briefly at close range.

She was modestly dressed, to be sure, but in quiet good taste in a dress of plain cream silk. She sported no other jewellery than a string of small pearls around her neck. She was no great beauty, either, but that was true of many heiresses, and he could only commend those who were responsible for her appearance in not succumbing to the desire to deck her about with the King's ransom which she undoubtedly owned.

Susanna, on her way back to the ballroom, was aware of his close scrutiny. She had seen him once or twice during the evening and his appearance had intrigued her. One of the other companions, to whom she had chatted while the musicians were playing and their charges were enjoying themselves in the dance, had told her who he was and that he was nicknamed the Wolf.

She thought that the name suited him. He was tall, with broad shoulders, a trim waist and narrow hips—in that, he was like many of the younger men present. But few had a face such as his. It was, she thought, a lived-in face, still tanned from the Indian sun, with a dominant jutting nose, a strong chin, a long firm mouth— and the coldest grey eyes which she had ever seen. His hair was jet-black, already slightly silvered although he was still in his early thirties.

Susanna had read that wolves bayed at the moon and that they were merciless with their prey. Well, the merciless bit fitted his face, so perhaps he bayed at the moon as well—although she couldn't imagine it.

Her mouth turned up at the corners as she thought this and the action transformed her own apparently undistinguished face, giving it both charm and character, which Ben Wolfe registered for a fleeting moment before she passed him.

So that was the young woman who was going to revive Babbacombe's flagging fortunes. He had seen prettier, but then, money gilded everything, even looks, as he knew only too well. He laughed soundlessly to himself. Oh, but Amelia Western's fortune was never going to gild Lord Babbacombe's empty coffers—as he would soon find out.

If Susanna could have read Ben Wolfe's most secret thoughts she would have known exactly how accurate his nickname was and how much he was truly to be feared. As it was she returned to the ballroom feeling, not for the first time, cheated of life: a duenna soon to

reach her last prayers, doomed to spinsterhood because
of the callous behaviour of a careless young man.

Francis Sylvester had never returned to England. He
had taken up residence in Naples and seemed set to stay
there for life.

Susanna shivered, but not with cold. She wanted to
be a child again, home in bed, all her life before her.
After she had been jilted, everyone had praised her
coolness, the courage with which she had faced life, but
once she had ceased to be a nine days' wonder she had
been forgotten. When Miss Stanton died and she had
returned to society as Amelia Western's companion,
there were few who remembered her.

She was perpetually doomed to sit at the back of the
room, unconsidered and overlooked. She had visited her
old home, but her mother and stepfather had made it
plain that they had no wish for her company, even
though the scandal surrounding her was long dead.
There was no place for her there, now.

'You're quiet tonight, Miss Beverly, are you feeling
a trifle overset?' asked one of her fellow companions
kindly.

'Oh, no,' replied Susanna briskly. She had made a
resolution long ago never to repine, always to put a
brave face on things. 'It's just that, sometimes, one does
not feel in the mood for idle chatter.'

'I know that feeling,' said her friend softly. 'You
would prefer a quiet room and a good book, no doubt,
to being here.'

And someone kind and charming to dance with,
thought Susanna rebelliously, not simply to sit mum-
chance and watch other young women dance with kind
and charming young men.

But she said nothing, merely smiled and watched Ben

Wolfe bearded again by Lady Leominster and handed over to Charlotte Cavender, one of the Season's crop of young beauties and young heiresses. For a big man who was rumoured to have few social graces he was a good dancer, remarkably light on his feet—as so many big men were, Susanna had already noticed.

She sometimes thought it a pity that her common sense, her understanding of the world and men and women, honed by her opportunities for ceaseless observation would never be put to good use.

Stop that! she told herself sternly, just at the moment that the patterns of the dance brought Ben Wolfe swinging past her. To her astonishment, he gave her a nod of the head and a small secret smile.

Now, whatever could that mean?

Probably nothing at all. He must have meant it for his partner, but she had gone by him before she had had time to receive it. Susanna watched him disappear into the crowd of dancers, and then she never saw him again.

It was a trick of the light, perhaps, or of her own brain which was demanding that someone acknowledge that she still lived other than as an appendage to Amelia, who, having been proposed to by young Darlington, would shortly not be needing her services any more.

Which would mean turning up at Miss Shanks's Employment Bureau off Oxford Street to discover whether she had any suitable posts as governess, companion or duenna for which she might apply.

The prospect did not appeal.

Now, if only she were a young man, similarly placed, there were a thousand things she could do. Ship herself off to India, perhaps, and make a fortune—like Ben Wolfe, for example.

Drat the man! Why was he haunting her? She had
never looked at a man other than in loathing since Francis's betrayal and now she could not stop thinking about
someone who, rumour said, was even more dubious
than Francis.

And he wasn't even good-looking and she hadn't so
much as spoken to him! She must be going mad with
boredom—yes, that was it.

Fortunately, at this point, Amelia returned and said
excitedly, 'Oh, Miss Beverly, I feel so happy now that
George has finally proposed. It will mean that once I'm
married I shall be my own mistress, do as I please, go
where I wish, and not be everlastingly told how a young
lady ought to behave.'

Susanna could not prevent herself from saying, 'You
are not worried, then, that *George* might demand some
say in where you go and what you do?'

'Oh, no.' Amelia was all charming eagerness. 'By no
means. We have already agreed that we shall live our
own lives—particularly after I have provided him with
an heir. That is understood these days, is it not?'

And all this worldly wisdom between future husband
and wife as to their married life had been agreed in less
than an hour after the proposal!

'Of course,' said Amelia. 'It will mean that I shall
not be needing a duenna after the wedding ceremony.
But then, you knew that would be the case when you
undertook the post. It's what duennas must expect,
George says.'

Amelia's pretty face was all aglow at the prospect of
the delights of being a married woman. She was a little
surprised that Susanna wasn't sharing her pleasure.

'He's promised to drive me in the Park tomorrow and
he's going to insist to Mama that I go without you now

that it's understood that we are to marry. You can have the afternoon off to look for a post, George says. He's very considerate that way.'

Susanna could have thought of another word to describe him, but decided not to say it.

'If your mama agrees,' she said.

'Oh, of course she will,' exclaimed Amelia. 'Why ever not?'

And, of course, Mrs. Western did.

She also agreed with her daughter that Susanna should—as a great concession—take the afternoon off to visit Miss Shanks about another post. 'I would not like you to think us inconsiderate,' she finished.

She must have been talking to George Darlington was Susanna's sardonic inward comment. But, again, she said nothing, which was the common fate of duennas, she had discovered, when faced with the unacceptable and the impossibility of remarking on it.

Fortunately for both Amelia and Susanna the afternoon was a fine one. The sun was out, but it was not impossibly hot, and after Susanna had seen that Amelia was as spick and span as a young engaged girl ought to be, she dressed herself in her most dull and proper outfit in order to impress Miss Shanks with her severe suitability and set off for Oxford Street—on her own.

It never failed to amuse her that although Amelia, only a few years younger than herself, was never allowed to go out without someone accompanying her, it was always assumed that it was perfectly safe for Susanna to do so. Who, indeed, would wish to assault a plainish and badly dressed young woman who was visibly too old for a nighthouse and too poor to be kidnapped for her inheritance?

So it was that, enjoying the fine afternoon, the passing show and the freedom from needing to accommodate herself to the whims of others, Susanna almost skipped along with no thought as to her safety or otherwise.

Nor did she notice when she had reached Oxford Street that she had been followed from Piccadilly by a closed carriage driven at a slow speed and with two burly men inside, so that when she turned into the small side street and the carriage and men followed her, she thought nothing of it until one of the men, looking around him to see that no one was about, acted violently and immediately.

He caught Susanna from behind, threw a blanket over her head and, helped by his companion, bundled her into the carriage, which drove off at twice its previous speed in the direction of the Great North Road.

Chapter Two

Susanna started to scream—and then changed her mind. She only knew that she was inside a carriage and had been snatched off the street by two men. Best, perhaps, not to provoke them. She was about to try to remove the restraining blanket from her head when one of the men removed it for her.

She found herself inside a luxuriously appointed chaise whose window blinds were down so that she had no notion of where she was, or where she might be going. Facing her, on the opposite seat, were two large men, both well dressed, not at all like the kind of persons one might think went about kidnapping young women.

She said, trying not to let her voice betray her fear, 'Let me out, at once! At once, do you hear me! I cannot imagine why you should wish to kidnap me. There must be some mistake.'

The larger of the two men shook his head. 'No mistake, Miss Western. We had express orders to kidnap you and no one else. And there is no need to be frightened. No harm will come to you. I do assure you.'

Somehow the fact that he was well dressed and decently spoken made the whole business worse. And what did he mean by calling her Miss Western?

Her fright as well as her anger now plain in her voice Susanna exclaimed, 'You are quite mistaken. I am not Miss Western, so you may let me out at once. In any case, why should you wish to kidnap Miss Western?'

'Come, come, missy,' said the second man, whose speech was coarser and more familiar than that of the first, 'Don't waste your time trying to flummox us. Sit back and enjoy the ride. This 'ere carriage 'as the finest springs on the market.'

Susanna's voice soared. 'Enjoy the ride, indeed! I can't see a thing, and I have urgent business to attend to this afternoon. You have made a dreadful mistake, but if you let me go at once I shall not inform the Runners of what you have done, which I promise you I surely will once I am free again.'

Number One drawled, 'That's enough. You're a lively piece and no mistake, but we have a job to do and no tricks of yours will prevent us from doing it, so my advice to you is to behave yourself.'

'Indeed I won't!' Susanna leaned forward and began to tug at the window blind with one hand whilst trying to open the carriage door with the other. 'I have no intention of behaving myself,' she shouted at him as he caught her round the waist and pulled her back into her seat.

He laughed and said, rueful admiration written on his face, 'Oh, my employer is going to enjoy taming your spirit, I'm sure, but I haven't time to argue with you. I shall have to tie your hands if you continue to try to escape. Sit quiet and do as you're bid without any more nonsense, or I'll tie your ankles together and gag you as well. Even if I was ordered to handle you gently, you're leaving me no choice.'

He spoke quietly, even deferentially to her, but Susanna had no doubt that he would carry out his threats. She sank sullenly back into her seat and tried to put a brave face on things.

They thought that she was Amelia—if so, the reason why they would want to kidnap her was plain. Amelia Western was a noted heiress and it would not be the first time that a man wanting money had carried off an heiress and married her. It was a risky business since the penalty for such an act was death or transportation if the parents or guardians of the girl pursued the matter. Some did not, preferring to accept the forced marriage, if the man were reasonably respectable, rather than have the girl's reputation destroyed.

Equally plainly they had mistaken her for Amelia— and how they had come to do so was a mystery. A further mystery was who could Amelia have possibly met in the recent past who was capable of carrying out such a criminal act? None of the men who had surrounded her since her entrance into society seemed likely candidates—or had Amelia been privately meeting an unknown lover and they had arranged this between them?

If so, why had she been snatched off the street? For, if Amelia had been conspiring with someone, it would have been simpler for her to have manufactured some excuse to meet him in secret to save him from risking exposure by kidnapping her in broad daylight.

Not that any of this speculation was of the slightest use when each yard the chaise travelled was carrying her further away from Oxford Street, Piccadilly and her temporary home there, and into the unknown.

And what in the world would be awaiting her at her journey's end?

She was not to know for some time. They changed horses at a posthouse on the edge of London where Number One put a hand over her mouth to prevent her from calling for help while Number Two made all the necessary arrangements at their stop—which included taking on board a hamper of food.

Number One unpacked the hamper and offered her a cooked chicken leg, which she refused indignantly.

'Don't like chicken, eh? How about this, then?' and he held out a ham sandwich. She shook her head so he gifted Number Two with the chicken and the sandwich before rummaging around in the hamper and fishing out of it a roll filled with cold roast beef, saying, 'Beef, perhaps?'

She waved it away with as much hauteur as she could summon, announcing rebelliously, 'I don't want to eat. Under the circumstances it would choke me.'

'Suit yourself, my dear. No skin off my nose. More for us, eh, Tozzy? My employer will be most disappointed. He particularly wanted you to be properly fed on the way home.'

'How very gracious of him,' Susanna snapped back. 'Even more gracious of you if you turned the chaise round and took me back to Oxford Street.'

'Can't do that, I'm afraid,' said Number One indistinctly since his mouth was full of the beef sandwich which she had rejected. 'How about some pound cake? No?'

It might be childish of her, but Susanna found that the only way to demonstrate her displeasure at what was happening to her was to turn her back on him and sniff loudly, like the cook in the Westerns' kitchen when something had happened to cause her aggravation—an event which occurred at least five times a day.

Eating over, silence fell.

Susanna resumed a more normal position, folded her arms, leaned back against the cushions and closed her eyes. She felt as exhausted as though she were a child again and had been running and jumping all afternoon with her cousin William—and whatever had happened to him? He had disappeared from her life when her mother had married again. And what a time to think of him!

The lack of light and the swaying of the chaise lulled her so that she was on the verge of dozing.

Number Two said softly to Number One, 'She's a good plucked 'un and no mistake. She'll be a match for 'im, that's for sure.'

'Oh, I doubt that very much,' yawned Number One. 'Never met anyone who was a match for him in all the years I've been with him. Pass a bottle of wine over, Tozzy, kidnapping's thirsty work.'

Even through her half-sleep Susanna heard what he said and was fired with indignation. Just let this journey be over so that she could tell their employer—whoever he might be—exactly what she thought of him for arranging a kidnapping at all, let alone one in which the wrong woman had been carried off!

Ben Wolfe was looking out of the window in the library of his great house in Buckinghamshire which had been known as The Den ever since six generations of Wolfes had lived there. Before that it had simply been called the Hall. It had been left derelict when his father had died and he had gone to India, but since his return he had spared no expense in returning it to its former glory.

He looked at his fob watch. If everything had gone as he had ordered—and he assumed that it had since Jess Fitzroy had never botched a job for him yet—it should not be long before the chaise turned into the sweep before the front of the house. He could then begin to take his revenge for the wrongs which had destroyed not only his family's wealth, but had driven his father into an early grave.

It was a pity that the girl was not particularly beautiful, but then, one could not have everything. He smiled as he thought of Babbacombe's anger when the splendid match for his son fell through and he was left penniless, ruin staring him in the face. He was absolutely sure that, even though he had carried their daughter off in order to marry her, the Westerns would find him an even more suitable husband for her than Darlington—once they had discovered the astonishing extent of his wealth and the Wychwood family's lack of it, that was, for he would take good care to let them know of it.

Even acquiring an Earl's title would not make up for that lack. Especially since someone as rich as Ben was—and with an old name into the bargain—would almost certainly be a candidate for a title of his own before very long.

Not that Ben cared about titles and all that flimflam, but the Westerns did.

He had just reached this point in his musings when the chaise turned into the sweep. As he had hoped, Jess had successfully carried out yet another task for him—and would be suitably rewarded. He had given orders for Miss Western, soon to be Mrs Ben Wolfe, to be taken initially to her suite of rooms on the first floor so that she might refresh herself after the journey.

After that she would be conducted to the Turkish drawing room—a salon designed and furnished by a seventeenth-century Wolfe who had been an Ambassador to that country—where the teaboard would be ready and where he would at last introduce himself to her.

As was his usual habit, he had planned everything carefully to the last detail so that nothing would go wrong and all would go right. Even the clothes he was wearing had been chosen with great care to give off the right aura of effortless self-command and good taste. They were neither careless nor were they dandified, but somewhere in between. His boots, whilst black and shiny, bore no gold tassels. His clothes had been cut for him by a tailor whose taste was impeccable—there were to be no wasp-waisted jackets or garish waistcoats for Mr Ben Wolfe.

He sat himself down to wait for Jess to report to him, after which he would visit the drawing room where Miss Western would be waiting for him.

Susanna stared numbly at the beautiful façade of The Den when a footman opened the chaise door and Number One helped her out. When she had first been kidnapped she had supposed that she might be taken off to some low nighthouse either in the Haymarket or London's East End. When, instead, they had obviously been driving into the country, she could form no idea of what her ultimate destination might be like.

Such splendour as Susanna saw all about her in the house and gardens awed her, and for the life of her she could not imagine why it had been necessary to carry

Amelia off and bring her here. Surely the owner of such magnificence would be able to court Amelia in proper form, with no need to treat her so cavalierly? And surely, also, the owner of it would be shocked to learn that he had merely acquired a plain and poverty-stricken duenna and not the wealthy heiress she had been guarding for the past half-year.

When she walked up the steps to the double doors held open by splendidly liveried footmen she found herself shuddering slightly, not from cold or fright, but for some reason which passed her understanding. It was as though, once she walked through them, she knew that, somehow, she would find herself in a totally new world, where nothing that had happened to her in the past mattered, only what would happen in the future.

And then this sensation disappeared as though it had never been and she was plain-spoken, downright, sane and sensible Miss Susanna Beverly again, who never suffered from whim-whams or premonitions and was about to give a piece of her mind to the fool or knave who had caused her to be kidnapped.

But not yet. She had to endure a fluttering little maid and a pleasant middle-aged woman who led her upstairs to a suite of rooms so beautiful and grand that she was overset all over again. Indeed, the splendours she saw all about her temporarily silenced her so that she did not complain of her mistreatment to the women even when they called her Miss Western and tried to persuade her to change into the beautiful garments laid out on the bed.

She shook her head in refusal dazedly, but she did use the other facilities offered her—to put it delicately—and finally washed herself and allowed her hair to be ordered a little by the maid.

Then she was taken downstairs by the motherly body into a drawing room which was even grander than the upstairs rooms, where she was offered a seat and tea, which she also refused. When the motherly body, shaking her head a little at her silence, retreated, she sat down at last—to stare at a wall full of beautiful paintings and prints of a foreign civilisation such as she had never seen before.

Outside the sun was shining. In the distance a fountain was playing. Standing in the window through which she was looking was a new pianoforte. Objects of great beauty and vertu surrounded her. It would almost be like living in a rare and well-arranged museum to take up residence here, she thought in confusion.

And then the double doors were thrown open, and a man walked in.

A man who was her captor—and he was, of all people, Mr Ben Wolfe looking his most wolfish.

Mr Ben Wolfe, who had nodded and smiled at her at Lady Leominster's ball.

This must, Susanna decided, be a nightmare. She would shortly wake up to find herself safely back in bed in the Westerns' Piccadilly home. Except that everything about her seemed as sharp and well defined as objects are in real life, not at all cloudy and shifting like those in a dream. Only Mr Ben Wolfe's presence partook of the dream.

And if he were truly here, in this disturbing and unreal present, then she would give him as short shrift as she was capable of offering in her unfortunate position. She could form no notion at all of why he had had her kidnapped or why he was bowing and smiling at her in a manner he doubtless considered ingratiating.

Well, she would not be ingratiated, not she! He could

go straight to the devil and ingratiate himself with him if he could. She would demand to be sent straight back home, at once, on the instant…

Except, except…it was already late afternoon. There was no way in which she could be returned before nightfall and offer any reasonable explanation of where she had been and what she had been doing. Indeed, by now, her absence would already have been discovered.

If anything, this dreadful thought inflamed her the further. So she said nothing, merely stared at Mr Ben Wolfe, who was bowing low to her. That over, he motioned her to a seat before a low table on which a tea-board was set out, saying, 'Pray be seated, Miss Western. You are doubtless wondering why you are here. May I say that I intend you no harm. Quite the contrary.'

It was the first time she had heard him speak. He had a deep gravel voice, eminently suited to his harsh features. Susanna's first impulse was to inform him immediately that he was much mistaken: she was not Miss Western, his hired villains having carried off the wrong woman.

She wondered briefly why Amelia was the right woman. For what purpose would *she* have been brought here? She made an instant and daring decision: she would not tell him straight away that she was not Amelia, and then only after she had discovered what his wicked game was. It would be a pleasure to wrongfoot him.

Aloud she said, 'No, I will not be seated. And I do so hope, Mr Ben Wolfe—you are Mr Ben Wolfe, are you not?—that you have a satisfactory explanation for my forced presence here.'

He smiled at her, displaying strong white teeth—all

the better to eat you with, my dear, being Susanna's
inward response to *that* for was he not behaving exactly
like the wolf whose name he bore in the fairy tale *Red
Riding Hood*?

Mr Ben Wolfe, on the other hand, evidently thought
that he was the good fairy in *Cinderella*, murmuring in
a kind voice, 'Do not be frightened. Miss Western. My
intentions towards you are strictly honourable, I do assure you. As for my reasons for bringing you here thus
abruptly, you will forgive me if I leave any necessary
explanation for them until later.'

'No, indeed, I do not forgive you at all. I don't believe in your so-called honourable intentions; I have no
notion of whether you intend to wed me or bed me. Or
neither. I do so hope it's neither. I should like very
much to return home untouched—and as soon as possible.'

His smile this time was rueful. 'No, I'm afraid I can't
allow that, Miss Western. You see, I wish to marry you,
to make you the wife of one of the richest men in England instead of one of the poorest. I'm sure, on mature
and rational consideration, you—and your family—
would prefer that.'

Susanna stared at all six foot one of masculine bra-
vura, superbly turned out from the top of his glossy
black head to the tips of his glossy black boots.

'Then, in the name of wonder, Mr Benjamin Wolfe,
why did you not approach my parents in proper form
and make an honourable offer in an honourable fashion
instead of having me carried off, hugger-mugger, like a
parcel from the post office?'

She was beginning to enjoy herself, hugging gleefully
to her bosom the knowledge that he was not talking to
his proposed forced bride at all but to her unconsidered

and poverty-stricken governess. He evidently believed her to be Amelia and had no suspicion that he was mistaken. The longer she continued to deceive him, the more her pleasure grew.

On the other hand, by the looks of him he had a fine and wilful temper, which offered her the problem of how he would react when she finally enlightened him as to her true identity. But that could wait. Susanna had endured her disastrous fall into penury by living only for the moment and ignoring the future. What will come, would come, being her motto.

Mr Ben Wolfe bowed to her again. 'My dear girl, I have already informed you that I have my reasons and will reveal them to you on a suitable occasion. That occasion is not now. Now is the time for us to come to know one another better. To that end, pray pour us some tea before it grows cold. We shall both feel better for it.'

'There are only two things wrong with your last remark, Mr Ben Wolfe,' returned Susanna, all sweetness and light. 'The first is that I have no wish to know you any better—quite the contrary. The second is that I have no wish either to pour you tea, or drink it myself—*I* should certainly not feel any better for it. A fast postchaise and an immediate return to London are the only requests I have to make of you.'

They were standing at some distance apart, for Mr Ben Wolfe had entered with no immediate desire to frighten his captive. On the other hand, he had expected to meet a young girl whom he could easily control by the gentlest of means. Instead, he was confronted with a talkative, self-possessed creature, older than her eighteen years in her command of language, who was evidently going to take a deal of coaxing before she agreed to become Mrs. Ben Wolfe without making overmuch fuss.

He decided to continue being agreeable and charming, praying that his patience would not run out. 'I regret,' he told her, bowing, 'that is one of the few requests which you might make of me which I must refuse. My plans for you involve you remaining here for the time being. Later, perhaps.'

'Later will not do at all!' said Susanna, who wished most heartily that he would stop bowing at her. Most unsuitable when all he did was contradict her. 'I have my reputation to consider.'

Mr Ben Wolfe suddenly overwhelmed her with what she could only consider was the most inappropriate gallantry, all things considered. 'No need to trouble yourself about that. I shall take the greatest care of you.'

'Indeed? I am pleased to hear it—but I am a little at a loss to grasp the finer details of that statement. I ask you again do you intend to wed me—or to bed me?'

This unbecoming frankness from a single female of gentle nurture almost overset Ben Wolfe. Nothing had prepared him for it. Might it not, he momentarily considered, have been more useful for him to have been equally as frank with her from the beginning of this interview?

No matter. He smiled, and if the smile was a trifle strained, which it was, then damn him, thought Susanna uncharitably, it is all he deserves.

'Oh, my intentions are quite honourable. I mean to marry you and to that end I have already procured a special licence from the Archbishop of Canterbury himself.'

Marriage! He proposed to marry her—or rather Amelia. In the cat-and-mouse game she was playing with him Susanna had almost forgotten that she was not the target of Mr Ben Wolfe's plans. For a moment she considered enlightening him immediately, but he deserved to live in his fool's paradise a little longer, for was there not an interesting reply which she could make to his last confident declaration?

'You do surprise me, sir. First of all, you seem to forget that you have not yet asked me whether I wish to marry you and, all things considered, I'm sure that I don't; secondly, aren't you forgetting that I am already betrothed to George Darlington?'

'No, indeed—for that is precisely why you are here.'

His eyes gleamed as he came out with this, and the look he gave her was so predatory that Susanna shuddered. She was playing with a tiger. A tiger who had intended to kidnap an innocent young girl and force her to marry him in order, apparently, to prevent her from marrying George, Viscount Darlington.

Now Susanna did not like George Darlington and, by the look on his face when he had uttered his name, neither, for some reason, did Ben Wolfe, but she didn't think that he deserved to be treated quite so scurvily as to lose his proposed bride, and when she had finally confessed who she truly was she would so inform her captor.

If he was prepared to let her get a word in edgeways, that was—for she was beginning to understand that Mr Ben Wolfe in a thwarted rage might be a very formidable creature, indeed.

Unconsciously they had moved closer and closer together so that, when Susanna echoed him again by murmuring 'By saying "Precisely why you are here", you mean—I take it—that you have kidnapped me in order to thwart George Darlington by depriving him of his bride—and her money,' he bent down to take her hand, saying,

'Yes—and you are a clever child to have worked that out so quickly. I think that I may be gaining a real prize in marrying you, Miss Western.'

Susanna smiled up into his inclined face. 'Oh, I think not, Mr Ben Wolfe. All of this would be very fine if I *were* Amelia Western but, seeing that I am not, you have given yourself a great deal of trouble for exactly nothing.

'Your hirelings have only succeeded in kidnapping not Miss Western, but her poverty-stricken nothing of a governess, Susanna Beverly, who possesses no fortune and no reputation, either. By carrying me off by mistake you have destroyed the last remnants of *that* for good— and gained only frustration for yourself.'

His response to this bold and truthful declaration was to smile down at her and say gently, 'Well tried, my dear. You surely don't expect me to believe that Banbury tale!'

Really! He was being as impossibly stupid as his two hired bravos—which was not his reputation at all.

'Of course I do—for that is the truth. I told those two bruisers of yours that they had snatched the wrong woman—but would they listen to me? Oh, no, not they!—and now you are as bad as they were.'

His face proclaimed his disbelief. She had carried being Amelia off so well that she risked being stuck with her false identity, if not for life, for the time being at least. So much for his immediately exploding into anger when she made her belated revelation!

Instead it was she who stamped her foot. 'Of course I'm not Amelia. Do I look like a simple-minded eighteen-year-old? Do I speak like one? Come to your senses, sir, if you have any, which I beg leave to doubt on the evidence of what I have seen of you so far. It is time that you recognised that you have organised the kidnapping of the wrong woman and are now unlikely to carry off the right one, for once I am free again I shall proclaim your villainy to the world. The punishment for kidnapping an heiress is either death or transportation. I have no notion what the penalty is for a mistaken kidnapping, but it ought to be pretty severe, don't you think? Unless, of course, you could manage to get it lessened on the grounds of your insanity.'

Susanna's transformation from a reasonably spoken young woman of good birth into a flaming virago was a complete one—inspired by the fear that, will she, nil she, having been kidnapped by mistake she was going to find herself married by mistake as well!

Ben Wolfe's face changed, became thunderous. He controlled himself with difficulty, and murmured through his teeth, 'Tell me, madam, were you playing with me then—or now? Was Amelia Western the pretence, or Susanna Beverly? Answer me.'

'I have already answered you. I am Susanna Beverly and therefore nothing to your purpose at all.'

The look he gave her would have stopped the late Emperor of France in his tracks it was so inimical, so truly wolf-like as he barked out, 'And how do I know that that *is* the truth? I assure you that you look and sound like no duenna I have ever had the misfortune to encounter. You are far too young to begin with. No, I fear that this is but a clever ploy to persuade me to let you go.'

'Well, I assure you that I don't find *you* clever at all. Quite the contrary,' exclaimed Susanna, exasperation plain in her voice. 'Call in that big man of yours and he will inform you that from the moment he threw me into your carriage I never stopped trying to tell him that he had carried off the wrong woman.'

Ben Wolfe knew at once that, whoever she was, there was no intimidating her—short of silencing her by throttling her—and he was not quite ready to do that, although heaven knew, if she taunted him much more, he might lose his self-control and have at her.

Choosing his words carefully, he said, 'Let us sit down, enjoy a cup of tea and talk this matter over quietly and rationally.'

Biting each word out as coldly as she could, Susanna said, 'If you offer me a cup of tea again, Mr Ben Wolfe, I shall scream!'

His answer was, oddly enough, to throw his head back and laugh. 'Well, I don't fancy tea, either. Would a glass of Madeira tempt you at all?'

'It might tempt me, but I shan't fall. A wise friend of mine once said that an offer of a glass of Madeira from a gentleman when you were alone with him was the first step on the road to ruin, so thank you, no.'

'Very prudent of you, I'm sure. Although, if you are Miss Western, you may be certain that I shall not attempt to ruin you. As I said earlier, my intentions towards you—or her—are strictly honourable. I intend to marry you—or her.'

'But since I am Miss Beverly, what will be your intentions towards *me*? Seeing that, by your reckless act, I shall have been irrevocably ruined?'

Before he could answer, Susanna added quickly, 'What I am at a loss to understand, Mr Wolfe, is how you came to mistake me for her. We are not at all alike. How did you discover who I was—or rather, who you thought I was?'

'Oh, that is not difficult to explain,' he returned, although for the first time an element of doubt had crept into his voice. 'At my express wish you were pointed out to me by Lady Leominster herself on the occasion of her grand ball the other evening. You were standing next to George Darlington at the time.'

'Was I, indeed? On the other side of the room? With another woman on his other hand?'

'Does that matter? But, yes—or so I seem to remember.'

Susanna began to laugh. 'Oh, it matters very much. One thing I know of Lady Leominster, but not many do, is that she cannot distinguish between her right or her left. Be certain, Mr Wolfe, that you have indeed carried off the duenna and not her charge. You should have asked to be introduced to Miss Western—but you had no wish to do that, did you? It would have saved you a deal of trouble and no mistake.'

Ben Wolfe, his mind whirling, tried to remember the exact circumstances in which he had seen the supposed Miss Western. Yes, it had been as she said. George Darlington had been standing between two women, and Lady Leominster had pointed out the wrong one—if the woman before him was telling the truth.

He smothered an oath. Her proud defiance was beginning to work on him—and had she not earlier told him to ask his 'big man' whom she had claimed to be when they had first captured her?

'For heaven's sake, woman,' he exclaimed, being coarse and abrupt with her for the first time now that it began to appear that she really might be only the duenna of his intended prey, 'sit down, do, don't stand there like Nemesis in person, and I'll send for Jess Fitzroy and question him. But that doesn't mean that I accept your changed story.'

'Pray do,' replied Susanna, whose legs were beginning to fail her and who badly needed the relief and comfort of one of the room's many comfortable chairs, 'and I will do as you ask. As a great concession, I might even drink some of the tea which you keep offering me.'

'Oh, damn the tea,' half-snarled Ben Wolfe before going to the door, summoning a footman and bidding him to bring Fitzroy and Tozzy to him at the double.

'By the way, before the footman leaves,' carolled Susanna, who was beginning to enjoy herself in a manic kind of way, very like someone embracing ruin because it was inevitable rather than trying to repel it, 'tell him to bring the reticule which flew from my hand on to the floor after I was dragged into the chaise. There is something in it which might help you to make up your mind about me.'

'Oh, I've already done that,' ground out Ben Wolfe through gritted teeth as he handed her a cup of tea. 'A more noisy and talkative shrew it has seldom been my misfortune to meet.'

'Twice,' riposted Susanna, drinking tea with an air, 'you've already said that twice now—you earlier announced that you had a similar misfortune with duennas. When I was a little girl, my tutor told me to avoid such repetition in speech or writing. It is the mark of a careless mind he said.'

She drank a little more tea before assuring the smouldering man before her, 'Not surprising, though, seeing that your careless mind has secured you the wrong young woman. You would do well to be a little more careful in future.'

This was teasing the wolf whom Ben so greatly resembled with a vengeance but, seeing that she had so
little to lose, Susanna thought that she might as well
enjoy herself before the heavens fell in.

Afterwards! Well, afterwards was afterwards—and to
the devil with it.

Ben Wolfe, leaning against the wall as though he
needed its support, looked as though he were ready to
send her to the devil on the instant. He did not deign
to answer her because he was beginning to believe that
she wasn't Amelia Western, and that, for once, he had
made an unholy botch of things.

No, not for once—for the very first time. He had
always prided himself on his ability to plan matters so
meticulously that events always went exactly as he had
intended them to and he had built a massive fortune for
himself on that very basis.

The glare he gave Miss Who-ever-she-was was baleful in the extreme, but appeared to worry her not one
whit. There was a plate of macaroons on the teaboard
and Susanna began to devour them with a will. She
hadn't eaten since breakfast and all this untoward excitement was making her hungry.

It was thus Ben Wolfe who greeted the arrival of his
henchman with relief. Tozzy, the junior of the two, was
carrying a woman's reticule, a grin on his stupid face.
Fitzroy, more acute, knew at once that his employer was
in one of his rare, but legendary, tempers and assumed
the most serious expression he could.

'Is that your reticule?' demanded Ben of Susanna,
who was busy pouring herself another cup of tea. 'I
thought that you didn't care for tea,' he added accus-
ingly, mindful of her former refusals.

'Oh, it wasn't the tea I didn't care for,' Susanna told

him smugly, 'it was the company and the occasion on which I was drinking it which incurred my dislike. I'm much happier now,' she added untruthfully, 'and, yes, that is my reticule.'

'Then hand it to her, man,' roared Ben who, being gentleman enough, just, not to shout at Susanna, shouted at Tozzy instead.

Tozzy, having handed the reticule back to Susanna, opened his mouth to speak, but was forestalled by the beleaguered Ben saying to Fitzroy, 'Look here, Jess, Miss Who-ever-she-is says that when you picked her up in Oxford Street—'

'Kidnapped me,' corrected Susanna, who was now inspecting the contents of her little bag and smiling at them as she did so.

'You picked her up in Oxford Street,' repeated Ben through his excellent teeth, 'and she told you that she was not Miss Western. Is that true?'

Jess looked away from his employer before saying, 'Yes. I called her Miss Western and she immediately informed me that she was not.'

'And who did she say that she was?'

'She claimed to be Miss Western's duenna, Miss Beverly. But you had pointed her out to me as Miss Western yesterday in Hyde Park so I knew that she was only saying that in order to try to make me let her go. So I took no notice of her.'

'You took no notice of her,' said Ben, who found that he had recently acquired the distressing habit of repeating not only what he had said, but everything said to him. 'Didn't it occur to you to tell me that she had made such a claim?'

'Not exactly, no. You've never, to my knowledge, ever made such a mistake before—indeed, I can't re-

member you ever making a mistake of any kind in any
enterprise we've been engaged on, it's not your way,
not your way at all…'

'Jess!' said Ben awefully. 'Shut up, will you? Just
tell me this. Which do you think she is? She has, in the
last half-hour, claimed to be both Miss Western and
Miss Beverly.'

Jess was too fascinated to be tactful. 'Both? How
could she do that?'

'Easily,' said Ben. 'Damme, man. Answer the question.'

Jess looked Susanna up and down as though she were
a prize horse. 'Well,' he said doubtfully, 'she's only
supposed to be eighteen. I'd put her as a little older
than that. On the other hand, she claimed to be a duenna
and, in my experience, duennas are usually middle-
aged; she certainly doesn't resemble or behave like any
duenna I've ever met and—'

'Jess! Stop it. You're blithering. I know what duennas
look like. Give me a straight answer.'

'Wouldn't it be simpler if you listened to me?' Susanna was all helpfulness. 'Perhaps you could explain
why, if I'm Miss Western, heiress, I should be kidnapped outside an office for the placement of young
gentlewomen needing employment, i.e. Miss Shanks's
Employment Bureau, and carry its card in my reticule.
Look,' and she handed it to Ben Wolfe who stared at it
as though it were a grenade about to go off at any moment.

'She has a point,' observed Jess gloomily.

'Does that mean, yes, she's Miss Western or, no,
she's Miss Beverly?' snapped Ben, tossing Jess the
card.

'No, she's Miss Beverly.'

'God help me, I think so, too. You picked up the wrong woman.'

'Kidnapped her, on your orders, which he faithfully carried out,' interrupted Susanna, her mouth full of the last macaroon. 'You really can't pretend that you're not the one responsible for me being here.'

Master and man stared at one another.

'Apart from gagging her to stop her everlasting nagging, what the hell do we do now?' asked Mr Ben Wolfe of Mr Jess Fitzroy, who slowly shook his head.

Chapter Three

'Missing?' said Mrs Western to Amelia's maid, who had been sent to remind Miss Beverly that she should have been in attendance on Amelia at six of the clock precisely to see that she was turned out *à point* in order to attend the little supper party which the Earl, George's father, was giving for them at Babbacombe House that evening.

'She's not in her room, madam, and the housekeeper says that she went out early this afternoon, saying that it would not be long before she returned. She has not been seen since.'

'You visited her room, I collect. Was there any sign that she had intended to be away for some time?'

The maid shook her head. 'Not at all, madam. The ensemble which she proposed to wear this evening was laid out on her bed, together with her slippers, evening reticule and fan.'

Mrs Western heaved a great sigh. 'How provoking of her! You are sure that she is not in the house—hiding in the library, perhaps? She spends a great deal of time there which would be better spent with Miss Western.'

'I enquired of the librarian, madam, but she has not visited it today.'

'I should never have hired her—although, until now, she has carried out her duties well enough—but tigers do not change their spots…or do I mean leopards? What are you smiling at, Amelia?'

'It's leopards, mama, I'm sure—or so Miss Beverly always says. But it's no great thing that she's missing. I am to marry soon and shall not be needing a duenna—and in any case, young women about to be married are always allowed greater freedom than those who are not. We could let her go immediately. I, for one, shall not miss her.'

'Not until you're married,' moaned Mrs Western. 'We must be seen to do the right thing.'

She snapped her fingers at the maid. 'Keep a watch out for Miss Beverly and tell her to report to me the moment she returns—she cannot be long now, surely. Her absence is most inconvenient.'

The maid bobbed a curtsy and said, 'Yes, madam.' Later, after the maid had spoken to the housekeeper, they agreed with Mrs Western that the duenna would shortly turn up. But no, time wore on—the Westerns left for Babbacombe House and still the duenna had not reappeared.

'Run off with someone, no doubt,' offered Mr Western when they reached home again and she was still missing. 'If she's not back by morning, we'll inform the Runners of her absence—just in case something odd might have occurred.'

'Never mind that, Mr Western—whatever the circumstances, you will agree with me that she's to be turned away without a reference.'

'Indeed, my dear. Amelia is right. She no longer

needs a duenna for these last few weeks before she marries.'

Susanna was not to know—although she had already guessed—the manner in which her disappearance was treated by the Western family and the way in which it would complete the ruin which Francis Sylvester had begun.

While Mrs Western and Amelia were discussing her fate so callously, she was sitting alone before the now-empty teaboard, Ben Wolfe and his chief henchman having retreated to Ben's study in order to discuss how to extricate themselves from the quagmire into which they had fallen as a result of kidnapping the wrong woman.

Not, Susanna concluded, wondering whether to ring the bell and ask for something more to eat, that there was such a thing as the right woman where kidnapping was concerned! And why was Mr Wolfe so bent on depriving George Darlington of his bride? There was a fine puzzle for her to solve.

The secret little smile she gave when she thought of what the two men might be planning in order to repair their present unhappy situation was quite a naughty one.

I really should not be amused, she told herself severely, for I can think of no happy way out of this brouhaha for myself. On the other hand… She paused, and thought carefully for some minutes. On the other hand, I must admit that Ben Wolfe seems to be a man of great resourcefulness, but he will need all of that to disentangle himself from the spider's web which he has created.

She was not far wrong about Ben. Once out of the sound of Susanna's mocking voice, constantly reminding him of what a cake he had made of himself, he had recovered the cold-blooded and cold-hearted equanimity which had taken him from poverty to immense riches.

'Don't say anything, Jess,' he had commanded, his right hand raised, when they reached his study, a comfortable room that was all oak, leather and bookshelves. 'I freely acknowledge my error. I am entirely to blame, and conceit has been my undoing. You carried out my orders to the letter and the only thing I can fault you for is not reporting to me the lady's reaction when you kidnapped her. What I have to do now is save the situation from becoming even worse than it already is.

'I cannot allow this innocent young woman to suffer as a consequence of my folly, but how to rescue her poses a number of difficulties. If you have any suggestions to offer, pray make them now.'

He flung himself into a high-backed chair which stood before a large oak desk on which pens, papers, sand, sealing wax, rulers and a large ledger were carefully arranged. As elsewhere in the house the room was meticulously ordered, a monument to the care with which Ben Wolfe normally arranged his life and that of those around him.

Jess looked down at him, a rueful smile on his face. 'If I had a magic sentence which, once uttered, put all to rights again, then I would offer it to you,' he said. 'But for the life of me I cannot think what would mend matters—or, indeed, if they could be mended. The young woman is here, will be missed by her employers and will have no tale to offer them which would not end in ruining us all—including her.'

'Job,' said Ben bitterly. 'I might have known that you would be Job's comforter. One thing, she cannot stay here long, in a house of men, with no duenna for herself, so that must be the first remedy—but how?'

He leaned forward, his elbows on the desk, his eyes closed. Jess had seen him do this many times before when he was concentrating, so he remained as still and silent as he could.

Ben began by reproaching himself for his carelessness. The young woman, Susanna, had the right of it. But enough of that. He needed a duenna for the duenna. But who? And how? How much time passed as he cleared his mind of thought and waited for inspiration to strike he never knew.

He lifted his head, looked at Jess, and said, 'I have it. Celeste. I wonder that I did not think of her before.'

'Celeste?' asked Jess, puzzled.

'Yes. Celeste. Madame la Comtesse de Saulx who is living not two miles away and whose reputation is beyond reproach.'

'You mean the Frenchwoman who has rented the Hall outside Lavendon. She is the epitome of all that is proper,' returned Jess. 'I had no notion that you knew her.'

'I know her, and she is not French—although she sounds as though she is.'

'And you think that she would agree to help us?'

Ben smiled. He had never looked so wolfish. 'Oh, I think she might be persuaded.'

He did not say, I know that she will and for reasons which I cannot discuss with you—or anyone else. All that remained was for him to ride over to her home, Primrose Hall, and ask her to help him—and immediately.

Jess watched him as he rose, saying, 'Ask Nicholson to have my curricle and my best pair of chestnuts ready as soon as possible. I'll drive over immediately. It's only a short run and she can come back with me straight away. Tell the housekeeper to prepare another suite of rooms for her and for her maid—and possibly an attendant if she wishes to stay overnight. I doubt that she will, but one never knows.

'In her hands, Miss Beverly's reputation should be quite safe.'

He bounded out of the room, all his usual violent energy restored.

Jess called after him, 'And I am to tell Miss Beverly of what you are planning?'

'You are to tell Miss Beverly nothing of that. Tell Mrs Ashton to attend on her and suggest that she goes to her room, change into the clothing provided for her, and be ready to eat an early supper with you, myself, and at least one other guest. That is all.'

Jess watched him go. Now, how in the world had he come to know Madame de Saulx? And know her well enough to demand such a favour of her? She was too old, surely, to be, or have been, his mistress; in any case, she was widely known for her virtue as well as her strong sense of propriety.

He shook his head. He had known and worked for Ben Wolfe for many years—but he still had no real notion of the true man he was, or of the many secret affairs which his employer chose to keep to himself.

Ben himself, cursing his folly, made short work of his visit to Madame de Saulx. He drove at a pace which, although it could not exactly be described as *ventre à terre*, was near to it. He knew that *Madame* would receive him immediately, not keep him waiting, at whatever hour he chose to arrive.

He was shown into a drawing room which already bore the marks of *Madame*'s impeccable taste, and it was not long before she appeared. She was in her middle fifties, was tall beyond the common height of women, and bore the remains of a great beauty. She was dressed modestly, although her turnout had that air of *je ne sais quoi* which most Frenchwomen of noble birth possessed.

Her shrewdness was demonstrated immediately when, after Ben had performed the common courtesies which a gentleman owed to the lady whom he was visiting, she said gently, 'Pray, sit down. I know by your face that you must have come on some matter of great moment, but we can still discuss it in comfort. I have no mind to have you pacing my drawing room like a caged tiger!'

Ben gave a short laugh and did as he was bid. 'How well you know me! I have come, as you have doubtless guessed, to ask a great favour of you.'

'You may ask as many favours of me as you please, great or small. Nothing I can do for you could equal the one great favour you did for me.'

'You exaggerate, but let me come to the meat of my problem as soon as may be,' and he immediately began to tell her the sad tale of how he had, by chance, come to kidnap the wrong woman, and how urgently he needed her assistance to save three reputations.

'*Bien sûr,*' she said, her voice and manner grave, 'that I shall certainly not ask you why you chose to do such a thing—but I can guess. What do you propose that will mend matters?'

'That you will come immediately to The Den to be introduced to Miss Susanna Beverly as a French noblewoman of impeccable birth, who is ready to assist her in every way after hearing of the sad mischance which I have so carelessly brought about. I have concocted an explanation which I believe will do the trick of allowing her to retain her reputation and which will also disassociate her completely from any connection with me—that is, if you agree to it.

'It goes as follows. You were being driven along Oxford Street when you saw this young gentlewoman overcome by faintness. Of your infinite compassion you stopped, assisted her into your chaise and took care of her. She did not recover for some time and, when she did, she was temporarily afflicted with a distressing loss of memory. Again, of your compassion, you drove her to your *pied à terre* in Stanhope Street near Regent's Park, where you cared for her until her memory returned. After which you immediately arranged to restore her to the family by whom she is at present employed.'

Madame clapped her hands together gently.

'Excellent. You should be writing plays for Drury Lane! I shall, of course, need to drive the young woman secretly back to London and make it known that I had recently arrived there in order to take part in the Season. I shall be happy to oblige you, seeing that I need to visit the capital in order to renew my wardrobe and visit a few old friends.'

'Excellent,' echoed Ben, looking happy for the first time for several hours. 'All that remains is for you to meet Miss Beverly as soon as possible. She seems a most respectable young woman, except that she said something rather odd to me, to the effect that, if it were known that she had apparently run off with me, it would finally destroy her reputation which was damaged already. Have you heard of any scandal relating to a young woman of that name? If you have, I think that you ought to tell me. It would be as well to know exactly where we stand.'

'Very true,' nodded *Madame* gravely. 'You and I, of all people, know the necessity of guarding our backs. The name is a little familiar—but I will try to gain her confidence this evening; if anything important crops up, I shall not hesitate to inform you.'

She smiled and said after a fashion as cool as his, 'By the by, I must congratulate you on your choice of words to describe the criminal act which you have just committed! To describe an innocent young lady's forcible kidnapping as ''a sad mischance'' is a feat worthy of the late Dr Johnson himself!'

Ben's grin was somewhat shamefaced. 'You never spare me, *Madame*,' he told her.

'Indeed not. There ought to be someone in the world who is capable of compelling you to face the truth about yourself occasionally, *mon cher*.'

And so it was arranged. On the one hand, in London, Susanna's future was being busily destroyed whilst, in the country, a practised pair of conspirators were equally busily trying to rebuild it!

Chapter Four

Whilst Ben was occupying himself at Lavendon by covering up his blunder, Susanna, at the urgings of Mr Jess Fitzroy, allowed the housekeeper, Mrs Ashton, and the little maid to accompany her upstairs, bathe her, and dress her in the modish clothing which lay on the bed in her suite of rooms.

It was many years since she had worn anything so fine, so expensive and yet so ladylike. Looking in the long mirror, she saw herself transformed. Mrs Ashton who had been a lady's maid herself long ago, not only dressed her hair for her, but also applied a *soupçon* of rouge with a fine hare's-foot brush, despite Susanna exclaiming that she never used it.

'You are a little wan, my dear. The tiniest application of colour to your cheeks will soon remedy that. There—' and she swung Susanna towards the mirror again so that she could see for herself that the ravages of the afternoon had been repaired.

'Now, you must go downstairs,' said her new guardian. 'I understand that it will not be long before the Master returns and, shortly after that, dinner will be served. It will be at an odd hour, to be sure, but then,

Mr Wolfe has his own ways of going on—as you have doubtless discovered.'

Oh, yes, Miss Susanna Beverly had already discovered that! She arrived in the drawing room to find Mr Jess Fitzroy there, dressed in a superfine blue jacket, cream pantaloons and the most elegant evening slippers—to say nothing of an artistically tied cravat and suitably dishevelled hair in the latest fashion.

He bowed to her gracefully. 'Allow me to congratulate you on your appearance, Miss Beverly. Most fitting.'

'Fitting for what, Mr Fitzroy—to be kidnapped again? And maltreated into the bargain?'

He bowed again. 'I pray you, forgive me for that— but do admit…my unfortunate behaviour to you was based on a complete misunderstanding.'

'And am I to infer from that, that all would have been well if you had carried off Miss Western and not myself? If so, I wonder at your morality, sir, as well as your common sense.'

By Jove, Ben had been right. The woman had a tongue like a viper and did not hesitate to use it!

Nevertheless, Jess Fitzroy had the grace to look a trifle ashamed of himself before he muttered, 'Why, as to that, Miss Beverly, there are reasons—'

He got no further before Susanna exclaimed, 'Pray do not enlarge on them, sir, for I am sure that I should neither approve of them nor like them!'

Jess was saved from having to reply by the arrival of Ben Wolfe, with Celeste, Comtesse de Saulx, on his arm. Both of them were dressed in the latest stare of fashion appropriate to their sex and to their different ages.

Ben, indeed, had for once allowed his valet to do his

best for him—why, he did not know. It was not that he wished to attract Miss Susanna Beverly in any way, far from it, simply that he wished to reassure both the Comtesse and her as to his claims to respectability.

The Comtesse had not only acceded to his demand that she return to The Den with him immediately, but she had also had herself dressed for dinner with exemplary speed after her arrival there. Ben's valet had passed on to him the welcome news that Miss Beverly had joined Mr Fitzroy in the Turkish drawing room where they were awaiting his arrival.

At least the argumentative virago had had the grace to give way over something. Ben had not relished the thought of another slanging match occasioned by his unwanted guest refusing to oblige him by dining with him. Not only that, when he walked in, he saw immediately that she had also obliged him by assuming the clothes which she had earlier refused.

But that was not all that he saw—or experienced—either when she rose to greet him, or when he took her hand to kiss its back after the continental fashion of which he knew Madame la Comtesse would approve. For, seeing Susanna for the first time as a woman, and neither as an object destined to bring about his long-awaited revenge on the Wychwoods, nor as the wretched nuisance who had been carried off as the result of his own folly, had the oddest effect on him.

That indomitable spirit, which had allowed Susanna to overcome the series of disasters which had afflicted her since her father's death, shone through the envelope of flesh which clothed it, and, in doing so, touched Ben Wolfe's own proud and unyielding soul.

There was nothing of the flesh about this experience for either of them. It affected Ben the more strongly and immediately precisely because it was so different from anything he had ever known before. It was not Susanna's fine eyes, or her tender mouth, nor her carefully arranged and lustrous hair, or even the delicate figure revealed by the arts of a Parisian dressmaker, attractive though these were, which were having such a strong effect on him.

No, it was something more, something which passed his understanding and which made him see Susanna in a totally new light. And when he took her small hand in his to kiss the back of it, a shudder passed through both of them.

Susanna's eyes widened and she withdrew her hand as though it had been stung. Nevertheless, so instantaneous was their reaction that even the keen-eyed Comtesse did not notice that Ben Wolfe and the pretty young woman whom he was now presenting to her were sharing something which neither of them could explain.

Why meeting Ben Wolfe again after a short absence should affect her so differently and so profoundly from her first sight of him, Susanna did not know. Perhaps, she told herself, it was my anger at being so vilely mistreated on his orders which made my first reaction to him one of acute distaste. That, and the harsh manner in which we both attacked one another.

But I must not trust him until he has proved that he is worthy to be trusted—he and this *grande dame* who has sprung from nowhere and whose reputation for virtue is such that the whole world knows of it.

As though he had just read her mind, Ben said, 'Madame de Saulx has kindly consented to join with me in arranging that you shall suffer nothing from the mischance which has befallen you today. We shall speak of it later at our leisure, after we have enjoyed the ex-

cellent meal which the butler tells me the chef has prepared for us.'

Thus, she had no alternative but to fall in with his
wishes when Madame de Saulx said approvingly in her
prettily accented English, 'What a splendid notion, *cher*
Ben. I hope Miss Beverly will understand that all her
troubles are now over, and that she has nothing more
to fear.'

'Other than that when I *do* return to the Westerns,
whatever explanation we may offer them, they will almost certainly terminate my employment,' Susanna
could not prevent herself from saying.

'Oh, as to that, my dear young lady,' *Madame* reas-
sured her, 'you need have no fear. One way or another
you will be taken care of. It is the very least that Mr
Wolfe can do for you after causing you so much mental
and physical agony as a consequence of his foolishness.
Is not that so, *cher* Ben?'

Susanna was pleased to see that, for once, '*cher* Ben'
looked a trifle discomfited by this rebuke. Jess Fitzroy
even smiled a little at it, only to earn from *Madame* a
rebuke of his own. 'And you need not smirk so con-
descendingly at your employer, Mr Fitzroy, for your
own part in this unhappy business is not without its
share of blame.'

Bravo, *Madame*, was Susanna's inward comment,
even as the butler entered to inform them that dinner
was served, and Mr Fitzroy proceeded to offer her his
arm so that they might properly follow Madame la
Comtesse and Mr Wolfe into the dining room where
she might forget for a time her unfortunate predicament.

'Allow me, Miss Beverly,' said Ben, 'to inform you
at length of the measures which I have taken to explain

your strange disappearance from London earlier today.'

They were all back in the Turkish drawing room again; the inevitable teaboard before them. They had just enjoyed the excellent meal which Ben had promised them. During it they had spoken only of the lightest matters, such as the health of the present monarch; the latest scandal about that old and faded figure, the Prince Regent; of his equally faded and scandalous wife, Princess Caroline of Wales; the recent birth of the Princess Victoria and even, at *Madame*'s instigation, of the change in women's dress brought about by the slight lowering of the waistline.

'So there you have it, Miss Beverly,' said Ben, after he had finished outlining his plans for Susanna's immediate future. '*Madame* has agreed to be our saviour and we can but hope that you will approve of the arrangements which we have made to bring about such a happy outcome.'

'I am struck dumb by your ingenuity,' returned Susanna, 'and can only hope that it will impress the Westerns sufficiently to save me. Were anyone with a reputation less than that of *Madame*'s to sponsor me, I believe that the task might be difficult, nay, impossible, but, as it is—' she shrugged her shoulders '—I can only thank her for her kindness and condescension in offering to assist me at such short notice.'

Madame's glance for her was an approving one. 'Properly and graciously spoken,' she said, 'as I am sure Mr Wolfe will acknowledge.'

Ben put down a china teacup which was so small that his big hand dwarfed it. 'With one small rider,' he added. 'Much, I fear, depends on the fact that Miss Beverly's own reputation is a spotless one. I was a little perturbed by a statement which she made to me earlier this afternoon to the effect that she possessed neither fortune nor reputation, and that by carrying her off I had destroyed the last remnants of the latter. I wonder if you would care to enlarge on that, Miss Beverly, so that we might all know where we stand?'

The white smile which he offered Susanna as he asked his question had her mentally echoing Red Riding Hood again: Oh, Grandma, what big teeth you have! It was plain that little said or done escaped him, and although she had no wish to tell Ben Wolfe of all people her sad story, let alone two other strangers on whose charity she now depended, tell it she must.

What was it that her father had said to her when she was a child? 'Speak the truth and shame the devil, my dear.' Well, she would do exactly that.

Aloud, after a little hesitation, she said, 'The explanation for my remark is a simple one. I believe that what happened to me should cause no one to think any the worse of me, but the world chooses to believe quite otherwise. Four years ago I was jilted by Lord Sylvester. He was cruel enough to leave me waiting for him at the altar where I received, not my bridegroom, but a letter informing me that he no longer wished to marry me.

'You must all be aware of what such an action does to the reputation of a woman, however innocent she might be, and I was truly innocent—but I was ruined, none the less. No man wishes to marry a woman who has been jilted.'

Madame said thoughtfully. 'So, you are *that* Miss Beverly, the late William Beverly's only child and heiress. I did wonder if you might be, but I thought it would be considered tactless to question you on the matter if you proved not to be her.'

Ben Wolfe, however, leaned forward in his chair, intent it seemed, on quizzing her further.

'You say that you are employed by the Westerns as a duenna. I was out of England at the time and consequently knew nothing of the scandal which followed. But if you *are* the India merchant William Beverly's heiress, how is it that you have descended into becoming a duenna, a paid servant? He was as rich as Croesus, to my certain knowledge.'

However painful it might be to tell them more of her sad situation, Susanna had no alternative but to do so.

'And so I thought when he died, some twelve years before I was to have married Lord Sylvester. My mother married again, one Samuel Mitchell, soon after my father's death, but after I was jilted my stepfather informed me that, contrary to public—and my—belief, my father had died a ruined man, and he had been keeping me since my mother's marriage.

'It was, he said, he who was providing my ample dowry in the hope that I would make a good marriage. Now that my chance of making any sort of marriage had gone, he was no longer prepared either to keep me or to be responsible for my dowry. Consequently it was necessary for me to find employment.'

No one spoke for a moment. *Madame* said gently, '*En effet*, he turned you out?'

'I suppose you might say so.'

'Oh, I do say so.' It was not *Madame* who answered her, but Ben Wolfe, and the look he gave her was quite different from any he had offered her before. There was pity in it for the first time.

Damn his pity! She didn't want it, or anything else

from him—especially the odd sensations which she was feeling every time she looked at him.

'You were not to know,' she told him.

'No, but nor should I have treated you so harshly this afternoon—but, in fairness to myself you did, at first, lead me to think that you were Amelia Western, which made it difficult for me to believe that you were telling the truth when you finally claimed to be Susanna Beverly. My apology to you for carrying you off, and then vilifying you, may be late but, believe me, it is sincere.'

They might as well have been alone in the room, so intent was each on the other. His grey eyes were no longer cold, his harsh features had softened into a smile. Susanna found it difficult to offer him one back. What she did do was acknowledge to him her own complicity in creating the situation which had set them so distressfully at odds.

'I should not have claimed to be Miss Western,' she admitted, 'but your cavalier attitude towards me—and indirectly towards her—angered me beyond reason. I am still at a loss as to why you should plan to do anything so wicked as carry off a young girl in order to make her your forced wife.'

As she said this, Susanna registered that Madame la Comtesse de Saulx was nodding her elegant head in agreement.

'That is neither here, nor there,' riposted Ben loftily.

Rightly or wrongly, Susanna could not leave it at that. 'And do you still intend to kidnap poor Amelia? If so, then regardless of anything which is done to assist me, I must inform the Westerns—'

Ben said, his tone regretful, 'Alas, no, that plan has been thwarted forever by the mistake which I made in identifying the wrong woman. Miss Western has nothing further to fear from me. More than that I cannot promise.'

So he was still considering further action of a lawless kind and, judging by what he had said in their first furious interview, it must concern the Wychwoods. But this was no business of hers. She owed them nothing. Her one concern was that young and innocent—even if silly and selfish—Amelia Western should be protected from the predator named Ben Wolfe.

Something of her emotions showed on her face, or Ben Wolfe was mind reading, for he said gravely, 'What are you thinking of, Miss Beverly, that causes your smooth young brow to furrow and your eyes to harden as they examine me in my own drawing room?'

'That you are a ruthless man, Mr Wolfe, and that I should not like you for an enemy—and that once you have set out to perform some action, whether lawful or lawless you are not easily deterred from carrying it through.'

'Bravo, Miss Beverly!' exclaimed Madame de Saulx, 'our friend Ben Wolfe is often in need of hearing some plain speaking and in this case you are the right person to supply it!'

Susanna's eyes glowed with honest indignation. 'He is not my friend, *Madame*, and it was an ill day when he mistook me for another woman. I shall accept his help in restoring myself, unstained, to society again, for he owes me that favour, but afterwards I shall thank him, bid him goodbye and try to forget that I ever met him.'

This brave and spirited declaration was admired by all three of her hearers, including Ben Wolfe. *Madame* clapped her hands together, and Jess could not restrain himself from saying, 'Well spoken, Miss Beverly, but may I be excepted from the interdict which you have proclaimed against Mr Wolfe since I should so wish to meet you again under happier circumstances?'

He avoided looking at Ben as he came out with this small act of defiance. His reward for it came when Susanna, regarding him thoughtfully, said, 'So soon as I am settled in life again, Mr Fitzroy, you may call upon me. More than that I cannot say. I must remember that you were merely carrying out your employer's orders, and only those like myself who are in a similar subordinate position can sympathise with the necessity to do so in order to earn one's bread.'

'Earn one's bread!' exclaimed Ben sourly, glaring at Jess's peacock-like splendour. 'I pay him much more than that, I think, if he can turn himself out like a Bond Street dandy, ready to make eyes at any pretty woman.'

Jealous! thought *Madame*, he's jealous because Miss Beverly spoke kindly to his aide, but not to him. Whoever would have guessed it? Now, what does that tell me? She examined Ben with knowing eyes. That's the first time in our long acquaintance that I have ever known him display such an emotion or care two pins about what any woman thought of him—or any man, either. Always excepting myself, that is.

Goodness, does that mean that he thinks of me as pretty? was Susanna's response. And could he possibly have been hurt because I spoke kindly to Mr Fitzroy and not to him?

Ben, indeed, scarcely knew what to think of himself. He waved a hand at Jess who opened his mouth to answer him. 'No,' he said, 'forgive me. I have made enough mistakes, as well as one unwanted enemy today, without my being graceless to my most faithful friend—

for that, Miss Beverly,' he added, turning to her, 'is how I think of Jess.'

Jess, surprised by this unwonted declaration mumbled, 'You do me too much honour, Ben,' while Susanna murmured,

'So you can be kind, Mr Wolfe, and, after a fashion, you have reprimanded me, for the Lord tells us to forgive our enemies, and now that you are not even my enemy I should have answered you more kindly.'

'And that,' announced *Madame* firmly, 'is enough of that. Heartsearching is a thankless occupation if overdone. Do you sing or play, Miss Beverly? Ben has a fine Broadwood piano and I have a mind either to play it, or to hear you play.'

'I can play a little, but I am a better singer,' answered Susanna.

'Good,' said *Madame*, 'then we shall entertain the company. Are you acquainted with Mr Tom Moore's songs?'

'Certainly. My favourite is "The Last Rose of Summer."'

'How fortunate, for it is also one of mine! And, that being so, let us perform it first of all. Shakespeare has said that music hath charms to soothe the savage breast. Let it soothe ours and we shall all sleep the more easily.'

Was it a coincidence that *Madame* was gazing at Ben Wolfe when she came out with this? Ben thought not. As he listened to Susanna's pure young soprano soar effortlessly towards the painted ceiling, the power of the music lulled his restless mind and his busy plotting brain into temporary tranquillity, as well as increasing his unwilling admiration for his unwanted guest.

What had he done to his calmly controlled existence

by dragging Miss Susanna Beverly into it? For the first time in his life he found himself considering a woman as something more than someone there to entertain him briefly and then be forgotten.

Chapter Five

'Has no one any notion where the wretched woman was going?'

Mr Western, on the urgings of his wife, was interviewing the servants two days after Miss Beverly's disappearance. Any hope that she might suddenly return was fading, and since an examination of her room had shown that she had taken nothing with her except the clothes in which she had left the house, it was beginning to appear extremely likely that some misfortune had befallen her.

The butler answered for his staff. 'None at all, sir. As you know, we had little to do with Miss Beverly, nor she with us. She exchanged no confidences with anybody—indeed, until she failed to return, no one was quite sure why she had left the house.'

'Then we must inform the authorities of her disappearance,' said Mr Western gloomily. 'She is, after all, of good family, and we must not appear to be negligent or careless concerning her safety.'

'Oh, we must be seen to be doing the proper thing,' said his wife contemptuously. 'For my part, I still think that she has run off with someone. Such creatures are more trouble than they are worth.'

'I'm sure I don't want her back,' offered Amelia.

'I shall start matters in train this afternoon,' said Mr Western. 'But first tell Cook to provide us with some nuncheon. Such matters are best discussed on a full stomach.'

'Or not at all,' commented his wife acidly.

They were about to enjoy the nuncheon when the butler entered, a strange expression on his face.

'Madame la Comtesse de Saulx has arrived, sir, and has asked to see you at once. She says that the matter is most urgent.'

'Madame de Saulx!' exclaimed Mrs Western, throwing down her napkin. 'What can she want with us?'

'She might have come at a more convenient time,' moaned Mr Western. 'Have you any notion,' he demanded of the butler, 'what this most urgent matter might be?'

'Only that she has Miss Beverly with her.'

'What?' exclaimed Mr Western, throwing his napkin down, too, and leaping to his feet. 'Have you admitted them?'

'Indeed, they are in the drawing room.' The butler smirked. 'One does not turn away such as *Madame*.'

'True, true,' said Mr Western. 'Come, my dear. As the young woman was our daughter's duenna, you must accompany me.'

'May I come too?' asked Amelia. 'I'm sure that I wish to know what Miss Beverly can be doing with the Comtesse de Saulx.'

Both her parents said together, 'No, it would not be proper.'

Mrs Western added, 'I promise to tell you all that transpires, my dear.'

'Not the same as being there,' grumbled Amelia, subsiding into her chair and picking up a buttered roll.

'Be sure not to overeat, my love,' ordered her mother. 'You are already a trifle too plump to be fashionable.'

Amelia made a face behind her mother's back as the door closed on it. It was bad enough that the duenna had bullied her about her eating habits, but it would be the outside of enough if her mother started singing the same tune!

Mrs Western was not singing any tune when she walked into the drawing room on her husband's arm to find there, as the butler had promised, not only the Comtesse, but also their duenna, dressed *à point*, although looking a trifle pale.

Susanna had been amused when, earlier that day, *Madame* had entered her bedroom in Stanhope Street carrying a bowl full of a fine white powder, a pot of oil and a large powder puff on the end of a stick.

'You look altogether too healthy, my love,' she proclaimed, 'for a young woman suffering from an unexplained fainting fit in Oxford Street. Permit me to remedy the matter.'

With that she sat Susanna down and tied a shawl around her shoulders before smearing oil gently on her face. Next she swirled the puff in the white powder before applying it to Susanna's too-rosy cheeks. She then produced a smaller puff with which she removed the surplus powder, leaving Susanna with an interesting pallor suitable for a convalescent from a sudden attack of some unknown, but mercifully brief, illness.

'Much better,' pronounced *Madame*, removing the

shawl. 'Try not to rub it off and your late employer will have no suspicion of the truth.'

'My late employer,' echoed Susanna, a trifle bemused. 'She has not yet dismissed me—although she doubtless will.'

'I assure you that she will not have the opportunity to do so, for Mr Wolfe and I are adamant that you shall not return to the Westerns. The reason, of course, being that you need to recuperate and, after that, you will become my companion—saving me the trouble of going to Miss Shanks's excellent bureau to find one.'

The mention of Mr Wolfe had Susanna up in arms immediately. 'Since when did he gain the right to decide my future?' she exclaimed, her eyes shooting fire.

Madame regarded her with approval. 'I admire your spirit, my dear, but he gained that right when he did you such a great wrong. To make up for that he has decided, with my help, to safeguard your future. Do I understand that you do not wish to become my companion?'

There was nothing Susanna would like better. From what she had seen of *Madame* and of her home, her own life would be infinitely more pleasant in *Madame*'s establishment than in any other in which she had ever worked. It was only Mr Wolfe's meddling hand that she resented.

'Of course,' she admitted. 'You are being most generous, and I must sound thankless, but—' She stopped, not sure how to continue.

'But you dislike the notion that Mr Wolfe had a hand in things. Believe me, he has a hand in more things than you can possibly imagine. Forgive him—particularly since to my certain knowledge it is rare for him to condescend to repair his mistakes—not that he makes many.'

Well, it would have to do and, sitting in the Westerns' drawing room, Mrs Western's baleful eyes on her, she was grateful to both him and *Madame* as *Madame* poured treacle over them, admitted to being Miss Beverly's good Samaritan and detailed the brief loss of memory which had resulted in her delay in returning Miss Beverly to them.

'Not that that return will be permanent, I hope,' she ended, bathing her hearers in smiling condescension. 'My physician has urged rest and recuperation for Miss Beverly before she returns to any duties she may have to perform. I understand that your daughter is soon to marry and that consequently you will have little further need of Miss Beverly's services. I suggest that it would be to the benefit of us all if you were to allow Miss Beverly to resign from your employment immediately so that she can become my companion as soon as her recovered health permits. I fear that at the moment she is still feeling weak.'

This last sentence was a signal for Susanna to lean back in her chair, hang her head while sighing gently before fetching one of *Madame*'s fine lace kerchiefs from her reticule in order to hold it before her eyes as though overcome.

This artistic manoeuvre was the result of some careful coaching by *Madame* before they left Stanhope Street for Piccadilly.

'I really do feel the most awful fraud,' Susanna had said whilst being instructed, 'and I am also fearful that I shall give myself away by laughing at the wrong moment.'

'Nonsense, child,' said *Madame* briskly. 'Only imagine that you are contemplating the death of your pet dog or bird—if you ever had one—and even tears will not be beyond you. Do you think that you *could* manage tears?' she added hopefully.

'I'd rather not,' said Susanna, wondering how *Madame* had gained such a reputation for virtue when she was the mistress of so many artful tricks. Nevertheless, in the Westerns' drawing room, she achieved the appearance of one suffering a major attack of the vapours by remembering her poor pug who had expired twelve years ago and whom she had forgotten until this moment.

Only *Madame*, thrusting a bottle of smelling salts under her nose and saying, 'There, there, dear child, we shall soon be home again where you may rest. We can collect your belongings on another day if you do not feel equal to the task today,' prevented her from succumbing to a severe attack of the giggles, something from which she had not suffered since she was thirteen.

Both Mr and Mrs Western were grateful to *Madame* for disposing of the duenna so easily and leaving them with nothing to reproach themselves had they turned her out with nowhere to go.

They parted with mutual expressions of admiration as though all four of them had been oldest and dearest friends for years—and Susanna was free once again.

Not before, however, Mrs Western, quite overcome by the graciousness of a grand personage whom she had never expected to find in her home, begged to be allowed to present Amelia to *Madame* while arrangements were being made to collect Susanna's few possessions and stow them in the boot of *Madame*'s chaise.

'By all means, nothing would please me more,' trilled

Madame untruthfully. 'And I am sure that Miss Beverly would wish to make her adieux to her late charge.'

Susanna was not sure that she would but, since polite deceit appeared to be the order of the day, she smiled her assent. She was not quite capable, she decided, of uttering an outright lie.

Her late charge, though, was delighted to be admitted to the great lady's presence and to discover that she was to lose her duenna immediately. Nothing would satisfy her but that *Madame* should recite all over again the saga of Susanna's misadventure and rescue.

'How convenient,' she exclaimed, 'for her to be able to turn a sad accident into something so fortunate in its consequences for us all! You are aware, I suppose, that I am about to marry Viscount Darlington, Lord Babbacombe's heir, in the near future.'

This was an arrogant statement, not a question, and *Madame*'s reply, had anyone cared to examine it, possessed more than a touch of ambiguity.

'Oh, then,' she murmured, 'you will truly be needing all the good wishes which I can offer you, my dear.'

'You are too gracious, Madame la Comtesse,' Amelia simpered back at her, oblivious of any double meaning—as were her parents.

Only Susanna understood that one was there for anyone who was acute enough to hear it. She wondered briefly why *Madame* should choose to exercise her wit on the Westerns, but decided that it was merely her idea of amusement. She was beginning to understand why she and Ben Wolfe were such great friends.

Thinking of him made her wonder what he was doing and where he was—and at the same time reproach herself for thinking about him at all.

* * *

Back in London again Ben Wolfe was reproaching himself for his inability to forget Miss Susanna Beverly. There were few idle moments in his busy days, but when they came along he found himself remembering her and the way in which she had sparked at him, had refused to bend before his will and had gallantly held her own in every one of their verbal encounters.

He had met prettier women—beautiful ones, even— but none of them had lingered in his memory as she had done. Standing before his desk in the house he owned off Piccadilly, he remembered the morning on which she and *Madame* had left The Den.

From the window of his study he had watched their chaise and the following heavy coach containing *Madame*'s most important servants and their luggage travel along the drive towards the main gates of The Den in order to make for the London Road.

He had let the heavy curtain fall as the carriages disappeared and turned to Jess Fitzroy, saying, 'And that's the end of that. Now I shall have to make new plans to deal with Babbacombe and his cub.'

Jess said, his voice as unemotional as he could make it, 'Do you think that's wise? Was yesterday's débâcle meant to be a warning to you from the gods? And is your interest in Miss Beverly truly at an end?'

'I don't pay you to quiz me,' returned Ben, seating himself at his desk, 'but for once I shall allow it—only don't let it become a habit.'

'Most gracious,' smiled Jess. 'But it would be wrong of me not to point out that the pitcher which too often to the well—you don't need me to finish that old saying, but you have gone to a great many wells lately.'

'Which, translated into plain English, means that you are advising me to abandon my vendetta against the

Wychwoods because you fear that my luck may be running out. Am I right?'

'That's about the sum of it,' replied Jess carelessly.

'I can't do that, Jess,' he said. 'I've waited long years for this, made myself a fortune to accomplish it. You have no idea what this means to me.'

'No,' agreed Jess. 'I don't want to know your reasons—unless you tell me them, nor will I refuse to carry out your orders. But a man must speak his mind occasionally.'

'Very true. And to your last question about Miss Beverly I will reply with another. Did you mean what you said when you asked if you might call on her?'

'Indeed. There is something about her which—'

'You needn't elaborate,' Ben growled. 'I accept that she might have certain attractions—for those who like noisy, self-assertive women, that is. So you want an argumentative wife?'

'Oh, matters haven't gone as far as that yet,' said Jess, grinning. 'But I would be pleased to meet her in happier circumstances.'

'Well, you are very likely to, for I need to return to London tomorrow, now that this business has fallen through. Be ready to leave before noon.'

'So noted,' returned Jess. 'Do you think,' he added provocatively, 'that there is anything significant in the fact that you refused to answer my question about her?'

The look Ben gave him was as fierce as his surname—which was unfair, he knew, for he could not have asked for a better lieutenant: a poor, but clever, gentleman who was willing to work for his living and whose loyalty was unquestioned.

So he said, a trifle less curtly, but still severe, 'Now

that is a question which I shall not dignify with an answer!'

In reply, Jess threw his hands into the air, exclaiming, 'Pax, I shall say no more—and carry out your orders to the letter!'

'See to it that you do. When we return to London I need to visit the Rothschilds, and you will immediately begin—most discreetly—to investigate the financial affairs of Bertram Wychwood, Third Earl of Babbacombe. I have lost one lever I intended to use against him and must now contrive to find another.'

He had said no more. Jess, who had hoped that he might learn the reason for the implacable hate Ben felt for the Earl, had shrugged his shoulders and left to prepare to return to the capital.

Ben was recalled to the present by the butler informing him that the chaise was waiting to take him on his delayed visit to Nathan Rothschild. He had called on him earlier before the attempted kidnapping of Amelia Western, only to find that he was away on business in the country but would return shortly when he would be informed of Mr Benjamin Wolfe's visit.

Shortly might mean now, and his business was urgent. Which meant that Ben was relieved to find Mr Nathan back at his desk and willing to receive him immediately.

The two men, young as the financial world counted youth, bowed and surveyed one another warily.

'I assume,' said Mr Nathan, 'that you have come to do business here, which does not surprise me, knowing of your operations in India. You are to be congratulated in achieving so much in so short a time.'

Ben was not to be patronised. He smiled, showing his teeth. 'Oh, I had the excellent example of you and

your family to urge me on,' he returned airily. 'I have
not come for a loan, but to discuss the extension of my
operations to the Port of London and to gain your co-
operation—for a consideration, of course.'

'Of course,' said Mr Nathan smoothly. 'But something tells me that that is not the only reason for your
presence here.'

'Ah,' returned Ben, showing his teeth again. 'You are
determined to live up to your family's reputation for
shrewdness, I see. No, I have a favour, perhaps two
favours, to ask of you. If you are prepared to assist me,
then I have further business to throw your way—if you
care to accept it, that is.'

This polite form of blackmail secretly amused Mr
Nathan, who was rapidly becoming aware that Mr
Wolfe was as formidable as his reputation and his name.

'I will help you,' he said, 'if it is in my power to do
so.'

'Excellent. I see that doing business with you, sir,
will be a pleasure. My first request is this: do you have
any knowledge of the affairs of the late Mr William
Beverly who, I understand, was a merchant of some
wealth who died about ten years ago? Most particularly
as to the extent of his wealth at his death."

'Beverly?' replied Mr Nathan reflectively. 'The name
is familiar, but as to the details of him, no. But take
heart—my chief clerk, Willis, is a mine of such information. One moment.'

He rang a small bell on his desk. The door opened
and an elderly man, a quill pen behind his ear, entered.

'Willis,' said Mr Nathan without preamble, 'this is
Mr Wolfe who wishes to know if we have any knowl-
edge of the affairs of the late merchant, Mr William
Beverly.'

'Mr William Beverly, sir? Oh, a very warm gentleman was Mr Beverly. Made a fortune in the late wars
whilst others were losing theirs. Came from poor gentry
stock as I recall. Had one daughter, an heiress—oh, very
warm she was, too. I have not heard what became of
her. Married well, I'll be bound. Brought her here once
when she was a little one, Mr Beverly did.'

He beamed at both men. 'Is there anything more you
wish to know, sir?'

Mr Nathan said proudly, 'Willis has the most remarkable memory—you may question him at your
will.'

Ben said slowly, 'Then it would not be true to say
that he died a poor man and that his widow and his
daughter needed financial assistance.'

'Indeed, not. A very Banbury tale that, I do assure
you. Very warm, Mr William Beverly.'

'Interesting,' murmured Ben, after listening to a tale
very different from the one Susanna had told him. 'One
further question, Mr Willis, of your goodness. Do you
know aught of Mr Samuel Mitchell, whom I believe the
Widow Beverly later married?'

'Oh, Mr Samuel Mitchell, a very sad story that. He
lost where Mr Beverly gained. Lately, his career has
been different, very different. He has recouped his
losses, one supposes, since he, too, is a very warm man
these days. Will that be all, sir?'

Ben nodded. 'I think so. May I compliment you on
your knowledge. I will not demean you by asking
whether you are sure of your facts: that Mr Beverly died
rich, and that Mr Samuel Mitchell, who was poor, has
recently become rich. On second thoughts, perhaps you
could tell me of the source of his new-found wealth.'

'There, sir, I must confess that I am nonplussed. A small mystery attaches to it.'

This guarded answer amused Ben. He smiled, and said smoothly. 'Your discretion is as remarkable as your knowledge. My thanks to you, sir.'

He bowed and, gratified, Mr Willis bowed back. He then looked at Mr Nathan for instruction, who nodded his head to indicate that he might return to his desk.

Mr Nathan said when the door closed behind Willis, 'You are thinking along the same lines as I am, Mr Wolfe?'

'Oh, I am sure of it, sir.' Ben's voice was grim. He said nothing further on the matter, although he was already turning over in his mind how he could use, on Miss Susanna Beverly's behalf, the disturbing information offered him by Mr Willis. Instead, he entered into business discussions with Mr Nathan over his own affairs at the Port of London.

He would have relished asking the knowledgeable Mr Willis about the financial affairs of the Earl of Babbacombe, except that the fewer people who knew of his interest in the Earl, the better.

What he did not admit to himself was that one of the benefits of the interview with Mr Willis was that it gave him an excuse to see Miss Susanna Beverly again—and soon.

Chapter Six

'I think,' said Jesse Fitzroy to Ben some days later, 'that you will be pleased to learn what I have discovered, both about Lord Babbacombe and the ineffable Mr Mitchell.'

After learning of Samuel Mitchell's sudden acquisition of wealth shortly after the death of Susanna's father and his marriage to Mrs Beverly, Ben had given orders to Jess to find out as much as possible about Mitchell and his firm.

'Do you want me to drop further enquiries about Lord Babbacombe, then?'

'Not at all. Carry on with them side by side—but give priority to Mitchell's business if there is any conflict of time. The other can wait a little. After all, it's waited for the last twenty-odd years.'

'Which do you want me to report on first?' asked Jess.

'Mitchell first,' replied Ben. 'That has more urgency and is probably more easily remedied—if matters are as I think they are.'

Jess pulled a piece of paper from his pocket and began to read from it. 'Before he married Mrs Beverly,

Samuel Mitchell was almost in Queer Street, only just staving off bankruptcy.' Echoing Mr Willis, he went on to elaborate, 'After that he became very warm indeed. He paid off his debts and launched several new enterprises but, some years later, shortly before he arranged his stepdaughter's marriage to Lord Sylvester, he started to fail again.'

He paused. Ben said impatiently, 'Spit it out, man—or is that all?'

'By no means. I contacted a friend of mine who has a connection with Mitchell's solicitors and another at Coutts where Mitchell and William Beverly banked. I also contacted the late Mr William Beverly's solicitors. I had to pay out good money to discover details from these and other contacts who prefer to be nameless. It appears that shortly after his marriage Mitchell paid into Coutts a large sum of money. He did the same at the time of Miss Beverly's proposed marriage. The sums were of an equal size, and added together they tally exactly with the sum of money left in trust to his daughter by Mr William Beverly. Mr Mitchell, who had been a friend and associate of Mr Beverly, was the chief trustee of Susanna Beverly's fortune.

'Further enquiries revealed that Mr Mitchell had, indeed, twice stolen from the trust, emptying it at the second time, after which he told Miss Beverly that she was penniless—without, of course, informing her that it was he who had made her so. My informant added that it is sadly true that money left in trust to young women heiresses is frequently stolen by the very trustees who are supposed to protect them.'

'As I thought.' Ben smiled wolfishly, adding, 'I won't ask how you penetrated Coutts's supposedly sacred records, I'd rather not know. What you can do for me now is set up a meeting with Samuel Mitchell—pretending that I am interested in doing business with him. On second thoughts, you won't be pretending, I shall be doing business with him—but not of a nature he will relish. I don't like swindlers who leave young women helpless and unprotected.'

'And Lord Babbacombe? You wish to hear of him?'

'Very much so.'

'Few details, I am afraid. He is virtually penniless, as you suspected. His son is to marry Miss Western in an effort to recoup the family fortunes—both of which facts you already know. What you may not be aware of is that he has mortgaged the family home and all his estates and that his lawyers have not informed the Westerns of that fact when drawing up the marriage settlements since that interesting piece of news has been kept from them by m'lord and his advisers. Were the Westerns to know, the marriage would, of course, fall through. Wealthy though Miss Western might be, her fortune would scarcely cover Babbacombe's losses.'

'Excellent, Jess,' said Ben, rising from his chair as he spoke. 'Remind me to give you a bonus for good work well done. Now, set about the Mitchell business at once. I would like to see Miss Beverly comfortable again as soon as possible.'

Unaware of the interest which Ben Wolfe was taking in her affairs, Susanna was finding life with *Madame* very different from life either in her stepfather's home or in the Westerns. She was being treated neither as somewhat of a cuckoo in the nest nor as a servant to be used and exploited.

Madame's paid companion she might be, but *Madame* treated her as a friend and as an equal. She insisted on buying Susanna an entirely new wardrobe, 'For,' she said, 'I cannot be accompanied by a young lady dressed like the under-housekeeper. Pray do not take that as a criticism of yourself, my dear. I know perfectly well the manner in which poor young duennas and companions are treated by their more thoughtless employers—and, from what I saw of the Westerns they were among the more careless it has been my misfortune to meet.'

She must have been talking to Ben Wolfe to come out with that piece of English slang, thought Susanna a trifle irreverently, or she is not quite so purely French as she claims to be. She was shrewd enough to notice that *Madame* occasionally forgot that she was a Frenchwoman and spoke perfect English without her pretty accent—although never in company, only when she was alone with Susanna.

As a consequence of *Madame*'s kindness, Susanna, when attending Lady Exford's ball for the French Ambassador a week or so after Ben's visit to Nathan Rothschild, was splendour itself. She was dressed in a deep rose silk turnout come fresh from Paris, beautifully cut and sporting the new lower waist and V-shaped neck. Its delicate colour flattered her dark hair and grey-blue eyes and gave a rosy flush to her creamy skin.

Although *Madame* had offered to lend her some jewels to go with it, Susanna had refused them, wearing only her small pearl necklace with its matching drop earrings and bracelet. Her fan, another present from *Madame*, was of a creamy parchment decorated with delicately painted rosebuds.

Thus attired, she came, early on in the evening, face to face with Amelia Western, who was on George Darlington's arm.

'Good gracious, what a surprise to find you here, Miss Beverly! I had rather thought that such an occasion would be beyond you,' was Amelia's graceless comment.

'But not beyond Madame la Comtesse de Saulx, I think,' retorted Susanna sweetly.

George Darlington, who had been staring at Susanna as though he had never really seen her before—but liked what he now saw—said gently to Amelia, 'Come, my dear. I am sure that—Miss Beverly, is it not?—will accept your congratulations on her good fortune in securing such a kind mistress. *Madame*'s reputation is a peerless one.'

Susanna was not sure that she cared for the look in George's eye. He had always previously passed by the somewhat dowdy and wan young person in a duenna's cap whom she had so recently been, and she was not sure that she wished him to notice her.

On the other hand, he was beginning to teach Amelia the good manners in which her parents were so singularly lacking, so he must be congratulated for that if for nothing else.

Amelia muttered something which could be construed as following her betrothed's advice. Her betrothed smiled fondly at her, saying to Susanna, 'We hope to see you, and *Madame*, later again this evening, but I have a duty to attend on my father as soon as possible to report to him on an errand which he asked me to perform this morning.'

His bow was low, but his eye was insolent and the look he gave Susanna was a meaningful one which she chose to ignore. She was helped in this by the arrival of someone whom she had not expected to see: Mr Wolfe.

Ben was turned out *à point* and was more over-whelming than ever with his combination of size and sartorial splendour, above which his harsh face seemed even stronger in a roomful of soft and over-civilised men.

He bowed most graciously to the three of them, finally turning to George, who was staring at his formidable presence, and saying, 'Forgive me for introducing myself, Lord Darlington. My name is Ben Wolfe. We have not been presented to one another, but you were pointed out to me by no less than our host, Lord Exford. I understand that you and your father have certain business interests in India—although we shall not talk of such affairs before the ladies.

'And, speaking of ladies, I hope that you will forgive me for ignoring the usual conventions by coming up to you as I did, and will consent to honour me by introducing me to your fair companions.'

He bowed again, straightening up to hear a trifle bemused George saying, 'Oh, as to the conventions, if Lord Exford is your sponsor here, then we may forget them. Allow me to present to you the lady on my arm: Miss Amelia Western, to whom I have the good fortune to be affianced. On her right is Miss Beverly, late Miss Western's duenna and now, I understand, the companion of Madame la Comtesse de Saulx.'

Ben bowed to each woman in turn, muttering, 'Charmed, madam.' To Susanna he said, lying in his teeth, 'I am acquainted with Madame de Saulx, but I have not yet had the honour of meeting her companion. I must compliment you, Miss Beverly, on becoming part of *Madame*'s household. She is a most gracious lady, as I am sure you have already discovered.'

Amelia, who did not look at all honoured by having

to meet Ben Wolfe, pulled mannerlessly at George's arm, annoyed that it was Susanna who was engaging Ben's interest.

'Oh, do come along, George,' she said with a pout. 'We have wasted enough time here and your father will be expecting us. I am sure that Mr Wolfe will be only too happy to entertain Miss Beverly—if she needs entertaining, that is.'

George said, 'Yes, my dear, Mr Wolfe will forgive us for leaving him after such a short time together, but we—that is, my father and I—may hope to meet him for a longer discussion.'

He bowed again to both Ben and Susanna before leading Amelia away. Ben watched them disappear through the double doors at the far end of the room, a wry smile on his face.

'Good God,' he exclaimed once they were out of earshot, 'is that little shrew the woman I was trying to kidnap? Thank the Lord I had you made off with instead! I should have strangled her within ten minutes of meeting her. I could not help overhearing the manner in which she spoke to you before I announced myself. It quite bore out what Madame de Saulx told me of her lack of manners.

'As for her fiancé, I disliked exceedingly the way he looked at you. His reputation is bad—I advise you to avoid him.'

This last came out in Ben's most imperious manner.

Susanna began to laugh. 'A fine case of the pot calling the kettle black, if I may say so, Mr Wolfe. Whatever Lord Darlington's reputation may be, I have not yet heard that it includes kidnapping young women.'

'Oh, pray do not hold that against me. After meeting Miss Western, I shall certainly never try to kidnap a woman again unless I have it on good authority that she is the most docile creature whom a man might want for a wife.'

There was no doubt that his eyes were mocking and challenging her as he said this. He was trying to provoke her, no doubt of that, either. Well, she would not oblige him, not she!

Susanna cast her eyes down and said, 'I shall remember that, Mr Wolfe, so it will not surprise you that I have no intention of becoming docile lest you try to kidnap me again. Once was quite enough. On top of that, you have involved me in telling a farrago of lies when I publicly pretended that we had never met one another before tonight. Even to save my reputation I find that a trifle above my touch.'

Ben leaned forward and said softly so that none might hear, 'Oh, no, it's not above your touch. You played your part to the manner born, my dear. And enjoyed yourself while you did. Now, let us find *Madame* and tell her that we have just met for the first time in Lord Exford's ballroom and that your reputation is therefore safe and sound.'

What could Susanna say to that? She opened her mouth to offer him a swift retort, but before she could she caught his wicked eye upon her. Consequently all that she could do was splutter, 'Oh, you are impossible, quite impossible!'

And all he said in answer was, 'So I am often told. Now let us find *Madame*.'

There was no putting him down. On the other hand, Susanna flattered herself that he was not able to put her down either.

'Shall we cry quits,' she murmured to him, 'the past quite forgotten and start again, as though we truly had met for the first time when George Darlington presented me to you?'

Ben said nothing for a moment before looking down at her from his great height. 'There is only one problem with that. I do not wish to forget the spirited young miss who sparked at me from the moment we first met. I think that I prefer her to tonight's proper young lady who only says what she ought.'

'Really, Mr Wolfe? Really? In that case am I to understand that you are giving me leave to be as impertinent to you *as* I please—*whenever* I please?'

'I would prefer that to being in the company of a bread-and-butter Miss Prim, so I suppose the answer is, yes, I am.'

This was becoming dangerous, was it not? Was Mr Wolfe descending from kidnapping her to engaging in a lesser, but more subtle, form of seduction? Did he find the newly polished Miss Beverly attractive? Or had George Darlington's obvious interest in her made him jealous?

'Dear, dear,' Susanna said, almost ruefully. 'I seem to have uttered a challenge to you which I had not intended. You were meant to say, ''Oh, no, my dear Miss Beverly, you misunderstood me quite,'' or some such nonsense, not fling the ball of conversation back at me quite so strongly.'

It was his head Ben flung back as he laughed aloud. Other heads turned to look at him in surprise. 'Ah, Miss Beverly, have you not yet discovered that I never do what is expected of me? No, no, that is not my way. And may I add that you possess the same talent—or, if you prefer, the same fault. It all depends upon one's point of view, does it not?'

To have discovered in a man whom she ought to

despise someone who said aloud what she sometimes thought secretly overset Susanna a little. To hold him off, she decided to be impersonal, to put the conversation on a higher plane—if she could.'

'Ah, then you agree with Prince Hamlet: "There is nothing either good or bad but thinking makes it so."'

'Prince Hamlet—who the devil's he?' asked Ben. 'Oh, I do beg your pardon, Miss Beverly. I should have said, "Pray, who is Prince Hamlet? And of what country is he a Prince?"'

Susanna could not tell whether he was joking or not, so she answered him in true Miss Prim fashion. 'Shakespeare's Prince Hamlet in the play of that name. I should not advise you to imitate him. He ended the play as a corpse on the stage—a noble corpse, but dead as a doornail all the same.'

'Oh, I do so agree with you. I have a rooted objection to ending up as a corpse—either on a stage or anywhere else—before my time, that is. I know little of Shakespeare, but I gather that a large number of the characters in his plays do come to an unfortunate end. By the by— you never told me of Hamlet's nationality.'

'He was a Dane, Mr Wolfe, and I do believe that you have been bamming me.'

'Not at all. A Dane, eh? I have never done business with a Dane. If one arrives in my counting house, I shall be sure to consult you as an expert on them. As it is, we have almost reached *Madame* and I must pay her my respects and relinquish you to the company of others. One thing before we part. Do you think that you could possibly refer to me as Ben in future?'

Susanna laughed up at him, unaware of how enchanting she looked and of how Mr Wolfe's heart twisted in his breast at the very sight of her as she teased him.

'What is it they say in the House of Commons? I demand notice of that question. And do we have a future—other than in chance meetings at balls and other public functions? For the moment I think that you must remain Mr Wolfe.'

'Oh, yes,' he said softly, 'we do have a future, you may be sure of that. It is that future of which I wish to speak to *Madame*. Oh, I almost forgot, Mr Fitzroy has had the impudence to ask me to pass on his respects to you—by which he showed his lack of respect for me. I hereby do so, and ask you to respect me by not respecting him.'

What impudence! 'You may be sure that I shall respect whomsoever I please, Mr Wolfe, and if I choose to respect Mr Fitzroy, so be it.'

'Oh, bravo,' he replied, and gave her one of his deep bows. 'We must cross swords again soon.'

'Whenever you please.'

Thus they parted, Ben to speak to *Madame*, who had been watching them approach, a curious smile on her face, and Susanna to carry out the errand *Madame* had asked her to perform earlier and which meeting George and Amelia had interrupted.

'Whenever you have a moment, child,' she had said, 'you might find the library for me and discover whether the Exfords possess a copy of *Les Maximes du M. le duc de la Rochefoucauld*. If so, I would wish to ask Lord Exford's permission to borrow it.'

The library was in a room at the end of a corridor just off the Grand Salon. Not surprisingly Susanna found herself alone in it. Books lined every wall and window ledge. A map table stood in the centre. Standing by it was a small man clad in the dark clothes of a scholar or a clerk. He looked up as Susanna entered and bowed in her direction.

'Ah,' he said, 'a refugee from the ball. How may I help you? If help you need.'

He was so quaint and old-fashioned that Susanna smiled. 'My name is Miss Beverly. I am here at the request of my friend and mistress, Madame la Comtesse de Saulx. She wishes to know whether the library contains a copy of M. de la Rochefoucauld's *Maximes*.'

He smiled at her. 'Indeed it does.'

'And would Lord Exford be prepared to lend it to her?'

'If Madame la Comtesse made such a request of him in proper form, I have little doubt but that he would agree to it.'

Susanna thanked him prettily, and looked wistfully around the room. She would have liked to explore the bookshelves filled with such treasures, but she had a duty to return.

On the other hand, she felt that there was one question which she could ask. 'I wonder if, before I leave, you would show me M. de la Rochefoucauld's treatise?'

'By all means,' he said. 'I will bring it to the map table for you. You must not soil your dress by carrying it. Pray take a seat.'

Susanna did as she was bid and presently the librarian, whose name, he told her, was Dr Strong, placed before her two elegant volumes bound in splendid red leather decorated in gold leaf, with the coat of arms of the Exfords on the front.

He opened the first volume for her, saying, 'I hope that you are a strong-minded young lady, Miss Beverly. The Duke was a very sardonic gentleman and his Maximes are cynical in the extreme.'

Susanna said gaily, 'You need have no fear, Dr Strong. Time and chance have shown me that the world is not a bed of roses.'

The books had been published in France and the type, though elegant and beautiful was a trifle difficult to read. And Dr Strong was right, Susanna soon found. *M. le duc* was indeed cynical. She laughed out loud at one gem. 'We all have strength enough to endure the troubles of others.'

Regretfully Susanna closed the book. She would read it when *Madame* borrowed it. Before she did so, however, she turned to the title page—to discover there an inscription in a woman's elegant handwriting.

'To Eleanor Exford on her marriage, from her true friends, Charles and Margaret Wolfe.' Beneath it a date had been written: 14th July, 1780. The book had been given to the present Lord Exford's late mother and father.

She stared at it. Were they in any way related to Ben Wolfe? And was it a coincidence that Madame de Saulx, who was Ben Wolfe's friend, should wish to borrow a book which had been the gift of persons called Wolfe?

Susanna shook her head. She was probably seeing mysteries where none existed. After thanking Dr Strong prettily, she made her way back to the Grand Salon and was about to enter it when she was stopped by a gentleman coming from the opposite direction. It was George Darlington, without Amelia hanging on his arm. It was not long since she had seen him, but now his face was flushed as though with drink.

Susanna knew that at such occasions there was often a small private room to which bored gentlemen retired to drink away from women and ceremony. She would have liked to avoid him but, on seeing her, he held out his arm, saying, his voice slightly slurred, 'Well met, Miss Beverly. Allow me to escort you back to the Salon. Or would you prefer that we delayed our return a little?'

'By no means, Lord Darlington. I have been performing an errand for Madame la Comtesse and I am already somewhat late returning…'

'Oh, come, *Madame* is not an ogre. She could spare you a few moments more. There is an anteroom not far away where we could enjoy ourselves a little. Neither of us would be missed, I am sure.'

He had taken a firm hold of her hand without her even willing it. Susanna tried to withdraw it, but in vain. He began walking her briskly towards the little anteroom which he had mentioned.

'Please release me,' said Susanna, trying to deter him by sounding as matter-of-fact as possible. 'I have no wish to accompany you anywhere, least of all to a small private room where we shall be alone. Pray remember that you are betrothed—and to the young lady who was recently my charge.'

'That has nothing to do with this,' said George. 'I had no notion that you were such a brisk little piece. Why should we not enjoy ourselves? Others do,' and he grasped her hand more firmly than ever.

This is ridiculous, thought Susanna, trying not to panic. First Ben Wolfe kidnaps me, thinking that I am Miss Amelia Western, and now Amelia's betrothed is trying to seduce me while Amelia is otherwise engaged in the Grand Salon!

Her adventures, or rather her misadventures, were rapidly becoming the subject of farce—except that George's intentions were not really farce at all. She couldn't scream for help—to do so would create a scandal which she would not survive, though George might.

Nevertheless she said, 'If you will not be a gentleman, sir, and release me, I shall be compelled to call for help.'

'Scream away,' said George unkindly, 'and complete the ruin which your being jilted started on its way.'

No doubt Amelia had informed him of that, which was why he was being so bold with her. They had reached the door to the anteroom and George began to drag her through it. The drink might have destroyed his common sense, but it seemed to have had little effect on his strength.

Afterwards Susanna wondered whether M. de la Rochefoucauld would have found a clever little phrase to describe or illuminate what happened next so far as its unexpectedness was concerned.

She had just begun to kick George's shins, hard, exclaiming, 'I really shall scream if you don't desist on the instant,' when a voice behind them said, 'What the devil's going on here?'

It was Mr Ben Wolfe. Before he had finished speaking, he seized George by his cravat and began methodically to strangle him. George, gasping for breath and slowly turning blue, was compelled to release Susanna in order to try to dislodge Ben's hands by pulling them away with both of his own.

George was not a small man, but he was no match for Ben. Susanna, released, staggered backwards. Ben said to her, over his shoulder, 'Leave us, Miss Beverly. I wish to teach Lord Darlington a lesson, but not in your presence.'

Feebly, as she afterwards thought, Susanna said, 'You won't kill him, will you? Think of the scandal.'

'What and hang for him?' said Ben through his teeth. 'Credit me with some common sense, Miss Beverly, and display your own by returning to *Madame*, and saying nothing to anyone of this.'

So they were conspirators yet again in a plot to save her good name. And common sense said that she obey him. Her last sight of George was as he sank to his knees when Ben loosened his murderous grip on his neck.

He didn't stay there long. Ben pulled him to his feet, thrust his face into George's and said in a voice which would have cut steel, 'Listen to me, Darlington, as you value your life. You are not to approach Miss Beverly again, neither are you to allow that wretched shrew whom you are doomed to marry to bait her in public or in private. Fail to oblige me in this and I will find an excuse to call you out and dispose of you for good.

'Now, give me your word and I will let you go, unscathed. Were we other than at a public function in Lord Exford's home I would have given you the thrashing you deserve, but I have no intention of providing society with a scandal to titter about.'

'Yes,' croaked George, fingering his abused throat. Ben had been careful not to mark him in any way.

'Yes, what?' exclaimed Ben, grabbing him by the cravat again. 'Say it clearly and plainly, if you please. I, George, Viscount Darlington, promise not to approach Miss Beverly again and I will also prevent Miss Amelia Western from abusing her. I also apologise for any unhappiness or distress I may have caused her.'

'Damme,' moaned George. 'You hardly leave a fellow a voice to say all that,' but he said it all the same.

'Good,' said Ben. 'Now, get out of my sight before I'm tempted to give a fellow what he deserves.'

George staggered away, to turn at the door and say, 'You'll pay for this, Ben Wolfe, see if you don't.'

'Oh, please,' returned Ben, 'pray try to make me pay as soon as possible. I shall enjoy giving you a second lesson in manners much more than the first.'

His victim could think of no clever answer to that but to give his tormentor his back and leave.

Susanna had made her way back to *Madame*, who was seated with a small crowd around her. *Madame* signalled to her to sit beside her before enquiring whether her errand had been a successful one.

'Very,' replied Susanna. 'The librarian, Dr Strong, will ask Lord Exford whether you may borrow M. de la Rochefoucauld's *Maximes*. He supposes that m'lord will give his consent.' She said nothing of the inscription which had intrigued her.

'Excellent,' said *Madame*. 'Mr Wolfe grew a trifle perturbed when you were so late in returning. He thought that you might have met with some mischance, so I suggested that he look for you in the library although I scarcely thought that you were in any danger there. He must have missed you on the way back.'

Susanna did not correct her. Secretly she was shocked at how greatly her ability to deceive had grown since she had met Ben Wolfe. His many naughtinesses must be catching, she decided.

Madame showed no sign that she thought that Susanna might not be telling the absolute truth. Indeed, when Ben returned she said brightly, 'You see, sir, your agitation over Miss Beverly's late return was unwarranted. Here she is, quite unruffled.'

Ben raised his thick eyebrows. 'Agitated? I was scarcely that. In any case, I never reached the library. I met an old friend and we had a most fruitful discussion. At least, I found it so. We were so long that I decided to return immediately, thinking that Miss Beverly might well be with you again by now. I see that I was right.'

Well, manhandling George was one way of having a fruitful discussion—on Mr Wolfe's terms! Susanna supposed. She wondered what having an unfruitful one with him might entail! George left dead on the floor, perhaps.

Aloud she said, 'Your care for me is exemplary, Mr Wolfe. I thank you for it.'

By the twitch of his lips Susanna knew that he had taken her double meaning.

'Not at all, Miss Beverly. I am always happy to be of service. I am not a dancing man, but I would be honoured to take the floor with you this evening—if you would so oblige me.'

His bow as he said this was a deep one. Susanna found herself trembling as he straightened up and she met his magnetic gaze. She had read of Dr Mesmer and his experiments, that it was possible to bend someone to your will by the power of that will. She could well believe that Ben Wolfe possessed that power.

It was the only explanation which she could find for the extraordinary effect which he had on her. Her mouth opened slightly, she licked her lips and swayed forward. She had a hard task preventing herself from stammering like a green girl at her first ball.

At the back of her mind was the memory of the summary manner in which he had treated that cur, George Darlington. Far from being horrified at his disposal of George, she had felt excited. Knights of old protected their ladies, she knew, but she was scarcely Ben Wolfe's lady. All the same it was comforting that someone cared enough about her to punish anyone who was mistreating her.

On the other hand, even as Ben led her on to the floor, she was remembering the harsh way in which he had spoken of Lord Babbacombe's family when he had been under the impression that she was Amelia—as well as his summary kidnapping of her. Perhaps there was more to his treatment of George than met the eye.

For a big man who claimed that he did not care for dancing, he danced surprisingly well, being very light on his feet as she had already noticed at the Leominster's ball. What disconcerted Susanna—and although she did not know it, Ben also—was that, as they touched, something like Dr Mesmer's famed electric response in frogs ran through them. That it was to do with Ben alone was made apparent by the fact that no other man's touch had ever brought about the same response.

But I am not a frog, Susanna thought wildly, so what can it mean? She tried not to catch Ben's eye as they moved through the stately parading of the dance, because if she did, that, too, possessed the power to excite her. And when they met, face to face, she had the oddest and most dreadful impression that all her clothes had fallen off. And if that was not bad enough, she found herself wondering what Ben Wolfe might look like with *his* clothes gone.

Of all improper thoughts for a respectable young lady to have! She would not have found any consolation in knowing that the totally unrespectable Mr Wolfe was having similar ones about her.

Unknowingly, her eyes dilated and shone. Her mouth opened itself slightly and the tip of a small pink tongue peeped out—a sight which drove Ben Wolfe mad. Like Susanna, he asked what was happening to him. Not because he was inexperienced in the ways of sex, but because, although he had always been kind to the women he was involved with, he had never felt anything for them such as he was beginning to feel for Susanna.

Mixed with an intense desire to have her in his arms or in his bed, was an equally intense desire to protect her. She had been right to see murder in his eye when he had attacked George. It had taken him all his willpower not to beat the wretch senseless for daring to distress her. He had no idea how to respond to such strange and new emotions. Particularly when they were so contrary.

Neither Ben nor Susanna had ever found dancing so exciting before. It certainly added spice to an otherwise rather formalised ritual. Susanna had heard that no less a person than Lord Byron had founded waltzing immoral. What *was* surprising was that she felt immoral performing the quadrille—his lordship had never gone so far as to suggest that!

As if that was not enough, further spice was added to an already interesting evening immediately after the dance was over. Ben had scarcely had time to escort Susanna back to her place beside *Madame* when he was accosted by a large middle-aged gentleman wearing a star on his breast.

'Lord Babbacombe,' whispered *Madame* to Susanna. 'Lord Darlington's father. Whatever can he want with Mr Wolfe?'

To pick a quarrel with him, apparently, for he said in a high, angry voice. 'A word with you, Wolfe, I will not call you sir. I wonder that Lord Exford has invited you to pollute his home. He cannot know of your dubious reputation or he would not allow you to cross his threshold. I understand that you have had the impudence to make yourself obnoxious to my son. Let me inform you that, if I have my way, every decent house in London will be closed to you.'

By the time that he had finished speaking he was scarlet in the face. The object of his anger remained impassive. Ben's face had never before looked quite so carved out of granite.

'I am here, as you are, I suppose, as a friend of Lord Exford, and I must inform you that, if your son conducts himself in good society as though his true home is a nighthouse in the Seven Dials rather than a gentleman's mansion, I shall be as obnoxious to him as I please whenever I find him misbehaving. Although I have to say that his deplorable conduct does not surprise me for I have always found ''like father, like son'' to be a useful maxim in the conduct of life—and of business.'

Lord Babbacombe was now, to Susanna's fascination, turning purple. 'Oh, business,' he snarled. 'Hardly the stuff of conversation in the company of gentlemen. Well, never say that I did not warn you what your fate might be. And, speaking of fathers and sons, your own father's conduct would scarcely bare inspection.'

Ben's expression fascinated Susanna. It never altered. He was as calm as Lord Babbacombe was noisy, and his calm did not desert him now.

'I trust that you have finished,' he said politely, 'since I came here to enjoy myself, not to listen to sermons from stupid old gentlemen. And as to business, I can understand your distaste for it, since you have been so unsuccessful in the practice of it. I bid you good evening, m'lord, in the hope that another day may find you in a better temper and your son likewise.'

He bowed and turned back to *Madame* and Susanna. Lord Babbacombe, now gobbling like a turkey, had no alternative but to accept the insults put upon him, or challenge Ben to a duel. As he had neither the mind nor the courage to do the latter he was left in a quandary.

What he would have liked to do was to order his footman to give Ben a beating, and throw him out of Exford House, but that being impossible, he turned on his heel and left, silently promising himself to take all the steps necessary to drive Ben Wolfe out of society.

Madame said gently, 'Was that wise Mr Wolfe? Lord Babbacombe is a power in London society.'

'So much the worse for London society, then,' returned Ben, his face implacable. 'My only regret is that you and Miss Beverly—to say nothing of several spectators—were compelled to listen to such an ill-tempered to-do. I hope, Miss Beverly, that my plain speaking will not result in you refusing to stand up with me in the next dance.'

'Oh, I am well acquainted with your plain speaking, Mr Wolfe, and I am in the best position to know that your remarks concerning Lord Darlington were no worse than he deserved.' She felt, rather than saw, that *Madame* was intrigued by her forthright defence of Ben, but had decided that, for once, she might indulge in a little plain speaking of her own.

'And I shall certainly agree to stand up with you in the next dance,' she added.

Susanna surprised even herself by her behaviour. On the face of it she should have been shocked but, after his failed kidnapping of her, the rest of Ben Wolfe's conduct seemed to her to be small beer at the very least.

Which was a piece of internal vulgarity she had better keep to herself!

'I wonder that you dare commit yourself to such a bad hat as I am, Miss Beverly,' said Ben with a wry smile, 'knowing, as you do, the very worst of what I am capable of performing. Who knows what might happen next?'

'Surely, sir, the evening can hold no more shocks for me, either verbal or otherwise,' she riposted.

But she was wrong. Ben had taken her hand and they stood side by side waiting for an opposite couple to appear so that the dance might begin. A tall gentleman with one of Lord Exford's sisters on his arm arrived to take his place. He was so busy talking to her that he did not turn to face Ben and Susanna until the very moment that the music began and it was too late for Susanna to react to his sudden appearance.

Ben Wolfe felt her tremble, but did not know that what had disturbed Susanna was the arrival of the latecomer.

He was Francis Sylvester, whom she had last seen the night before he had left her at the altar.

Chapter Seven

'Susanna,' said Francis agitatedly as he passed her in the dance, 'can it possibly be you?'

As he ought to have known she could not answer him immediately for the dance had rapidly returned her to Ben's side. Nor, when they were next face to face again, hands held high, did he allow her to speak, bursting out instead with, 'I had heard that you had left your parents' house and were no longer in society.'

She barely had time to retort, 'Then you were wrongly informed,' before she was back with Ben, who hissed at her,

'Who the devil is that fellow who is pestering you each time you pass him?'

Fortunately the dance took her away from him, too. And who gave him leave to question her so summarily? Or Francis, either, for that matter. Both men had glared at her as though she had offended them. She decided to speak to neither of them, treading through the patterns of the dance in silence.

So when Francis asked her as they crossed again, 'Whose party are you with, Susanna, to whom I may pay my respects when the dance is over?' she said nothing, turning her head away from him before rejoining Ben—who demanded of her exasperatedly,

'Is that fellow still troubling you?'

She didn't answer him either—which was all that they both deserved, seeing that Francis had jilted her, and Ben had kidnapped her, neither of which acts could possibly be described as gentlemanly. Her temper wasn't helped by her noticing that both men were now scowling blackly at one another whenever they crossed.

'What in the world are you doing with *him*?' Francis snorted at her. 'Don't you know how dubious his reputation is?'

Susanna could not prevent herself from riposting, 'No more than mine was and is, Francis, after you had finished with me.'

That should have finished *him* but, judging by his wounded expression, hadn't, for when he next twirled her around he came out with, 'I never intended that, you know.'

'Then what did you intend?' she shot back at him before moving on to Ben, who muttered at her,

'Is he *still* importuning you? Do you want me to deal with him also, when the dance is over?'

Susanna nearly came out with, 'Heaven forfend', murmuring instead, 'Best not, he's Lord Sylvester.'

This made matters worse, for Ben immediately hissed at her, 'The swine who jilted you, eh? I will deal with him as he deserves.'

'Oh, not that,' she said. 'What little good reputation we still possess would be quite destroyed, and having escaped hanging for George, you would swing for Francis instead. Neither of them are worth it and I should have to retire to a nunnery to escape public obloquy.'

Fortunately Ben's sense of humour revived itself

when he saw that she was smiling as she spoke. 'True,' he said, his lips twitching again and his harsh face lightening a little. 'I admit that I am being somewhat extreme, but he's exactly the kind of soft fool I most dislike.'

Susanna refrained from pointing out to him that most of the men in the room were soft fools if you compared them with Mr Ben Wolfe, but that didn't justify him threatening them all with violent death as a consequence. She also reflected that, until she had met him, her life had been conducted after a fashion which could only be described as dull and boring, whereas now even attending a ball at Exford House had become almost dangerously exciting!

There was no time for further talk with him, or with Francis either, who next had the impudence to ask, 'Are you married, Susanna? I trust that that great oaf, Ben Wolfe, is not your husband if you are.'

'No business of yours if he is,' she told him briskly, over her shoulder, as she left him for the last time.

The dance over, Ben seized her arm proprietorially and virtually dragged her over to where *Madame* was sitting, but he didn't succeed in throwing Francis off the scent. He doggedly followed them, bowing to *Madame* and ostentatiously avoiding any eye contact with Ben who had been compelled to release Susanna once she was under *Madame*'s wing again.

Francis bowed to them all. He was, Susanna noticed, as superbly turned out as he had been when he had been her supposedly faithful suitor. Yet Ben was right: his face was soft, something which she had not noticed when she had been a green girl. His public manners, however, were still superb.

'We met in Paris, I believe, Madame la Comtesse,'

he said, 'at a reception given by M. de Talleyrand. I am happy to renew your acquaintance, and would wish to renew that of Miss Beverly—if she is still Miss Beverly, that is.'

Madame's manners were, as always, impeccable. 'Lord Sylvester,' she acknowledged. 'Yes, I remember the occasion. And Miss Beverly is not married, but I am not sure whether she will wish to renew her acquaintance with you. She must speak for herself.'

'Then I must beg of her that she will allow me to speak privately to her—for a few moments only,' he said hastily, 'for I have to inform her of something meant for her ears alone.'

Susanna looked away from him. 'This comes a trifle late, m'lord, if it is an explanation of your behaviour of four years ago.' Or an apology, she was going to add, but he did not allow her to finish, saying,

'I know that I did you a great wrong, but I wish to remedy that. I ask you to allow me to speak to you in memory of what we once were to one another.'

She could almost feel Ben Wolfe's hard eyes on her, willing her to refuse him, but that very fact compelled her to accede to Francis Sylvester's wishes. To neither of them would she give the right to determine her conduct. She would speak to Francis of her free will, and that same free will would determine the nature of her reply to him. Her decisions would be her own.

'Very well, Lord Sylvester,' she said, rising. 'I will allow you to address me privately, but for a few moments only, and on the understanding that you will make no attempt to detain, or control me, physically.'

'He'd better not,' growled Ben under his breath, earning himself a sharp tap of her fan from *Madame* who was watching with interest the play of emotion on his usually impassive face.

Lord Sylvester held out his hand. Susanna shook her head as she joined him, and, not touching, they walked out of the Grand Salon and into the self-same anteroom into which George had earlier dragged her.

He turned to face her, indicating that he wished her to sit while he spoke to her. Susanna shook her head again. 'I would prefer to remain standing,' she said, as coolly as she could.

Francis inclined his handsome blond head. His looks were the exact opposite of those of Ben Wolfe—but they had lost the power to attract Susanna.

'Very well,' he said, his voice melancholy. 'I wish to tell you how sorry I am that I behaved to you as I did four years ago. But I had no alternative. I was heavily in debt, but the moneylenders, knowing of our marriage, were holding off. And then, two days before the wedding your guardian, Mr Samuel Mitchell, came to me and told me that, contrary to public belief, you were not an heiress. That he had discovered that your father had left you nothing, and that consequently I was right up the River Tick again. That the moneylenders had word of this and there was a writ out against me, consigning me to the Marshalsea since I would now be unable to pay my debts.

'Consequently, to escape imprisonment I would have to fly the country at once. He said that he would help me on condition that I said nothing of this, for he would put matters right with you and ensure that you did not suffer as a consequence of your marriage failing. He told me what to say in my letter to you, and I set sail for the Continent on the following day. You may judge of my surprise when I heard not long ago that you had left your home soon after we should have married.'

Susanna, shocked by this surprising news, stared blankly at him. Could Francis possibly be speaking the truth? Had her stepfather been playing a double game with her? And if so, why? She remembered that, immediately after Francis Sylvester's rejection of her Samuel Mitchell had informed her that he had known since her father's death that he had died penniless and had deliberately kept the truth from her until Francis's dereliction had made that impossible.

Could she trust no one? Was everyone lying to her? Samuel Mitchell, Ben Wolfe and now Francis Sylvester. The room swung about her. She put out a hand to grasp the back of an armchair in order to steady herself.

'Am I to believe a word that you are saying?' was all she could manage.

Francis, shocked by her pallor, said, 'I swear to you, by all I hold holy, that I am telling you the truth. I loved you then, and I love you now. I fled because I could not condemn you to a marriage with a man who would shortly enter a debtors' prison, or to a narrow life in Calais never to revisit your home again. Forgive me for deceiving you so vilely four years ago, but, seeing how much I loved you, I thought that it was for the best.'

He might, perhaps, be telling her the truth, but Susanna dared not trust him. Her common sense, which rarely deserted her, had her asking him, 'If that is so, why are you able to return now?'

'Because an old aunt, whom I scarcely knew, died, leaving everything to me. Enough to pay my debts and enable me to live a decent life again in England. I have forsworn gambling and the wild life which went with it. I am a reformed character, and I wish to make a new start—with you, if you will accept me.'

He made a move to take her hand, but she pushed him away. She could not bear to be touched by him.

'Accept you!' she exclaimed bitterly. 'You do not know what you are asking, nor what my life has been since you left me at the altar. As for forgiveness, you may have that, but only because I must not forget the Christian faith by which I live and which bids us to forgive sinners. But marry you! Never, not if you were the last man in the world.'

To her horror, for horror it was, he went down on his knees before her, half-moaning, 'You cannot mean that.' This time he clutched at her hands and would not let them go. Susanna sought to release herself, but he was obdurate. He was not yet trying to force her as George had done, but she feared that he might.

'Listen to me—' he began.

Attempting to pull away, she exclaimed, 'No, I will not…'

At which point the door opened and it was Ben Wolfe again who strode in saying, 'For a short talk, you said, and you promised not to detain her, but, damme, I find you at it after all.'

His expression was so ugly that Susanna, freeing herself from a startled Francis Sylvester, caught him by the arm, exclaiming, 'No, Mr Wolfe, do not attack him, I was only trying to prevent him from proposing to me and from holding my hand while he was about it.'

'What! And give himself the pleasure of jilting you twice, I suppose,' was all the answer she got, but he made no further attempt to assault Francis, simply adding, 'If you dislike his advances, then I offer you my arm to escort you out of his unwanted presence.'

Francis, his face white now, said angrily, 'I was merely trying to make Miss Beverly an honourable proposal. Can you claim to wish to do as much?'

'Certainly,' almost shouted Ben, coming out with something which he had never thought to hear himself say. 'Miss Beverly, if you will only consent to marry me, I shall apply for a special licence tomorrow.'

The look which he threw Francis was a triumphant one.

But he did not triumph with Susanna.

She jumped back from the pair of them, exclaiming, 'Oh, you are impossible, both of you—and for quite different reasons. You are only alike in wishing to make my life miserable, and I certainly don't want to marry either of you.'

Which, she later dismally acknowledged, was not a true statement at all so far as one of them was concerned, but she wasn't going to allow anyone—even someone she was beginning to love—to bully her into doing anything.

And as the two men turned to her, both speaking at once, she said as coldly as she could, 'As you claim to be gentlemen, pray allow me to depart without troubling me further.'

Her head high, she walked past them to the door, pacing slowly along the corridor, delaying her return to the Grand Salon, for after what she had just passed through she did not know whether to laugh or to cry.

After that, the evening resumed the normal course of such evenings. Francis Sylvester disappeared, not to reappear again. Susanna could only imagine what Ben had said to him before he returned to talk to her and *Madame* as though nothing untoward had occurred. She could not help wondering of what he was thinking—

and all the time she spoke and laughed and danced without an apparent care in the world, although not again with Ben, who stood silent behind *Madame*'s chair.

Was he regretting his rash proposal—or her rejection of it? At the end of the evening when *Madame* rose to take her leave, Ben bent over Susanna's hand in farewell, murmuring in a voice doubtless meant to be reassuring, 'I do not think that that fellow will trouble you again, Miss Beverly. If he does, pray inform me immediately.'

Miss Beverly! So they had returned to their previous relationship with one another as though his proposal of marriage had never been made. In theory, this should have pleased Susanna but, in practice, made her feel cold and desolate.

He had only proposed to her in order to annoy Francis and to put him off—and he had succeeded. It was simply one more of Mr Wolfe's many deceits performed to allow him to remain in control of his life—and the lives of others.

She took this sad and lonely thought to bed with her.

As for Ben Wolfe, his night was spent in wondering at himself. In the name of all that was holy, how had he come to propose marriage to Miss Susanna Beverly when he had always told himself that—other than for revenge on the Babbacombe—he would never marry? In retrospect, his rashness appalled him. She might have accepted him on the spot, then where would he have been?

Properly caught—but she had not accepted him. Instead of being pleased, he was feeling glum—which was ridiculous, for he had had no real desire to marry her, had he? He had merely been putting down that ass Francis Sylvester, hadn't he?

So why was it that he couldn't sleep, and was behaving like a moonstruck boy whose love had turned him down flat? Yes, he must be moonstruck, fit for Bedlam: hard Ben Wolfe, who was slowly being overcome by a pair of fine eyes and a brave spirit such as he had never met in a woman before.

And, when sleep came at last, his dreams were filled with visions of Susanna.

'A letter for you, my dear,' said *Madame*, passing it across the breakfast table to her several days later when the Exfords' ball and its many incidents was becoming a memory.

'For me?' Susanna looked up in surprise. She could not remember when she had last received a letter. The invitations to the many social events which she was attending were made to *Madame*: and she had lost all her friends from her old life after Francis had jilted her.

The letter looked official. It was addressed to her in a clerk's copperplate script and it invited her to attend the offices of Messrs Herriott and Bracewell as soon as possible, where she might learn something to her advantage. She passed it over to *Madame*, saying, 'Whatever can it mean? Do you know anything of this?'

Madame shook her head. 'No, my dear. I am as surprised as you are. Do you know of the firm?'

'Only that it was Papa's. I never had dealings with them after he died. Everything was done by Mr Mitchell even before he married Mama.'

'Indeed,' remarked *Madame* drily, thinking of a conversation which she had had with Ben Wolfe. 'I think that you ought to visit them as soon as possible. You may take the carriage this afternoon.'

'But you were going to the Park…'

'Oh, that can wait,' said *Madame* airily. 'This is more important.'

It was a somewhat puzzled Susanna who was shown into Mr Herriott's office later that day. He rose to meet her, offering her a chair and a glass of Madeira in that order.

'Thank you, no,' she said to the Madeira. She saw that Mr Herriott had another portly middle-aged gentleman with him and assumed that it was his partner, Mr Bracewell. Stranger and stranger, she thought, surely my business cannot be so important that it needs the two senior partners to conduct it.

'First of all,' began Mr Herriott, whose face looked as though he had drunk more than his share of Madeira in his time, 'we are here to offer you an apology for what is a dereliction of duty on our part. It has recently come to our notice that you have been under the misapprehension that your father left you a pauper. That the money set out in his will was non-existent and had been lost by him before he died.

'Regrettably we were unaware of this but, once it was brought to our notice that your stepfather, Mr Samuel Mitchell, had misappropriated a sum upwards of one hundred thousand pounds, it was our duty to remedy the matter, in so far as we could.'

Susanna was not so innocent that she did not grasp that Mr Herriott was using grand language to obscure his own share of guilt in the matter. It had been his duty to protect her interests—something which he had singularly failed to do.

'Immediately we became aware of the true situation, we set matters in train. Mr Mitchell has been compelled to make over to you the balance of your fortune left

after his depredations had reduced it. You will immediately receive the sum of some sixty thousand
pounds—or, rather, the yearly interest of that sum. As
for Mr Mitchell, he will escape conviction and transportation only because he has co-operated with us in
restoring your fortune to you, and because we believe
that you would not wish your mother and your half-
sisters to be left in penury and without a husband and
a father. He has sufficient capital left to enable them to
live in modest comfort.

'If, of course, you felt that this punishment was not
enough, then we would inform the proper authorities,
but we believed that you would not wish your mother
to be punished as well.'

Susanna hardly knew what to say. Mr Herriott rose
and poured her a glass of water. 'Drink this, Miss Beverly, I am sure that this news has come as a great shock
to you.'

She drank the water greedily down before saying,
'So, when my stepfather virtually turned me out of the
house in order to earn my own living, he was actually
using my money to improve his own circumstances?'

'Yes. It appeared that, shortly before he married your
mother, he had lost a great deal of money in speculation
and he used part of your inheritance to overcome that.
Later, after your marriage with Lord Sylvester was arranged, he had another run of bad luck, he said, and
embezzled most of the rest of it to make up his losses.'

Susanna thought of what Francis had told her at the
Exfords' ball—and knew that he had been speaking the
truth.

Her distress was patent. Not so much because of the
loss of the money itself, but because of the hard life she
had led until Ben Wolfe had had her kidnapped. The

only good thing in the whole vile business was that it had prevented her from marrying Francis Sylvester.

'Does my mother know?' she asked at last.

'I fear so.'

'I ought to help them…' she began.

'Indeed not,' said Mr Herriott vigorously. 'He has caused you a great deal of misery and I understand that neither he nor your mother ever offered you any help during your last few difficult years. They are not in penury and must learn to live on what is theirs and not on what was stolen from you.'

'But surely my mother had no notion of Mr Mitchell's wickedness?'

'Possibly not.'

Susanna stared at the breakfront bookcase opposite to her, filled with law books.

'How did you come to know of this?'

'Oh, only recently—and our sources must remain secret. Legal etiquette, you understand.'

Susanna didn't; it all seemed most odd to her. Since Madeira had not served its purpose in preparing her for such good news, Mr Bracewell joined in the discussion by ringing for tea instead and offering Miss Beverly both congratulations and condolences.

'I understand that you are comfortably placed at the moment,' he said kindly.

'Yes, I am the companion of a very gracious French noblewoman, Madame la Comtesse de Saulx.'

'So we understand. You realise that the house in which Mr and Mrs Mitchell have been living is yours, part of the estate which your father left you. They quitted it today.'

So Mr Mitchell had turned her out of her own home.

'Time's whirligig,' she said aloud.

'I beg your pardon?' said Mr Bracewell gently.

'Shakespeare,' answered Susanna numbly. '"Thus the whirligig of time brings in his revenges."'

'Ah, yes,' he answered her, smiling. 'The ancients' Wheel of Fortune. First we are down and then we are up.'

'Or the reverse in Mr Mitchell's case,' put in Mr Herriott, who appeared to be enjoying the Mitchells' downfall.

'May I assure you, Miss Beverly,' he continued, 'that the interest on your fortune will be paid to you quarterly, and that you may return to your home as soon as it is convenient to you. You may call on us for any assistance you may require when you take up your new life. Before you leave, I must ask you to sign some necessary documents to enable us to do so.'

What a difference a fortune makes to the manner in which you are treated, thought Susanna sardonically. Yesterday I was an unconsidered nobody, grateful for *Madame*'s kindness, and today, all is changed. The world is bowing and scraping to me and my lightest wish is law.

This was not the sort of comment she cared to make to the Messrs Herriott and Bracewell, however.

She drank her tea and signed the necessary documents, both gentlemen assuring her of their good wishes and their desire to help her at all times. Mr Herriott, as the senior partner, escorted her to her carriage, returning to his office to find that Mr Bracewell had been joined by a third party, Mr Ben Wolfe, who had slipped in from another room.

'Your partner assures me,' he said to Mr Herriott, 'that all went swimmingly this afternoon, and that Miss Beverly is now in command of her fortune again.'

'Indeed,' said Mr Herriott, bowing slightly. 'I wish that you had allowed Mr Samuel Mitchell to be prosecuted for his misdeeds—even if you did compel him to make restitution. It is a bad principle, I fear, to allow the wicked to go unpunished.'

'Not exactly unpunished,' drawled Ben comfortably, drinking the Madeira which Susanna had refused, 'seeing that he was compelled to disgorge himself of virtually everything he possessed. Furthermore, I wished, as I am sure you do, to spare Miss Beverly as much public pain as possible, as well as ensuring that she remains unaware that it was I who uncovered Mr Mitchell's wrong doing. I have no wish to profit from that.'

'Very noble of you,' returned Mr Herriott insincerely, for he thought that Mr Ben Wolfe was as devious a schemer as he had ever encountered. 'It does you nothing but credit, sir.'

'It does, doesn't it,' agreed Mr Wolfe amiably, 'which was probably why I did it, don't you think?' He threw his head back and laughed. 'But of course, you do. Who knows how it may yet profit me? At the moment, though, I must thank you both for your co-operation in this matter, especially insofar as it relates to keeping my intervention a secret.'

He refrained from pointing out that, despite their dereliction of duty in allowing Mr Mitchell to deceive them, he was allowing them to take the credit for unmasking him.

Allies were always useful, especially in the game he was about to play—and now he had two powerful ones.

Chapter Eight

Susanna was seated in *Madame*'s small drawing room, trying to come to terms with the sudden recovery of her fortune, when the butler announced that Mrs Mitchell had arrived and wished to speak to Miss Beverly.

She put her canvaswork down and composed herself. Ever since she had told *Madame* of her good news she had felt that she was living in a dream. *Madame* had begged her to remain with her as a friend, rather than as a companion, 'Although,' she had added, 'I shall quite understand if you wish to return to your old home immediately.'

'I don't know what I wish,' Susanna had told her. 'If I am honest, I would like to accept your kind invitation, if only because it will give me time to consider my future arrangements.'

She was not sure that she wanted to return to her old home: it held too many unhappy memories—and she certainly didn't want to live there on her own. She was contemplating a number of possibilities when her mother was announced.

Mrs Mitchell scarcely waited for the butler to depart before she rounded on Susanna—*Madame* had already tactfully left the room so that mother and daughter might be alone together.

'Was it you who ruined poor Mr Mitchell and banished us to a back street in Islington? Someone must have told a pack of lies to condemn us to poverty so that you might live in splendour. We were given an hour to leave our own home and were not allowed to take anything with us except the clothes we stood up in. Your poor sisters were even compelled to leave their little treasures behind. Such unkindness! I would never have thought a daughter of mine would treat me so cruelly.'

She paused to draw breath before continuing her tirade, looking around the room and exclaiming, 'You seem to be comfortable enough here without needing to vent your spite on us in order to make yourself more comfortable still.'

After hurling this dart at Susanna, Mrs Mitchell threw herself on to the nearest sofa and began to howl into one of the cushions on it in the most abandoned fashion, before throwing it on one side and preparing to reproach her daughter again.

Susanna, her face white, had retreated a couple of paces backwards, fearful that her mother might attack her physically. She said, as gently as she could, before Mrs Mitchell could speak again, 'I had no knowledge of Mr Mitchell's theft of my inheritance until three days ago, nor was I aware that you had already had to leave your home. But aren't you forgetting something, Mother?'

'Forgetting! I!' screamed her mother. 'No, I am forgetting nothing. Oh, the humiliation! The pain!'

'You are forgetting,' said Susanna steadily, 'that your husband, Mr Samuel Mitchell, not only stole my inheritance, he also made sure that my marriage with Francis Sylvester would fail, and after that he turned me out of my home—not yours or his—to earn my own living. My father left you a fortune of your own which passed to Mr Mitchell when you married him, but, not content with that, he made sure that he enjoyed mine. I lost everything—my inheritance, my good name, and my home—through his machinations. It is you who should apologise to me for the wrongs I have suffered, not me apologise to you.'

'Oh, "How sharper than a serpent's tooth it is / To have a thankless child,"' intoned her mother, quoting from Shakespeare and rolling her eyes towards heaven. 'Your father had no business leaving so much to you. Mr Mitchell has five of us to keep and there is only one of you.'

'Well, Mr Mitchell made sure that I remained only one when he wrecked my marriage, so you had better reproach him. No, Mother—' as her mother raised her arms to heaven like an Old Testament prophet, ready to rain fire and brimstone on her '—I am sorry that Mr Mitchell has brought this disaster on you. It was none of my doing, and I agreed with my lawyers that he should not be arrested for his misdeeds. Had I insisted, he would have either been hanged or transported, for those are the punishments for embezzlement. Be thankful that you still have him, and pray that he uses his talents for business more honestly in the future.'

'No,' said her mother, pushing her open hands at Susanna as though she was about to attack her, 'no, I will not listen to you. I am sure that my poor husband is innocent and that the truth will come out one day. Until then I have no wish to see you again.'

'Well, you have lived without seeing me for the last four years, so a longer parting will make little odds.'

She stopped, and then tried to take one of her mother's hands, 'Oh, Mother, remember that I am your child as well, and try to understand how I must have felt when I learned the dreadful truth. And how I feel now when you disown me so cruelly although I have done you no wrong—and have even saved your husband from the implacable hands of the law despite all that he has done to me.'

Her mother pushed her away. 'That is enough. I won't hear any more. Stay with your fancy French-woman—oh, how it hurts me to think that she may be enjoying herself in my home while I suffer the privations of poverty.'

Ignoring Susanna's pleading face, she walked to the door. 'You need not have me shown out. I want no favours from you or anyone who lives with you. I know that you disliked Mr Mitchell, but I never thought that you would have gone so far as to ruin him—and us.'

She went. Susanna sank on to the sofa which her mother had briefly inhabited and found that, broken though she was, she could not cry. Or rather, she thought grimly, I will not.

Madame came in a few moments later, took one look at her and rang for the teaboard.

'Dear child,' she said kindly, 'I will not ask you what passed. Knowing the world as I do, I assume that your mother was far from kind to you. No, do not answer me. There is nothing which either of us can say at present other than to admit that life is often too difficult for us to bear. The only comfort which I can offer you is one that I have found to be true—''This, too, will pass,'' which is cold comfort enough, I admit. Now, drink your tea.'

Susanna reflected sadly that these days everyone seemed determined to make her drink some liquid or other. Mr Wolfe had begun this apparent ritual and everyone else she had encountered had followed his example. Nevertheless she did as she was bid, wondering what else the afternoon had in store for her.

She was not in the least surprised when Mr Wolfe was announced—he seemed to haunt her these days. Even her refusal of his proposal—of which she had not informed *Madame*—did not seem to have deterred him.

In *Madame*'s little drawing room he seemed larger than ever. He refused the tea which *Madame* offered him, saying, 'Another time, perhaps. It is a fine day, I have a new carriage outside and four splendid horses and am determined that, if you have no other engagement, you will allow me to drive you both to Hyde Park to enjoy the sun.'

He could have said nothing more calculated to allow Susanna to recover herself. Before her mother's unhappy visit she would have thought that her reaction to it would have been to wish to hide herself away. Instead, she was possessed with a fierce determination to show the world that she would not be put down. Which was stupid, she thought wryly, because no one but her mother and herself were aware of what had so recently passed between them.

Knowing Ben Wolfe as well as she did, she also knew that his new carriage would be as splendid as his horses and that it would be a privilege to sit behind them. Nevertheless, having agreed almost immediately, she was a little perturbed to hear *Madame* say that she was suffering from a light megrim and would prefer not to sit in the hot sun—if Mr Wolfe would be so good as to allow her to make her excuses.

'In that case,' began Susanna, a trifle unhappily, 'perhaps I—'

For once *Madame*'s perfect manners deserted her. She cut Susanna off in mid-sentence, announcing briskly, 'Do not allow my malaise to prevent you from enjoying a well-earned excursion, my dear. Without yet being past your last prayers, you are mature enough to sit beside Mr Wolfe in a public place such as Hyde Park without causing scandal.'

'Or perhaps because I have already caused so much,' Susanna riposted lightly, 'one more *bêtise* will not count against me!'

'Nonsense,' said *Madame* and Ben together.

'Your presence in *Madame*'s home,' said the latter, 'will suffice to stifle any scandal. And you need a run in the Park. You are a trifle pale this afternoon—too much staying indoors, I presume.'

Madame again answered for her. 'You mistake, Mr Wolfe. Miss Beverly has recently received two pieces of news, one good and the other much less so. The first is that she has received notice that her fortune, which her lawyers had allowed her to be cheated of by her stepfather, has been restored to her, so she is no longer dependent on cold charity. The second is that her mother has visited her and has been most unkind to her because of the change in her own circumstances. Not that she has told me so directly—it is what I have gathered from her manner.'

'Is this true, Miss Beverly?' asked Ben, his face grim. He had, at *Madame*'s urgings, taken a seat, and he leaned forward from it to add, 'Most unwarranted, if so, seeing that by all accounts her husband stole your inheritance from you.'

'Both statements are true,' she told him, 'but I confess to feeling a trifle unhappy that my good luck is at the expense of my mother and half-sisters' bad luck.'

'Do not reproach yourself,' he said earnestly. 'You have had a great wrong done to you, and your mother and sisters have been living a comfortable life while you have been struggling. You were turned out of your home, were you not?'

Susanna nodded a brief agreement.

'Well, then!' said Ben sturdily. 'Your sentiments do your soft heart credit, but I advise you to forget the unhappy past, accept my invitation and tell me what you think of my carriage and four.'

'But I am not really dressed to go to the Park,' objected Susanna.

'Nonsense, you look as you always do whatever you wear, quite *à point*. You simply need to equip yourself with a parasol to arm yourself against the sun and a light shawl to protect your arms.'

Madame nodded agreement and sent her away to dress herself as Ben had advised. Once Susanna was out of the room, *Madame* rose and walked to the mantelpiece to rearrange some objects of *vertu* there.

'Do I detect your fine Italian hand in this sudden access of wealth which Miss Beverly is enjoying?'

'Now, why in the world should you think that?'

'You forget how well I know you, *cher ami*! What I don't understand is why you don't simply propose to her and have done with it.'

Ben said in his most winning voice, 'Oh, but I have, and…' He paused tantalisingly.

Madame turned to face him. 'You really are provoking,' and her voice had quite lost its pretty French accent and was disturbingly downright in the English fashion. 'I am growing too old to be teased.'

'Never—you are timeless, as you well know,' he said. 'But, all the same, I will oblige you and finish my sentence. She refused me. Perhaps because neither the manner of it, nor the occasion on which it was made, could be described as either tactful or auspicious.'

'You are, as usual, being remarkably cold-blooded about the whole business,' said *Madame* sternly, 'but that is your way. Are you cold-blooded about her? Do you feel anything for her?'

'You are not to ask me that. I can only tell you that I would not hurt her for the world. She has been hurt enough.'

'Only that? Is that all you feel for her?'

'Better that than loud protestations of undying love which mean nothing.'

If *Madame* thought that he was not quite telling her the truth, she did not say so. In any case, the arrival of Susanna, looking enchanting in cool pale blue and cream, with kid shoes, bonnet and parasol to match, brought an end to their conversation.

'Charming,' said Ben, bending over to kiss her hand. 'Quite charming. I shall be the envy of Hyde Park.'

He was not far wrong. On his own he would have created gossip, because all the world was excitedly chattering about the mysterious nabob, and the new *on dit* running around the *ton* suggested that he was not a member of the Wolfe family at all, but merely an adventurer who had assumed the name and had subsequently misappropriated what was left of the Wolfe estates.

Escorting Susanna, however, who had remained anonymous for the four years since her jilting when she had made such a scandalous, if fleeting, impression on the London scene, he was the subject of even more gossip and interest. Pieces of excited conversation flew around the Park such as:

'Who is he with?'

'Oh, is that the young woman whom Sylvester jilted? What a beauty she is now. Where has she been?'

'Madame la Comtesse de Saulx is sponsoring her, you say? Then what is she doing with *him*? *Madame* is respectability itself.'

'Had her fortune restored to her, I understand. Is that why Wolfe is with her?'

'And *Madame* is sponsoring Wolfe, as well, is she? Odd, that! Best go over and pay our respects. Wouldn't want to be backward in coming forward if he is the coming man, which they say he is.'

And so on…

Susanna was sublimely unaware of the excitement which she was creating. She only knew that she was happy. Ben had driven the carriage into the shade of some trees and his two grooms were holding the horses steady. She and Ben became the subject of a little court. Men and women on foot, either because they had walked to the Park or had left their horse or carriage for the moment, made their way to them out of sheer curiosity if nothing else.

'I had no notion that you were so popular, Mr Wolfe,' said Susanna, intrigued by all this excitement.

'I am a novelty,' he whispered to her. 'In a few months I shall become a commonplace and a new sensation will be found to exclaim over. And you are a novelty as well, a beautiful woman whom, I dare say,

few know. And remember, the story of your lost-and-
found inheritance is probably an *on dit* already. Prepare
to be boarded by ambitious and fortune-hunting suitors.'

'I hadn't thought of that,' Susanna admitted artlessly.
She had been so busy worrying about all the other im-
plications of her new-found wealth that she had forgotten that one.

'Best to remember it.' Ben's voice was now sober,
its usually wryly jesting overtones absent for once.

'Yes, I suppose so.' She sighed. 'Ah, well, I suppose
every silver lining has its cloud.'

Before he could answer her, a mature beauty on the
arm of a large man in the uniform of a Hussar approached them and began to gush at Ben as though he
were alone.

'So happy to see you. You remember me from India,
I trust. Charlotte Campion I was then, but my husband
died of a fever out there and here I am, home again and
married now to Colonel Bob Beauchamp—you know
him too, I believe.'

'We have met.' Ben's voice was dry. 'You will allow
me to present Miss Susanna Beverly to you. Miss Beverly, Colonel and Mrs Beauchamp.'

'Ah,' said Mrs Beauchamp, at last acknowledging
Susanna's existence. 'So you are the little heiress who
has recovered her lost fortune!'

She said this as though Susanna's carelessness had
caused this sad mishap through conduct on a par with
her mislaying her reticule or her kerchief.

'An heiress, true, but not little,' said Ben before Susanna could answer—something, she thought crossly,
which was happening to her too often these days. She
was perfectly capable of defending herself, both Ben

and *Madame* were doing it a little too brown by deciding otherwise.

She was reduced to smiling vaguely at Mrs Beauchamp whilst wondering if she had ever been Ben's mistress—or even a passing lover. Her manner seemed to suggest so.

Colonel Beauchamp had produced a monocle which he jammed in his right eye to enable him to survey Susanna more closely after a fashion for which she did not care.

'Must come to supper with us soon,' he offered. 'Eh, Charlie?'

'Oh, indeed. I can gossip about old times with Ben and you can tell Miss—Beverly, is it?—all about Waterloo, leaving out all the gory bits, of course.'

'Supposing I wanted to hear about the gory bits,' Susanna raged at Ben when the Beauchamps had departed after Mrs Beauchamp had hurled a few more poisoned darts at Susanna. 'What then? How well did you know her in India?'

To his inward horror, Ben realised that he was delighted to detect a note of jealousy in Susanna's response to Charlotte Beauchamp's overblown charms. He must be going mad. Worse, it was even madder of him to stoke the fire by saying confidentially, 'Very well. Every man in Indian society knew her very well.'

'How fortunate for them all,' said Susanna tartly, 'to find someone so obliging.'

'True,' said Ben naughtily. 'Particularly when there was such a dearth of females who were.'

He was highly entertained when Susanna closed her parasol, produced a fan and began to wave it vigorously in front of her, saying crossly, 'You really should not

talk like this to me, you know. I am an unmarried female whose innocence ought to be protected.'

'I am taking my tone from you,' retorted Ben primly.
'If you wish to discuss something less…inflam-
matory…we can embark on some more respectable
topic.'

'Oh, so you admit that the lady is not respectable.'
The accusation shot out of Susanna without her willing
it.

What on earth is the matter with me, she thought
dismally, that every time I am with Mr Big Bad Wolfe
I find myself saying the most dreadful things and behaving like Lady Caroline Lamb at her worst? I never
do it with anyone else. Quite the contrary, I am usually
as solemn as a parson or a judge—more, in fact. I really
must compose myself.

Ben watched the play of emotion on her face, guessing a little of what she was thinking.

'Cannot you think of anything suitable to discuss?'
he offered helpfully. 'If you cannot, might I suggest we
converse on the state of the King's health. I hear that it
is declining rapidly.'

'I shall decline rapidly if you don't behave yourself,'
retorted Susanna, watching another group of curious
sightseers approaching their carriage. Among them were
the Westerns and Amelia. Amelia was wearing a brilliant purple walking dress which did nothing for her
complexion. Her mouth was turned down at the corners,
too.

'Whatever can be the matter with her?' whispered
Susanna to Ben. 'She is generally so high-spirited as to
be unendurable.'

'Her marriage to Lord Darlington will not take place,'
Ben whispered back. 'Yours is not the only sensation

here today. The *on dit* is that Babbacombe's financial situation is so dire that the Westerns cried off shortly after learning of it. Apparently they concluded that even to gain a title was a game not worth the candle if by doing so they risked bankruptcy themselves in order to save Babbacombe. Smile at them; for the moment you are up and they are down.'

Susanna duly obeyed him when they finally reached the carriage. It appeared that the Westerns had decided that they might recognise Mr Wolfe and his companion after all.

Preliminaries over, Amelia said to Susanna, 'I suppose that I ought to congratulate you, so I will.'

'Thank you,' said Susanna, ignoring the graceless nature of this remark and wondering what to say in reply, but Amelia, joining the growing throng of those who never allowed her to finish a sentence, added immediately,

'I suppose that you have heard of my bad news?'

'Mr Wolfe has just informed me of it.'

'No doubt—he seems to know everything. Who would have thought that Lord Babbacombe would be so deceitful? M'lord told Papa a series of lies when the marriage settlement was being arranged. His estates were heavily mortgaged, he was deep in debt, the moneylenders were after him, and only an anonymous letter informing our lawyers of the true state of things prevented us from becoming part of his general ruin. I was sorry to lose George, of course, but I'm sure that you will agree that I could not marry him and end up a pauper.'

'But I thought that you shared a deathless love with him?'

Oh, dear, now she was beginning to sound exactly like Ben Wolfe himself, coolly sardonic!

Amelia stared at her. 'Deathless love would be hard to manage in a garret,' she said at last.

'Oh, indeed. On the other hand, I believe that deathless love is hard to manage anywhere.'

And now I've done it again. I must stop before I say something which I shall regret.

Ben, who had been conversing with the Westerns—on a respectable topic, Susanna hoped—overheard this and made his contribution to the wake for George and Amelia's marriage.

'If you believe in love, that is. In any case, outside of novels, it seems to me that love and marriage have little to do with one another.'

Well, one might have expected Ben Wolfe to say something like that. It killed the conversation dead. Amelia dabbed at her eyes with her handkerchief, but whether she was crying for George, or the loss of his title, was difficult to guess.

After that the conversation went even further downhill until at last the Westerns drifted away, leaving Ben and Susanna alone for a moment.

But not for long.

The next to approach them was, improbably, Jess Fitzroy, riding a superb grey. He swept off his hat to Susanna and said cheerfully to Ben, 'Good afternoon, sir.'

'Very good for you,' returned Ben, 'if you have nothing better to do than ride in the Park.'

'Oh, all in the way of business,' replied Jess, not a whit disturbed. 'I not only have information for you which cannot wait, but I have also been gathering even more as I made my way around the Park.'

'Urgent or not, the business must wait until we return home,' replied Ben. He was quartering the Park with his eyes and, when he finished, said affably to Jess, who was smiling at Susanna, 'You could do me a service if you would, Jess. You could take Miss Beverly for a short walk, for I believe that I see another person who has urgent business with me approaching. She will not wish to listen to a dull recital of Stock Exchange prices, I am sure.'

Now how did she know that he was not telling the truth? Susanna had a mind to refuse him and see what he said to that. Forestalling her—as usual—Jess said cheerfully, 'Are you sure that Miss Beverly wishes to take a stroll around the Park?'

'Nothing would please me more,' said Susanna before Ben could answer. She was tired of having others anticipate her wishes for her.

'Very well,' said Jess, dismounting and throwing the reins of his horse to one of Ben's attendant grooms, before handing Susanna down from the carriage.

'Do you wish me to walk Bucephalus with us, Miss Beverly? Or would you rather take a turn without him?'

'Oh, let him walk with us,' said Susanna, gratified that someone had taken the trouble to ascertain her wishes. 'He is very beautiful, is he not? Have you had him long?'

Jess took the reins from the groom. 'Alas, he is not mine, Miss Beverly. He is Ben's…I mean, Mr Wolfe's. He allows me the use of him.'

Susanna noticed, as she had done before, that Jess Fitzroy had the speech and manners of a gentleman, something which intrigued her. How had he come to be Ben Wolfe's faithful dogsbody?

'Where did you meet him?' she asked, apparently idly.

'In India,' Jess responded frankly. 'I was an officer in the regiment in which he was a sergeant. I was lucky to have him. I was a raw fool and he saved my bacon once or twice in several frontier skirmishes. He left the army shortly after that and set himself up in business.'

He paused, before adding, 'I respect you enough to be honest with you. I was a fool, do not ask me how. I was duped by others and ended by having to resign my commission. There I was, penniless, with no family, other than the knowledge that my grandfather had been the natural son of Frederick, Prince of Wales, and that I was his only descendant. I had no prospects, no near relatives, and nowhere to go. Ben found me, offered me work and I have been with him ever since. I owe him everything for he saved me from being a pauper.

'Do not be deceived by his manner. Oh, he is hard, I grant you, but he is true, as true as a new-minted golden guinea. On the other hand, if *you* are not true— then look out is all I can say!'

'You can say that, Mr Fitzroy, even after he tried to kidnap Miss Western?'

Jess smiled wryly. 'I did not say that he was virtuous, Miss Beverly. Virtue is quite another matter and is rarely found—even amongst those who claim most loudly that they possess it.'

Susanna said nothing for a moment. She honoured Mr Fitzroy for being frank with her so she asked him another question.

'You spoke almost dismissively of virtue, sir. Does that mean that neither you nor Mr Wolfe practise it?'

'On the contrary: but acts of kindness individually performed do not in themselves constitute virtue, as I

am sure you understand. Mr Wolfe looks after people—
but in doing so not all his acts are virtuous. The world
in which we live is a cruel one, and the good do not
survive in it if their only defence is their virtue—more
than that is frequently necessary.'

Susanna did not ask him what 'more than that' might
entail. Her own experience had taught her that much of
what he had just said to her was true. She had been
good and her goodness had not prevented Mr Mitchell
from ruining her—quite the contrary, it had made it
easy for him to do so.

A sudden thought struck her. A thought which she
did not wish to share with anyone until she had examined it carefully. Her life had been growing increasingly
difficult until she had met Mr Ben Wolfe. From that
moment on everything had changed.

She had been introduced to *Madame* and all her fears
for her immediate future had disappeared. And then,
suddenly, mysteriously, her fortune had been restored
to her, and she was again Miss Susanna Beverly, the
heiress, no longer a poor dependant on the charity of
others.

Jess Fitzroy had said that Mr Wolfe looked after people, and he had undoubtedly looked after Jess. Had he
looked after her? Who else knew her who was powerful
enough not only to discover Mr Mitchell's theft of her
inheritance, but was also able to restore it to her?

And if her reasoning was correct, how did that affect
her feelings for him? She must be grateful—but might
he expect more from her than that? And if so, what?
By helping Jess, Ben had gained a faithful servant and
an honest henchman—what might he expect to gain
from helping her?

A man who was not virtuous—even if true—might

have a hidden reason for his charitable acts. She looked sideways at Mr Jess Fitzroy and half-thought of saying something on these lines to him.

Reason told her that might be foolish—he was Mr Wolfe's faithful servant, not hers. On the surface he was everything a gentleman ought to be, but she must not forget that he had kidnapped her on Mr Wolfe's orders and it was to him he owed allegiance.

'You are quiet,' Jess said at last. 'But then, I like a quiet woman.'

Susanna laughed, and her laughter drove away her darker thoughts. 'You did not think that I was quiet when you snatched me from the street—on the contrary.'

'Ah, but you were defending yourself, were you not? And that is what I meant by goodness not being enough. To have acted like a perfect lady would not have helped you in your dealings either with me or with Mr Wolfe. He admired the manner in which you stood up to him and refused to be put down. And then, when all was settled, you reverted to being a perfect lady and allowed yourself to be good again.'

'You tempt me, Mr Fitzroy, to ask you whether you learned your deviousness from Mr Wolfe—or did you always possess it?'

The look he gave her was an admiring one. 'And you tempt me, Miss Beverly, to remark that you needed no lessons in that line from Mr Wolfe since from the first moment you met him you also were deviousness itself. That is why he admires you.'

So Mr Wolfe admired her—and what was she to make of that? She was about to answer Jess—or, rather, ask him another question—when she saw that they had walked in a half-circle and were almost back to their starting point.

She could see Ben talking earnestly to a man in dark unfashionable clothing who was sitting beside him in his carriage. She thought suddenly that Jess's arrival in the Park might not have been accidental, even though Ben had twitted him on it.

'You have honoured me by giving me your confidence, Mr Fitzroy,' she said at last, discarding her question, 'and I will not betray it. I had, I must admit, wondered about your name. You do not have a great look of the Royal Family.'

'No, indeed, and that is a relief. I take after my grandfather's wife or so my father told me. And, yes, I would prefer it if you did not inform Mr Wolfe of what I have said of myself—or of him. And now that is enough of me.'

'Oh, I have learned to be close-mouthed in a bitter school,' Susanna told him, 'for if I did not look after myself, no one else would.'

Jess did not inform her that she, like himself, now had a benefactor in the unlikely person of Ben Wolfe, for he had been forbidden to do so. He would not be surprised, though, if Miss Susanna Beverly did not work that out for herself quite soon. He was not to know that she had already done so.

After that they talked idly until Jess, seeing that Ben's visitor had disappeared, walked Susanna back to his employer's carriage again, mounted his grey and bade them adieu.

His business apparently over—and Jess disappearing into the middle distance, doubtless to carry out more of his errands—Ben gave Susanna his full attention. His first sentence proved that, even when apparently conducting business, he still had time to watch what was going on about him.

'Jess had plenty to say to you,' he remarked drily as he drove slowly along, 'and you seemed to be equally loquacious. Was it the weather or the current *on dits* which occupied you?'

'Neither,' said Susanna briskly. 'The weather has been unchangingly temperate recently, and I know little of any *on dits*. Instead we enjoyed a short philosophical conversation on the nature of virtue.'

'Of which Jess knows a great deal, I am sure,' remarked Ben, a trifle ironically.

'Oh, one need not practise something in order to discuss it,' retorted Susanna. 'Otherwise it would be difficult to discuss anything—paintings or poems, for example, seeing that most of us are neither painters nor poets.'

Few men, and no women, ever spoke to Ben Wolfe in such a downright fashion. He gave a short laugh and said, 'I shall make it my business, Miss Beverly, to choose my words very carefully when I discuss anything with you. You would have made a good career in the world of business had you been a man.'

He had almost said 'been lucky enough to be a man,' but had revised that statement before he made it for he was sure that Miss Beverly would have had said something sharp in reply. He thought that she was happy to be a woman even if, in many ways, she possessed the kind of acuteness which was commonly thought to be confined to men. Besides, he had absolutely no wish for her to be a man!

'Is that intended to be a compliment, Mr Wolfe?' she asked him gravely.

'Many would think it so.'

'But am *I* to think it so?'

The look she gave him as she said this set Ben groaning inwardly. He wished that they were alone, not in a crowded Park with idle, curious and malicious eyes upon them. He would have kissed her for her impudence, there, at the corner of her smiling mouth. And then he would…he would…

Stop that, he commanded himself sternly. This is neither the time nor the place…

And stop that, too. I have no wish to be any woman's slave—even one as clever and desirable as Miss Susanna Beverly.

'I meant it as such,' he came out with at last, Susanna meanwhile wondering why it took him so long to answer her.

'Then I will accept it as such.'

'And in the meantime,' he ground out, 'you will oblige me by cutting that obnoxious puppy, George Darlington,' for he had just seen George tipping his hat and smiling at Susanna for all the world as though he had not recently attempted to assault her in Lord Exford's study.

'You know, Mr Wolfe,' Susanna told him after doing as he wished, 'I don't really need a duenna when I am with you. You perform that service so admirably I wonder that you do not take it up as a profession!'

He replied to her in kind, 'I would if it paid as well as being a financier in the City.'

'I must remember that,' she said, 'if I lose my fortune again and need to find a well-rewarded occupation.'

'You did not lose your fortune, Miss Beverly, you had it stolen from you. Remember that if you begin to feel mercy towards those who robbed you.' His voice was both stern and forbidding.

'You surely do not mean that my mother—?'

'Your mother, from what you have said of her, turns a blind eye to her second husband's actions. I cannot believe that she was completely unaware of his misappropriation of your inheritance.'

In fact Ben, from his investigations, knew that what he was saying was true. Equally, Susanna, with a sinking heart, was sure that what he was telling her was the truth because he had been her unknown saviour.

For a moment she debated whether to tell him that she was aware of that, but decided against it. If he wished to keep his secret, then she would take no steps to make him aware that she had discovered it.

Jess Fitzroy is right. I am as devious as he is. Knowledge is power, as the old saying has it, and although I cannot yet conceive what power over him this knowledge gives me, I will continue to keep my secret—as he keeps his. Like it or not, what frightens me the most is the knowledge of the attraction he has for me so that simply sitting by him excites me strangely.

And the most exciting thing of all is that that is another of my secrets, from him and the world.

Thus, side by side, they drove back to Stanhope Street, chatting amiably together, neither of them giving the slightest sign that what was growing between them was slowly becoming so powerful that they would be unable to deny it—either to themselves or to the other.

Once back at *Madame*'s Ben refused an offer of early supper. 'Alas, I must decline,' he said, 'I have another engagement, made only this afternoon. What would please me is if you would both consent to dine with me on this coming Friday evening. Pray forgive me for asking you at such short notice.'

'Not only do we forgive you,' said *Madame*, 'but we

shall be delighted to attend as we have no other engagements—is not that so, Miss Beverly?'

'Indeed,' said Susanna who, beneath her quiet acqui-
escence was all agog at the prospect of dinner with Mr
Wolfe. If his country home was The Den, what was his
London home called? The Lair, perhaps?

She hugged this gleeful thought to herself as *Madame*
discreetly questioned her about her ride with Ben and
she as discreetly answered, amused, as always, at the
distance she had come from being the naïve girl whom
Samuel Mitchell had cheated so easily.

Chapter Nine

'I say, Gronow, ain't that Ben Wolfe? Who let him in? All sorts of stories goin' around about him. No one knows who the devil he really is.'

'Best not let him hear you say so,' returned Captain Gronow, looking up from his game of whist to rebuke the speaker, his partner, James Erskine. 'He's a devil of a fellow for anything you care to name: rapier, sabre, pistols or fists. What's more, he's a member here. That Indian nabob, Wilson, put him up for membership and he was accepted before the *on dits* started their rounds. Whatever else, he's the dead-spit image of his supposed father, the late Charlie Wolfe, but on which side of the blanket…who knows or cares?

'In any case, your turn to play—you haven't forgotten that we *are* playing at whist and not at gossip.'

Since Gronow possessed all the athletic attributes which he claimed for Ben Wolfe, James Erskine flushed and played the card which he had been holding in the air. 'Only asking, old fellow, only asking,' he muttered.

Ben, watching them from where he was propped against the mantelpiece, a glass of rather inferior port in his hand, would not have been surprised to learn that he was the subject of their conversation. Only that morning Jess Fitzroy, as tactfully as he could, had told him of the unpleasant rumours about him circulating around London.

'So that was why I caused such a commotion in Hyde Park yesterday,' he had said. 'I might have thought that it was the splendour of my turnout, but no. Try to find out where this nonsense came from—who started it on its way.'

'Difficult, that,' said Jess, shrugging his shoulders. 'I'll do my best, though.'

Ben had said no more. He thought he knew who had started the lie on its way, but he wanted hard evidence before he took any action. He drank down the remains of his port and turned to speak to his friend, once his patron, Tom Wilson, who was standing near him.

He had only exchanged a few words with him when someone tapped him aggressively on his shoulder, causing him to turn in the opposite direction—to discover that he was facing George Darlington.

'You wish to speak to me?' he asked. He kept his voice low and his manner courteous. He had no wish to embarrass Tom Wilson to whom he owed a great deal, including his membership of White's.

George, however, was suffering from no such constraints. 'I have no *wish* to speak to you,' he said roughly, treading on the word wish. 'But I am compelled to do so in order to ask you what you are doing here in a club reserved for gentlemen. You, being neither a gentleman nor entitled to the name you pretend to, have no business here.'

'Steady now, young fellow,' exclaimed Tom before Ben could answer. 'He is here because he has been properly elected at my sponsorship and that of Lord

Lowborough with whom we were both acquainted in India.'

'Oh, India,' jeered George, 'one might claim to be anyone in India, eh, Father?'

George's father, Lord Babbacombe, who had been a little way behind his son because of handing his hat and greatcoat to a footman, said approvingly, 'Indeed, that is so. We order matters differently in England as this fellow will soon discover. I shall make a complaint immediately to the committee and ask them to revoke his membership forthwith. To my certain knowledge he is an impostor. Charles Wolfe's only son, Benjamin, died in childhood.'

'A fate likely to overtake your son at a somewhat later stage in his life,' ground out Ben through his teeth, 'since I am giving him notice that I shall be sending my seconds to him to arrange for us to meet on the field of honour so that I may repay him for the insult which he has put upon me.'

'You may send as many seconds as you please,' returned m'lord, 'but no son of mine, nor any other gentleman, will soil his hands by engaging in an affair of honour with a cheat and impostor. Be warned, sir, I shall shortly be laying before the proper authorities evidence of your crimes. I say nothing of the fact that you have spent your time since you returned to England attempting to ruin me financially. That has nothing to do with the case, other than to prove that you have no shame and that the word honour on your lips demeans it.'

'Attempting to ruin you,' said Ben, his eyebrows rising. 'I believe that I have gone further than that—for a reason which you well know and which I shall not mention here.

'I take note that your son, having insulted me, is neither ready to take the consequences, nor to speak for himself. I wondered where the courage—which he so recently lacked—came from when he taunted me a moment ago, but I see that it was because he had no intention of proving either his courage or his honour. I don't find that surprising since he apparently possesses neither virtue.'

He swung round on George, who had stepped back to allow his father to fight his battles for him.

'Do you intend to allow me to insult you at will? I shall certainly do so if you don't remove yourself from my sight.'

His whole appearance was so threatening that George retreated even further backwards, his face paling, proving, if proof were needed, that Ben's impugning of his courage was no less than true.

Tom Wilson put a hand on Ben's arm. 'Come,' he said, 'you have made your point. If the young fellow won't fight, we all know what to think of him.'

Captain Gronow, who had abandoned his card game, came over to them. 'What's to do?' he asked, being very much a man who was sought after to pass judgement when such quarrels had reached *point non plus*.

Before Ben could answer Gronow's question, Tom Wilson put his oar in again. 'I am a third party here, albeit I am Mr Wolfe's friend. The matter lies so,' and he gave a brief and accurate account of what had passed.

'Hmm,' said Gronow, managing to make that mild exclamation sound magisterial. 'A serious business, I see. My own feeling is that Lord Darlington should not have gone as far as he did unless he intended to back his accusation with the force of arms. On the other hand,

Lord Babbacombe has some right on his side when he argues that the accusation, if true, relieves his son of defending himself against someone whose own honour is dubious. The matter is at a stand-off until Mr Wolfe's claim to be who he is has been proven beyond doubt.'

Tom Wilson said indignantly, 'I have known Ben Wolfe since he was eighteen and he has borne no other name.'

'Which proves nothing, Tom,' said Ben savagely. 'You are but an India merchant, and who I claimed to be at eighteen is neither here nor there—as you well know. I thank you for your defence, but...' and he shrugged his shoulders.

Captain Gronow's reply was mild. 'Until matters are settled, all parties must agree to let them rest. No unproven accusations and insults should be exchanged, and consequently there should be no duelling, either provoked inside these walls or outside of them. I think that is clear, you will agree.'

He was one of society's arbiters, and most of the men who had clustered around Ben and his two accusers would consider what he had said to be fair and reasonable. Both parties could do nothing but accept what he had said.

'This is not the end of the affair,' exclaimed Lord Babbacombe. 'You heard what I said. I shall pursue you until I have broken you, as you are breaking me. I believe you to be the person behind the collapse of my son's marriage to Miss Western.'

'Come, come, m'lord,' said Gronow, the only person brave enough to say such a thing to a peer of the realm, 'you have no proof of that. No proof at all. Let us, as I advised, leave the matter where it stands.'

Even Babbacombe could not refuse to agree with

him, especially when he was surrounded by nodding heads all agreeing with Gronow. There were those who hastened to put their name in White's famous betting book, wagering good money that Ben Wolfe and either Babbacombe or Darlington would meet one dawn at Putney to put the matter to the final test of a duel, even though they dare say nothing aloud.

His face furious, Lord Babbacombe walked away with his son, exclaiming vigorously that he had no mind to remain at White's while it was polluted by Ben Wolfe's presence. Ben himself made no effort to leave. He picked up his glass of port and coolly continued his conversation with Tom Wilson as though he had never been interrupted.

Tom heard him out before saying bluffly, 'Well, at least one thing that m'lord said was true. You are, I am reliably informed, responsible for his financial ruin.'

'Now where did you hear that?' Ben's reply was almost indifferent.

'Oh, you can't keep such matters secret.'

'I know. Every camp has its traitor. Be sure I shall find mine.'

Tom clapped him on the back. 'I wouldn't like to be in his shoes. If you leave him the wherewithal to buy any, that is.'

'Are you referring to the traitor—or Lord Babbacombe?'

'Either or both,' said Tom with a grin. 'Take your pick.'

'Oh, I will. Another thing you may be sure of.'

His friend nodded. One thing he *was* sure of was that he would not like to have Ben Wolfe for an enemy.

'You would do well not to underrate Babbacombe,

though. He has powerful friends, and it would be advisable to take his threats seriously.'

'Oh, Tom, I always take everything seriously. As you should know.'

They had been friends since Ben had left the Army in India and had used his savings and his winnings at cards to start up his own small business. By chance he had done Tom Wilson so great a favour that Tom had rewarded him not only with money, but with help and advice in his new career.

Later Tom was to think, a trifle ruefully, that the help and advice had been scarcely necessary, for Ben had soon carved out for himself an empire even greater and more prosperous than his own. But being Ben's friend, he had discovered, brought its own rewards. Jess Fitzroy had not lied when he had told Susanna that Ben looked after people. When ill luck overtook Tom, it was Ben who had bailed him out, and helped him to recover most of what he had lost and enabled him to make an even greater fortune.

And now they were both in London, enjoying their success, and building a new life in the land which they had left behind as very young men.

'Did you ever think, Ben, when you were a penniless private soldier, that one day you would be drinking with the nobs in the best gentleman's club in London?'

It was a question which invited 'no' for an answer, but Ben lifted his refilled glass and grinned at his old friend. 'Oh, yes. Even then I dreamed of a day like this. And what I should do when I achieved my dream.'

'You mean—about Babbacombe?' asked Tom shrewdly.

'Among other things, yes.'

His face when he came out with this was so grim that

Tom shuddered. Ben had served under the Duke of Wellington when he had been what Napoleon had sneeringly called 'a mere Sepoy general', and he thought that, like Wellington, Ben had steel in his soul.

He pitied Babbacombe and his cowardly cub of a son from the bottom of his heart, but he also knew that if Ben Wolfe was pursuing them they deserved to be pursued.

'So,' said Susanna prettily to her host, 'you didn't name your home in London "The Lair" as I thought that you might. Croft House seems a pretty innocent place for a Wolfe to live in.'

Ben smiled at her. They were in the drawing room, waiting to go into dinner. 'I might have known,' he told her, 'that I would suffer the edge of your tongue. My London home is called Croft House because the Croft family lived here until they died out some fifty years ago. But now that you have mentioned it I shall probably change it to The Lair—it might frighten off housebreakers and scapegallows.'

'Scapegallows?' exclaimed Madame de Saulx. 'That is a new word for me. Pray, what does it mean?'

'Oh, you must ask Mr Fitzroy that—it is he who collects thieves' slang for me.'

Jess smiled and bowed to *Madame* before saying, 'A scapegallows is a criminal who has done exactly that. He has escaped hanging by some artful means and returns to prey on us again. At the moment, there is a new and violent crew of them—their word for gang— stopping honest citizens in the street at night and relieving them of their valuables. The watch seems unable to protect us from their depredations.'

'Best not to go out alone at night,' said Tom Wilson practically. 'I never do.'

'Wise advice,' drawled Lord Lowborough. 'Coming back to it, I find that London is a paradise for rogues of all degrees. There are nearly as many swindlers in the City in the day as there are pickpockets in the streets at night.'

'Oh, come, Lowborough,' exclaimed Tom. 'That's stretching it a little, ain't it?'

'Hardly,' murmured Ben, smiling.

'And you should know.'

Lowborough smiled back at him. He had been young Henry Forster, a poor lieutenant in Wellington's Indian army, three lives from a title, when Ben had been his sergeant. As an almost penniless boy, he had been helped by Ben Wolfe after Ben's rise to fortune nearly as much as Jess Fitzroy, except that his unexpected accession to his title had suddenly transformed him into a rich magnate who needed no man's help.

Unlike many, he had been as grateful to Ben when he was rich as he had been when he was poor, and their friendship had continued unabated. He had married into the Milner family and his pretty wife, Jane, was sitting next to Susanna, listening in some astonishment to the lively conversation going on around her. The Milners were devout Christians and discussions about swindling and thieves and thief-taking were not the staple of their normal conversation.

She whispered to Susanna, 'Are Mr Wolfe's dinners always like this?'

'I don't know,' Susanna whispered back. 'This is the first of his which I have attended.'

'Henry swears that Mr Wolfe is the cleverest man he knows, and he always says and does the unexpected.

Looking at him, I find that I can quite believe that to be true. He frightens me a little. Doesn't he frighten you? If you will forgive me saying so, you didn't seem frightened when you quizzed him about the name of his house.'

Does he frighten me? thought Susanna. I can't honestly say that he does. He didn't frighten me when we first met because I was too angry with him to be frightened of him, and he doesn't frighten me now. On the other hand, he does disturb me in the oddest way. If I were a character in a novel, I should probably believe that I was falling in love with him—although I can't imagine him falling in love with me.

'No,' she told Jane honestly. 'He doesn't frighten me, he intrigues me.'

She was watching him laughing at something Lord Lowborough had said, his head flung back, his strong white teeth gleaming, his eyes shining, looking for all the world like the wolf he was named after. She was surer than ever that he was her unknown saviour—and by what devious means he had saved her she did not yet care to know.

'You have heard, I suppose,' Jane said, 'that Lord Babbacombe, who is a distant relative of the Wolfes, swears that he is not a Wolfe at all and has no right to the name or to the house and the remnants of the Wolfe lands which he claimed when he returned from India. He says that he will go to law to prove it.'

Susanna swung her head around to stare at Jane. 'No, I had not heard that. Is it true—or is it idle gossip?'

'Oh, I overheard Henry telling a friend that Lord Babbacombe and Mr Wolfe had a set-to at White's the other night. He said that Mr Wolfe challenged Lord Darlington to a duel for insulting him and Lord Darlington refused on the grounds that he did not fight men who had no right to the name they bore. Even if that name was tarnished by the scandals around the late Mr Wolfe.'

'He would,' said Susanna curtly. 'He is too cowardly to face Mr Wolfe—or any other man in a duel.'

'Well, I'm glad that Henry is Mr Wolfe's friend,' said Jane, 'for I can't imagine anyone wishing to face him in a duel. Henry says…' and she began to describe her husband's account of Ben's prowess as a swordsman, marksman and pugilist.

One thing was plain to Susanna—beside the proof of Ben Wolfe's many-sided talents—Jane Lowborough was so besotted with her husband that 'Henry says' prefaced most of her conversation.

What worried her, though, was Lord Babbacombe's reported attack on Ben. If Ben hated Lord Babbacombe—and her memory of what he had said of him at the time of his kidnapping told her that he did—then, equally, for whatever reason, Lord Babbacombe hated Ben. And what were the scandals which surrounded the late Mr Wolfe? They must be old ones, for she understood that Ben Wolfe's father had died when he was little more than a boy.

'Did your husband tell you, or have you any notion, why Lord Babbacombe dislikes Mr Wolfe so much?'

'Oh, the rumour is that it was Mr Wolfe who ruined him financially—which was why Lord Darlington's marriage with Miss Western was called off, and possibly why Lord Babbacombe is accusing him of impersonation now.'

She paused reflectively. 'I had no notion when I married Henry that life would be so exciting. Papa was a country Rector, you know, and the most excitement we

ever had were the disputes among the men about who
was the best shot and among the ladies about who
should organise the flowers in church, or go first into
dinner. One can scarcely imagine Mr Wolfe and Mr
Wilson troubling themselves about such innocent matters.'

'Ah, Lady Lowborough,' said *Madame* on overhearing this, 'you intrigue me.'

She had been conversing with Mrs Wilson and Mrs
Dickson. Mrs Dickson was the wife of another of Ben
Wolfe's financial allies. She had been, before their re-
spective marriages, the companion and friend of Lady
Devereux, famous for her wit and her eccentricity.

'If you are discussing innocent matters with Miss
Beverly, then I fear that you may be the only pair in
the room who are. Mrs Dickson and I have discovered
a common admiration for the late M. de la Rochefoucauld, who cannot in any circumstances be described as
innocent. We have been shocking Mrs Wilson with his
cynicism.

'As for the gentlemen of the party, their conversation
is never innocent, and we must hope that dinner will be
soon announced so that it becomes trivial again when
they decide that they must spare the ladies' delicate
feelings.'

Jane Lowborough gave a little gasp on hearing such
frank heresy. Susanna, on the other hand, was as entertained as she always was when *Madame* spoke her
mind.

Mrs Dickson remarked approvingly, 'Well said. I am
sure that they will deal only with crinkum crankum in
our presence.'

'Crinkum crankum?' queried *Madame*. 'Pray, what

does that mean? My command of English does not extend to understanding that.'

'Women's nothings,' returned Mrs Dickson. 'Most of the men are not very good at it. Real crinkum crankum is dress and gossip and the latest Gothic novel—about which none of them know anything.'

'I wouldn't bet on Mr Ben Wolfe being ignorant of such matters,' offered Susanna, 'he seems to know everything.'

Privately she was amused at the turn the evening's conversation had taken with earnest discussion on thieves and society slang being intermingled with lofty discussions on French philosophers.

Dinner being announced had them all parading into the dining room. Susanna was led in by Jess Fitzroy; *Madame* was Ben's partner. Dinner-table conversation, as prophesied, was light in the extreme.

The only serious remark came from Tom Wilson, who told Ben to watch his back and earned in response, a light-hearted, 'Don't worry, Tom, I always take more notice of my enemies than my friends.'

How typical of him, was Susanna's immediate reaction. He was sure to say the very opposite of what one might have expected! She said so to Jess. 'I shall take a deal of notice of your judgements in future, Mr Fitzroy, particularly to those concerning your employer.'

'Oh, all my judgements are worth heeding, Miss Beverly,' he told her, giving her his most dazzling smile. He really was the most handsome man, so why his golden beauty and regular features were unable to excite her in the same way that Ben Wolfe's harsh and craggy face did was a puzzle which Susanna was unable to solve.

In fact, she seemed to be surrounded by puzzles. Why

had *Madame* been so eager to borrow Lord Exford's copy of La Rochefoucauld's *Maximes*? Did the inscription in it have any significance? What were the scandals about his father to which Jane Lowborough had referred? Was Ben Wolfe truly entitled to his name? Why did he wish to ruin Lord Babbacombe and his family? And why had he wanted to kidnap Amelia?

Were all these things connected in some way? It was difficult to see how her new friend and patroness Madame de Saulx was involved, other than that she was also the most unlikely friend and patron of Ben Wolfe.

'You are quiet tonight, Miss Beverly,' remarked Jess as they were served the next course. Ben Wolfe's dinners were organised after the Russian, not the English, fashion with footmen handing the food around rather than all the courses being put in the centre of the table.

Susanna's eyes were alight with mischief as she answered him. 'Does that mean that you usually find me noisy?'

'On the contrary, you have a low voice, which I assure you is what pleases men most in women, but you commonly use it well and wittily. Tonight, though, you are a trifle subdued. I trust that you are not feeling low.'

'Oh, no, I am in rude health, but…' For a moment Susanna considered asking Jess the nature of the scandal about Ben's father, but decided against it.

'But?' he prompted her.

'But I have been reading M. de la Rochefoucauld's *Maximes* and his cynicism has left me feeling a little melancholy.'

There was a certain amount of truth in that statement, but not much, Susanna reflected, but it was the best explanation which she could offer to satisfy Jess at such short notice.

'Then allow me to dispel your melancholy by regaling you with some of the more amusing rumours circulating about town at the moment.'

The greatest rumours, thought Susanna, as Jess was as good as his word, telling her of the Prince Regent's latest efforts to rid himself of his unwanted wife, were those concerning their host, which were hardly the subject for wit at his own dinner table! However, she laughed obligingly at Jess's spirited delivery, so much so, indeed that Ben leaned forward and remarked, 'You seem to be enjoying yourselves a great deal at your end of the table, Jess. May we all be allowed to share your jokes?'

The true reason for his intervention was his very real jealousy at the sight of another man entertaining Susanna and fixing admiring eyes on her.

He gained his reward when Jess looked away from her and turned towards him, saying, 'I was informing Miss Beverly of the Regent's remarking that he could not wait to rid himself of his elderly, plain and illdressed wife to his latest female favourite who is, if anything, even older, plainer and worse dressed.'

'An old Hanoverian custom, I understand,' remarked Lord Lowborough. 'Ever since the Royal family came over to rule England in 1714, their monarchs have always favoured plain women. I understand that, when the Regent becomes King, he will immediately press for an Act of Parliament to be passed to permit him to divorce his wife. Divorced or not, he will not allow her to be crowned with him.'

Ben was happy to notice that talk now became general, centred mostly on the Regent's affairs, with Jess's attention diverted from Susanna, who conversed instead with Lord Lowborough, who was recently and safely married to a wife whom he loved. No danger there from him: Susanna might talk to him as much as she wished.

Later, alone with the women, whilst back in the dining room the men drank port at their leisure, the conversation again turned to the Princess of Wales, the Regent's unhappy wife.

'One has to say,' remarked Madame de Saulx, 'that the poor woman has a certain amount of right on her side. Whilst we may not agree with the London mob that she is a totally wronged woman, nevertheless we must always remember that she was given in marriage to a man who treated her abominably from her wedding day onwards. She may have acted unwisely on occasion, but how has *he* behaved?'

It was plain that all the women agreed with her over the Regent's bad behaviour, even if they did not condone his wife's. 'Nevertheless,' said Jane Lowborough slowly, 'I am happy that she is rarely received in good society. None of our husbands would be safe, I understand, if she were.'

'True,' said *Madame*. 'And more's the pity. The greater the persecution which she suffers, the more she becomes a driven woman.'

After that the conversation took a lighter turn, ending with a discussion of the first Canto of Lord Byron's latest poem, *Don Juan*, which, among other things, contained an unkind portrait of the poet's estranged wife.

'But,' said *Madame*, when that subject was almost exhausted, 'we must confess that, as always, he mingles his satire with the most divine poetry. Who can disagree with him when he writes,

> Man's love is of man's life a thing apart,
> Tis woman's whole existence…

For do not men have many worlds to range to which
we are not admitted? We are but wives or daughters:
but they are not only husbands or sons.'

Susanna clapped her hands together and exclaimed
impulsively. 'How true—and how ironic that a man like
Lord Byron, who has always behaved so badly towards
women, should at the same time be aware of how cir-
cumscribed we are.'

She was thinking of the ruin which had almost overcome her when she was neither wife nor daughter, just
an unconsidered and unwanted spinster with no profession, and no occupation. Even the meanest of younger
sons had more than that to expect from life.

No time to revisit the unhappy past, though, for the
men were returning and the present became all-
consuming again. Ben made his way to where Susanna
and Jane were and took a seat between them.

'Lowborough has proposed a game of whist,' he told
them, 'and, since the party is large enough to make up
three tables, I hope that the ladies will all consent to
play.'

Jane said, a trifle agitatedly, 'I'm afraid that my card-
playing skills are not good enough to allow me to take
part. We rarely played at home, and Henry has been
trying to teach me.'

'And I am in a similar situation,' added Susanna.

As might have been expected, this did not deter Ben
Wolfe at all. 'Splendid,' he exclaimed, lying in his
teeth. 'I can think of nothing better than spending an
evening trying to teach my partner how to play. Now,
if you partner your husband, and Miss Beverly agrees
to partner me, we can have a happy hour enjoying our-

selves and leave such experts as Madame de Saulx and
Tom Wilson to play the game with those others who
share their grim determination to win. They can play
for money; I propose that we play for bonbons, eh,
Henry?'

Madame said, 'That's the most remarkable proposal
I've ever heard, seeing that it comes from a man who
once earned his living playing every card game ever
invented!'

'Did you?' asked Susanna, fascinated by this new
revelation about Ben's past. 'Earn your living by playing cards, I mean. Oh, forgive me, I shouldn't really
question you about such matters—or so I used to tell
my charges.'

'*You* may question me about anything, Miss Beverly,'
said Ben. 'And yes, I did. But I have forgotten everything I ever knew.'

'And that's a Banbury tale if ever I heard one,'
drawled Lord Lowborough. 'Seeing that you emptied
everyone's pockets playing whist the other night at
White's.'

'Oh, I only forget everything I know about cards
when I play with those innocents who genuinely know
nothing—other than anything necessary to teach them
the rules of the game, that is.'

'You should have been a lawyer, Ben,' laughed Tom
Wilson, 'or a member of Parliament, you play with
words so well. I propose that we play cards immediately
so that we may have the pleasure of watching you join
with Lowborough in playing for nothing rather than for
something. I cannot believe that you ever did such a
thing before.'

'I agree,' said Ben, rising. 'Let us begin, if only to
stop these unwarranted attacks on my reputation. Before

we do, however, I hope my two pupils already know that there are fifty-two cards in a pack.'

'Really?' exclaimed Susanna, putting on what Ben recognised as her teasing face. 'I thought that there were only twelve.'

Before Ben could tease her back, Jane Lowborough said mournfully, 'Oh, are there? I had thought that the number was fifty-two—but I suppose that I am wrong. I am usually wrong about figures.'

'Nonsense,' said Ben firmly. 'Miss Beverly knows exactly how many cards there are in a pack. She is teasing us so that when we begin to play we shall underrate her and thus enable her to win more bonbons than she ought.'

'Exactly,' said Lord Lowborough. 'Jane, you may sit opposite to me, and I shall endeavour to explain the game as we go along. Wolfe, you may do the same for Miss Beverly—but none of your tricks, mind.'

'As though I would,' returned Ben, putting on a mournful face. 'The footmen have finished setting out the tables, so let us begin. The rest of the party may arrange themselves as they please.'

Afterwards, Susanna was to remember that evening as one of the last for some time that she and the rest of the party spent in innocent pleasure. Ben used his tutoring of her as an excuse to tease her. He also whispered confidentially to her while he taught her—despite Lord Lowborough's warning—some of the tricks of the game. For the last few years Susanna had been outside the magic circle of fun and laughter at such parties, condemned to watch others enjoy themselves, and now she was inside that circle again.

The evening passed so quickly that she could scarcely believe that it was over when *Madame* whispered to her that it was time to leave and their carriage was waiting for them.

'Oh, I have enjoyed myself tonight,' she told Ben before they left.

'So you will come again soon?' he asked, taking her hand and pressing it gently.

'Of course, if you invite me,' she told him, a little breathlessly, her eyes shining as her whole body vibrated at his touch, telling her that for good or ill she had fallen in love with Ben Wolfe.

'Never fear,' he said. 'You will always be at the top of my guest list.' He relinquished her hand reluctantly.

Jess Fitzroy, watching them, knew that he had lost her, but then, he had never possessed her and now never would. Damn you, Ben Wolfe, he thought, if you mistreat her, however loyal I have been to you in the past, my loyalty would not survive that!

He was not the only one who had guessed Susanna's secret. Madame de Saulx, seated opposite her glowing protégé on the drive home, was also aware of it and was making Ben a similar promise to that of Jess's.

If Ben could not see what a suitable wife Susanna would make for him, seeing that she was one of the few women who would stand up to him, then he was less shrewd than she had always thought him.

Despite the success of his dinner party, Ben found it difficult to sleep that night. It was not only the memory of Susanna's face which haunted him, but something which Lowborough had told him: that, as well as the rumours which Babbacombe was spreading about his legitimacy, he was also resurrecting the old scandal about his father and mother.

He thought grimly that, whilst he was redressing

other people's wrongs, he ought to find time to right some of his own.

Morning found him tired but resolute. He had business to attend to at his counting house in the City of London before he talked in the afternoon with the Rothschild brothers, with whom he was engaged in discussions about enlarging trade with the United States as well with the East. He acknowledged that his ambitions were limitless—but then, they always had been, even when he had been a private soldier.

Yet, to his surprise, he found that memories of Susanna's face laughing up at him whilst he was teaching her to play whist came between him and the papers which he was studying—something which had never happened to him before.

He smiled ruefully to himself before attending carefully to what Mr Leopold Rothschild was saying to him in his beautifully furnished office.

'My brothers and I will be happy to do business with you, sir. Your reputation as a man of your word is good, your honesty as a man of business is unimpeached, and our investigation of your financial situation shows that the claims you make in your propositions to us are accurate.

'You will forgive my plain speaking, I hope, but our reputation has been built on taking only those risks which are unavoidable—we see little danger of them occurring in our future dealings with you.'

Ben inclined his head. Mr Leopold was a man after his own heart, downright and straightforward—in speech, if nowhere else.

'I prefer plain speaking myself to the other kind,' he told them. 'I take it, then, that our lawyers will draw up the necessary papers between them, ready for us to sign as soon as possible.'

'Indeed, and in the meantime, let us shake hands upon the bargain we have made as surety of our respective goodwill.'

It was done. All that remained was for him to return to his office and alert Jess and his clerks, inform the lawyers and complete the deal.

It was well into the dusk of the evening by the time that Ben had finished working. He had sent Jess off in the gig to carry out some necessary errands relating to the business with the Rothschilds, telling him that he need not return to collect him. He would walk home.

Jess demurred. 'You heard what was said last night—about it being unsafe at present to walk London's streets unaccompanied after dark. Let me call for you when I have finished.'

'I thank you for reminding me, but the journey home is not long and I have been cooped up all day. I have a stout stick with me. Do you go straight home when your work is over. You may report to me there later tonight.'

There was no arguing with him. Jess shrugged his shoulders and drove off. Later, Ben wished that he had listened to him for he was tired and impatient: the day had been harder than he had expected and the walk home seemed less attractive than he had earlier thought.

He took tight hold of his stick—it was almost a cudgel—and set off through the City's maze of streets. He was almost out of it when disaster struck.

A group of men, armed with bludgeons, sprang out of an alley to attack him on a deserted street. He was fortunate enough to glimpse them coming and guess

that their purpose was to attack him. Rather than try to
defend himself he began to run at top speed, away from
them. Only to find himself faced by two more men who
had been hiding in a doorway, one of them being armed
with a pistol, the other with a cudgel.

Nothing for it but to try to tackle them. He raised his
own cudgel to strike the pistol out of the fellow's hand
and send it skittering into the gutter, although concentrating on him meant that he took a blow on the shoulder from his pal.

Ben, reeling from the blow, was sent backwards and
to the ground, to come up holding the first robber's
pistol which he fired at the man with the cudgel, hitting
him in the shoulder. Clutching it, and dropping his
cudgel, the robber staggered off to escape further punishment. The man whose pistol Ben had snatched from
the gutter picked up the cudgel, raised it, and ran at
him.

By this time the first group of robbers had caught up
with him, ready to finish him off, but the noise of the
pistol shot had brought workmen from a nearby yard
into the street where, after watching the struggle for a
few moments they took Ben's part and a general mêlée
broke out. At the same time two watchmen, just beginning their rounds, arrived to join in the battle.

The thieves, now heavily outnumbered, began to run
off, pursued by those men who were armed with the
hammers with which they had been working.

Ben, who had taken several more blows and was now
unsteady on his feet, sat down on a nearby wall, still
clutching the pistol. Now that the fracas was over, men
and women who had been watching from windows and
doorways began to emerge from the houses and work-
shops which lined the street.

The man who had been in charge of the rescuing workmen came up to Ben to offer him further assistance. On reaching him, he exclaimed, 'Ben! It is Ben Wolfe, isn't it? I couldn't see who you were in the mêlée. Are you hurt? Should we send for an apothecary?'

It was George Dickson, his friend, business acquaintance and recent dinner guest who owned the saddler's yard from which the workmen had come.

Ben shook his dizzy head. 'Bruised,' he said briefly. 'Nothing serious, thank God—and I owe my safety to you and your men. I can't thank you enough. Without your timely help I should probably be lying dead in the road. One of the ruffians attacking me had a pistol. I shot him with it, but he wasn't mortally wounded, just ran off. That's my cudgel over there. I lost it in what followed.'

'Trust you to shoot a man with his own weapon,' said George, who was himself an old soldier. 'Come in and let us look after you. Emma can make you a cup of tea—or you can have some brandy if you prefer it.'

Still talking, he led the dazed Ben into his living quarters which were above his shop and office. The watch, who had failed to catch any of the ruffians, resumed their rounds and, the excitement over, the spectators went indoors again.

'The streets are no longer safe,' mourned Emma Dickson as she applied salve to Ben's bruised face. 'But I haven't often seen such a large number of men attack one person before. I saw everything from the window, including George's men rush out to discover what was what when the shot was fired. It was lucky that they were working late on a commission tonight, or you would have had the worst of it.'

'Yes,' said Ben, drinking first the tea and then the

brandy. 'My thanks to them, and to Dickie are heartfelt.'
Dickie had been George Dickson's nickname ever since
he had been a trooper in the army: his friends still used
it.

What the worst of it was he did not tell them immediately. The pistol which he had scooped up from
the gutter was an expensive piece, and he was sure had
been meant to finish him off. That, and the large number
of men involved, convinced him that this had been no
chance attack. It had been planned and he had been
followed, almost certainly from his counting house.

How many nights had they been watching him—and
who had paid them to kill him? The pity was that they
had all escaped in the confusion which had followed
Dickie Dickson's intervention, thus preventing any hope
of questioning any of them.

Useless to repine. Tomorrow he would set men on
their trail. He knew that he had enemies—no man in
his line of business could escape them—but an enemy
who wanted to kill him—now, that was quite another
thing!

As Dickie Dickson said in his quiet way when he
offered to drive Ben home in his gig, 'You ought not
to leave unescorted, they might still be waiting for you.
That was a hardened crew of bludgeoneers with an upright man in charge—the one with the pistol, I suppose.
Who dislikes you enough to want to half-kill you, Ben?'

He didn't need to tell Ben that an upright man was
the captain of a crew or the leader of a gang: like him,
Ben was *au fait* with thieves' slang.

'And a good pistol, too,' said Ben, thinking that
Dickie might prove a useful ally. 'One of Manton's best
with a hair trigger.'

He showed it to him, saying, 'Either stolen or given

to him to finish me off when the bludgeons had done their work. You might as well know that I think that murder was their aim—theft would have been a bonus. I'll accept your kind offer of a ride home.'

Dickie nodded thoughtfully. 'I thought murder was on their mind—and wondered if you did. Would you like me to make some enquiries? I promise to be discreet.'

'Only if you let me pay you.'

When Dickie raised his hand and made protesting noises, he said, gently enough, 'You have a business to run and a young family to look after—I know I'm a friend, but I'm not going to trade on that.'

Later that night Emma Dickson said briskly to Dickie, 'I thought more highly of Ben Wolfe tonight, George, than I did when I first met him in his drawing room last night. His bark is worse than his bite and his courage is undoubted. I wouldn't like to be on the wrong side of him, though.'

'Nor I,' said Dickie, 'but he ought to guard his back. I've offered him the service of a bruiser I know to act as a bodyguard and he's almost agreed. He doesn't like to depend on others, but there are times when one has to.'

'Like Dev and Dickie were,' said Emma sleepily, referring to her husband's David and Jonathan-like friendship with Jack, Earl Devereux, when they had been soldiers together.

'Exactly,' said Dickie, 'and now, do your duty to me, wife.'

'That's what Ben Wolfe needs,' murmured Emma, turning happily into her husband's arms. 'A wife.'

Chapter Ten

Ben said nothing of the attack on him, and the only others who had immediate knowledge of it were Dickie and his wife, and Jess Fitzroy, whom he told when he reached home, so it was surprising that, by the next afternoon news of it was circulating in the *ton*. Since Dickie never mixed with the *ton* and Jess had been sworn to secrecy, it told Ben that the only person who could have set the story on its way was the person who had ordered the attack.

He puzzled over the motive for such an odd action and concluded that the notion was that it proved Ben Wolfe to be a shady character if someone was determined to maim or kill him.

He passed a restless night pondering on who his enemy might be. He finally determined on three names: Samuel Mitchell, Lord Babbacombe and Herbert Jamison, with whom he had had some dealings which ended in acrimony as a result of Jamison's dishonesty. The result for Jamison had been bankruptcy, but Ben did not honestly believe that he could have behaved otherwise.

Babbacombe and Mitchell had reason to hate him, but would they kill him? For what purpose?

When morning came he decided against going to his counting house—his face was heavily bruised and he did not wish the sight of it to encourage gossip. Instead he sent for Jess, on whom he could rely, with instructions, not only for him, but for his clerks, regarding both the business with the Rothschilds and the attack of the previous night. He also complainingly agreed with the doctor whom Jess had called in that he should rest for two or three days before returning to work.

By mid-morning on the second one he was already feeling better and ready for action again, but he also felt regretfully compelled to keep his promise to Jess that he would obey doctor's orders.

That afternoon *Madame* and Susanna were enjoying themselves at the piano. *Madame* was playing and Susanna was singing, when Lord and Lady Exford were announced. Both of them looked exceedingly grave. *Madame* rose to greet them and offered them refreshments. Lady Exford settled for tea but Lord Exford, usually an abstemious young man, asked for sherry.

'For,' he said, 'I have just heard some unwelcome gossip. It appears that Mr Wolfe was attacked three nights ago when he was walking home from his counting house in the City. Report has it that he was only saved from being injured by the intervention of a group of workmen. Report also says that he is confined to his home until his injuries improve.'

He looked at *Madame*, and said heavily, 'As if that were not enough, someone has also revived the old scandal about his father. This, as you must know, *Madame*, affects me since my late mother, as well as

Charles Wolfe's wife, was involved, and the last thing which Lady Exford and I wish is that it shall become the commonplace of gossip again.'

Susanna, drinking her tea, now had an explanation for the inscription in the *Maximes*—the Wolfes and the Exfords had been friends—but none for the nature of the scandal.

She would not have been human if she were not curious, but she said nothing. *Madame* commiserated with the Exfords without giving anything away, but the effect of their news was to throw a cloud of melancholy over the afternoon.

After they had departed, *Madame* did not take her seat at the piano again, but instead came and sat near Susanna, saying, 'I did not like to speak of the matter with the Exfords present, but it seems to me that, since the rumour is going the rounds, you ought to know the truth of it lest you unwittingly say something untoward. The truth being almost certainly different from the rumour. I must warn you that it is not a pretty story and will be painful for me to relate.

'When Ben Wolfe was but a boy his mother and father were bosom bows with the late Lord Exford and his wife, all of them being of a similar age. I am speaking of some twenty-five years ago. The Exfords were staying with the Wolfes at The Den when, one afternoon, Lord Exford went shooting with some local gentry and Charles Wolfe was engaged in business with the then Lord Lieutenant of Buckinghamshire at his seat, Beauval, nearby.

'The two women decided to go for a walk in the grounds without taking an attendant footman. Mrs Wolfe was a skilled amateur painter and Lady Exford was carrying a book: the *Maximes* of M. de la Rochefoucauld. Both the men returned home in the early evening to find the servants in an uproar. Their wives had not returned although they had been gone for over three hours and a search party was being prepared by Mr Wolfe's agent, one Thomas Linacre.

'They were not in the spot by a small stream where they had told their lady's maids that they were going: Mrs Wolfe to sketch, Lady Exford to read, although her book—the one I have borrowed from Lord Exford— was found thrown down nearby, together with the shawl she was wearing. There was no sign of Mrs Wolfe and she has never been seen since that fatal afternoon. Her sketching equipment was found floating downstream later that evening. Lady Exford was eventually discovered some distance away from her book and shawl. She had been dragged into a copse and left for dead after being criminally assaulted.

'When she recovered consciousness her memory had gone. The last thing which she could recall was being in the drawing room after nuncheon. She remembered nothing about her and Mrs Wolfe's decision to go for a walk and what had occurred during it. Consequently she had no notion of what might have happened to Mrs Wolfe. One might have said that nature was merciful to her, given what she must have suffered, except that that mercy left such a dreadful mystery unsolved. She never recovered her full health and died within the year...' *Madame* paused.

Susanna was puzzled. 'But why did that create a scandal involving Mr Wolfe? From what you have told me he was far away at the time.'

Madame sighed. 'As soon as the matter was investigated a number of contradictions came to light. It turned out that no one could say with any certainty that the two women *had* left together. The stories of the servants differed. And although there were plenty of witnesses to testify that Lord Exford was with a group of gentlemen all afternoon, it turned out that Mr Wolfe had left the Lord Lieutenant's home after spending only an hour with him. Yet he did not arrive back at The Den until two hours later, although the journey from Beauval should have taken him no more than half an hour.

'Lord Babbacombe's agent testified to having seen him not far from the spot where Lady Exford was found around forty minutes after he had left Beauval. As though that were not enough, Lord Babbacombe, who lived nearby, testified that, at a dinner he gave the night before, Lord Exford and Mr Wolfe had had a fierce argument, although Lord Exford later said that what had passed was of little import since each had been joking with the other.

'He would never hear a word said against Mr Wolfe although gossip began immediately that Mr Wolfe had come across Lady Exford alone, had made advances to her which she had refused, that he then overcame and mistakenly left her for dead, but was interrupted by the arrival of his wife—whom he then killed in her turn. All this despite the fact that both couples, until then, were famous for their happy marriages and for their friendship, and with no evidence to support such a theory.

'But an *on dit*, although supported by no real evidence, once started on its way is hard to refute. No action was taken against Mr Wolfe because the evidence that he might have been involved was so tenuous. At the same time his financial situation became difficult—some said because either grief, or guilt, had caused him to become careless. He never ceased to search for his wife. Eighteen months later he was found dead, again in odd circumstances, and it was assumed that he had committed suicide. His death proved that his ruin was absolute and he left his son penniless. Young Ben was sent to an elderly relative who turned him out when he reached sixteen, giving him only enough money for a passage to India where he enlisted as a private soldier.

'The rest you know.'

Susanna sat transfixed.

'So it was Lord Babbacombe who started the rumours on their way—which explains why Mr Wolfe hates him so.'

Madame nodded. 'Exactly—and there is another twist to the story. Ben Wolfe was his father's only male heir. If he were proved to be not the late Charles Wolfe's son, then the Wolfe estates would revert by a female entail to Lord Babbacombe—since his mother was Charles Wolfe's father's only sister.'

'And were Lord Babbacombe and Charles Wolfe friends?'

'Not particularly. Charles Wolfe and m'lord both wished to marry the same young woman, who later became Charles's wife and Ben's mother. Lord Babbacombe was particularly eager, he said, to discover Mrs Wolfe's fate, for he claimed to be still in love with her and disappointment at losing her had prevented him from marrying another. What *is* true was that he did not marry George Darlington's mother until some years after Mrs Wolfe's disappearance.'

Susanna said shrewdly, 'So you are hinting that Lord Babbacombe has a direct interest in trying to prove Ben Wolfe an impostor? But surely he would gain very little in inheriting what is left of the Wolfe estates, seeing that the majority of them were sold after Mr Wolfe's suicide to pay off his debts, leaving him only The Den and its immediate surroundings?'

'I warned you that I was not about to tell you a pretty tale and where the truth lies is unknown, and may, indeed, never be known. After all, this happened twenty-five years ago. There is another problem: the agent who reported seeing Mr Wolfe near the spot where Lady Exford was found himself disappeared shortly after telling his story to the magistrates. That was one reason why Mr Charles Wolfe was never arrested.'

She fell silent, but not before adding, 'Now you know why Mr Ben Wolfe is such a strong and stern man: he has had much to overcome. It is to his credit that he has carved himself a fortune and been able to restore his family home to its former glory. But his misfortunes have inevitably left their mark on him.'

'You have spoken of his family home,' said Susanna slowly. 'Does that mean that you do not believe him to be an impostor?'

'Oh, yes,' said *Madame*, 'I am sure that he is not. As sure as I am of anything. Lord Exford must think that he is not, too, and he must believe that Ben's father was innocent of wrong doing or he would not receive Ben in his home. As for what Lord Babbacombe has to gain, it is possible that if a Writ of Ejectment were to be served on Ben by Lord Babbacombe and the courts found against him, they might rule that Ben should pay heavy damages to m'lord for having cheated him of his inheritance.'

Seeing Susanna looking puzzled, she said, 'If someone thinks that their rightful inheritance, or their property, has been stolen by an impostor they take out this Writ to compel them to come to the Law Courts in order to prove that they are the rightful owner. If the person on whom the Writ is served loses his case, he is ejected from his property and it is restored to the complainant. It is a long, complicated and expensive procedure as those who have used it have often found. Some seventy years ago James Annesley regained his home and his title through such a Writ.'

Susanna made up her mind. 'You will not think me forward, I hope, if I ask that we may visit Mr Wolfe as soon as possible to show that we, at least, believe that the rumour about him being an impostor is a lie. Of what happened to his mother and Lady Exford twenty-five years ago I cannot speak. Time, perhaps, may yet tell.'

'Of course I do not think you forward, and I heartily agree with your suggestion. I shall ask John Coachman to drive us there this afternoon instead of to our usual rendezvous in Hyde Park. We must assure Ben that he still has loyal friends who will rally around him in his time of need.'

'If he is well enough to receive us,' qualified Susanna.

'True, if he is not we may put off our visit until he is, and grace the Park instead.'

Ben *was* well enough to receive them and they found him in his drawing room before his escritoire where a pile of papers and ledgers betrayed that he had been working. He rose to meet them, pleasure written on his stern face.

'I never knew who my true friends were,' he told them, 'until I was attacked. There has been a small procession of them here over the last two days. Lord and Lady Exford have just left. They told me that they had visited you and informed you of what happened three nights ago. What no one has told me is who informed society of it, seeing that I have said nothing, nor, I am sure, has my rescuer, or Jess, who is busy doing my work for me.'

'Not all of it,' said *Madame*, gesturing towards the laden escritoire. 'Perhaps your servants started the story on its way.'

'Oh, that!' he exclaimed of his pile of papers. 'That's some small nothings. And you may be right about the servants.'

Susanna, who had been relieved to see that although his left eye was black, and that side of his face was bruised, he was not, as she had feared, so badly injured that he was crippled in any way.

'Lord Exford told us that you were walking home on your own—which surprised us after all the warnings we have been given about not going out alone at night.'

Ben smiled ruefully. 'Foolish of me, wasn't it? It served me right for being conceited, I suppose. I had imagined that I could fight off one or two men, but it was a small army who attacked me. It was fortunate that by chance the attack occurred outside George Dickson's place of business. He and his men rescued me or I should have been cats' meat by now.'

Susanna shuddered. 'Never say so! You will take more care in future, I hope.'

'If you agree to order me to do so, then I will, Miss Beverly. I only exist to oblige you.'

He had bent forward a little to answer her, and his voice was teasing her, but his eyes told her a different tale. Madame de Saulx, watching them, thought that Ben Wolfe's hard heart was at last being touched by a woman—something which she had thought she would never see.

'I wish I could believe that,' Susanna told Ben, forgetting that they were not alone, intent only on answering the unspoken message of his eyes.

'Believe it,' he said, astonished to discover that his gratitude for his salvation lay partly in his barely conscious desire to know more of the woman who intrigued him so. He suddenly knew that he did not want to go to his grave unloved and unmourned. More than that—since he had met Susanna he had become aware of how lonely he was and, what was worse, was likely to remain, if he let no one into his life.

For a long moment they looked into one another's eyes before Susanna half-whispered, 'I think that I will, Mr Wolfe.'

'Good,' he said, straightening up again and resuming all his usual arrogance, 'for you must understand that my word is my bond, and what I promise, I always fulfil.'

She could believe that of him, and it almost frightened her, for it told her what a dreadful enemy he would make. On the other hand, it meant that he would also make a staunch friend—as Jess Fitzroy had once assured her.

She told him so—that she would sooner have him for a friend than an enemy.

'Which shows your good sense,' he said, smiling at *Madame* as he spoke. 'And now, may I offer you some refreshment? Ladies usually require tea, and I can ring for some immediately. My cook has, I am told, a nice line in Sally Lunns; perhaps you would care to sample them.'

Susanna laughed. 'I always associate you with food,

Mr Wolfe. May I remind you that from the very first moment that we met you have been plying me with it. Yes, pray bring on the Sally Lunns and the tea.'

Ben smiled, not something which he often did. 'You also remind me that I once asked you to call me Ben. Pray oblige me on that. There can be nothing improper in it when Madame de Saulx is happy to humour me by doing so.'

Susanna cast her eyes down primly and muttered. 'Yes, Ben. Certainly, Ben. By all means, Ben.'

Ben could not help himself. He bent down, caught her chin in his hand and tipped her face towards him—to find that she was quietly laughing at him while teasing him with a show of grudging agreement. Had *Madame* not been there he would have swept her into his arms and taught her what was what in double quick time. As it was, he released her, muttering softly, 'Minx,' and nothing more.

The rest of the afternoon passed like lightning. Tea was brought in and after it Ben asked *Madame* and Susanna to play and sing for him on his new Broadwood piano.

'I cannot play myself,' he said, 'but one of my happiest memories is of my mother playing and singing nursery rhymes to me when I was a little boy. I must hope that my visitors will oblige me by performing on it.'

Of course, they promptly did and Ben had the pleasure not only of hearing Susanna sing some old Scottish airs, but of watching her mobile face as she did so. Her voice was light but true, and delighted him more than those of the most celebrated Grand Opera divas.

On the way home *Madame* said thoughtfully, 'In all

the years I have known him I have never before heard Ben Wolfe speak of his mother. I believe that to be your influence, my dear. You know how to talk to him without being either frightened of him or flirtatiously forward—he must feel safe with you.'

'If so, I wish my influence over him would extend to compelling him not to take unnecessary risks as he did the other night,' sighed Susanna, thus revealing to *Madame*—if such a revelation were needed—how much she was beginning to care for Ben.

She need not have worried. Grumblingly Ben consented to Dickie Dickson finding a reliable bruiser for him to act as bodyguard. He was provided with a former soldier who was a useful hand with a pistol and who would keep an eye on Ben as discreetly as his duties would allow.

'I feel a rare old woman,' he told Dickie and his guest in Dickie's snug little parlour on his way to the counting house on the first day that his physician thought it wise for him to go out again. 'A fine milksop you have been making of me!'

Dickie's guest—who looked something like the bruiser who was sitting outside in Ben's landau, keeping watch—smiled. 'No one looking at you, sir, would think that.'

'I should have introduced you when you came in,' said Dickie apologetically. 'Allow me to present to you my friend and patron, m'lord Devereux, here on one of his rare visits to town.'

Earl Devereux stood up and extended his hand. 'Jack, please. I was Jack long before I became Earl Devereux and I still think people are referring to my father when the name Lord Devereux is mentioned. And as to a bodyguard for you, I would have offered myself, only I am too busy these days to find the time, but Jem Walters is a good fellow, as we both have reason to know, eh, Dickie—I mean, George!'

Dickie nodded soberly. 'Oh, we are all respectable, these days, so I suppose that you must call me George. But speaking of the attack on you, Mr Wolfe, I have had some of my men on the *qui vive* for any information they can gather, and one of them says that the word is out that a deal of money awaits anyone who can do you an injury, preferably a mortal one. Where the money is coming from is unknown—but the other rumour is that a gentleman is behind it.'

Ben nodded. This was similar to information that Jess had gathered for him, and which had made him grudgingly agree to a bodyguard, since an attack might come at any time, and always from persons unknown to him.

What he did not know was that Jess Fitzroy had already carelessly let slip to Susanna and *Madame* that someone was out to injure him. Or had he been careless, Susanna thought afterwards? Had his slip been intentional?

In any case the information started her busy brain working. Someone must hate Ben very much to want to do such a thing. She knew that a man in his way of business must make enemies, but that someone should wish to kill him seemed an excessive reaction.

On the other hand, supposing he had virtually ruined someone? Would not they want revenge?

An icy hand clutched her heart, for she knew what Ben must have done to Sam Mitchell to make him disgorge her fortune. Was Sam his mysterious assailant?

And if he were, was she not in some measure responsible?

The thought was unendurable. She sprang to her feet and went to the little study where *Madame* was writing letters and said, 'May I borrow the carriage this afternoon? I should like to visit my mother.'

Like to visit her mother, indeed! She had not the slightest wish to see her, or her stepfather, but if she visited them she might learn something which would either bolster her sudden suspicion—or dismiss it.

'Of course, my dear. You share in the expense of living here, so you have only to ask.' Susanna, indeed, had made it plain from the moment that she recovered her fortune that now she was no longer a paid attendant she was as responsible as *Madame* for the upkeep of the house in which they resided.

She knew where the Mitchells were living; her mother had sent her a bitter letter giving her the address in Islington where they were renting a house, ending with the words, 'You see to what straits you have reduced us.'

They were, indeed, settled in the wrong end of Islington when she reached there in her modest carriage, grateful that *Madame*'s taste did not lend itself to a chariot emblazoned with a lozenge showing the arms to which she was entitled. Such an equipage might have caused commotion in the humble street.

A woman's face appeared—and then hastily disappeared—at the tiny bow window when the footman travelling behind handed her down and followed her to knock on the door before he returned to the carriage.

The face belonged to a slatternly servant girl who drawled, 'Yus?' at her after she opened the door just enough to show Susanna a tiny hallway with a steep flight of stairs facing the door. There was another door to her right, and a half-open one at the end of the hall. There was no carpeting on the worn boards of the hall or staircase.

Susanna swallowed. Her mother had not exaggerated the depths to which she and her family had sunk. She clutched at her reticule and offered the sullen girl—little more than a child—a watery smile.

'Please inform Mrs Mitchell that her daughter is here to see her.'

Before the girl could as much as move the door to the front room opened and her mother appeared.

'I thought when I saw the carriage that it might be you. What do you want?'

Her voice was as cold as she could make it, and she did not invite Susanna into the house.

'I would like to speak to you, Mother—if you will invite me in, that is.'

'Certainly not. Say what you have to say to me now—and go.'

'Very well, but I think that you would prefer to hear me out in private, rather than in the street.'

'Go to the kitchen, Polly,' was all that that earned her.

'Yessum,' drawled Polly.

'Yes?' said her mother to Susanna, motioning her just inside the front door after the girl had left them, exactly as she might have asked a disobedient servant to explain herself.

'Mother, I want you to know that I had no notion of what was being done for me when my inheritance was being recovered. I am certainly not happy to see you and the girls in such reduced circumstances. I only ask you to remember that it was Mr Mitchell's actions which have brought you here, not mine.'

'Oh, yes?' sneered her mother. 'You expect me to believe such a Banbury tale as that when it was that man with whom you and that Frenchwoman are so friendly who brought this upon us? If that is all you have to say to me, you may leave at once.'

So it *had* been Ben Wolfe who had found out the truth about her fortune and had returned it to her.

'You must believe me, for I would not lie to you.'

'And did you also tell him to make sure that Mr Mitchell can find no employment after being branded an embezzler by him, and that we live on the edge of starvation?'

'If that is so, I am sorry—although I do not believe Ben Wolfe to be as vindictive as that.'

'Oh, it's Ben Wolfe, is it? What did you pay him with? Your money—or your person?'

She walked to the street door to fling it open, saying, 'Please leave, I have nothing more to say to you.'

Susanna stood in the open doorway, her face agonised, but determined to say what she had to, whatever her mother might think or do.

'But I have something to say to you, Mother, and in saying it I mean to help you. Please tell Mr Mitchell that if it is he who is employing men to injure or kill Mr Wolfe he is risking death or transportation, for Mr Wolfe is not only determined to track him down but he also has powerful friends who will see that he is suitably punished.'

She had barely finished speaking when the door at the far end of the little hall opened and Sam Mitchell stood there. He was so changed from the man she had once known that he was barely recognisable. He had not shaved for some days, his linen was filthy, his clothes dishevelled and he was clutching a bottle in his hand. He must have been listening to their conversation through the half-open door.

'What the devil's that you're threatening me with, girl? Do I look as though I've the dibs to pay a crew to nobble the swine who nobbled me? If I had, I would, but I haven't, and that's flat. You've brought me nothing but bad luck and now you promise to hand me over to the Runners.'

He took another swig at the bottle. 'Tell your bully boy that. And if I did know who was after him, I wouldn't peach on him, that I wouldn't, but I don't— and if I did, I'd help him if I'd so much as tuppence.'

A final swig and he was staggering back into the room. Mrs Mitchell finally gave way and began to cry bitterly.

Her bravado had not moved Susanna, but her despair did. She stepped forward and took the sobbing woman in her arms. Her mother made no effort to throw her off.

'Oh, Mama, don't. It's not your fault. Oh, this is terrible. Here.' She pulled her handkerchief from her reticule and began to wipe her mother's eyes with it. Her mother lay unresisting against her so Susanna walked her gently into the small front room and sat her on a greasy sofa.

After a time her mother subsided into weak snuffles, finally wailing, 'You see how he is. Nothing which I can say or do will move him.'

How to comfort her? Susanna opened her reticule and pulled out the handful of guineas which she had put there before she had left *Madame*'s.

'Oh, Mama,' and it was the childish name for her

mother which was wrenched from her again. 'There is so little I can do to help you. The trustees who administer my money are firm with me because of their previous breach of trust. They don't want to make another mistake. I can settle nothing on you, but take this.'

She thrust the guineas into her mother's lax hands. 'Use it to make life for yourself easier. Don't let him know you have it or it will go on drink. I will try to send you a little when I can—but I fear it won't be very much.'

All her mother's defiance had leached out of her. She clutched the guineas to her bosom before putting them into the deep pocket of the apron which she was wearing.

'I can't forgive you,' she said pathetically, 'but I can't forgive him, either. Which leaves me with nothing. Go now, before he comes out again. He hasn't mistreated me or the girls yet, but I fear that one day he might when the drink is in him. I hope you believe him when he says he knows nothing of any wrong doing.'

Susanna thought that she did believe Samuel Mitchell's denials. 'When the drink's in, the truth comes out', was a saying she had heard as a child and she thought that in this case it might be true.

She kissed her mother on her withered cheek—for she seemed to have aged twenty years since she had last seen her—and took her sad way home to Stanhope Street.

Ben Wolfe's carriage with its silver trimmings was outside. A large man was standing beside it, talking to the driver who was holding the horses. Susanna hoped that he was the bodyguard of whom Jess had spoken. Inside she found Ben talking to *Madame*. His face lit up when he saw her.

His greeting of her was, however, prosaic. 'I thought that I might have missed you. *Madame* tells me that you have been visiting your mother.'

Susanna thought for a moment before she answered him, considering whether or not to tell him the truth about her errand. She concluded that truth might be the best.

'Yes. She is living in poverty in a back street in Islington. I had an important question to ask of her and my stepfather.'

She concluded that Ben Wolfe must possess some sort of ability to divine what it was that those around him were truly thinking of or doing before they had told him, for he said immediately after she paused for breath, 'Why do I believe that your question had something to do with me?'

A little gasp of surprise was forced from her. 'Now, how did you know that? It is precisely why I went.'

'Nothing, something,' he said softly, aware that *Madame*'s shrewd eyes were on them both. 'Something in your expression, or your posture, I must suppose. It's an odd gift I possess which has sometimes proved useful, not only with men, but with animals. I can always tell a wicked horse from a good one.'

'And which do I qualify as,' Susanna could not help retorting, 'a wicked one? Or a good one?'

'Mixed a little, I should say,' he told her, keeping his face straight.

Susanna began to laugh. 'I asked for that,' she admitted.

And then, growing sober again, she continued with, 'It was not an amusing question I had to ask her, nor was her behaviour to me amusing, either. On the contrary.'

She hesitated, for now she must tell him that she had guessed of his intervention over the matter of her fortune.

'You see,' she said, as quietly and calmly as she could, 'I guessed that it was you who had pursued Mr Mitchell in order to recover my inheritance, and since it must be supposed that you are being attacked by someone who considered that you had wronged him, it occurred to me that your unknown enemy might be him.'

Fascinated, Ben stared at her. 'May I ask how long you have known about my part in your recovered inheritance?'

'Almost from the day it was restored to me,' she confessed, 'for who else did I know who was powerful enough to right my wrongs?'

'And you said nothing,' he marvelled. 'Most women would have been chattering about it for evermore.'

'Well,' said Susanna, 'I supposed that had you wished me to know, you would have told me. Only the notion that Mr Mitchell might be your enemy caused me to use my knowledge and then to tell you what I think I may have learned.'

Both *Madame* and Ben were staring at her in astonishment.

Ben said at last, 'Never tell me you went there and asked him point-blank?'

'Not quite.' Susanna was a trifle uncomfortable over admitting what she had done when they were both looking at her as though she were an odd specimen in a case in a museum. 'But when my mother was so unkind to me and blamed me for her penury, I felt free to warn her what Mr Mitchell's fate might be if he were your attacker... Why are you both looking at me like that?'

Ben answered before *Madame* could. 'Well, if you must know, I was thinking of how you behaved when we first met, which should have told me that little was beyond you in terms of daring. But do go on. I am sure, again by your expression, that you have not concluded this remarkable narrative.'

'Nor I have,' said Susanna, smiling at him now she understood that his surprise at her forward conduct was laced with admiration. 'The moment I finished warning her, Mr Mitchell suddenly appeared from the back room. He was most unlike himself,' she finished thoughtfully.

'May one ask in what way?' intoned Ben sweetly.

'He was dirty, badly dressed and quite drunk. Not falling down drunk, you understand, just tipsy and still able to converse—'

'We both thank you for the definition, most helpful,' interrupted Ben. 'Do go on. What next?'

'Well, between swigs from the bottle he was carrying, he said that he had had nothing to do with the attack on you because he couldn't afford it, but he applauded it all the same. He said that I had brought him bad luck. I am inclined to think that he was telling the truth.'

'He's right about the bad-luck bit,' offered Ben, grinning. 'What makes you think that he wasn't lying about the attack on me?'

'They are most desperately poor,' said Susanna earnestly. 'I'm sure that he couldn't afford to hire bully boys, although he might like to.'

Ben thought for a moment. 'I'm almost certain that you are right. But, Susanna, I want you to promise me something. That you'll never do such a thing on your own again. It might be dangerous. You should have told me, and I would have gone to interview him.'

'Oh, I couldn't have done that. You see, if I hadn't received any kind of assurance, I didn't want you to know that I had guessed that you were my benefactor. Surely you can understand that?'

His eyes on her were assessing. 'Yes, we are more alike than anyone might think. It gave you a kind of power over me, didn't it?'

Susanna flushed scarlet. 'I suppose so, yes. I have to keep my end up you see, and you are such a superior creature in so many ways. Being a man to begin with… It doesn't leave a poor girl much in the way of feeling that she is in control of her life. Keeping from you the knowledge that I was aware that you were my benefactor was a small victory.'

Silence fell. Ben said at last, 'I see.'

He couldn't say, Thank God you're not a man because I want to take you in my arms and do with you all those exciting things which men and women can do together—particularly because you are such a gallant creature. I have a feeling you'd be gallant in bed, too.

So he said nothing.

Mistaking his silence—and the slightly strained expression on his face—for disapproval, Susanna said earnestly. 'It was also a way of thanking you for your kindness—to be able to find out whether or not Mr Mitchell was guilty. The only sad thing is my poor mother. She is being punished, too. I know you won't approve, but I gave her some ready money and I intend to give her more. On condition that she doesn't give it to him to buy drink.'

'Dear girl,' said Ben fondly, 'if she loves the wretch, and from everything you tell me she does, of course, she'll give it to him to buy drink. But if it makes you happy to throw your money away on them, don't let me dissuade you.'

Madame spoke at last. 'Everything you have told us does you credit, my dear, and I'm sure that Ben knows that. He's only worried about your safety.'

'Well, I'm worried about his, so that makes us quits,' said Susanna cheerfully. 'May we talk about something else?'

'Not before I have thanked you,' Ben said. 'You understand that I must ask Jess to try to confirm what you have told me—but that is merely a precaution. A wise man always checks any information which he is given, he never merely takes it on trust.'

Susanna nodded. 'I can see that,' she told him, her face so earnest and confiding that it nearly unmanned him.

'But if Mr Mitchell proves not to be your enemy, then it narrows your search, does it not?'

'Exactly,' said Ben. 'You would be a most useful addition to my staff, Miss Beverly, if you can understand that without me telling you.'

'Susanna,' she said. 'I insist that you call me Susanna. We are friends now, are we not?'

'Friends!' Ben almost snorted. 'Yes, I suppose you may say so.'

Judging by their expressions during this interchange, *Madame* thought that friendship was far too mild a word to describe what existed between Ben and Susanna. The only problem was why it was taking so long for them to understand that. On second thoughts, though, it was possible that their difficult past lives had made it impossible for them to trust another completely. It was easy to detect how powerfully Ben was attracted to Susanna, but Susanna, for all her charming artlessness, was a far more difficult person to read.

That she liked Ben was plain—but was liking all that she felt for him? If so, it was a pity, for they were so well suited to one another that, for a moment, *Madame* was tempted to play matchmaker. Only for a moment, though. Ben and Susanna were both so strong-minded that they would strongly resent feeling that she might be manipulating them, and she liked and respected them both too much to risk losing their friendship.

Best simply to wait and see, however much that might exhaust her patience while she watched them refuse to admit what was before their very eyes—that theirs would be a marriage made in heaven!

Chapter Eleven

'Whoever is after you, it's not Sam Mitchell,' Jess told Ben later that week. 'He's neither the money nor the determination to plot to murder you. He's either sitting at home drinking, or sitting in the nearest dirty tavern drinking—take your pick. From a man who was once something of a thruster, he's turned into a maudlin sot. The way he's going on, he and his family will shortly be reduced to lodging in the nearest work-house—he's heavily in debt with no way of honouring any of it.'

Ben groaned. 'Never say so, and his poor wife is Susanna's mother and the two girls are her half-sisters. If I know her, she'll find some way of squandering her little fortune on them.'

Jess forbore to say that only someone as rich as Ben would describe Susanna's fortune as little—instead he waited for the instructions which he knew from of old would shortly be forthcoming.

'I want an assistant to Dawes, the Clerk of Works down at the docks,' Ben said at last after staring glumly into space for some time. 'The man I've got there at the moment isn't up to snuff. Mitchell was a clever fellow—if dishonest. There's not much he could get up to with Dawes's eagle eye on him, and he'd earn just enough to keep his family in reasonable comfort. Send Tozzy to the inn he's frequenting, get to know him, and then offer him the post—telling him it's a chance to earn an honest living. Susanna Beverly was right, I've made his name mud—so, if I'm to stop her from trying to rescue him, it is I who must give him something to enable him to haul himself out of the mire.

'Tell Tozzy to warn him that if he gets up to his old tricks he'll soon be rotting in Newgate Prison. My mercy for him only extends so far.'

'Will he consent to work for you?' asked Jess, a trifle artlessly.

'Now, Jess, you know better than that. No one knows that Marsden and Sons is part of my empire. And Tozzy's not to tell him who owns Marsden's, of course. Just that Marsden's wants a competent man, and he was that—once.'

Jess gone, Ben stared at the opposite wall dispiritedly as he contemplated what his affection for the clever little hussy he had fallen in love with had let him in for. No less than rescuing the rogue who had swindled her in order to prevent her from being so unhappy at her mother and sisters' fate that—in a ridiculous act of charity—she would throw away the inheritance he had rescued for her.

And if Mitchell was sensible enough to accept this lifeline, neither he nor Susanna was to be told that it was Ben Wolfe who had thrown it to him—although, knowing her, it was quite possible that she would twig what he had been up to!

He smiled. It would add spice to his life, watching and waiting to discover whether she would. He might even have a little bet with himself about how long it would take her.

In the meantime, he would take himself to Louis Fronsac's fencing salon where Jack Devereux had promised to give him a lesson with the rapier and where he might learn whether there was any current gossip which might give him some clue as to the identity of his enemy.

Fronsac's was busy when he reached it. Jack was already dressed in formal clothing for fencing: black silk knee-breeches and a white silk shirt. Before his accession to the Earldom, he had been one of the salon's instructors and still kept his talent honed by practising there whenever he was in town.

Ben had been first rate when using both a sabre and a foil as well as a pistol when he had been in India. He was, though, astonished at Jack's expertise, which was beyond anything which he had ever previously encountered in an amateur.

He told Jack so.

Jack laughed wryly. 'I had to earn my living teaching others after I left the Army, and I soon discovered that fencing is an art as well as a science. Most people's problem is that they see fencing purely as a science. What they don't understand is that you are facing a man whose character, physique and personality must be taken into account when you fight him, as well as his skill. That is where the art of it comes in.'

So saying, he disengaged before starting the bout again—and promptly slid through Ben's guard for the fifth time. This time Ben stepped back, raised his foil in a gesture of submission and remarked thoughtfully,

'You are telling me that I am going at you like a bull at a gate, no subtlety, just using my strength.'

'Exactly, and most of the time you will succeed by doing that, but not when you meet a master,' was Jack's reply. 'However, because you can say that, there is hope for you. You have a chance to improve. For the moment, though, take a rest,' and he gestured at a row of benches on the side wall.

Blowing hard, his own shirt clinging to his back, Ben sat down, lifting the protective mask from his face, causing a young sprig who had just entered to exclaim, 'Good God, is there nowhere safe these days? Nowhere one can be certain of not meeting the riff-raff!'

It was George Darlington who had arrived while Ben and Jack were fencing and had not recognised Ben until he had unmasked.

Ben sighed. Jack said quietly, 'Ignore the young fool. He's a spoilt boy, the unpleasant sprig of an unpleasant sire.'

He had not needed Jack to advise him but, knowing that Jack was a hot-tempered man who did not suffer fools gladly, he also knew that he must have good reason to suggest that he did not rise to young Darlington's bait.

Young Darlington, however, had no mind to let the matter rest. Secure in his rank and surrounded by a group of his friends, he was foolish enough to forget the lesson Ben had taught him at the Leominsters' ball and continued to insult him.

'I had thought,' he said, 'Mr What-ever-your-name-is, that the attack on you the other evening would have convinced you that you are not wanted in London. One supposes that you find it impossible to take a hint—else you would not attend a place where gentlemen congregate.'

On hearing these words, Jack Devereux gave a low moan. Small chance now that Ben Wolfe would restrain himself after being offered such an insult.

He wronged Ben, though. Suppressing his very real desire to seize young Darlington by the throat and throttle the life out of him, Ben merely looked coolly around while saying politely, 'Are you referring to me? Or is some other unfortunate the victim of your bile?'

Several of George's companions tittered at this. George himself flushed scarlet, and answered in a high voice, 'You know perfectly well that my remarks were addressed to you. Who else in this room is so patently not a gentleman? Who else uses his hands to hump loads in the port of London?'

'Why, no one,' riposted Ben. 'Looking around me, I can't see anyone other than myself, or Devereux perhaps, who is in sufficiently good condition to do any such thing. Lifting a lady's fan—or her skirts—looks beyond most of you.'

Jack Devereux did not help matters by laughing loudly at this sally, and saying, 'Oh, come, Darlington. Give over, do. Neither Wolfe nor I intend to be provoked into folly by your lack of manners. Go and insult someone who punches your own weight—I commend you to the dwarf at Greenwich Fair.'

'My quarrel is not with you, Devereux,' said George, a trifle fearfully, for everyone in the room knew that Jack was a master of weaponry and was not to be trifled with by anyone. 'My quarrel is with *him*—and his presence here.'

'And with Louis Fronsac who runs this salon,' said a new voice, that of Fronsac himself, who, attracted by the noise, had left the private room where he had been instructing a personage so grand that he never used the public rooms. 'It is I who determines who practises here, not some young gentleman with his mother's milk still on his lips. If you have a quarrel with Mr Wolfe, then pursue it somewhere else.'

Furious, George said unwisely, 'I would have thought that since we pay you highly we have a right to say with whom we might mix.'

'Then you thought wrongly. Indeed, since you are here and have chosen to pick a quarrel with Mr Wolfe and Lord Devereux, then you must settle your difference with one of them in a practice bout with the foils, or suffer banishment from my salon in future. The choice is yours.'

George looked wildly around him. His supporters remained silent. Louis Fronsac was held in high esteem, not only by the Grand Personage who stood in the doorway of the private room, but by most of society. He had hoped to bait Ben, secure in the knowledge that if Ben challenged him he could always refuse to fight someone so patently not a gentleman. Louis Fronsac had taken that choice away from him.

Louis stared at George, raising high-arched brows. He was a handsome man in early middle age who had been an *émigré* from France during the late Revolution there: a member of a noble family who had chosen—like many—not to return to his native land.

'You have not answered me, *Monseigneur*. Either agree to a practice bout—or leave. Have no fear, you will only be fighting with buttoned foils. Whether Mr Wolfe or m'lord will insist on meeting you at dawn tomorrow for a more serious bout is their choice to make once they leave my rooms.'

Neither Ben nor Jack spoke while Louis was laying down the law. There was no need. He was doing their work for them. Desperate, and aware that he was about to be humiliated, George ground out, 'I'll fight him,' pointing at Ben.

Louis Fronsac smiled thinly. 'Not like that,' he told him. 'What Mr Wolfe is, is neither here nor there. *You* pretend to be a nobleman—and a gentleman. That being so, challenge him in proper form or forfeit those titles yourself.'

'Bravo,' said the Grand Personage from the doorway, leaving George no choice but to do as he was bid.

He bowed, lifted a tormented face and said through gritted teeth, 'I would be honoured, Mr Wolfe, if you would agree to a practice bout with the foils.' He added conciliatingly, 'M. le Marquis de Fronsac, to give him his proper title, will agree to adjudicate between us, I am sure.'

Ben, his face a polite mask, bowed back. 'It will be a great pleasure, m'lord, to oblige you. A very great pleasure.'

Jack Devereux choked back a laugh at this two-edged reply. Ben might not be his equal with the foils, but he was more than a match for anyone he had ever tutored at Fronsac's: the Grand Personage included.

'Very well,' said Louis. 'I will give you ten minutes to prepare yourself whilst I clear the room and ask his Royal Highness to be good enough to allow me to con-clude his lesson later—or resume it at another time. You will excuse me while I consult him.'

His Royal Highness, it appeared, was more than happy to abandon his lesson in order to watch a practice bout which promised more fun than most. A chair was fetched for him by one of the courtiers who had been attending him in the private room, and was placed in a most favourable position.

'Haven't enjoyed myself so much at Fronsac's for years, what!' he exclaimed loudly. 'Nor since I was last on a man-of-war.'

'You must understand,' Jack whispered to Ben while they waited, 'that HRH's presence made it impossible for the young idiot to back down. The Duke of Clarence suffers neither fools nor cowards gladly.'

Ben nodded a trifle glumly. This piece of flummery— for such he thought it—was not of his making, nor to his liking. 'You can say that,' he whispered back, 'since no one is asking you to make a raree show of yourself.'

'Oh, come,' riposted Jack briskly, 'the only person in this room who answers to that description is young Darlington. All you need to do is make sure that he learns his lesson: not to taunt those who are in a position to make him pay for his folly. It's a great pity this bout is only a practice one. A bit of bloodletting would do him no harm at all.'

Ben privately agreed with him, but said no more, simply moved into the middle of the room to wait for his enemy—wishing that it was the father, not the son, he was about to face. Jess Fitzroy's enquiries were making it more and more likely that Babbacombe was behind the attack on him.

Fronsac was pitiless. He made young George go through all the lengthy formalities required of one who was fighting another gentleman and George could do nothing about it. At this late stage, to withdraw under any pretext would place his own reputation for courage and fair play at risk. After all, most would ask where was the harm in a bloodless bout.

'Three hits or three disarmings and the bout is over,'

declared Fronsac, immediately before the antagonists assumed the *en garde* position, both stripped to their shirts and breeches. Ben was fighting barefoot and George was wearing light shoes. The spectators lined the walls, standing: None could be seated now that the Duke was—unless he gave the word, and he was not doing that.

The contrast between the two men could not have been greater. On the face of it George, tall and slim, ought to have the advantage over Ben who was also tall but built like a bruiser—their skills being equal, that was.

The younger and less experienced men were betting on George. Most of them knew that Ben had served in the ranks and would therefore, in their opinion, be less skilled with a small sword, always considered to be a gentleman's weapon. Older heads were betting differently. Some of them had been watching Ben and Jack Devereux fence and had noted that Jack's superiority was not all that great.

Clarence did not bet at all, but kept up a loud running commentary on the bout which began slowly, both participants being wary of the other.

Ben was keenly aware that he was the outsider here—even though it was plain that George was not greatly liked. He soon knew that George was in no way his equal and that he could therefore do one of two things. He could either restrain himself and fight a tame draw, or he could throw tact and caution to the winds and teach George a shameful and humiliating lesson.

He had just decided on the former—which would save everyone's face—when, in a lull in the bout with the pair of them warily circling around one another, he heard a voice behind him drawl, 'The big fellow's all wind and importance, ain't he? No finesse there—ought to be in his proper place, the prize ring, not pretending to equal his betters. Glad my tin is on Darlington.'

Red rage roared through him: the rage which he had known from childhood but which he usually kept under strict control as a wise man would keep a fierce dog on a leash. Occasionally, though, the rage, like that of the dog's, would be so strong that it would snap the leash and run riot.

The world around him disappeared. All that was left in it was George opposite to him and the fierce desire to show those who secretly mocked him that he was not to be trifled with, for, although the rage was red, inside it he was icy calm.

In a moment he was through George's weak guard like a knife slicing through butter to catch George's foil near the hilt with his own. Then, he fiercely twisted his wrist with such force that George's foil was first thrown into the air before falling to the floor.

Both men stepped back, consternation written on George's face and cold savage glee on Ben's as they unmasked.

Clarence clapped his hands together, his florid face on fire. 'Bravo, Wolfe, never seen that better done.'

Ben inclined his head in acknowledgement. Louis Fronsac stepped forward and said, 'First point to Mr Wolfe. Pick up your foil, m'lord, and the bout may start again.'

Again they circled around one another while Ben debated what to do next. He made up his mind quickly, presented his whole left side, apparently unguarded, to George and as George gleefully went in for the touch, he side-stepped, and on the turn wrapped George square on the breast.

'A hit,' someone shouted, as Louis Fronsac separated them again.

'You tricked me,' muttered George through his teeth before they resumed their masks.

'So I did,' rasped Ben. 'I'll show you another ploy in a minute, if you'll only be patient.'

The room had fallen silent. The duel was turning into a massacre, as Ben disarmed George again, and for good measure rapped him on the breast having done so. The rage had begun to diminish and for a few moments he allowed George a respite, dancing around him, apparently offering him the chance of a hit, almost inviting him to try one.

George, though, was beginning to learn his lesson. He would not be caught again by such an obvious trick, but alas, the third hit which finished the bout was accomplished by a reverse thrust on high which came as such a surprise that George lost his balance and sprawled on the ground so that all Ben had to do was to stand over him and touch his breast lightly again.

The voice which had mocked Ben now mocked George. 'The young cub should be grateful he didn't provoke Wolfe into a real duel,' it said. 'He would have been dog's food by now.'

His rage's appetite satisfied, Ben found his triumph to be an empty one—a common aftertaste, for he disliked not being in total command of himself. He swung round on the mocker and said through his teeth, 'Since you are such an authority, sir, would you care to engage me, and make a better fist of it than Darlington?'

He did not wait for an answer, but swung away, intent on changing into his street clothes and leaving, but he was stopped by the Duke who had risen from his chair, exclaiming peremptorily, 'Come here, Wolfe, I wish to speak to you.'

Ben did as he was bid, bowing as he approached Royalty. The Duke said genially, 'They tell me that you were a soldier in the army in India—and in the ranks at that. You are a gentleman—why in the ranks?'

'I had no money, Your Highness, and no real home. To enlist as a private soldier gave me both. I feel—and felt—no shame at earning my living in the only way I could.'

He was aware that he sounded defiant and wondered for a moment whether he had been wise.

The Duke suddenly gave a great bellow of laughter. 'You are an honest man, Wolfe, and have given me an honest answer. You have also provided me with amusement in the way in which you disciplined Babbacombe's young puppy. My gratitude is such that should you need a favour, you may call on Clarence to provide you with one. What do you say to that, hey?'

What could Ben say? He was well aware of the caprices of the Royal Family, from those of the mad King George III downwards. Clarence was brave, choleric— and irresponsible. He might forget immediately what he had promised—but he might not. Everything and nothing was possible.

So he bowed, and murmured, 'I shall not forget your kindness, sir.'

'See that you do not, what? See that you do not! And hello to you, Devereux,' he said to Jack. who was standing beside Ben, before calling to his equerry who had been standing at a respectful distance. 'Time to leave, I have had my fun. Fronsac may give me another lesson on another day.'

Jack murmured in Ben's ear, 'Put not your trust in

princes, Ben. He'll probably forget you before he climbs into his coach. On the other hand, Clarence is the best of a bad lot. And before I forget, why did you trick me into believing you a relative novice with the foils? Fronsac tells me that one of your moves was a favourite of his old master Jean Dupuy, and that if he taught it to you he thought you were something of a master, too, because only a master could perform it. Is Fronsac right?'

Ben shrugged a little shamefacedly. 'A man does not confess to everything he knows—or can do—if he is wise. You should know that, Jack. As for Dupuy, he ended up in India teaching anyone who would learn. I was one of those who wished to.'

'I'll remember that the next time we practise together—for I shall give you no leeway at all. I was easy with you—but never no more—that I promise.'

'I shan't come to Fronsac's again,' said Ben dourly. 'I lost my temper, and I don't care to put myself in the way of doing so again.'

'Fool's talk,' said Jack rudely. 'Don't let the smug swine who run London society drive you away. Take no notice of them. I never do.'

This was so patently true and was said in Jack's most aggressive manner, which drove Ben's megrims away and set him laughing.

'Well, I see that I cannot play the coward when you do not, so I'll withdraw my resolution.'

'Then we may still be friends. I see that that cub you've just thrashed is sulking in a corner. He grows more like his father every day. A word of warning, Ben, Babbacombe is dangerous because he is stupid. Guard your back against the bludgeoneers.'

'You have heard something?' asked Ben quickly, thinking of the recent attack on him.

Jack shook his head. 'No, I only have my hard-earned knowledge of the world and the fools and knaves who live in it to guide me. I see that you have agreed to employ a bodyguard—most wise of you. But remember, a man may be attacked in other ways than the physical.'

Jack Devereux was a good friend, and would also be a dangerous enemy, thought Ben as he was driven to *Madame*'s once his session at Fronsac's was over. He had tickets for a performance at Astley's Amphitheatre and thought that Susanna—and *Madame*—might be pleased to accompany him. These days it was always Susanna he thought of first.

In fact, if he were truthful he thought of her first, last and always—a new thing for him.

Madame, the butler informed him, was not at home, but Miss Beverly was, and he would ask if she were prepared to receive him.

Ben stood in the grand hallway with its black and white flagged tiles and its vases of flowers on tall occasional tables, hoping against hope that Susanna would break all the rules of conduct and entertain a single gentleman on her own. The expression on the butler's face when he returned gave nothing away.

He put out a hand for the hat which Ben was holding and enunciated clearly and disapprovingly, 'Miss Beverly will receive you, sir, in the small drawing room. Please follow me.'

His heart beating violently, Ben allowed himself to be ushered into the room where Susanna rose from her chair after putting down the book which she had been reading. She looked so enchanting that Ben could barely wait for the butler to leave before he told her so.

Susanna, her own heart bumping in the most alarming way—for was she not breaking every rule by which she had lived all her life?—said as soberly as she could when he had finished, 'You need not flatter me, Ben. I am dressed quite simply because I did not foresee that I should have company this afternoon—*Madame* has gone to the French Embassy to visit an old friend.'

'Then you should always dress simply,' declared Ben in his usual downright fashion, 'for it suits you even more than dressing grandly does—and I must thank you for receiving me when you are on your own.'

'More flattery—' Susanna smiled, '—and, seeing that we are now old friends, I have allowed myself the luxury of your presence.'

Ben could not help himself. The sight of her in her plain white muslin gown with its pale blue ribbons and its modest high neck, her hair dressed simply, so that one curl was allowed to coil around her graceful neck, was having the most disturbing effect on him, so that he blurted out, 'Friends! I should hope that we are more than that!'

And then, as she offered him a dazzling smile, he continued, the words pouring from him like water cascading downwards, out of control, 'Marry me, Susanna, at once, or I shall immediately expire, or dissolve spontaneously into a flaming pyre like the ones on to which Indian ladies fling themselves after their husbands' death.'

This extraordinary proposal, totally unlike anything which a young gentlewoman of quality ought to expect, might have overset many young women, but it was so like the man making it in its downright extravagance, that it had no such effect on Susanna.

'Do but consider what you are saying, Ben! Did you really come here this afternoon to propose to me?'

'No,' he said, all sense deserting him, aware only that he would go mad if somehow or other he did not get her into his bed. 'Not at all, but the sight of you provoked me to it. Have you no notion of the effect which you have on me? Have had since I first clapped eyes on you. Only the presence of *Madame* in the past and now the conventions which bind us both in the present are preventing me from falling on you and physically demonstrating the passion which I have come to feel for you. It is highly inconvenient—particularly since you are not at all the kind of young person whom I have always thought of marrying!'

As soon as he had finished speaking, Ben knew that he must have dished himself by being so tactlessly truthful. Yes, he had thought that he would marry a biddable, pampered young woman whom he could shape and mould to his heart's desire, not someone like Susanna whose character and temperament had been sharpened and strengthened by the troubles through which she had passed—but he shouldn't have said so.

Before she could answer him he apologised humbly, 'Forgive me, that was no way to speak to the lady whom I have come to desire beyond reason, but I have been a blunt man all my life, and it is difficult for me to change now.'

Susanna, her whole body singing a triumphant song, yet could not contain her amusement at her suitor's bluff and brusque proposal.

'Why should I wish you to change?' she enquired sweetly. 'I like you as you are. I admit that you could have made me a more elegant proposal. There are women who might be offended on learning that their suitor thought his passion for them to be inconvenient, but I am not one of them. In return, may I inform you that you are the last man I could ever have imagined either proposing to me at all, or to whom I could consider giving a favourable answer—which makes the fact that I am about to say "yes" to you even more remarkable. I once thought Francis Sylvester to be the kind of paragon whom I would wish to marry—and I cannot imagine anyone more unlike you than he is!'

Ben stood dazed, trying to work out exactly what she was saying to him. 'Do I infer that you are accepting me?' he came out with. 'If so, your answer is a good match for mine in its crossgrainedness!'

'True,' replied Susanna, 'but that is probably why we shall deal well together. Who else would wish to marry either of us? Seeing what an unlikely pair we are.'

He exploded into laughter, throwing his head back, behaving as usual totally against all the rules of polite society which demanded that a gentleman should never display strong emotions in public: a laugh should always be a pleasantly controlled thing—if one had to laugh at all, that was. Susanna's amusement at his frank enjoyment of her saucy sally set her laughing, too.

Wiping the tears from her eyes, she said, 'Oh, dear, now you have set me off as well. The late Lord Chesterfield would have been most ashamed of us.'

'Why so?' asked Ben curiously, his life not having been spent in reading elegantly phrased letters by elegantly living peers.

'He wrote letters to his son on how a gentleman ought to behave in which, among other things, he said that no true gentleman—and presumably gentlewoman—ever laughs aloud. The letters were published because it was believed that his advice on etiquette was so wise that all the world ought to know of it.'

Ben thought for a moment before answering her. Then, 'You really ought to marry me, if only because you know so much of these matters and I know so little. Between us you could turn me into a paragon who would know everything about Prince Hamlet and when to simper rather than laugh aloud.'

Susanna shook her head. 'Not at all. I much prefer you as you are. If I had wanted to marry a simpering gentleman, I should have accepted Francis Sylvester's second proposal.'

'Does that mean that you have accepted *my* second proposal?'

'I think so.'

'That is not an answer which a man of business like myself understands.'

'Which is precisely why I made it.'

Her face on throwing this conversational titbit at him was so *piquante* and alight with mischief that Ben's self-control flew away. He gave a little groan—and swept her into his arms.

His little groan was matched by her little cry on finding herself brought smack up against his broad chest.

He brought his mouth down on hers with a movement so swift that there was no stopping him. Susanna's heart beat rapidly as a consequence of fear as well as of passion. He was so big and strong, such a bear of a man, that she was momentarily afraid that his lovemaking would be as fierce as his name and appearance.

But no such thing. His mouth on hers was so tender and gentle, the big hands which rose to cup her face were so delicate in their handling of it that fright flew away and only passion reigned supreme. She moaned again and raised her own hand to stroke his face, letting her fingers run along his jaw in line with the shadow of his beard which grew so rapidly that by evening he was compelled to shave again.

And then delicately, oh so delicately, his mouth teased hers open and Susanna was ready to swoon when his tongue met hers and made it dance in unison with his. Only the right hand that he had taken from her face in order to cup her head kept her on her feet.

Francis's few kisses, perfunctorily snatched whenever, for a few moments, they were left alone, had not prepared her either for Ben's lovemaking or the strength of the passion with which she responded to it.

'Please, yes, please,' she muttered hoarsely and knew not for what she was asking, only that there was something more to come and that by contrast with what she had already enjoyed, it would be even more powerful and fulfilling.

He dropped his mouth to the hollows of her neck and began to celebrate them; at the same time his hand began to rove down her back to the base of her spine to cup her buttocks, creating a sensation which made her writhe and twist against him.

This, in turn, had such a powerful effect on Ben that his rapidly slipping control nearly disappeared altogether, so that it was fortunate that—as though they were taking part in a bad French farce, by Marivaux, perhaps—the drawing door opened to reveal to Madame de Saulx that her two protégés were so closely entwined that they might as well have been one.

The sound of her entry and her muttered, 'Ahem', set them springing apart, rosy-face, dishevelled—and guilty.

Ben, who, for obvious reasons, remained half-turned

away, said with great joviality as soon as he had physically recovered and had rearranged his clothing, 'My dear *Madame*, you will be delighted to learn that Miss Beverly has agreed to marry me—and as soon as I can acquire a special licence—and with as little flummery as possible.'

Susanna, who had been carrying out some rearrangement herself, to *Madame*'s amusement riposted with, 'Oh, I'm sure I never agreed to any of that.'

'Indeed, but you did,' replied Ben. 'I distinctly remember that you said "yes". You did qualify it by remarking that, in effect, no one else would marry either of us—but that does not affect your agreement, as I am sure *Madame* understands.'

'And *Madame* will offer you both her congratulations,' said that lady calmly, secretly delighted that one of her fondest wishes was coming true. 'On mature reflection, Ben, I think that you will agree that your marriage must be no hole-in-the-corner affair, for that would reflect, not only on yourself, but on your bride. That does not mean that you must carry on as though you were one of the Royal Dukes tying the knot, simply that you must fulfil the duties which you owe to your station.'

Ben, busy thinking that hard though it might be to propose, the act of marriage itself seemed to be even harder, nodded a reluctant agreement.

'More particularly,' continued *Madame*, ignoring his reluctance, 'since, given your present situation of being under attack from Lord Babbacombe's spiteful accusations, you must not be seen to be afraid to appear in public.'

Susanna stifled a giggle at the expression on Ben's face indicating that to suggest that he was afraid of anything was a statement so monstrous that it was not worth contradicting.

Madame, seeing that Susanna was now composed again, moved over to her to kiss her on the cheek and whisper congratulations to her.

'He is a good man,' she said, 'and you have made a wise choice—as he has. I wish you well. You will, of course, be married from here.'

Somehow, until *Madame* uttered that last sentence, Susanna had not fully grasped what she had done in accepting Ben so lightly. It was as though they had been jousting with words quite bloodlessly and suddenly that joust had become a real, and not an imaginary, one and both of them had been laid low! So low that the carpet had nearly become their bed.

Thus, even before they had fully grasped what they had done, they had fallen prey to a mutual passion so profound that had *Madame* not arrived when she did they might have consummated it on the spot.

Did she wish to repudiate her agreement to marry him? No, she did not. Unwise it might be, but her own reactions to Ben's caresses had shown her two things. The first was that, however fierce he might be, however like his namesake the untamed wolf which roamed the forests, in appearance and manner, his lovemaking to her had been both considerate and kind to the untried woman that he knew she must be. And secondly, her own response to it had been breathtakingly spontaneous. She had proved herself not only willing to meet and match him in the lists of love, but that she was ready to dare all in marrying him.

Their fiery coming together had shown how tepid her relationship with Francis Sylvester had been: a mere extension of friendship with no passion in it.

She was prepared to be the wolf's mate—and would glory in being so.

Unknown to herself, her face told *Madame* everything. Later, alone for a few moments with Ben, she said to him with some severity in her manner, 'You must be kind to her, *mon cher*. Yes, I know she is a strong woman, but it is plain that she has not known what it is to be loved and cherished and you must supply that lack.'

'Oh, I will,' he told her, 'but, and I must tell you this, my own passion for her frightens me. She is so small and delicate, and I am so large. Wolfe my name is, bear I sometimes feel myself to be.'

Madame smiled a subtle smile. One thing Ben Wolfe did not know of himself was how much his face changed and softened when he looked at Susanna. She was prepared to bet that the desire to love and to protect his mate was strong within him and would not be denied. She had long thought that the woman whom he married would be lucky—but only if she could meet his strength with her own quite different brand.

In Susanna Ben had met his mate and his equal and it would be her pleasure to see them flourish together, their respective miseries long behind them. She could only pray that the troubles which surrounded him would soon be over and that their life together would be set fair.

Chapter Twelve

The buzz about Ben Wolfe's origins rose to a roar. Rumours flew about: that Lord Babbacombe wished to go to law, but pursuing a Writ of Ejectment through the courts would prove both long and costly and Babbacombe, unfortunately for him, was on his beam-ends. It was known that the moneylenders would no longer accommodate him and that no bank would advance him so much as a half-penny. He was in immediate danger of ending up in a debtor's prison since he had been living on tick and borrowed money for years.

Ben Wolfe, on the other hand, was rolling in it, as the saying went, and since possession was nine-tenths of the law, remained ensconced in The Den in the country and in his town house in London.

M'lord called in the Runners, but all their pushing and probing gave him no harder evidence than he already possessed—other than that there had been a country rumour about the time of Ben's birth that his supposed mother was not his real one—but no reliable witnesses could be found to testify that this was true. Another rumour was that a child had been born to Mrs Wolfe but that it had died immediately and an orphan brat had been substituted in its place to prevent Lord Babbacombe from being the then rich estate's heir. This, too, was supported by no witness whom a court of law might believe.

Lord Babbacombe, rolling his eyes and looking melancholy, said repeatedly to anyone who would listen to him that it was monstrous that a poor man like himself should be unable to do anything to right his wrongs, particularly when his enemy was so stinking rich.

'Ill-gotten gains,' he always ended mournfully.

He also stirred the pot vigorously by keeping the old gossip about Mrs Wolfe and Lady Exford alive.

Ben's defenders—who were not many, seeing that he was somewhat of an outsider owing to his strange career—were powerless to silence the uproar.

'You could bring an action for slander against him,' Lord Exford said, doubtfully, 'but once one goes to law the outcome is always uncertain.' He never ceased to believe in Ben, as did Jack Devereux who laughed scornfully at the very idea of going to law.

'Leave it,' he said. 'By next season there will be another *on dit* to engage the *ton* and by then Babbacombe should be safe in the Marshalsea—or worse.'

Ben, engaged in the preparations for his marriage to Susanna, was in agreement with Jack, although the whole rotten business distressed him, not for his own sake, but for that of his future wife's. He also thought that Babbacombe and his claque would not let the matter rest.

'It's *point non plus* for me, I'm afraid,' he told *Madame* and Susanna almost apologetically. 'There's nothing I can do to silence him, short of calling him out, and then he's likely to refuse to meet me on the grounds that I'm not really a gentleman, just some nameless bastard masquerading as one.'

'But Lord Exford says that you are the image of your father,' protested Susanna, Madame de Saulx nodding her agreement.

Ben grimaced. 'Oh, that proves nothing. Someone made that point to Babbacombe and his answer was that I was Charles Wolfe's bastard by a village girl who was conveniently handy for substitution. He has an answer for anything.'

'And many believe him,' said *Madame* sadly.

'Well, I don't.' Susanna was robust. 'You're not to let it worry you, Ben.'

But he did worry, all the same. He did not mind people giving him their shoulder, but it hurt him when they did it to Susanna.

He knew that Susanna had met Amelia Western at Lady Leominster's and that she had rudely accosted Susanna with, 'Can it possibly be true that you are about to marry that impostor Ben Wolfe?'

She shuddered delicately while murmuring, 'You must know that if you do I cannot possibly continue to receive you when I am married. I am sure that you are aware that I am promised to Sir Ponsonby Albright, who has the strictest notions of propriety—as I do, of course. I trust to your good sense to cry off before you become a social pariah.'

'Having been a social pariah once, and survived it, I don't regard that state with quite the same horror that you do,' returned Susanna drily. 'And as I happen to be marrying Ben because not only do I love him, but trust him, your notion that I should cry off is repugnant to me.'

Amelia sniffed. 'You never showed much common

sense about these matters when you were my duenna,' she announced, 'so one can't expect you to display any when your fortunes are so unaccountably changed. We part, I fear, not to converse again.'

And what a relief that will be, thought Susanna, but did not say so.

'I don't think that I ought to marry you until this is settled one way or another,' Ben told her one afternoon in Hyde Park when a peer who had been one of his friends, and had dined with him several times, cut him dead.

'Nonsense,' she said. 'I don't value any of these people. Think how they all behaved towards me when I was in trouble.'

'Nevertheless…' He sighed.

'No.' Susanna was definite. 'I will not have my life— and yours—at the mercy of a spiteful old man. I know that you need to live in London, but it is populous enough for us to choose for our friends those who do not believe these slanders.'

She reflected for a moment. 'In one way,' she said thoughtfully, 'it might be better if Lord Babbacombe were rich enough to bring a Writ of Ejectment against you. The whole thing would then be decided one way or another.'

'Except,' said *Madame*, her face troubled, 'that it still might drag on for months or years and if the Writ by some mischance resulted in the court finding for Lord Babbacombe, Ben might end up in prison for personation for fraudulent reasons by falsely assuming the Wolfe name in order to gain The Den and the remainder of the estate. Worse, he might also lose much of his hard-earned wealth by having to pay Lord Babbacombe heavy damages for depriving him of his property and forcing him to go to law to recover it.'

'*Point non plus* it is, then,' Susanna agreed ruefully.

It was not to remain so. The Duke of Clarence gave a great dinner for men only to which Ben, Lord Exford and Jack Devereux were invited. Lord Babbacombe was conspicuously not present. Before it, the Duke took Lord Exford on one side. 'What's this about my friend Ben Wolfe, what, what?' he demanded.

Lord Exford looked at him and wondered how to be tactful. Common sense took over. Nothing about His Royal Highness, William, Duke of Clarence, was remotely tactful. So as precisely as possible he informed the Duke of the rumours and slanders which Babbacombe was promoting, the possibility of his taking out a Writ of Ejectment, and the difficulty of silencing both him and his son.

'Never liked the man,' bellowed Clarence. 'Played cards in an odd way—didn't do to say so, what! So my friend is in trouble and no way out.'

'He's at *point non plus*, in this matter,' agreed Lord Exford, echoing Ben.

'And raising the old scandal about your poor mama. Can't do anything about that, but the other, yes. Have Erskine to dinner, lean on him, eh? Don't want any more noble scandals, eh, what? Public getting restive.'

By Erskine he meant the law lord who had once been Lord Chancellor and was highly respected in consequence.

Lord Exford betrayed his puzzlement. Clarence said, his rosy face beaming goodwill, 'A private court of adjudication, what? If Erskine thinks that Babbacombe has right on his side—which I beg leave to doubt—then I shall help him with his Writ. If, on the other hand, he finds for Mr Wolfe, then Babbacombe must apologise and withdraw. Simple, ain't it?'

One thing was to be said for him, Lord Exford decided. Downright and slightly simple he might be, but he ordered himself and his life better than his much more clever elder brother, the Prince Regent, who lacked the unselfconscious and childlike honesty which was Clarence's hallmark.

'And will Lord Erskine agree to preside over such an unofficial court?' asked Lord Exford.

'He'd better,' retorted the Duke with a twinkle in his eye. 'Both parties would have to agree that his decision would be binding, of course. Otherwise, no point.'

What he did not say was that if either party refused to agree to such a request their social ruin would be inevitable.

'An impromptu court of law. Trust Clarence to think of anything so unlikely,' was Ben's first remark when Lord Exford told him of the Duke's decision.

'Aye, but on the other hand it could bring the whole matter to a head. You would do well to prepare yourself for it.'

Susanna and *Madame* nodded their agreement. One way or another it would end what had become a constant irritant and would—if satisfactorily settled—mean that Susanna and Ben could be married without a shadow hanging over them.

'Suppose Lord Babbacombe does not agree?' Susanna asked Lord Exford. He shook his head before replying, 'He cannot gainsay a Royal Duke. The only way out for him would be to apply for a Writ of Ejectment immediately and he cannot afford to do that.'

'As for preparation,' Ben said, 'I have to tell you that I have had Jess Fitzroy and a couple of my most trusted men secretly investigating the servants and villagers who live around The Den to discover what they can about both the circumstances of my birth and the strange disappearance of my mother. I gather that Babbacombe has had a couple of Runners doing the same thing, but most of the local people are loyal to my family and have given nothing away. I ordered Jess to inform those whom he questioned that they must tell him the truth about these matters, however unpalatable it might be for me to learn it. I have no wish to be surprised by the revelation of events long gone either in a true court of law or an unconventional one such as the Duke proposes. I wish to know the worst, as well as the best, of my case.'

'Very wise,' agreed Lord Exford.

Susanna said to Ben when Lord Exford had gone, 'You are not happy about this, are you?'

'No,' he said, walking restlessly towards the window to look out of it at the busy street below. They were in a drawing room on the first floor of *Madame*'s house near Regent's Park. *Madame* was seated on the sofa before an empty hearth. She watched Susanna walk to where Ben was standing in order to take him by the hand.

'Lord Exford believes that the Duke is doing this to help you. He calls you his friend, Mr Wolfe.'

Ben gave a short laugh and turned to look down into her earnest, anxious eyes. 'I am not sure whether he will help me. I believe in letting sleeping dogs lie. I do not think that Lord Babbacombe will be able to find any evidence substantial enough to help his cause in a court of law—should he ever get there. Given time the whole business would, I believe, have blown over of its own accord. It is thirty-four years since my birth and twenty-five years since my mother disappeared. During that time people's memories have faded and become unreliable—my own included. In a sense the Duke, although he does not mean to, is indulging Lord Babbacombe and keeping the scandal alive.'

'I know,' she told him simply, 'and I agree with you. Nevertheless, the thing is done, and there is, as Lord Exford told me yesterday, no gainsaying a Royal Duke, and perhaps Lord Babbacombe may not agree to submit to such a tribunal.'

'Perhaps—but I think that he will. Looking on the bright side, our mutual friend, Lady Leominster, who was the direct cause of bringing us together, has invited us to dinner in order to demonstrate her faith in us. And the fact that *Madame*—' and he turned to bow to Madame de Saulx '—as well as Lord Exford, continue to be my friend is a plus on my side.'

'And your own character,' added *Madame* rising to join them at the window, 'which is that of an honest man. One thing is significant: there have been no more attacks on you since the failed one.'

Ben smiled wryly. 'Oh, there are two reasons for that. Babbacombe hopes to destroy me by spreading scandal, and the fact that I never move without a bodyguard has spiked his guns.'

'And the Rothschilds are still dealing with you,' said Susanna who was beginning to take an interest in Ben's business affairs, 'which must stand for something.'

'Only that a good business deal takes precedence with them over the whim-whams of the *ton*,' said Ben cynically. 'Nothing must interfere with the making of money.'

'Ah, that is truly a case of the pot calling the kettle black,' commented Susanna, her face full of mischief, 'since I believe that is your motto, too.'

'Minx,' exclaimed Ben, bending down to kiss her soft cheek, regardless of *Madame*'s presence—or rather because her presence meant that he could take his caresses no further. 'I see that I shall have a useful helpmate. If the future Mrs Wolfe is going to be as keen a businessman as her husband, I shall have to find her an office!'

'Which must wait until you are married.' *Madame* smiled.

'And that cannot be,' said Ben firmly, 'until this wretched business with Babbacombe is over. When I marry Susanna I want no cloud in my sky.'

'Which means,' said Susanna, 'that you anticipate giving Lord Babbacombe a legal black eye in this odd arrangement which the Duke has set up!'

'Exactly,' said Ben, kissing her again. 'And now I must leave you both. I have work to do before I call on you to take you to Lady Leominster's.'

'Oh, I do hope that he is right to be optimistic,' Susanna sighed to *Madame* when he had gone, 'but I cannot help but feel that the Duke has made him a hostage to fortune.'

'No need to repine,' returned *Madame*, putting an arm around her shoulders. 'My instincts tell me that Babbacombe must lose. You see, I don't believe that he ever intended to go to court—he simply hoped that he could drive Ben out of society by blackguarding him so much that he would turn the whole town against him. The Duke has forced his hand, and now he must prepare to back his slanders with evidence. That, I believe will be difficult—and almost certainly impossible.'

Nevertheless, Susanna went off to dress for the Leominsters' dinner with a heavy heart. It was for Ben that she feared, not herself. She had been through the fires of rejection and knew how much they hurt, and although she had come through strengthened, she knew that the fires had burned and changed her.

Her love had had a hard life and it was time that he found peace. It would be her duty, once they were married, to see that he achieved it. She was only sorry that he would not marry her until the enquiry was over, for she wished to demonstrate to the whole world how much she loved him, and that no stupid slanders could affect that love.

The Duke's court of enquiry moved at a greater speed than the courts in which a Writ of Ejectment would have been debated. Lord Babbacombe asked for more time to prepare his case: Ben, having heard from Jess, allowed that he was ready at any time that the Duke commanded.

The Duke, wishing to appear fair, gave Lord Babbacombe the extra time he asked for.

'But no more, mind,' he told m'lord sternly. 'I have set this court up to bring matters to a speedy conclusion, not allow it to drag on. It does society—and the country—harm to allow these matters to be aired so publicly and so lengthily.'

'Stretching it a bit, ain't he?' was one comment. 'What's Ben Wolfe's legitimacy got to do with the country's interests?'

'Only,' said Lord Exford severely, to whom the comment was made, 'that in these troubled times when the Radicals are gathering again, anything which shows the aristocracy and gentry in a bad light adds fuel to the would-be fires of revolution.'

Most of the cousinry—for the aristocracy and gentry were heavily inter-related—agreed with Lord Exford. The only thing which they lamented was that the enquiry was to be held in private.

'Which means that we shall miss all the fun,' was the complaint of many.

Which was what the Duke intended. Later, when his brother's marriage to Princess Caroline was dragged through Parliament, the courts and the press, it was generally agreed that the Duke had shown wisdom in his arrangements.

Lord Erskine hummed and ha'd at this bypassing of the courts, but agreed with the Duke that since Babbacombe persisted in his slanders, and was not able to find the money to launch his Writ, this suggestion to end the matter was as good as any.

'Why does not Wolfe bring an action for slander against the feller?' he asked Clarence. 'That would settle things.'

'Pride,' said the Duke simply. 'I understand that he says that he will not waste his time bringing Babbacombe to book, for it would mean that he would be taking his accusations seriously. Since Babbacombe would certainly not agree to a duel with a man he claims to be a common impostor, then my friend Wolfe says, ''To hell with him and his lies, I shall not demean myself by recognising him or them.'' This wretched business must not be allowed to drag on, so my solution is what lies before you in the document which my secretary has prepared. Both parties have agreed to accept your judgement, and after it, whichever way it goes, will let the matter die immediately.'

Lord Erskine was now an old man whose wits—honed by a lifetime in the law—were still undiminished by age. He fell in with the Duke's wishes after some mumbling and chuntering.

'Although I fear that you may find that the losing party will not keep to the agreement about letting the matter drop.'

'Oh, as to that,' said Clarence cheerfully, 'he will face social ruin if he goes back on his word. It would not be well seen. You shall have a room at St James's Palace and as many secretaries and aides as you please. You have only to say the word.'

Lord Erskine said several words—as did the rest of society when the news of the enquiry became public—as it inevitably did. Lord Babbacombe, when questioned, looked noble, saying, his eyes rolling, 'I could not but agree to anything which His Royal Highness might propose. We are each allowed a counsel to represent us and may produce our own witnesses. I could not ask for more.'

Ben said nothing. 'Better so,' he told *Madame* and Susanna. 'I shall save my remarks for the enquiry itself.'

Clarence decided that it was to be held at St James's Palace and that ladies were not to be admitted, only a few men who might be regarded as the cream of society and who would be there to see fair play. Lady Leominster was delighted that her Lord was to be among them, but annoyed that she might not be there to enjoy the fun, although privately Lord Leominster had informed her that it would be very dull. 'Lord Erskine will make sure of that,' he said.

'You may be sure,' she trilled at Ben, 'that Leominster will see that you are not thrown to the wolves. And Lord Granville will be there, which is very proper, for all the world knows that he is not only shrewd but will, in his calm way, see fair play for all parties. The spectators will not be allowed to take part, of course, but their very presence will act as a useful check on folly. Leominster says that witnesses will be called and that both parties have handed in a list to Lord Erskine.'

Her Lord, standing by her, added his own gloss on the matter. 'The Law Lords have been saying that it is all most irregular but, seeing that Babbacombe cannot afford to go to court and that Mr Wolfe will not, they agree that it is the only way out of a dangerous impasse.'

Which seemed to be the general feeling. Society, sharply divided as to who was right and who was wrong in the matter, agreed only on that—and the fact that the Duke had insisted that the matter be settled as soon as possible.

'Bad enough for the Princess of Wales to be a thorn in everyone's flesh,' as Mr Canning said privately to Lord Granville on hearing that he was to be present, 'without having this scandal hanging over us for months. The radical newspapers would fill their columns with screams about "old corruption". That scoundrel, Leigh Hunt, has already been gloating over it, reviving the old mystery about Lady Exford and Mrs Wolfe.'

'So I understand.' Lord Granville was frosty. 'Fortunately, Exford is Mr Wolfe's friend, which ought to put a damper on too much unpleasant speculation. Erskine has told me that he has instructed both Babbacombe and Wolfe not to discuss the matter with others either in public or in private before the enquiry is held.'

'And a blessed relief that is,' said Mr Canning, agreeing with *Madame* and Susanna, who were saying the same thing to Ben when they were picnicking by the Thames at Richmond one sunny afternoon.

Susanna was charming in a simple white high-waisted frock with a pale blue sash, and a small blue bow at her neck. Ben was more formally dressed and had already complained that 'the ladies are more able to endure the sun than we are, seeing that they wear about half the quantity of clothing with which we are encumbered.'

They had been speaking briefly of Lord Erskine's interdict. 'Not that Ben has been giving anything away,' said Susanna, laughing up at him. 'He's been keeping mum, but I believe that he has been thinking quite a lot.'

She knew that he had been closeted with Jess Fitzroy that morning, going over evidence which he had been collecting in Buckinghamshire.

'None of it is substantive,' Ben said wryly. 'We shall be trading in gossip and hearsay, and how the truth can be arrived at in such a climate is beyond my comprehension. Jess has heard that Babbacombe has been secretly claiming that he has two witnesses who will win his case for him, but he cannot discover who they are. Neither can Jackson, the ex-Runner I have been using, so perhaps it's nothing more than Babbacombe's flim-flam.' He added, still wry, 'At least, I hope so.'

'I wish that we could be there to support you,' said *Madame*. 'But I believe that the Duke is probably keeping the ladies away in order to ensure that the audience will be small and informal—which is probably wise.'

They had finished eating their cold collation and were reclining on the grass. Ben took Susanna's hand in his.

She pressed it gently, both of them wishing that this wretched business had not arrived to delay their wedding. Each ached for the other. For the first time Susanna understood what the poets meant when they spoke of love as a flame. It was burning strongly inside her breast—and in Ben's.

Madame, watching them, suddenly declared that she was drowsy and would like to rest. 'But you, on the other hand, are both young and lively, so I suggest that you go for a stroll. There is a fine promenade by the Thames called Cholmondely Walk which will offer you some splendid views of Twickenham Bridge in one direction and Richmond Bridge in the other. Or you may meander into the pleasant grove which lies behind us. Arcadia is another name for the river at Richmond.'

And so it proved. First they wandered along the promenade, admiring the ducks and rails who were taking their ease on the river, before striking off into the trees where they found themselves alone.

'At last,' murmured Ben, taking her into his arms. 'I think that *Madame* knew what a temptation you presented to me in your pretty summer frock and provided us with an opportunity to indulge ourselves.'

He ran his right hand through her hair before gently kissing her as passionlessly as he could.

'I must restrain myself,' he muttered into her ear, 'for I am in danger of celebrating our wedding night, here on the grass, before the parson has made all legal and proper.'

Susanna knew how he felt for she was experiencing the same wild desire as Ben was. She had not truly known herself, she decided ruefully, for always in the past she had thought of herself as cool and contained and now her whole body was throbbing, demanding a fulfilment which it had never known before.

'Alas, this is not the time or the place,' she said sadly, breaking away from him. 'If we were simply a shepherd and his love in the Arcadia of which *Madame* spoke, then we might have met and loved in innocence—with no consequences. But we are not—and must wait. Fortunately, we may not have to wait long.'

'Yes,' he said, standing back. But he could not prevent himself from putting out a tender finger and running it along her upper lip. Susanna turned her head to kiss the caressing hand.

Ben stood spellbound. For one brief mad moment he thought that both *Madame* and propriety must wait. And then sanity returned. He dropped his hand to take hers again, to swing her towards the path back to the world where duty waited for them.

'Not long,' he agreed with her. 'Next Monday we meet at St James and, please God, matters will be settled once and for all.'

The sun made shifting patterns of light on the river and threw a golden glow over everything. Men and women in their summer finery passed them chatting happily. A dog ran towards them and barked defiantly at Ben, who bent to stroke it behind the ears. It stood passive, allowing him to caress it, and when he stopped nuzzled at his boots asking for more.

An elderly lady walked up to claim him, smiling at the handsome pair Ben and Susanna made in the peace and quiet of the early afternoon. When they reached her, *Madame* was resting on the grass, half-asleep. One of the footmen was standing guard.

She opened her eyes as they walked up. 'Back so

soon,' she murmured drowsily, 'I would have thought that you'd have been away longer.'

'Another time,' said Ben gently, 'another time. We shall soon return, I trust, to pay the river homage. Now, I fear, we must leave for Jess told me that Jackson would be back later this afternoon, and I must not keep him waiting. Duty calls.'

It would always call Ben, and he would always answer it, thought Susanna as they were driven home. Which is one of the reasons why I love him.

Chapter Thirteen

'Nothing so far,' said one disgusted gossip to another of what was now known as Lord Erskine's enquiry. 'My information is that so far it has been all guesswork, rumours and hearsay. First Lord Erskine addressed them all on the rules of the court and then the attorneys spoke at length—and so two days were taken up. Then some affidavits were read when Lord Babbacombe's action began, mostly from those too old and stupid to appear in court. Lord Erskine ruled that their evidence should be struck out as it consisted merely of country gossip. Lord Babbacombe made no objection as he said that there was better evidence to come.'

'And that was that?'

'So I understand.'

'Much ado about nothing, then?'

'So far,' agreed the first speaker, 'but we are only at the beginning. My informant said that Ben Wolfe looked ready to sleep by the end of the day.'

'He's confident, then?'

'Appears to be—which is not the same thing.'

Ben, whom *Madame* had invited to stay with her for the duration of the enquiry, but who had refused on the grounds that he wished to give his enemies no ammunition with which to accuse him of impropriety, chose instead to call at the end of each day with the latest news.

'So far,' he told them at the end of the third day, 'you have missed nothing. We are proceeding as in a normal trial. First Lord Babbacombe will state his case, and then I shall state mine. At the end, after due consideration, Lord Erskine will give his judgement. So far it seems likely that we shall remain at *point non plus* for Erskine has so far heard nothing to enable him to come to a conclusion. On the other hand...' He paused and frowned.

'What is it, Ben?' Susanna said as calmly as she could. She thought he looked ill, and wondered how well he was sleeping.

'Nothing? No, that is a lie,' he said energetically. 'The evidence today from some old woman who used to work in the kitchens at The Den had a strange effect on me. Of course, I can have no knowledge of what my father may or may not have done at the time of my birth, since I was then a newborn babe. But...'

He paused again. 'The oddest thing is happening. I have never been able to remember much of my childhood and virtually nothing of what happened when my mother disappeared, but suddenly memories of that time are flooding back. I remember playing battledore and shuttlecock with her on the terrace at The Den, that she watched me when I was taught to ride. I remember my father praising me because I learned so quickly... All that had gone, apparently beyond recall.'

Again, he fell silent. Neither Susanna nor *Madame* said anything. He turned away from them for a moment before turning back to continue. 'I could not even re-

member her face, or whether I grieved at her disappearance, but now I know that I did, and that from his
behaviour my father became a broken man. It is as
though what happened was too terrible for me to hold
on to. Now, even as I speak, more and more of the past
comes to life again. Yesterday I could not have told you
what my mother looked like—my father destroyed all
her portraits, he could not bear to look at them—but
today I could see her in my mind's eye, a woman
younger than I am now, who would be in her fifties if
she had lived... I am convinced that she died either on
that day, or soon after.'

There was such a look of anguish on his face that
Susanna rose and went to him, to put her arms around
him, regardless of *Madame*. She felt him shudder at her
touch and, when he bent his head, his hot tears fell on
the hand which she put up to comfort him.

'I never cried then,' he said, 'and I suppose that I
forgot because it was too painful to remember. Besides,
my life was hard once my father died and it took me
all my time to endure and survive in the present without
grieving for the lost past.'

He took the tiny handkerchief which Susanna offered
him, and dried his eyes with it.

'You will think me maudlin and unmanly,' he said
ruefully, 'but I cannot ever remember crying or grieving
before—it is a new sensation for me. Perhaps I should
try to forget the past again.'

'No!' exclaimed Susanna and *Madame* together.

Susanna, indeed, added her gloss. 'You surely do not
wish to lose your mother for the second time. It cannot
be hurtful to remember past happiness with her and your
father—and if the enquiry has restored them to you, it
cannot be a bad thing.'

'Wise girl,' he said, his eyes dry again, and he bent his head to kiss her tenderly on the cheek. 'You have a touch of my mother about you and I never knew that until today. You are not at all like her in looks but in your brisk, but loving-kind, manner.'

He guided her to the sofa where they sat decorously side by side. 'Jess tells me,' he said at last, 'that one of Lord Babbacombe's two key witnesses will be on show tomorrow. She worked in the nursery when I was born, and later married one of the workers on his estate. She refused to talk to Jess and told him that what she had to say was for m'lord Erskine and no one else. He thought that she was extremely hostile when speaking briefly of my father. Jess joked that his own famous charm made no dent on her patent dislike of him. Jackson had a go at her and fared no better.'

'If Jess cannot charm her, then no one could,' Susanna declared. She could see what attracted other women to Jess even if he did not in any way affect her as Ben did. She had long ago decided that she liked large, dark and fierce men more than smooth, fair and mild ones.

'So tomorrow may be a crucial day,' commented *Madame*.

'Very much so. It will be the first hard evidence offered. On the other hand—' he paused again '—on the other hand, what has passed so far is difficult to refute—or prove—simply being rumours which left Babbacombe with little hard ammunition to shoot at me. Still, we shall see.'

'And you will stay for supper?'

'If I may?' His eyes were on Susanna as he spoke. 'I must tell you that I never valued the company of women until I enjoyed that of yours and Susanna's. You may both take the credit for civilising me.'

It was plain that he meant what he said. Susanna, remembering what he had hinted earlier about his hard life, understood that the softer side of human intercourse had been missing from it. The women whom he had met as a common soldier and then, later, as a hard-working merchant were unlikely to have had the same interests—and advantages—that she and *Madame* had been blessed with.

Hard though her life had been after Francis had jilted her, she had always remained in polite society, even if only at the edge of it—Ben, on the other hand, had been banished to the outer depths.

Supper over, *Madame* offered him a bed for the night because she thought that there was a desolation about him. He shook his head at her. 'No ammunition for Babbacombe,' he announced, more cheerful than he had been all evening. 'I shall call on you tomorrow—and with good news, I hope.'

Ben had no real hope of any such thing. Both Jess and Jackson had prepared him for the worst well before the enquiry.

'The woman was undoubtedly present at your birth. She is the only reliable witness that they were able to find. Your father's steward agreed that Mrs Harte was indeed the Joan Shanks who assisted at your mother's accouchement. We can't attack her as an impostor coached by Babbacombe and his men—only as a possible liar.'

Ben's attorney had agreed with them. 'We have to break her,' he advised. 'Try to catch her out, suggest that Babbacombe has bribed her. She is their strongest card.'

She was to be the first—and possibly the only—witness of the day. It was cold and grey for summer: rain was sliding down the panes of the long windows. Inside, the candles in the chandeliers had been lit and a fire was blazing in the large hearth. Lord Erskine was seated at a long table covered with law books, his clerk by his side busily taking down every word.

A large armchair placed at an angle to the table accommodated the witnesses. The major participants in the action were seated on each side of a gangway which ran the length of the hall. Behind them was the small audience of gentlemen and noblemen, all of them grave and reverend signiors, who behaved themselves impeccably throughout the hearing as befitted their station and their years. Lord Granville was on the front row. When he cared to attend, the Duke of Clarence and his suite were seated in a gallery at the back of the room from where they could look down and see all that passed.

An usher called out in a loud and important voice, 'Mrs Thomas Harte', and a stout woman of middling years was escorted to the witness stand by a footman. She was dressed in a decent black gown with a white linen fichu, edged with lace and fastened by a small brooch, her only piece of jewellery. Her answers were given in a clear, composed voice touched with a rural accent. Any hope that she might be awed into making mistakes by her grandiose surroundings and the presence of the great men who were listening to her soon disappeared.

Lord Babbacombe's attorney, a Mr Gascoyne, took her gently through her story.

'You are Mrs Joan Harte, are you not, formerly Miss Joan Shanks?'

'Yes, sir.'

Mr Herriott, Ben's attorney, leapt to his feet. 'M'lud, may we have evidence before us that this woman is who she claims to be?'

Lord Erskine looked towards Mr Gascoyne. 'You have this evidence, I assume, Mr Gascoyne.'

'Indeed, m'lud.'

'And it has been shown to Mr Wolfe and his attorney?'

'Indeed, and I believe that Mr Wolfe remembers this woman as being part of the household when he was a boy.'

Lord Erskine addressed Ben. 'Do you confirm that, Mr Wolfe?'

Ben remained silent for a moment. He was staring at Mrs Harte. Something about her troubled him, but he could not say what. He was silent for so long that Lord Erskine said testily, 'Did you hear me, Mr Wolfe? Do you remember this woman? Can you confirm that she was Miss Joan Shanks, who is now Mrs Thomas Harte?'

Ben jumped. More than one of those present thought that it was unlike him to be so *distrait*.

'Forgive me, m'lud. Yes, I believe her to be who she says she is.'

If his answer was a trifle equivocal it was deliberately so. He could not say what it was about her which troubled him, but something did. An elusive memory rode at the borders of his mind and refused to be identified.

'You may continue questioning the witness, Mr Gascoyne,' snapped Lord Erskine, not best pleased by Mr Ben Wolfe's absent-mindedness which he considered derogated from his court's dignity.

Mr Gascoyne smiled reassuringly at Mrs Harte and began his examination.

'You were employed as an assistant nursemaid to Mrs Wolfe before her accouchement?'

'Yes, sir.'

'And you were present throughout the delivery of her baby boy?'

'Yes, sir.'

She had been well coached. Her answers to Gascoyne's questions were all brief and to the point, without embroidery.

'What happened after the baby was delivered?'

'The doctor and the midwife were alarmed because it was not breathing properly. It was the wrong colour they said. Blue, not pink.'

Listening to her, Ben found that it was difficult to believe that they were talking about him in the long ago, before he had either memory or real consciousness.

'And did this condition continue?'

'It did.' Again the brief, stark answer giving nothing away.

'Were the doctor and the midwife alarmed?'

'Yes.'

'How long did this go on?'

'For two days. The little boy, Ben, they called him, could scarce suck his mother's milk because of his difficulty in breathing.'

'And what happened at the end of two days?'

'The child began to fail. The doctor said that he was not long for this world.'

'But the child did not fail—or so the gentleman calling himself Mr Ben Wolfe claims.'

Mr Herriott jumped to his feet and protested at this. 'That is a most improper statement. I must remind you, m'lud, and Mr Gascoyne, that nothing has yet been proved affecting Mr Wolfe's legitimacy.'

'Very true,' said Lord Erskine. 'Please refrain from making such statements, Mr Gascoyne, and address yourself solely to your witness's evidence.'

'I obey you, m'lud. And did the boy die, as the doctor prophesied?'

'He did, sir. On the third day.'

For the first time there was noise in the court as this stark answer sank in.

'You were present?'

'Yes.'

'What happened then?'

'Mrs Wolfe screamed that Ben had stopped breathing. The midwife ran over to the bed and took the child from her. Mr Wolfe was sent for.'

She stopped. Again she had been so simple and straightforward when she answered that everything she said seemed to bear the ring of truth.

'And what happened when Mr Wolfe arrived?'

'He took the child from her and left the room.'

'Did he return?'

'Yes, but not before Mrs Wolfe had a screaming fit.'

'What happened when he returned?'

'He brought in a baby wearing Ben's clothes and laid it in Mrs Wolfe's arms.'

Again there was a murmur. Ben leaned forward. What was it about the woman? Dame Memory flashed her skirts at him again, but would not show her face. His puzzlement over this prevented him from being shocked at her evidence which proclaimed him to be an illegitimate impostor—albeit unknowingly.

'You say a baby wearing Ben's clothing. Was it not Ben?'

'No, sir. This baby was like him, but he was bigger and he was the wrong colour.'

'The wrong colour? How so?'

'He was pink. The true Ben had always been blue. At the end he was purple.'

'Did no one question this apparent exchange?'

'No, sir.'

'Why not?'

'Mrs Wolfe was too far gone to understand and the midwife was tiddly.'

'Tiddly?' queried Lord Erskine, his voice austere.

'I believe she means drunk,' explained Mr Gascoyne, while Mrs Harte nodded agreement.

'Very well. Continue.'

'Where did the new baby come from?'

Mr Herriott leapt to his feet. 'I protest at a question which asks the witness to assume something. If she has no direct evidence of an exchange, she cannot answer the question.'

Before Lord Erskine or Mr Gascoyne could say anything, Mrs Harte explained mildly, 'Mr Wolfe's by-blow by Lucy Withers, one of the parlour maids, was born on the same day as Ben Wolfe. Her baby was so big and strong it killed her. It was very like the true Ben Wolfe. Mr Wolfe exchanged the two babies and gave it out that Lucy Withers' baby had been the one that died.'

She came out with this although the two attorneys and Lord Erskine were all trying to silence her. Ben doubted whether Mr Gascoyne was trying very hard and believed that it was more than likely that he had instructed her to continue with her account if ever he was challenged.

If true, Mrs Harte's story was a hammer-blow for

Ben. Lord Babbacombe was grinning, George, seated by him, was clapping him on the back. Here was no village rumour, no hearsay, but a decent, quiet woman who had been present at the birth, the death and the substitution. Lord Babbacombe's witness was like to win the case for him.

The woman herself sat there quite still, in no way discomfited by having every eye upon her. She apologised to Lord Erskine for having continued to speak after Mr Herriott's protest. He accepted her apology, saying sharply to Mr Gascoyne, 'Pray instruct your witness not to volunteer information unless she is first asked to offer it by you.'

Mr Gascoyne also apologised to m'lud, his head suitably bent, adding afterwards, 'I have no further questions for Mrs Harte, m'lud, her evidence now speaks for itself'—earning himself yet another rebuke from Lord Erskine, but gaining the advantage that the woman's last words would be remembered as destroying Ben's case.

Mr Herriott, invited by Lord Erskine to cross-question the witness, murmured something to Ben, to which Ben nodded agreement, before he rose to say, 'In view of the grave nature of Mrs Harte's evidence and the fact that neither my client nor I were aware of its nature until she gave it, I would ask m'lud to adjourn the court so that we may determine what course of action we need to follow to counter it.'

Lord Erskine stared at the ceiling as though asking God to advise him, before looking up at the gallery at God's nearest representative on earth, the Duke of Clarence, for guidance. He took the Duke's imperceptible nod to mean that an adjournment should be granted and so ruled.

'You may have until tomorrow morning, Mr Herriott.

In view of the gravity of the evidence of which you have spoken, I must ask all present not to discuss what has passed today with anyone outside of this court. That is all.'

He rose, and swept out of the chamber.

'You knew nothing of this?' demanded Mr Herriott of Ben that evening after they had dined in Ben's London home. 'If you did, you should have informed me at once.'

'Two of my people questioned her,' Ben said. 'Both of them are skilled in such matters, one of them being an ex-Bow Street Runner, Jackson by name. Neither of them got any change from her.'

'Jackson, hmm, a good man,' murmured Mr Herriott. 'That woman's a cool piece. You're sure she was employed at your home when she said she was—and in the capacity which she claimed?'

'Both of my men were sure that she was. They went to a great deal of trouble to check that. The devil of it is that most of the servants at the time are either dead or gone elsewhere and cannot be traced. It is on her evidence—and her husband's—that Babbacombe's case relies. We have no one to counter them with.'

Mr Herriott sniffed. 'Whether she's telling the truth is quite another matter, of course. Now, let us sit down and take her evidence to pieces. If either of your men is here, send for them at once.'

Ben nodded. He had had to forgo his nightly rendezvous with Susanna, sending her and *Madame* a brief letter informing them that something quite unexpected had occurred during the day's hearing, and that he needed to spend the evening with his lawyers planning their next moves.

Jess was sent for and was questioned ruthlessly by Mr Herriott, but the lawyer could not fault him in any way.

'So, what do we do next?' he asked. 'For once, Mr Wolfe, your guess is as good as mine, perhaps better.'

'I don't know,' said Ben slowly. 'If I did, I would tell you. The thing is, there is something *wrong* about that woman, something I can't put my finger on.' He did not tell Mr Herriott what he had once told Susanna—that he could smell wrongness and evil. With Mrs Harte it was the former—but what about her gave him that impression he could not think.

Mr Herriott stared at his puzzled face before saying, 'If anything occurs to you, you will, of course, inform me. We really need some hook, some device or ploy, to break that woman's confounded certainty. She's the best kind of witness. Doesn't say too much, keeps her head. One thing, Fitzroy said that she married one of Babbacombe's people. Could Babbacombe have bribed her through him? Who exactly was Tom Harte?'

Jess said, 'He succeeded the agent who disappeared after the disappearance of Lady Exford and the murder of Mr Wolfe's mother.'

'Did he, now? That might bear investigating. Had this Harte a good reputation?'

'The best,' said Jess reluctantly. 'That's the devil of it. He and his wife are both highly regarded, being good churchgoers with well brought up, well-behaved children. They can't be faulted. I suspect that he's Babbacombe's next key witness'

'So—' Mr Herriott swung on Ben '—it's up to you now—try to think what's wrong with her—it might help us, or it might not. God knows we need help. Or the sort of miracle that doesn't happen nowadays. Tomorrow I'll try to break her, but as it is, it's bricks without straw.'

But next morning, sitting there, demure, in the big chair, Mrs Harte looked more unshakeable than ever when Mr Herriott took her once again through her evidence. Questioning everything she said, he was quite unable to disturb her.

The devil of it was that she never repeated anything—exactly—something which might have hinted that she had been coached. Ben, watching her, was more baffled than ever as she ran rings around all Mr Herriott's clever tricks by being apparently transparent and truthful in all her answers.

Only once was she a little shaken. He had asked her how she could be certain that the baby Mr Wolfe had brought back was not the one he had taken away. 'You said that it was because the new baby was pink, whereas the old baby had always been blue—'

He paused.

'Purple,' she offered helpfully. 'I said that he was purple at the end.'

'So you did. You appear to have an excellent memory for what happened over thirty years ago...' He paused again. 'What puzzles me is this: if you knew that Mr Wolfe had switched the children, why did you never tell anyone? Lord Babbacombe, for instance. He was the heir and his man, Harte, was courting you at the time. You must have known that Mr Wolfe had committed a crime—and against your future husband's employer.'

It was the first time that she seemed to be a little wrong-footed. She did something that Ben had seen her do before when a question momentarily took her by surprise. She put up a hand to fiddle with the brooch which fastened her fichu—and as she did so, Ben's memory took on a life of its own, and he knew, at last, what it was about her that was wrong.

'I was afraid of what might happen to me if I told the truth,' she said at last.

While she spoke Ben was thinking furiously, testing his newly won memory until he was certain that it had not deceived him. Mr Herriott, pausing temporarily in his cross-examination of Mrs Harte, bent down to pick up a piece of paper on which Jess had prepared some questions for him. As he did so, Ben caught him by the sleeve.

'A moment,' he said urgently.

'What is it?' Mr Herriott was irritable. 'M'lud will not like it if we hold matters up.'

'This. Will you allow me to question her? I have just realised what is wrong with her, but it would be lengthy and difficult for me to instruct you at this late date. If I begin to make a fool of myself, I promise to sit down immediately.'

'Very well. Desperate situations demand desperate measures and, God knows, ours is desperate enough.'

'M'lud,' he said, appealing to Lord Erskine, who was about to protest their whispered conversation, 'my client begs leave to question Mrs Harte himself. He has new and vital information relating to—' He turned to Ben and hissed, 'Relating to what, for God's sake?'

'Her truthfulness,' Ben whispered back.

'Her veracity, m'lud,' translated Mr Herriott into legalese for m'lud.

'Very well, Mr Herriott.' Lord Erskine was reluctant, but was wishful to appear fair. He knew, like everyone in the room, that Mr Ben Wolfe was nearly dished.

Indeed, when both participants to the enquiry, and their lawyers, had entered, shortly before Lord Erskine came in, Lord Babbacombe had smirked at Ben, exclaiming loudly and exultantly, 'I wonder at you, Wolfe—or whatever your true name is—still having the gall to continue with this matter. Better to cut line and cut losses. The longer this case goes on, the bigger the damages I shall claim when I go to the law courts to win it.'

Ben had said nothing; had simply given him his shoulder. Now he rose to his feet to walk slowly towards Mrs Harte. She showed no emotion when he smiled at her and said, 'I have not seen you since I was a little boy and you were Joan Shanks, but I should have known you anywhere.'

Her only response was to stare stonily at him.

Ben made nothing of that but simply continued to speak, in the same even tones which the lawyers had used. 'I believe that you were somewhat of a favourite with my late mother, were you not?'

Her right hand rose to finger her brooch nervously before she replied, somewhat reluctantly, 'Yes, I suppose I was.'

'I knew my memory could not be at fault,' he told her gravely. 'I think, however, that yours might be.'

Mr Gascoyne leapt to his feet. 'I protest, m'lud. Mr Wolfe is going nowhere. He is simply making speeches, not asking questions.'

Ben bowed first at him and then at Lord Erskine who said sharply, 'Do not make speeches, Mr Wolfe. Confine yourself to asking the witness questions.'

'I do beg your pardon, m'lud. I am not versed in the law, but now that you have so kindly instructed me, questions it shall be.'

He turned again towards the witness. 'That is a very pretty brooch you are wearing, Mrs Harte.'

Her hand dropped from it as though it had been scalded. Mr Gascoyne leapt to his feet, howling, 'I protest, m'lud, he is making speeches again.'

Before Lord Erskine could reply, Ben forestalled him by saying, 'Grant me a little patience, m'lud. I shall now ask Mrs Harte a question.'

It was her turn to be bowed to before he threw a gentle question her way, his voice honeyed. 'Pray tell me, Mrs Harte, who gave you that trinket? I believe that I have seen it before. It is an inexpensive fairing, is it not?'

This time the jack-in-a-box which Mr Gascoyne had become was almost gibbering. He shouted in m'lud's direction, 'What the deuce have these questions got to do with anything in the case?'

'Something which I am asking myself,' said m'lud, gazing severely at Ben. 'Is there any point to all this, Mr Wolfe? Because if there is not, I must ask you to cease this line of questioning.'

Beside Ben, Mr Herriott was moaning gently to himself. He saw his case—and his reputation—declining into ruin.

'It is very much to the point, m'lud, and if you will instruct the witness to answer it, you would earn my undying gratitude.'

Mr Herriott's moans grew louder. He rested his head in his hands, declining to look at his principal, or the court.

Lord Erskine said frostily, 'I don't want your gratitude, Mr Wolfe, undying or otherwise, but to please you and in the hope of bringing this matter to a speedy end

I shall instruct Mrs Harte to humour you. Were we in a real court of law I should not do so.'

He leaned forward to say gently and kindly to the witness, 'Pray answer Mr Wolfe's questions, madam.'

She stared at Ben before saying, defiance in her voice for the first time, 'Why, your mother gave it to me. It *is* inexpensive, tin and glass, but I treasure it in her memory.'

'Do you, indeed? That is most gracious of you. Tell me, when did she give it to you?'

She smiled at him for the first time. 'That is easily answered, sir. The day I was promised to Tom Harte.'

'Which was?'

'A fortnight before she disappeared.'

'A fortnight before she disappeared. You are quite sure of that?'

'Quite sure, sir.'

Mr Herriott, agonised by this series of *non sequiturs*, pulled at Ben's coattails to urge him to sit down. Ben ignored him and tried not to catch the eye of Lord Erskine or the by now baleful glare of Mr Gascoyne.

Instead he said to her, his voice still honeyed, 'Do you know, Mrs Harte, I do believe that you are not telling me the truth, the whole truth and nothing but the truth.'

Her hand flew to the brooch again. 'Oh, but I am.'

'No, and I can prove you to be a liar. If I am not mistaken, that brooch was bought at Lavendon Fair and given to my mother on her birthday, the very day she disappeared, and I was the one who paid for it, and gave it to her. I bought it out of my pocket money.'

She was now as agitated as she had been calm. 'No, it is you who are lying. You have been living a lie all your life. It was as I said, she gave it to me on the day I was betrothed to Tom.'

Pray God, thought Ben, that time has not betrayed *me*, nor erased my handiwork of over twenty-five years ago.

'You see,' he said, and his kind smile never wavered, 'I was only a little boy of nine then, and I was so proud of my gift that I scratched my name and the date on the back. I don't suppose that you ever saw it, or, if you did, thought that the marks were other than random. Pray give m'lud the brooch that he may inspect the back of it.'

He knew that he was taking an enormous risk, but as Herriott had said the night before, they needed a miracle and perhaps here was one for the asking—if the marks were still there.

'You see,' he said, more into the silent room than to the now-unhappy witness, 'I gave my mother that brooch a fortnight *after* the day on which Mrs Harte claimed that my mother gave it to her. Two points must follow from that false statement. One, that if she has lied about that, then she can lie about anything, including my birth, and two, when I kissed my mother goodbye on that last terrible afternoon she was wearing my brooch to please me—so how did Mrs Harte come by it?'

Everyone was staring at the pair of them. Ben was still smiling his now terrible smile at the white-faced woman who was shrinking away from him in her chair.

Lord Erskine said at last, 'Pray hand me the brooch, Mrs Harte, so that I may inspect it.'

'No,' she wailed. 'It's my brooch. I made a mistake...my husband gave it to me...'

She got no further. Lord Erskine had motioned to one

of the ushers who came forward, his hand outstretched, ready to take it from her. Her face a rictus of shame, she unfastened it and handed it to him.

Regardless of whether or not Ben's childish marks were on the back of it, she had given herself away by trying to change her story.

Lord Erskine took the brooch, turned it over, picked up a quizzing glass and inspected the back.

'What do you claim to have scratched there, Mr Wolfe?'

'My name, Ben, and the date, 12.6.94.'

M'lud bent his head, raised it and said, 'The marks are just visible, Mr Wolfe, and confirm that what you have said is true. Bearing in mind your second point, I shall ask the court's tipstaff to detain Mrs Harte for questioning in connection with your mother's death, which, I understand, has been a mystery ever since the day you gave her your present. I am afraid that the court must retain it for the time being.'

Mr Herriott's face was one smile. Mr Gascoyne was shaking his head ruefully, and Lord Babbacombe looked ghastly as his strong case against Mr Wolfe dissolved before his very eyes.

Chapter Fourteen

'That was deliberate, was it not?'

Ben smiled, a lethal smile. 'What was deliberate, Mr Herriott?'

'All that clowning which you did. Pretending not to know the rules of evidence, bringing Lord Erskine into the case, making the witness think first that you were harmless, and then that you were not.'

'If you say so, Mr Herriott.'

'Oh, I do say so. You did not make a great fortune out of mere guesswork, I am sure.'

'No, indeed. But I also took risks. The brooch was made of tin. Mrs Harte has been wearing it for over twenty-five years. I took an enormous risk in assuming that the marks were still legible enough for m'lud to read them.'

Mr Herriott shook his head admiringly. 'By God, that *was* a risk.'

'But one worth taking, you will agree. You will be admired as the man who had the sense to allow his principal to take over, and the case to be won thereby, will you not?'

For, after hearing Mr Harte's halting evidence, and

warning him not to incriminate himself in matters not relevant to the court of enquiry, Lord Erskine had given judgement.

'Unless Lord Babbacombe has further direct evidence to present, which I understand is not the case, his action against Mr Benjamin Wolfe must fail. Without independent evidence to support that of Mrs Harte and her husband, it would be dangerous to find for him, given her proven lack of veracity in relation to an even more important matter.

'I now declare this court of enquiry closed and urge both parties to keep to their agreement that, whatever the result, they will not take any further action regarding the question of Mr Ben Wolfe's legitimacy and will refrain from comment on it. The matter of Mrs Wolfe's reappearing brooch will be passed on to the proper authorities for investigation.'

The usher shouted 'All rise,' and Lord Erskine left the room. Lord Babbacombe swung round to address his attorney. 'And that's it? Have you nothing more to say?'

Mr Gascoyne shook his head gravely. 'No, m'lord. Mr Wolfe sank your witness. Or, rather, she sank herself by lying about the brooch. Whatever can have possessed her?' and he fixed Lord Babbacombe with a glittering eye.

'But that,' persisted Lord Babbacombe, 'did not necessarily mean that she was lying about Wolfe's birth.'

'No, indeed, but you heard what his Lordship said— that it meant that her evidence could not stand on its own. Since we could produce no other witness to the birth, he was compelled to disallow what she had said— and so your case could not be sustained.'

'But she told her husband—'

'What she said to her husband was hearsay and, as such, could not be admitted into an English court of law.'

Lord Babbacombe, in an agony of frustrated rage, would not be silenced. 'A more nonsensical rule I have never heard—and besides, this was not a true court of law.'

Mr Gascoyne began to gather up his documents, 'Unfortunately you, and Mr Wolfe, both agreed that the rules of an English court of law should obtain at this enquiry. No, I am afraid that you must grin and bear it—'

'Pray cease patronising me, you damned pen pusher,' snarled Lord Babbacombe, 'and do not trouble to send me a bill for your inefficient conduct of my action for, thanks to you, I have nothing left to pay you with.'

He stalked off, his head in the air, his unhappy son George trailing after him.

'Could have told you he would turn nasty if you lost,' remarked Mr Herriott cheerfully, 'which you were bound to.'

'No such thing,' returned Mr Gascoyne, snarling nearly as fiercely as his late patron. 'Nearly dished you, didn't we? And would have done so if that silly bitch had held her tongue.'

'Ah, but you hadn't coached her on the questions Ben Wolfe asked her, had you? How much did Babbacombe pay her to lie for him, do you think? Or was it only a promise of money in the future? For sure, she will get none now—and, by the by—how did she come by the brooch?'

Which sally he repeated gleefully to Ben when talking to him in the anteroom outside the court. He was still laughing when the Duke of Clarence walked in, his royal hand outstretched towards Ben.

'Never enjoyed m'self in a courtroom so much before, Wolfe. Wouldn't have missed it for the world. A pleasure to watch you demolish that lying old besom. My congratulations, didn't believe a word of what she said, although she said it well. Too well for my money, but you pinned her down royally.'

He laughed heartily at his own pun. 'Royally, since I was there—and at last you may find out what happened to your poor mother. Erskine said we weren't to gossip about today's excitements, but I'm willing to bet they will be the talk of the town tomorrow.

'And now you can marry your pretty girl with a light heart, what, what! I'll send you a fine piece of silver for a wedding present. No tin and glass this time, eh, what!'

'Did he really say that?' asked Susanna when Ben visited Stanhope Street that night to tell them that he was still legitimate Ben Wolfe, and the melancholy news that his mother's death was to be investigated again.

'Indeed, he did.'

'And this woman, Mrs Harte, I suppose that the fairy stories about your birth which she told yesterday were the reason why you did not visit us last night. How could she lie so convincingly that you nearly lost your case?'

Ben shrugged. 'I suspect, and Herriott thinks so too, that she was well paid to do so by Lord Babbacombe.'

'You're not happy about your mother's death becoming a topic for rumour again, are you?' asked Susanna shrewdly.

Ben, who looked better than he had done for weeks, said slowly, 'Not really, but you must understand that the discovery of the brooch changes things completely. For where did it come from? Mr Herriott swears that Lord Babbacombe must be involved—although I understand that there was no question of that at the time. Mrs Harte began to say that her husband had given it to her. Was that the truth—or another lie? She's lodged in Newgate tonight and tomorrow the law will harry her until she does tell the truth—if she knows what truth is.

'What is strange is that the strains of this enquiry, as I told you a few days ago, caused me to remember a great deal about my life both before and during the day on which my mother died, things which I had completely forgotten. A week ago I could not have identified Joan Shanks as she then was, and I had no memory of my birthday gift to my mother. That I fortunately recovered in court whilst she was testifying.'

Madame, who had so far said nothing, now rose and walked to the fireplace to look down into the empty hearth, her back to Ben and Susanna, who stared at her breach of manners in some astonishment—she was usually so circumspect.

'There is something of which I should have told you before, Ben,' she said in a low voice before turning to face them both. 'It was wrong of me to keep quiet. I did not think that anything I knew was important and, like you, Ben, I had forgotten, almost deliberately, much of what happened on the day that your mother disappeared.

'You see, at the time I was staying at Lord Exford's, the daughter of his cousin who had married a Frenchman who became an *émigré* during the revolution of '89. I was then twenty years old. I am sure that you have no memory of me, for what little boy of nine would know much of one young woman among many, and one who took little interest in him.

'Later I married another *émigré* who had become an India merchant and there, in India, I met you again, much changed from what you had been when I last saw you. I saw no reason to remind you of the unhappy past, the less so when you helped me when my husband died suddenly. Like you, I wished to forget that unhappy day.

'But now, I too, must try to remember it, for as your memory saved you in court today, mine might contain something which did not seem important to me at the time, but which might help to solve the mystery surrounding my two lost friends. When I asked Susanna to recover La Rochefoucauld's *Maximes* for me I was, for the first time, revisiting the country of my youth.'

'But why should you feel regret,' Ben said, 'at saying nothing to me of this? It does explain, perhaps, the affinity which I felt for you when we met in India—and the many kindnesses which you have done for me since—including helping me when I found myself in difficulties after kidnapping Susanna.'

'You must understand,' said *Madame*, 'that in some way I felt that I owed you something, having known you as a happy child before your life fell apart—and you ended up, penniless, in India. I could not but admire your courage and resolution in making yourself such a successful life after such an unpromising start.

'And, more to the present point, although Lord Erskine would undoubtedly not accept it as evidence, I never heard anything to suggest that you were other than Charles Wolfe's legitimate son. You are most remarkably like him.'

She resumed her chair before going on, 'As to your
mother's disappearance…since you told us of the mysterious reappearance of her brooch I have been trying
to recall something of that day. I do remember that I
had a slight summer cold; consequently, when your
mother asked me to accompany her and Lady Exford
on their walk, I refused her kind invitation. Would that
I had not—perhaps my making it a party of three might
have averted a tragedy. But how can I logically assert
that? As it was I watched them walk down the terrace
steps and into the Park, not knowing that I was never
going to see them again.

'I also remember your father leaving us to visit Lord
Beauval. He usually accompanied your mother on her
painting and sketching expeditions and reproached himself bitterly afterwards for having not been with her that
day.'

She stopped, to put her head in her hands for a moment. Neither Ben nor Susanna said anything, except
that Susanna went over to her to take her in her arms.
Madame lay there for a moment before continuing.

'I have been trying to remember whether or not I saw
Lord Babbacombe that day. I don't think that I did. You
must understand that he was then a handsome young
man and I was very taken with him until, one day, his
dog snarled at him and he beat it cruelly with his crop—
he thought that he was alone. He did not know that I
had seen him coming up the drive and was on my way
to meet him. I turned back and went into the house. I
never felt the same about him again.

'There was one thing, though. You remember that I
told you that Lord Babbacombe testified that Lord Exford and Mr Wolfe had had a fierce argument at a dinner
he gave the night before, which Lord Exford always

denied—well, I was at that dinner and I can remember no such argument. What I do now remember is that later, after dinner, Mrs Wolfe went upstairs to the room which had been set aside for the ladies' coats, jackets and shawls, saying that she was feeling the cold. I was careless of servants those days and would have sent a maid to collect it—and so I told her.

'She laughed and said that Jane, her lady's maid, deserved to enjoy her evening in the Babbacombe kitchens and that she was strong enough to climb the stairs and collect her own shawl. When she came downstairs again she seemed very agitated. So much so that I remember asking if anything was amiss. She said "no", but when Lord Babbacombe returned from some errand she asked him if he would allow her and Charles to leave early— she had begun to suffer from a slight megrim, she said. I thought nothing of it at the time, and it was only this wretched business of a court of enquiry which set me trying to recall the past again.

'What if the fierce argument was not between Lord Exford and Mr Wolfe, but between Lord Babbacombe and Mrs Wolfe? Did he try to accost her when he found her alone? Both of them were certainly absent at the same time. Lord Babbacombe had taken it very ill that your mother had refused him, Ben, but later he appeared to forget his anger and he became friendly again with both your father and your mother. He said that he would never marry, having lost the woman he loved, and indeed, he did not, until after your mother's death.

'None of this may mean very much, I know. Lord Babbacombe was never suspected of being involved in your mother's disappearance and was only lightly questioned by the authorities. His agent testified that they had spent the afternoon together at Babbacombe House and that it was on his way home shortly after that he saw Charles Wolfe when he was supposed to be some miles away.'

Ben, who had been listening eagerly to her, his face fierce, said, 'Suppose that the agent was lying? At Lord Babbacombe's orders. Is it preposterous to suppose that Lord Babbacombe was behind the disappearance of my mother and the attack on Lady Exford?'

He struck his hands together. 'So far we have no evidence of any such thing—other than the ferocity with which he has pursued me—and the fact that my mother's brooch has reappeared on the breast of the wife of one of his servants. Until Mrs Harte and her husband have been questioned, we are making bricks without straw. We must contain ourselves and wait for the tidings which tomorrow will surely bring us. I have never felt so helpless before.'

He was thinking that always before in his life, once he had reached manhood, he had been in control of events. Even in the enquiry it had been he, who in the end, had dictated matters, he who had blown down Lord Babbacombe's house of cards. He wanted to do—what?

There was such a look of anguish and frustration on his face that Susanna was now compelled to leave *Madame* and comfort him.

'Come,' she said, putting her arms around him and stroking his warm cheek gently, before releasing him in order to sit by his side again. 'You have been patient all your life. You can be patient a little while longer, I am sure. Neither you nor *Madame* have anything to reproach yourself with.'

'I have,' *Madame* said sadly. 'I should have told Ben the truth about myself long ago, but I said nothing in order to spare him. We both thought that the past was over and done with and that we could forget it.'

'We were both wrong,' Ben said. 'Once I returned to England it lay in wait for me. Whilst I was a nobody in India it hibernated, but when I arrived here, rich and relatively powerful, it revived again. While I was on the other side of the world Lord Babbacombe must have felt safe—indeed, he *was* safe. But when I returned one of my first tasks was to try to account for my father's sudden ruin, and after much investigation I found, to my surprise, that Lord Babbacombe had engineered it.

'That was when I tried to revenge myself on him by kidnapping his son's rich bride and marrying her—but I ended up by kidnapping Susanna by mistake! After that I decided that revenge, too, was a mistake and decided to let the past stay dead. But Lord Babbacombe was a fool, for he allowed his hatred of me and mine to remind the world of it by constantly attacking me so that the old ghosts began to walk again, clamouring for justice. The only thing which surprises me is that I never thought to connect him with my mother's disappearance before.'

'Ah, but he thought that he could destroy you, didn't he,' said Susanna sensibly, 'by proving you to be both illegitimate and dishonest? Let us pray that by making that mistake he may have destroyed himself.'

'The Duke of Clarence said that you were my pretty girl: he did not know that you were my wise girl, too. He also told me to marry you straight away,' said Ben. 'Will you? I think that I was wrong not to marry you before. I must not let my past destroy my present, and with you by my side I think that I could face anything.'

'Tomorrow, if you wish,' exclaimed Susanna joyfully. 'Yesterday would have been better!'

Ben's face cleared as she uttered this naughty joke. The misery he had worn on it since he had destroyed Mrs Harte's credibility, at the cost of reviving his anguish over his lost mother, disappeared.

'You are right. Life must go on. All I would ask is that we should wait until the Hartes have been questioned. I should not like the prospect of their revelations hanging over our wedding day.'

'I'm willing to agree to that,' Susanna told him. 'Only if, whatever happens, you marry me as soon as possible afterwards. No further delays, if you please. At least Francis Sylvester managed to get me to the church—we have not been in sight of it yet!'

'Oh, but even if we marry in church, I want the ceremony to be as private as possible since church has unpleasant associations for you. I certainly don't want many curious spectators who have only turned up because we have both been objects of scandal. If *Madame* agrees that we can be married from here, I propose that we invite only our most immediate friends—like the Dicksons and Lord and Lady Devereux. The only thing is, I can't offer you a honeymoon at present, I've too many deals tied up—but once they have been concluded then you may choose to go where you please: France, Italy or the moon!'

'Wherever you are, is where I please to be,' Susanna told him, her face rosy with suppressed joy. 'I think that the moon might be taking things too far. Later on we can arrange together where we might like to take our ease.'

They had forgotten *Madame*. She watched them, a wistful expression on her face while she remembered her own happy hours with her dead husband.

'Of course, you may be married from here,' she told

them when they at last came down to earth again. 'And
I approve of the wedding being as soon as possible. You
have both already waited far too long to be happy.'

Tom Harte was in a small dark room in Newgate
Prison, facing two Bow Street Runners. He had been
arrested shortly after his wife and taken for questioning.
He was a big, burly man, usually rosy faced and jovial,
but on the morning after the collapse of the enquiry he
was neither of these things.

Immediately afterwards he had tried to approach Lord
Babbacombe to ask him for help and advice, but
m'lord's lawyers would not allow him within yards of
their client, having him escorted as quickly as possible
out of St James's Palace. After that rebuff he had considered fleeing London, but had rapidly decided that he
had no stomach for living as an outlaw.

Now, facing his interrogators, he had no notion of
what his wife might have told them on the previous day.
His face grey, his manner hangdog, he at first tried to
deny that he had given her the brooch.

The larger of the two men laughed. 'That is not what
she says. She asserts that you gave it to her not long
after Mrs Wolfe's disappearance, saying that you had
found it.'

'So I did,' he said eagerly, 'Now I remember. That
was it.'

'She also said that you told her to tell anyone who
was curious about it that Mrs Wolfe had given it to her
a fortnight before her death—although why you should
have thought anyone would be curious about such a
trumpery thing…' He paused before saying with a nasty
grin, 'Unless, of course, it was because you knew that

it had been in the possession of a woman whose disappearance was a mystery.'

Tom Harte closed his eyes in agony. To tell the truth would free his wife—but would destroy him. Who would have thought that a worthless trinket, carelessly given to his wife, would have the power to bring him into the shadow of the gallows.

The second Runner saw his face change, and his head begin to hang.

'Of course,' he said slyly, 'if you were not a principal in the matter of Mrs Wolfe's disappearance, but merely an unconsidered servant who felt compelled to defend and obey his master, then to confess all might be to earn something of a remission from the utmost penalty of the law. To that end I will inform you that there is a warrant out for the arrest of Lord Babbacombe on a charge of murder and kidnapping.'

He leaned forward to tweak Tom Harte's slovenly cravat to pull him forward a little in order to thrust his face into his victim's, growling, 'Have a little common sense, cully, and save yourself. You cannot save him!'

Tom Harte was not to know that unless he confessed the notion that Lord Babbacombe was involved had no hard evidence to back it—only Mrs Harte's tearful cries and recriminations and that the warrant had been sworn simply to compel m'lord to answer questions relating to Mrs Wolfe's disappearance.

His face turned from dirty yellow to dirty white.

'I wasn't there,' he stammered, 'not I. Vincent was, I know. M'lord's agent, he was. Him as lied about seeing Charles Wolfe where he wasn't. He and m'lord were as thick as thieves. Used to go hunting the common molls together—both in the town and the country. Vincent was m'lord's poor relation who been at Oxford with him.'

This information came out in a frantic rush. The Runner said, 'Whoa, lad, steady on. A little more slowly. My fellow cannot hear you properly. What happened—"there", I believe you said?'

'Seems that they'd been drinking all morning and went for a walk—to clear their heads, Vincent said. Very merry they were, laughing and singing. They found Mrs Wolfe painting on her own, by the river, t'other lady had gone for a walk.'

He put his face in his hands. 'I don't know exactly what happened. Seems that m'lord said something wrong to Mrs Wolfe and she answered him sharply. M'lord was tipsy and took it amiss. He struck her in the face and she was knocked to the ground, half-stunned. He laughed and fell on her—and then someone screamed, Vincent said. It was Lady Exford who had come to rejoin Mrs Wolfe.

'M'lord shouted, "Silence her, damn you"—or something like that—so Vincent did. And since m'lord was having his fun with Mrs Wolfe, he had his with Lady Exford. Only when it was over they found that Mrs Wolfe was dying—she'd struck her head on a stone when she fell—and that Lady Exford was unconscious, and likely dying, too. That's when Mr Vincent fetched me. They dragged Lady Exford into the undergrowth to hide her, and m'lord ordered me to carry Mrs Wolfe to the mausoleum in the grounds of Babbacombe House where we opened one of the old stone coffins and put her in. She was dead by then.'

'And before that,' said the Runner savagely, throwing him violently to the ground, 'you took the brooch from

Mrs Wolfe's dress and later gave it to your wife—adding grave-robbery to your crimes.'

'It weren't valuable,' howled Tom.

The second Runner, who hadn't yet spoken, said coldly to him, stirring him with his foot, 'You disgust me. Tell me, was it you who did for Vincent—or m'lord?'

'It weren't me. I swear God it weren't. We thought we were home dry when Lady Exford was found and couldn't remember anything, but then Vincent got the shakes. He couldn't sleep, he said, the women were haunting him and he was all for giving himself up. I know he told m'lord so—and then he disappeared. M'lord told me him and Vincent was drunk and so were not responsible for what they had done. "T'were an accident," he said. And then m'lord said that Vincent had shot himself in the mausoleum and that was the end of that. "We are safe," he said, "now that there are only the two of us." And then he made me agent.'

Runner number one said, 'Take him away. Be a pleasure to see him swing.'

Tom's howls increased. 'You promised…if I talked…if I told, you said…you know you did…'

'More fool you. And your biggest folly was to steal a tuppenny fairing and give the law the chance to do you. Stand up, man.'

'No,' he wailed, 'no.'

So they dragged him from the room.

All this Mr Herriott told Ben Wolfe when Ben visited him in his chambers the next afternoon.

Ben listened in silence as the dreadful events of that long-ago afternoon were slowly unfolded.

Mr Herriott nodded. 'I am grieved to have to tell you

this sad news, but better I than another. The officers of the law were sent to Lord Babbacombe's home with a warrant for his arrest even before Tom Harte had confessed, but he had fled it the night before. Another set of officers have gone to Babbacombe House with a warrant to search it and the mausoleum. Babbacombe's flight, however, would appear to prove his own guilt and the truth of Tom Harte's story.

'And had you not recognised your mother's brooch, the mystery would still remain a mystery. Both Babbacombe and Harte must have felt safe after all these years.'

'Until I returned to England and began to unravel the true cause of my father's ruin. No wonder I was pursued so relentlessly. M'lord was undoubtedly the man behind the attack on me.'

'It would seem so. It is, alas, yet another scandal in high life. Babbacombe will have to be tried by his peers in the House of Lords—the last time that happened the wretch, one Lord Ferrers, was found guilty and hanged with a silken rope.'

Ben said grimly, 'Which would hardly lessen the magnitude of the sentence.'

'Indeed. I am sure that you will be glad when this sad business is over.'

Ben said, 'I hope that you will not think me heartless, but I intend to marry as soon as possible. I am in process of arranging for a special licence. My future wife is a sensible young woman who will be a great comfort to me—as she has been already.'

'Then you are a lucky man, sir. And I wish you well.'

'In return for which, Mr Herriott, I will send you an invitation to the ceremony which will be held as privately as possible. You deserve that for having to suffer my amateur attempts at usurping your role in the enquiry.'

'Best not let the Duke of Clarence know,' remarked Mr Herriott with a grin, 'else he will demand to be present, and, if I know him, that will certainly put paid to any attempt of yours to keep it private!'

He and Ben enjoyed the joke together, before Ben left to call at Stanhope Street and take Susanna for an airing in Hyde Park. The strange thing was that, now he knew the truth, terrible though it was, a huge burden which he had not known he was carrying had been lifted from his back.

Chapter Fifteen

Any hope that Lord Babbacombe would be swiftly caught and brought to justice soon faded. He had disappeared completely. The Runners sent to track him down reported that the rumour was that he had left England immediately and disappeared on to the continent.

Their investigations at the Wychwood mausoleum on Lord Babbacombe's estate proved that Tom Harte's story was true, and Ben and Susanna's wedding was delayed yet again when they went north to Buckinghamshire to give his mother's remains a Christian burial. Vincent was given a suicide's one, at a crossroads, even though Lord Babbacombe might possibly have killed him.

Custom and etiquette should have made them delay the wedding even further, but Ben would have none of it. 'I have grieved for my mother for twenty-five years,' he said, 'and for me she died on the day on which she disappeared. I shall love her and grieve for her no less if I love and marry Susanna. Remembering her, it is what she would have wished.'

Since he had unlocked his memory, recollections of his lost past had come flooding in. In them he was playing cricket with his mother and father on the lawn before The Den, holding her hand at the Fair where he had bought her the brooch, and watching her enjoy herself at the coconut shy stall. He remembered, too, that she had lifted him up on to her shoulder the better to see Mr Punch perform.

She had been jolly and kind, and he was sure that she would have approved of Susanna if only because Susanna greatly resembled her in her liveliness—as Madame de Saulx confirmed.

More than one person—for many came to congratulate him on his victory in the enquiry and to commiserate with him over the news of Lord Babbacombe's destruction of his family—remarked that he must be greatly wishful to see his accuser brought to book before the House of Lords.

'Yes and no,' he replied. 'I would like to see him punished, but on the other hand I hate the notion that the whole dreadful business will be rehashed again— and in public, too. If it could be done in private and without fuss—that would be different. No mummery of a trial and of silken ropes for execution can bring my mother back.'

Many could not understand him, but Susanna did. 'You are really a very private person, Ben,' she told him when they were, at last, preparing for the wedding, 'but because you are big and strong and powerful in every way most people think that you have no tender feelings at all. *Madame* and I both know better than that.'

'You always think the best of me,' he said gravely. 'You forget that I am a hard businessman.'

'Most sensible of you,' returned Susanna, 'for if you were not you would not be so successful and I should not be marrying you—or you might be marrying me for my money, which you only retrieved for me because you *were* a hard businessman—with tender feelings.'

'Oh, I do like the idea that I am marrying such a hard-headed wife,' he returned, kissing her and beginning to make gentle love to her, for *Madame* had left them alone for a little and as a couple about to be married they might be allowed to enjoy themselves without prying eyes following them about.

Five minutes later Susanna sat up and began to re-arrange herself. They were both finding it harder and harder to prevent themselves from anticipating their wedding day.

'Which we mustn't,' she told him severely, 'because think of the *on dits* which would run round if we had to put the wedding off yet again and our indiscretion meant that we had an early baby. I don't worry for my sake, but for yours. We must have no scandal of any kind attaching itself to us which might give the gossips another field day at our expense.'

'Goose,' he said, kissing her affectionately before re-tying his cravat which she had pulled undone. 'We need fear no further delays, I am sure. Jackson told Jess and myself yesterday that they had quite certain information that Babbacombe boarded a packet for Calais on the morning after he fled. Harte and his wife are in New-gate, awaiting trial and George Darlington, like his father, has also disappeared. There was talk that he might buy a commission in the Army, seeing that his father has been declared bankrupt. Once the news of Babba-combe's infamy became known, the banks and the mon-eylenders foreclosed on him at once.'

'Nevertheless,' persisted Susanna, 'I have the oddest feeling that all is not yet quite over. I suppose that it

comes from living with uncertainty these last few
months—and years, for that matter. I woke up with
gooseflesh this morning after a bad dream. I can't remember what it was, just that it was bad. No, you are
not to look at me and tell me that I am suffering from
female whim-whams!'

'I wouldn't dream of daring to do any such thing.
What I do think is that the sooner we are hitched, the
better.'

'And so do I.' Susanna was fervent. 'Jess talked
about you being turned off—which I thought was slang
for being hanged, but he said no, that it was also used
to describe a man when he was about to be married, for
being married was, for many men, equivalent to a hanging! I asked him what the equivalent slang was for a
woman, but he didn't know.'

'Oh, Jess,' said Ben dismissively. 'He had a bad experience with a woman in India and tends to see them
and marriage through jaundiced yellow spectacles. I did
worry once that he might be after you.'

'Well, worry no longer. I like Jess—but not to marry.
He must find his own young woman.'

They were still engaged in happy badinage when *Madame* came in and reproached them both for not spending the day having the final fittings for their bridal wear.

'After all,' she told them severely, 'you have the
whole of the rest of your lives in which to gossip together. At this rate you will both be wearing what you
stand up in—and that would never do.'

Despite all Madame's predictions their wedding day
found them both in splendid fig. Susanna's dress was
made of a delicate cream silk. It was high-waisted, in
the latest fashion, and boasted a boat-shaped neckline.

Her only jewellery was a small necklace of pearls. Her little kid slippers were cream with silver rosettes. She carried a bouquet of cream and pale pink carnations and a tiny wreath of them circled her head.

Ben, who never normally cared to rival any of the dandy set, had surpassed himself. His cream breeches, his black coat, his cravat were all so splendid that Jess told him that he was barely recognisable. As for his hair, his barber had excelled himself.

'You look a proper gentleman at last,' Jess said approvingly. He, of course, was as well turned out as ever.

'I look a proper noddy,' grumbled Ben. 'I thank heaven that I don't have to deck myself out like this every day. Everything's so tight I should never get any work done and we should all starve and be turned out into the street—you included.'

'Not me,' said Jess sweetly. 'Thanks to you I've a little something of my own for the first time in my life. Now, one more twist to your cravat and you'll be fit to be presented at court. Oh, by the by, did I tell you that the Duke of Clarence has invited himself to the ceremony? He will respect your wish that you have a private party at The Lair after it, but he does insist that he has a right to see you turned off, seeing that it was his court of enquiry which saved your bacon. His words, not mine.'

Ben closed his eyes. His wishes for a quiet informal ceremony were, it seems, not to be heeded by anyone. He would have preferred to be married in his working clothes with Susanna in the pretty cotton dress which she had worn at Richmond. Well, it was not to be, but no matter, by evening they would be safely hitched, and he and Susanna could get down to the real business of marriage.

Even thinking about it ruined the tight and perfect fit of his breeches. He could only hope that Jess was so busy chattering that he didn't notice, or, if he did, that he would have the common sense not to say anything.

The church they were being married at was not too far from Croft House, Ben's home in Piccadilly, now always jokingly referred to as The Lair since Susanna had christened it that on her first visit. It was a medium-sized mansion, a little set back from the road, with a small drive, bordered with shrubs and trees, which led up to an imposing front door. He could hardly wait to walk up to it with Susanna on his arm, his wife at last.

And who would have thought, on the day which had seen Susanna kidnapped by mistake, that he would ever be doing such an unlikely thing—he who had vowed that he would never marry!

He was still wondering about the mysterious workings of Fate when he was at last in church waiting for Susanna to arrive. His Royal Highness, the Duke of Clarence, and his suite were already seated in the front rows. Behind them were Susanna's mother, her stepfather and their two pretty blonde girls. The groom had no relatives other than Madame de Saulx so his part of the church was given over to Jess, Tozzy and numerous others of his staff. Ben's wish for a private marriage was being only partly met.

Mrs Mitchell, delighted that Susanna was marrying wealth and birth, as well as a man whom a Royal Duke called friend, had graciously forgiven Ben for restoring her fortune to Susanna. She, the girls and Mr Mitchell had spent the previous day at *Madame*'s and it had been agreed that the past should be forgotten. Ben refrained from saying that great wealth and consequence gilded everything—if one's daughter was marrying it, that was.

*   *   *

Afterwards, Susanna remembered little of the ceremony. She only knew that Ben was with her and that she was with Ben. The contrast with her previous failed wedding day could not have been greater. The Duke came up to them after they had been pronounced man and wife and the parson had given them his blessing, in order to add his congratulations.

'I would have entertained you all at St James's Palace, Mrs Wolfe,' he roared, 'except that your husband does not wish to share you with anyone and insists on taking you home with as little ceremony as possible.'

'He is a very private man, Your Royal Highness,' replied Susanna demurely, as she had earlier said to Ben, 'and ceremony does not sort well with him.'

'Oh, he's a true old soldier, one sees well, blunt and down to earth. Well, well, let me wish you both happy, eh, what? And if your husband should ever wish a favour he knows where to find a friend in need. You hear me, Wolfe. I always mean what I say.'

'You know…' said Susanna when they were finally seated in Ben's splendid new curricle, decorated with white ribbons to celebrate his wedding, in which he was to drive her to The Lair. The rest of the party and the carriage in which she had been escorted to the church, were to follow behind. 'You should not mind that the Duke invited himself. The moment I informed my mother that he was going to be present and that he counted himself your friend, all was forgiven. The man who was the friend of a royal prince was not to be sneered at and must be recognised. Even Mr Mitchell was won over. My mother said that he had acquired a new post, down at the docks, which was enabling them to live in a little comfort.'

She looked sideways at her husband. 'I wonder who found that for him.'

'No, you don't,' he told her, skilfully negotiating a herd of cattle being driven by a sullen boy, 'you know—or, rather, you guessed—that it was I who arranged it. He does not know that, and you must not tell him—or your mother.'

'No, they would not like it. My mother even hinted that you might not be best pleased that he had found employment. Why did you do it?'

'She is your mother, and the girls are your half-sisters. I did not do it for them. I did it for you.'

That did not need saying, Susanna thought, and said aloud, 'It was a kind action, all the same.'

Ben said simply, 'I did not wish to see you unhappy at the thought of their poverty and squandering your money on them. This way we are all happy.'

'Indeed we are, particularly me.'

'I refuse to allow you the particularly. It is I who am particularly happy,' he teased her.

'Both particularly happy, perhaps?' she teased back.

'Agreed. Both of us. So noted, as I say to my clerks.'

They had reached The Lair and outpaced their followers. Their grooms who were wearing white wedding cockades on their jockey caps, jumped down to hold the horses for them.

Ben leapt out to hand down his bride. She was still clutching her bouquet of pink and white carnations. In the excitement of the Duke's intervention at the end of the wedding, she had forgotten to throw it to her sisters.

'You may do so later at the wedding breakfast,' Ben had told her.

Now she took his arm and they began to walk towards the door.

Afterwards, Susanna was to ask herself why the premonitions of disaster with which she had been plagued had disappeared completely on her wedding day. Excitement no doubt, she later concluded.

So it was that, when they were halfway to the front door, which was being held open by two footmen, she was almost as surprised as Ben when a man jumped out from the trees and bushes in which he had been hiding to wave a pair of pistols wildly at them.

It was Lord Babbacombe. His clothing and appearance were as wild as his behaviour. Ben held Susanna's arm firmly, wondering what action he could take. He could only be grateful that Babbacombe had not shot them down on the spot, for his intention was plainly evil.

His first words revealed his fell intent—and the reason for his delay. 'Well met,' he cried. 'I would not have had you, Ben Wolfe, go straight to your maker without knowing that I had repaid you for ruining me and making me gallows meat.

'Stand aside, Mrs Wolfe. I should not like to shoot you by accident.'

'No—' began Susanna defiantly.

She was silenced by Ben, who said gently, without taking his eyes from Lord Babbacombe, 'Do as he says, Susanna. Madmen should always be humoured.'

'And who made me a madman,' roared Babbacombe, 'but you and your mother! She should have married me—and then none of this would have happened. Well, at least if I hang, it shall be for killing you—and you shall not see me swing. Why did you not stay in India, why?'

He raised one of his pistols.

Susanna, who had obeyed Ben and moved a little away, knew that she was about to lose him.

'No,' she shrieked, 'you shall not kill him,' and she flung the bouquet which she was carrying straight into Babbacombe's face as, startled by her cry, he turned his head in her direction.

It was enough for him to be so disorientated that he involuntarily fired the pistol he had raised, and for Ben—the shot going high and missing him—to leap upon him and to try to wrest the second pistol from his grasp.

They both fell to the ground, struggling. Susanna, delighted that her intervention had saved Ben from certain death, now had to watch him trying to overcome Babbacombe. As they writhed on the ground there was a second shot.

For a moment the world reeled about her at the thought that Ben might have been killed, until he stood up, unharmed, his bridal clothes torn and awry while Babbacombe lay supine on the ground. Susanna hurled herself on Ben, exclaiming, 'Oh, Ben, I thought I had lost you!'

And then, 'Is he dead?'

Ben held her for a moment, their two hearts beating as one, sharing the joy of danger passed.

'You saved me,' he said at last, kissing her. 'You, the Wolfe's mate, saved me. And no, I don't think he's dead, just sorely wounded.'

The footmen, paralysed by the sight of their master and mistress in danger, were now running towards them. The outriders of the wedding party, who had arrived in time to see the end, also ran up.

'What is it? What is it?' they cried, at the sight of

Lord Babbacombe lying on the ground, semi-conscious, blood running from a wound in the chest.

Jess, who together with Jack Devereux had reached them first, said shortly. 'Stand back, everyone. It's Lord Babbacombe. He tried to kill Mr Wolfe—and failed. I'll send for the Runners. Leave me to deal with matters, sir, while you and Mrs Wolfe go into the house.'

Ben, used to being the one in charge, was ready to argue until Susanna said, her voice shaking, 'Yes, indeed, very sensible of you, Mr Fitzroy. We owe a duty to our guests. Come, Ben, you know that Jess is quite capable of looking after matters properly for you.'

Ben, oblivious to those about them, put an arm around her and kissed her, saying, 'Since you saved me, my love, you shall have your way.'

'Saved you?' exclaimed Mrs Mitchell shrilly—she had arrived well after the whole matter was over. 'Whatever can you mean?'

'We shall explain to you once we are indoors. Do not let this wretched business mar our happy day,' said Ben urging them all in, except the footmen who were placing Lord Babbacombe on a makeshift stretcher.

'Carry him into the summer house and you, Tozzy, find the nearest doctor and bring him here,' were the last words Susanna heard as Ben ushered her through the front door of her new home.

Madame de Saulx was on her left, not clucking and exclaiming like her mother, but saying gently, 'What a brave and resourceful creature you are my dear, I arrived in time to see you throw your bouquet at that murdering wretch. I picked it up for you since it deserved not to be trampled on but to be preserved as an emblem of your courage.'

'I wasn't brave,' responded Susanna numbly. 'I did what I did without thinking.'

'The truest bravery of all,' said Ben kissing her again. 'Take that from an old soldier. And now if the company will excuse us for a moment, let us retire upstairs in order to repair the damage which recent events have done to our bridal wear.'

Jess and Jack Devereux watched them walk away. 'I tell you, Fitzroy,' Jack said, 'that young woman is a fit wife for Ben Wolfe. I would never have thought that he would find anyone who could match him for sheer courage and initiative, but he's certainly married a nonpareil.'

Jess nodded and said briefly, 'I know—and once she looked at him any hopes I had of winning her dropped dead. I wish that I could say the same of Babbacombe. He's still living—just. For Ben Wolfe's sake, I hope that he doesn't survive to go to trial. Ben doesn't deserve to have the whole wretched business rehearsed again.'

'Agreed,' said Jack, taking his wife by the arm, 'but now that he has a helpmate worthy of him, she can share his burdens.'

It was a good epitaph for his own lost hopes regarding Susanna, Jess thought, and then set about organising matters indoors until Ben and Susanna came down, looking refreshed, and ready to face the congratulations of their guests, not just on their marriage, but on their very survival.

Later, much later, the house to themselves, Ben and Susanna were at last alone in their bedroom.

Susanna had exchanged her cream silk wedding dress for a cream cotton nightgown. Ben was wearing a linen one, open at the throat. Trying to overcome her natural shyness, she said, laughing, 'We are nearly as muffled up in our nightwear as we were in our wedding clothes.'

'True,' said Ben slyly, 'but not for long, I hope. No, do not blush, my darling. No woman who has just saved her newly married husband's life should blush.'

'Oh,' she said, turning her face into his chest as he put his arms around her, 'you are over-praising what I did. I'm sure that you would have found some way of overpowering him if I had remained a mere spectator.'

'No,' replied Ben, his voice sober. 'For he was about to shoot me—and would have done so had you not thrown your bouquet into his face. I know the look in an enemy's eye when he feels ready to attack. Who would have thought that he would have deceived everyone by hiding himself away in England, and waiting for an opportunity to murder me?'

'Yes,' said Susanna, shuddering. 'It is wrong and un-Christian of me but, like you and Jess, I hope that he does not live to be tried. And now, may we forget him, for he failed and what started nearly thirty years ago is over, and we may make our own lives with that shadow removed from it. You can remember your mother as young and lovely, and I can forget Francis Sylvester and the pain he caused me.'

'You are right, my love—which is a distressing, but useful, habit of yours. Yes, tonight is ours and the future. Come to bed, Mrs Wolfe, and begin to celebrate it.'

Celebrate it they did, and the last memory of the unhappy past disappeared when Lord Babbacombe died of his wound in prison. The Den and The Lair became happy homes again, full of joy and laughter when Susanna and Ben raised what Ben called their wolf pack.

'The wolf and the wolf's mate must have cubs to carry on the line,' he said to Susanna one fine afternoon at The Den some years later, watching their children playing on the lawn, 'and make the future secure for all the Wolfes to come.'

'None of whom,' riposted Susanna naughtily, for she loved to tease him, 'would have existed if, on a long-ago day, you had not kidnapped the wrong woman.'

'The wrong woman then, but the right woman now—and forever,' was his loving reply.

'I have no answer to that,' she said—and kissed him.

*   *   *   *   *

Don't miss the conclusion of Paula Marshall's
Regency duet in Volume 12 of the
The Regency Lords & Ladies Collection,
available in June 2006.

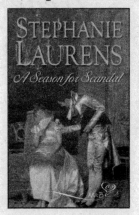

Rome invaded
his country,
she conquered
his heart

LYNN
BARTLETT

Defy the Eagle

62AD AND BRITANNIA IS AT WAR...

ROWAN'S REVENGE
by June Francis

Owain ap Rowan had sworn to track Lady Catherine
down. And in Spain he believed he had finally found
her. Her guilt was obvious – no innocent lady would
disguise herself as a boy! But could he be sure that
the beautiful Kate was, in truth, the lady he sought?
With so many secrets between them, he must not
yield to her seductive spell…

THE LAST BRIDE IN TEXAS
by Judith Stacy

Elizabeth Hill couldn't believe her bad luck!
As if she hadn't provided enough gossip for the town
already, she had to be caught up in a daring daylight
bank robbery…and even though the mysterious
stranger Connor Wade was a genuine hero, she was
in need of saving. But Connor knew that if he
could just get past the prickly exterior, the woman he
would find would be more than worth the effort…